DANGERFIELD'S PROMISE

Interior illustration courtesy of Larry Purdy.

TERRANCE C. NEWBY

outskirts
press

ACKNOWLEDGMENTS

It has taken me over 15 years and numerous drafts to produce this novel. I am indebted to so many people who helped me develop the manuscript and grow as a writer that I cannot name them all. But there are some to whom I owe a tremendous debt that must be acknowledged.

To Sara Schwebs, Claire Newby, Jane Newby, and Adam Newby; thank you for your love, dedication and patience over the past 15 years. I hope the next book does not take as long, but I make no promises.

To Roger Barr, Cynthia Kraack, Jim Lundy, Charles Locks, Ames Sheldon, Kathy Kerr, and Loren Taylor; I am grateful for your insightful comments and critiques, awed by your talents as writers and playwrights, and eager to continue to learn from all of you. You have all helped me grow as a writer and storyteller, and I am forever thankful.

To the Jefferson County Black History Preservation Society; thank you for sending me your 2005 publication detailing the life of Dangerfield Newby and his family. I have changed some of the names, dates, and events found in the historical record, and created others, but your book provided valuable background that proved crucial to the arc of the novel.

And to all the members of the Newby family in America; I have not met all of you, but we should all be very proud of the heroism and sacrifice of our distant ancestor, whose contribution to American history should be celebrated and explored long after we are gone.

AUTHOR'S NOTES

This book is a work of fiction based in part on real historical events and real people. That some of the events and people depicted in this book have actual historical roots does not take this book out of the realm of fiction. I took great pains to adhere to known history where appropriate, and when adherence to known history advanced the story. At other times, I created fictional characters, conversations, relationships, and events, and weaved them into the known historical narrative. Inquisitive readers likely already know about John Brown's raid on Harpers Ferry, and Dangerfield Newby's participation in that raid. But there is much that is not known about Dangerfield's life before he joined Brown's fateful campaign at Harpers Ferry. Because this back story is not known, it must be invented. I have attempted to weave fiction with history, much as memoirists recreate past events through the lens of imagination.

Again it bears repeating – this is a work of fiction, viewed through the lens of history.

BOOK I

CHAPTER 1

Outside the dying woman's room, a dozen or so family members shuffled about, some crying softly, others thumbing through an old picture album. Dr. Michael Turner sat alone on a cracked, greasy vinyl chair, a forlorn piece of furniture that seemed built just for this place; probably hundreds of people before him had sat on this chair, waiting for a friend or relative to die. Turner stole a furtive glance at his watch, and wondered silently how long he would have to wait. He was certain everyone else did not want this to end, that the others were desperate to spend a few more minutes with the old woman, to hear one more laugh, and to endure one more story. He had heard all of the old woman's stories before. Tales of ghosts and spirits, of long-dead aunts and uncles who came back from the dead, of rooms in her childhood house that were haunted, of distant relatives who could find no peace. The others believed this stuff; he never did. Michael Turner did not want any more ghost stories. He wanted to go home.

One of the doctors emerged from the room, tapping her pen. Turner thought she was too young to be a doctor, her sleek blonde hair pulled back in a ponytail. "Dr. Turner," she said without bothering to look up from her clipboard, "your grandmother would like to talk to you. Alone." His cousins halted their conversations and looked at him, some envious, others relieved. Once again, Turner was the chosen one, a role he had never wanted.

He already knew all of Grandma Lorraine's stories: Great Uncle Billy, killed in a car crash, who still showed up on foggy nights at the front door, holding the steering wheel from the Buick 70 Roadmaster he wrapped around a tree; Baby Michael, her two-year old son who died after he fell down the stairs and broke his neck, and who still peered out from his nursery wearing the blue denim jumper he had on when he died; great-great grandma Tillie, born into slavery, who drowned in the Ohio River while trying to escape her plantation in Kentucky, and still showed up behind the woodshed on cold winter nights, frozen and translucent, searching for firewood to warm her dead frozen soul.

Turner had heard all of this before, and never believed a word of it. He had no reason to think his dying grandmother had anything different to say this time. But this was probably her last time, so he thanked the young doctor, trudged dutifully into the tiny room, and slid a folding chair next to the creaking metal bed.

"I'm here, Gran," he said wearily. He clutched the old woman's hands and held her gracile, coal-black fingers in his. She was lying with her head and back elevated on the inclined bed. The old woman turned slowly and peered at him through her clouded eyes. "I didn't think you would be here," she wheezed softly. "Sometimes you don't seem to have much time for your family, with your job and all. But we understand. I do, anyway." The old woman closed her eyes. Unmoved, Turner looked at his watch. "Gran, I think the others might want to be here too," he said. "They don't want to miss anything you have to say. I don't want to deprive them."

"If you got someplace you need to be, then leave," she said. Turner slumped in his chair, his shoulders sagging. "I will have plenty of time for the others," she said. "I got nothing but time."

Turner said nothing. After a few minutes, she coughed, and willed herself to speak. "I know you don't believe the stories I used to tell about our family," she whispered. "Educated doctor like you, you don't have time for ghost stories, and an old woman's nonsense." Turner waited. "Your stories are good stories, Gran," he said, not quite convincing himself.

She peered at him intensely through her opaque eyes. "Not just good, they're true," she whispered. "And even if I am the only one in this whole world who believes them, that makes them true to me." Turner chose not to challenge the old woman's irrefutable logic.

She wheezed and moved her emaciated frame closer to the edge of the bed. "Something I been meaning to ask you for a while now," she said softly. "I should have asked you before now, but you weren't around much at family gatherings, and when you were, it always seemed like you were in a hurry to leave. There were things I wanted to tell you, tried to tell you, but there was never a good time."

Turner grimaced. "I am sorry Gran, I wasn't around as much as I should have been, it's just that . . . never mind, I am here now. What do you need to tell me?"

"Did you ever learn about John Brown and what he did in Harpers Ferry?" she asked. Turner arched his eyebrows, paused, and stated what he knew: that John Brown was a zealous but misguided abolitionist who thought he could end slavery by taking a small group of men and hijacking an entire town. "Brown had good intentions but bad planning, and his men had no military training and little experience," he offered. "They had righteous indignation, but without training or experience, they had no chance of success."

His grandmother looked at him and mustered a weak smile. "So that's all they taught you in school," she said softly. "All that education, and you don't know nothing about your history, your own people, about what's important," she said. "I never got past eighth grade, but I know about the things that matter to folks."

Bested again by an old woman's homespun arguments, Turner sat and waited. "God himself sent John Brown to Harpers Ferry to free the slaves," she said. "And one of your relatives was with him. Your own flesh and blood. Did they teach you that in school?"

"No," muttered Turner softly. He pulled his chair closer, and leaned in.

The old woman coughed again and groaned. Neither spoke for a long time. Turner slid his watch from his wrist, and put it in his coat pocket. "Dangerfield Newby was one of John Brown's raiders," she said. "He was the first one of Brown's men to die at Harpers Ferry, fighting to free the slaves. He's related to you, on your mother's side. Your mother never told you before she died, but she wanted me to tell you. When she got real sick, she asked me to promise her that I would tell you about Dangerfield Newby, about your history. That's why I asked you to come here, so I could tell you about your family."

Turner leaned in closer. "Why didn't you or Mom ever tell me this," Turner asked. "This actually sounds interesting." He immediately regretted his choice of words, but, as was often the case, it was too late. The old woman continued. "Your mother never told you because she was just like you – she never had time, and she figured you might learn it in school. And I never told you because I didn't think you would care. Young folks don't seem to care much about history, especially when it's their own. And you were never around long enough for me to tell you."

Turner blanched. "Dangerfield was born in Virginia, near to where I was born," she continued. "His slave owner was also his father – he had some children with one of his slave girls, and Dangerfield was one of 'em." She paused to cough and rest, and after a few moments, continued.

"Before he died, Dangerfield's father freed all of his slave children, including Dangerfield. Well, Dangerfield had married an enslaved woman, who lived on a plantation not far from his. He had six or seven kids with her, but her owner wouldn't let her go. So Dangerfield joined up with Old John Brown, because he figured the only way to free his wife and family was with a gun. He promised his wife that he would come and get her off that plantation, and rescue her and his children. He died in Harpers Ferry trying to keep that promise."

After this exertion, the old woman paused, and rested her head against a pillow.

Turner leaned in urgently. "But how do you know we are related to him?" The old woman wheezed, and her clouded eyes became darker, but she said nothing. Turner squeezed one of her fingers, and repeated his question. Finally, she spoke. "Nobody knows for certain because nobody kept real good records of slave births. But my maiden name was Newby, I was born close to where Dangerfield was born, and I know from my mother and grandmother that my great-great grandfather was a white slave owner who had a bunch of children with one of his slaves. And I told all this to your mother before she died. All this might not prove anything, but it is part of our family history." Turner waited for more, but the old woman said nothing.

Turner leaned in closer, and now he was only inches from her time-worn face. Sensing his next question, she coughed and began speaking: "Dangerfield was shot on a bridge during the raid. After he was dead, the townsfolk cut off his ears and kept 'em for souvenirs. Then, they took his clothes, and fed his body to the hogs. Folks in Harpers Ferry say you can still see his ghost roaming the streets on foggy nights, looking for his wife and family, trying to keep that promise he made to his wife."

Turner leaned his frame against the back of the small folding chair, and stretched his legs. "This is fascinating, Gran. But how do you know all of this?" The old woman mustered a weak smile. "They used to teach us things in school," she said. "Everything I told you is in books somewhere. And even though I never spent a lot of time in school, I remember the important things."

She paused, and Turner waited. "But most of what I know about family comes from my mother, and her mother, and on and on and on," she said. "And I know Dangerfield's ghost still roams the earth, because his spirit never found peace. He couldn't keep that promise to his wife, and when a good man dies before he can keep an earthly promise, his spirit won't rest until he keeps that promise." She closed her eyes while mustering the strength to speak again. "I always wondered what happened to that poor man's wife and children after he died. Seems like nobody knows for certain. Some folks think his wife and kids were sold South."

Turner smiled at yet another one of the old woman's countless ghost stories. He pulled his watch out of his coat pocket, and quietly slipped it over his wrist. "Gran, I think you should get some sleep," he said as he stood up and stretched. "Do you want me to send in the others?" "Yes," she croaked softly. "Send them in now. Now is a good time. Tell them to hurry." Turner clasped her hand, squeezed her spindly, coal-black fingers, and kissed her softly on the forehead. He turned, and left the room.

—◦《◉》◦—

MAY, 1848, CULPEPER COUNTY, VIRGINIA.

As he did every day during planting season, Dangerfield arose before dawn, dressed quickly, and left the house for the fields. He walked over to the trough that the cattle drank from, and splashed water on his face. He walked to the fence line, and cut a small twig from a young tree. After dipping the twig in the trough, he chewed it for a while, and then ran the twig back and forth over his teeth. When he finished, he spat out the remnants of the twig and the water, and walked into the barn.

Dangerfield worked the fields for two hours, then waited for his sister Anna Mae to deliver the morning meal. Anna Mae was tall and willowy, with a honey-colored complexion, long, dirty-red hair, and Henry's high cheekbones. This morning, she wore her hair pulled back, and covered with a bright yellow scarf she had made out of some old curtains. She carried the morning meal in a large metal bucket.

Dangerfield plopped several spoonfuls of corn meal into his tin. Anna Mae watched him silently. He finished eating, and was about to resume his work in the fields when Anna Mae touched his shoulder.

"Henry says he wants to see you at the house."

"Why?"

"Don't know why. He just told me to get you and bring you up to the house before you go back to the fields."

"Somebody with him?"

"Not yet. But I heard him tell Miss Elsey that Marse Jennings was coming this morning all the way from Warrenton."

"Miss Elsey say anything?"

"No."

Dangerfield scratched his chin and thought for a moment. "You go on back, and tell him I'll be up directly."

Anna Mae looked at him silently. He watched a single tear trickle down her cheek.

"Don't start that," said Dangerfield. "Aint' nothing going to happen to me. I will be fine."

Anna Mae wiped her face with her sleeve, turned, and ran back up to the house. He watched her as she ran. Then he turned back, and surveyed the property. The corn crib was rickety, but full of last year's crop; the hogs were as fat as ever; the barn leaned to one side, and the door was falling off the hinges, but it was stuffed with the best hay crop Henry had ever had. The place needed some work, but Henry was not desperate for money, certainly not desperate enough to sell his own children.

He strode up to the house, and knocked on the door. He heard Elsey's slow shuffle as she approached the door. Elsey opened the door, and looked out just long enough to see that it was him. "Day, Miss Elsey," he said firmly, removing his hat. Elsey lowered her eyes without ever looking at him. Her voice cracked as she spoke: "I'll go and fetch him," and she turned without another word. He waited on the front stoop.

He heard Henry's footsteps behind him, and turned around.

"Morning, Henry," he said.

"Yes, it is a good morning," said Henry, looking past him.

"You asked for me."

"Dr. Jennings is coming by sometime this morning from Warrenton," said Henry. "He just added a hundred new acres to his farm, and needs more able-bodied men. I told him about you, and he wants to have a look at you."

"How long a ride is Warrenton from here?"

"About 20 miles or so. Two, maybe three hours, depends on weather, your horse, and how hard you ride."

Henry looked down and spat.

"I ain't planning on selling you to Jennings or anybody else, so you can put that thought out of your mind now," explained Henry. "Thought maybe you could help him out two or three days a week, but you still belong here. Jennings will pay me a fair price for the time you spend."

Dangerfield slowly loosened the grip on his hat.

"So, you don't aim to sell me to Jennings?"

Henry laughed. "Elsey would never let me back in the house. I don't plan on selling you or anyone to anybody. I just thought you could help Jennings, and he would pay me for your time. And I wanted you to know before Jennings got here."

"That sounds like a fair arrangement," said Dangerfield.

Henry smiled. "Jennings and I have quite a few arrangements, some fair and some not."

Both men turned at the sound of a horse trotting down the path. A tall man riding an enormous black horse with a regal bearing approached, and called out.

"Good Morning, Henry."

"Good Morning, Dr. Jennings."

"Day, Marse Jennings," said Dangerfield."

Jennings remained on his horse, and surveyed what he saw in front of him.

"Well, Henry, it appears to me that your barn could use a bit more care than it is getting now," pronounced Jennings.

"That may be true, although I have enough hay in there to keep it from coming down," replied Henry. "Stuffed to the rafters with the best hay I've had in years."

"And the corn crib is a fair sight," scoffed Jennings. "You must not have enough Negroes on hand to keep the place up."

"I don't lack for help," said Henry. "Between butchering last year's hogs and bringing in all that hay and corn, we've had work a'plenty. I expect to have even more hogs next year. Might even consider selling a few if you need any. I seem to recall you ran short of hogs last year. And the year before last. And the year before that one, if I recall."

Jennings looked down at Dangerfield, who stood next to Henry.

"This the one you told me about?"

"One and the same."

Jennings walked his horse slowly around both of them. "Is he good with horses?"

"Best I have on the place."

"Can he butcher hogs and cattle?"

"Taught him myself."

Dangerfield watched Jennings as the rider slowly circled both of them.

"Tell me Henry, how many Negroes do you have now?"

"Enough to get work done."

"And how many of those are your children? I know you have quite a few with Elsey. I assume she must be the primary house servant."

Henry looked up at Jennings and then spat near the horse's hooves as he circled. "Don't see how that might be any concern of yours, Dr. Jennings."

"Now Henry, forgive me for saying this so directly, but I believe the best way to increase your Negro help is to buy them at auction. Makes it difficult to part with them if they are your flesh and blood. Besides, you'd have to knock up all your housemaids at once if you aim to increase your slave help that way. Wouldn't do to have all your housemaids knocked up that way at the same time. Not very efficient."

Dangerfield gripped his hat, never taking his eyes off horse or rider.

"What happens on this place between me and Elsey, or anyone else, is my concern," said Henry in a low growl as he removed his hat. "I'll thank you to keep that in mind when you set foot on my land, Dr. Jennings."

Jennings loosened the reins and lowered his hat against his brow as he faced the morning sun. He watched slave and master closely.

"Well now, Henry, I think I understand. This one has a fair likeness to you, and of course Elsey. I can see why you won't part with him."

Henry said nothing.

"I'll pay you six hundred dollars if you sell him to me," said Jennings. "That's a fair offer, Henry, and you won't see a better one. I will see to it he's treated well."

"I ain't looking for a better offer. I told you I'd let him work for you, but he ain't for sale. Nothing has changed."

"Seven hundred dollars, and you can have two of my house servants, and a young field hand," countered Jennings.

Dangerfield watched as the two men discussed his fate as though he were not present. Henry slowly wiped his brow. "Seven hundred dollars, eh?"

"I'll make it seven hundred and fifty, and you still get the two house servants, and the young buck." Jennings waved his arm as he surveyed the crumbling outbuildings. "I say, Henry, you could take the money and buy yourself two young bucks at auction. You'd have three new young bucks and the two house servants."

Just then, Elsey came out of the house and stared at the men. She held a broom in one hand and a cast iron pot in the other. Her black skin shone in the morning sun. Elsey assessed the situation for a few moments, glowered at Jennings, then banged the end of the broomstick against the bottom of the pot. The sound of hickory against iron shattered the day's quiet. Jennings' horse bucked and spun, catching him off guard. His feet flew out of the stirrups, and the reins arced wildly above his head. He went airborne, landed cross-wise in the saddle, and his shiny black hat flew off his head and was trampled under the angry hooves. Jennings grabbed the pommel, regained his seat and the reins, and calmed his horse, speaking in soft tones. He bridled the horse and spun toward Elsey.

"Henry," she said evenly, "breakfast is ready. You better come on." She turned toward the house, then turned back. "Day, Marse Jennings," she said brightly. "That horse of yours got some fire in him, don't he." She gave an enormous satisfied smile, and went back inside.

Henry smiled softly and put his hat back on. He turned and faced Jennings, who looked silently toward the house.

"I thank you for your kind offer, Dr. Jennings. As you can see, I don't presently need any more house servants. And this one's not for sale at any price," said Henry, pointing at Dangerfield. "You can have him two days a week, thirty dollars per week. I'll send him by next week Wednesday."

Jennings dismounted slowly, and picked up what remained of his hat. "Henry, you'd do well to apply the rod to your Negroes. Improves discipline," said Jennings as he stood and examined his crumpled and dusty hat.

Henry turned and spat at the horse's hooves. The big black animal snorted, and looked wall-eyed toward the house and Elsey. "You'd do well to apply the rod to your horses, Dr. Jennings. Improves discipline." He turned and walked toward the house and his waiting breakfast. "Good day, Dr. Jennings," said Henry, bowing with a great flourish before entering the house.

Dangerfield looked toward his new part-time master. "Day, Marse Jennings," he said weakly.

Jennings saddled up, gingerly placed what was left of his tattered hat on his head, and trotted off down the path toward Warrenton. Dangerfield watched him until the dust had settled and no trace of horse or rider remained.

CHAPTER 2

The rest of Turner's family was crowded around the door as he exited his grandmother's room. Turner brushed past them as he walked out. Vernita Williams, his cousin, tugged at his sleeve as he tried to pass. Vernita and her husband Frank lived in St. Paul's east side in a tumble-down duplex. Her word was law for almost everyone in the family.

"What did she have to say," said Vernita.

"Not much, just a few stories," said Turner. "Same as always, more ghost stories."

"You were in there a long time for just a few stories."

"Nothing new, at least nothing you haven't heard before. You know more of her stories than I do."

"Maybe that's because I been around more."

"What's that supposed to mean?"

"Not supposed to mean anything. I'm just saying you ain't around much."

"You expect me to apologize because I have a job, because I moved away to go to college, because I tried to make something of myself? When I moved back home to go to med school, I didn't exactly have evenings and weekends free," said Turner. "I still don't."

"This ain't about you at all," snapped Vernita. "In case you hadn't noticed, your grandmother is dying. This is supposed to be a time when we come together."

"Well, Vernita, we certainly are together," said Turner.

"And she picked you to hear her last words."

"There weren't any last words. She is still alive, Vernita. Go in there if you want. She asked for you and the others. Gran wants to see all of you now."

"I intend to see her," said Vernita. "But first, I need to hear what she had to say from you. I need to know why she wanted to talk to you alone, apart from the rest of us. The rest of us never left her, stayed here, took care of her, looked after her. You left and came back maybe twice a year. And now, she wants to talk to you alone, while the rest of us have to wait on you to tell us what she wants, tell us what she knows. Thank God you chose to grace us with your presence."

"I never asked for this," hissed Turner as the rest of his family slowly edged away from the escalating argument. "Maybe if the rest of you had any good sense and ambition, she might share more, and trust you with secrets. Maybe Gran has figured out that anyone who can't make something of themselves can't be trusted with anything worth knowing."

"So that's it," said Vernita, her voice a raspy whisper. "We can't be trusted? Only the brilliant doctor, with his blonde wife and his big house in the suburbs, can be trusted? You think you're the only one worthy of carrying this family?"

For the second time in as many minutes, Turner had stepped on a verbal land mine that he had planted. "Look, I am sorry. Oh, for Christ's sake, Vernita, go on in and talk to her. She asked for you, and the others. It was the best history lesson I have ever had. She told me things I never knew."

"Praise the Almighty, it is a special day when you learn something."

"You better get going, Vernita. And send the others. Anything she has to say, she's going to say soon. I don't think she has much time."

Vernita turned and entered the room, closing the door firmly behind her. Turner brushed quickly past the others as he left. No one else said a word to him.

Turner walked out of the hospice into the parking lot, and found his car. He slid his lean, angular frame into the front seat of his gray BMW 325, and started the engine. He gunned the engine, jetted out of the parking lot, raced out in front of traffic, and headed for home. As he cruised past the other cars, he thought about what his grandmother had told him. Who was this distant relative, who had fought to free the slaves alongside John Brown? Why hadn't his mother, or anyone else, told him this story before? And was he really related to Dangerfield Newby? How would he find out? And what had happened to Dangerfield's wife and kids after he was killed at Harpers Ferry? And why did his grandmother tell him, and not the others?

Turner did not have the luxury of contemplating these questions for long. Just as he reached the exit that would take him home, his cell phone rang. Vernita spoke. "You better get back here. She's taken a turn for the worse. Doctors don't think she'll make it through the night."

Turner got off at the next exit, turned around, and sped back to the hospital.

Vernita and the others were outside his grandmother's room, clamoring around one of the doctors, the same pen-tapping, too-young blonde woman who had summoned Turner earlier. "What are her vitals," Turner asked the doctor without waiting for her to speak. The young doctor extricated herself from the crowd of relatives and approached him. "Dr. Turner," she said politely. "Let's talk privately, if that's alright with you." Turner nodded, and put his hand on Vernita's shoulder as he brushed past her. Turner and the doctor went to an empty room next to the old woman's room.

"She won't make it through the night," said the doctor. "Most of what she is saying is incoherent, and her blood pressure is erratic. Her pulse is weak. Her time is coming. None of this should surprise you. I know you have seen this before." Turner spun around to leave, but the doctor grabbed his arm. "She asked for you a few minutes ago. I think it would be better if you spent a few minutes with her by yourself before you bring the others in. You seem to calm her." The young doctor smiled at Turner, but he did not see it. He had already left the room.

The old woman lay on her side. The window was open, but there was no breeze outside, and the tiny room was stifling. He could hear her talking, muttering to someone unseen, unknown to him, and probably long dead. He walked to the side of the bed and grasped her hand, but she did not notice. She kept talking, muttering, pleading with the unknown souls on the other side. Turner wanted to ask more questions about Dangerfield Newby and John Brown, to find out more about his mysterious and heroic relative, but he had seen enough dying people in his career as a doctor to know that his questions would go unanswered.

He squeezed her hand, and heard her say "Yes, yes, you will, you will. You will find them, I know you will. You keep on looking 'til you find 'em."

"Who are you talking to, Gran?" said Turner. The old woman said nothing, but smiled, and gently squeezed his hand. She turned quickly, and gazed at him intently. Turner flinched at the sudden movement. "You was always special, boy," she whispered. "You may not know it, but you was always special. Still are. Just know what it means." She closed her eyes.

As she did, Turner felt a strong breeze, and saw the wind suck the curtain against the screen of the open window. He felt a sudden chill, and went to close the door, but it was already closed. He walked toward the window and looked out at the giant American flag in the yard. It hung limp and still. And then Turner knew without turning around that it was over. He pushed the window sill down, closed the old woman's eyes, and trudged outside to deliver the news to the others.

CHAPTER 3

A week after the funeral, Turner was at home, lying in his own bed. He could not sleep, so he watched his wife as she slept. He watched her, listened to her breathe, saw how her golden hair rose and fell over her body. He slipped his hand underneath her nightgown, and softly ran his hand along her leg, caressing her thigh. She rolled over and smiled, but said nothing. Turner kissed her on the cheek, quietly left the bed, and went downstairs.

He surveyed the contents of his study. His medical diploma from the University of Minnesota; rows of medical books lining the walls; the picture of him and Tracy on their wedding day; pictures of him and Tracy on a camping trip in Colorado; fading pictures of his parents; and newer pictures of Tracy's parents. On his desk was a framed, black-and-white photo of his mother shaking hands with Martin Luther King, Jr. after one of his sermons. His mother had written the date on the back of the photo: "April 9, 1967, New Covenant Baptist Church, Chicago, Illinois." His mother was a strong-looking, pretty woman, with big almond-shaped eyes accentuated by the black horned-rim glasses popular then. She is grasping Dr. King's hand firmly, and wearing a reserved smile, clearly in awe of him, but not overwhelmed. Dr. King, a full head taller than her, is smiling politely, face turned toward the camera while accepting her outstretched hand. His narrow black tie is loosened at the neck, and just slightly askew.

Turner's mother had given him this photograph ten years ago, but he had never studied it closely until now. Turner looked at the date again, and realized that the picture was taken exactly two years to the day before he was born. His mother had never mentioned that, and Turner had never bothered to ask. While he was growing up, his mother rarely discussed her involvement in the civil rights movement, except to say that she met Turner's father at a rally in Atlanta, and they married shortly after that. His father was equally silent about his work in the movement. Turner remembered his father telling him once that "your mother preferred Dr. King's approach, while I preferred Malcolm X and the hardliners. Opposites attract, which is why I married your mother."

Other than these two morsels of information, Turner knew almost nothing else about his parents' history together in the civil rights movement. Even as his mother was dying of cancer, she said very little about her civil rights work. Once, when visiting her at the hospital after it was clear that cancer would take her life, he asked her what it was like being in the center of such an important movement. "We didn't do anything to be important. Everything we did was important, but not to us. None of it mattered unless we made things better for the next generation. We had already suffered the worst of what they could throw at us. We only wanted to make things easier for the children we wanted to bring into this world. That's it."

Turner's father was even more reticent. Ever the dutiful and loyal husband, he stayed by his wife's side until her death. After she died, he retired and moved to California. He never remarried, but he kept in touch with his children. In an unguarded moment several years after Turner's mother had died, Turner's father had told him, "You will never know the things people did for you and your generation, even before you were born. You can't possibly imagine the sacrifices we made for the children we didn't even have. And if your mother and I never talked about it, that's only because it doesn't matter now. We did what we had to do. We made things better for the next generation." These explanations were good enough for Turner, and they were the only ones he would ever get.

And as he surveyed the contents of his study, Turner realized that his life was a monument to that generation's success. Turner had enjoyed a comfortable middle-class upbringing, and all the rewards that such an upbringing provides into adulthood. He had attended good schools and gotten good grades; had gone to college and then on to medical school; had graduated near the top of his class, and had gone on to become a successful internist. And although as a child he had to endure the occasional racial insult or insensitive comment, he had never felt that his skin color held him back. Now, comfortably ensconced in a large house, with a new car, a pretty wife and a successful medical career, Turner realized that he had never known true hardship or suffering. He did not know what it felt like to risk everything for people he did not know. He had never been asked to risk everything he had for any cause or movement. And now, with the death of his grandmother, he realized that another door had closed, and with it, another chance to ask the questions he should have asked many years ago.

CHAPTER 4

On the day he was to start working at the Jennings farm, Dangerfield awoke even earlier than he usually did. He pulled on Henry's old riding boots, and a coarse, yellowing cotton shirt. He wore the same pants he had slept in the previous night.

Anna Mae had gotten up earlier, and was waiting for him when he exited the house, heading for the barn. She was not carrying the usual bucket of thin, weak corn mash or the tin spoon, but instead held a plate, a fork and a knife.

"Elsey told me to fix you some breakfast before you leave today."

Dangerfield looked at the plate. It was piled high with ham, biscuits, gravy, and eggs. Dangerfield remembered the rumors he had heard from the slaves Henry had purchased years ago that field slaves ate like this only on two occasions: Christmas, and about a week or two before their owner was to sell them to someone else. If you were going to sell a slave, you wanted him well fed and healthy before the new owner could inspect him. Dangerfield knew it wasn't Christmas.

"Elsey told you to fix me all this?"

"She says you goin' over to Marse Jennings to do some work today. It's a long ride, and she want you to eat before you leave."

"She say anything else?"

"About what?"

"She say how long I'm stayin' with Marse Jennings?"

Anna Mae peered into his eyes intently. "No, but I know Henry don't aim to sell you to Jennings. I heard Elsey tell Henry yesterday morning she'd lay a pot alongside his head if he sold you to Jennings."

Dangerfield chuckled, picked up the fork, and tucked into the ham, eggs and biscuits.

"Elsey won't let Marse Henry sell any of his children he had with her," said Anna Mae softly as she looked back toward the house. "Not the field hands, or the house servants neither."

Dangerfield studied her closely: her long ruddy brown hair, which she had up in a bun; her almond-shaped eyes; her tan complexion; the freckles that dotted her face.

"So he won't sell you neither," he said as he continued eating.

"Least not as long as Elsey in the house."

Dangerfield continued eating. "You seem to know enough about what happens to the field hands. We don't know much about what happens inside the house."

Anna Mae smiled and twirled the hair at the back of her bun. "'Aint nothing happens in the house that concerns you much. Anything you need to know, I'll pass it on."

Dangerfield kept eating, but his eyes never left her face. "I suppose we are all pretty lucky Elsey's in the house," he said.

"Henry made sure Elsey knew how to read," Anna Mae replied. "He thinks all the house servants should read. Helps him out with things. And he told me to teach you how to read. I suspect he knew I was teaching the others, but never said nothing. Marse Henry about the only man in his position allows his slaves to read. I reckon you all about the only field hands in Culpeper County know how to read almost as well as a white man. Elsey keeps him in line about the only way she knows how."

Dangerfield finished his ham and eggs, and sopped the gravy with the biscuit. "I guess you don't worry much about Marse Henry selling you someplace."

Anna Mae's face darkened, and she looked down at her shoes. She took the empty plate from his hands. "You'd best be goin' now. Got a long ride and long day ahead of you." She took the plate, the fork and knife, and turned toward the house.

Dangerfield stared at her as she left; he watched his only connection to the outside world turn and walk away from him. In that moment, he realized that his sister had provided him with virtually everything he knew about life outside the farm – apart from bits and pieces of what he heard at Sunday church, Dangerfield and the others knew almost nothing about how other people lived. Henry did not discuss outside business with him.

"Anna Mae," he called out. She turned slowly and faced him.

"Thank you for the fine breakfast. You thank Miss Elsey for me."

Anna Mae smiled, but not as brightly as before. "You'd best be going now." She turned and entered the house, closing the door behind her.

Dangerfield turned from the house and walked toward the stable. Henry was waiting for him.

"Day, Marse Henry," he said.

"Yes it is," Henry replied. "I talked with Jennings last week when we were both in town. He wants you to help him with his livestock. That, and he's got a new horse that ain't broke yet. I told him you'd get a saddle on him before week's end."

"Yes, Marse."

Henry walked to the end of the stable and opened the stall gate of his favorite horse, Solomon. Solomon was a magnificent animal, a big beautiful bay stallion, over 16 hands high. The top of his withers was level with Henry's nose. Henry took Solomon by his halter and walked him out of the stable into the early morning light. His long, thickly muscled legs quivered and pulsed with each step, and his broad chest heaved. Solomon snorted, shaking his head from side to side with anticipation.

"You aim to take Solomon for a ride this morning,'" asked Dangerfield.

"No, but you will. I reckon you'd better take Solomon for your first day at Jennings' place. Need to make certain you get there and back. Solomon knows the way day and night."

Dangerfield stood silently. He had walked Solomon in the stable from time to time, but he had never ridden him. No one but Henry had ever ridden Solomon. Dangerfield watched as the big bay pranced and bucked in the early morning light. Henry saddled him, bridled him, and gave him the bit. Solomon snorted and curled his lips upward as he clamped down on the bit. Henry took the reins and slowly looped them around the pommel. He kept his hand on the pommel and motioned for Dangerfield to step forward. Solomon watched Dangerfield approach, and stamped his hooves, moving sideways. "Hush now," hissed Henry.

Dangerfield put his right hand on the pommel, and slid his left foot into the stirrup. He swung his right leg over Solomon's back, and just as he got both boots into the stirrups, Solomon bucked and twisted under the weight of an unfamiliar rider. Dangerfield pressed his weight down into the saddle and squeezed his legs tightly against Solomon's belly. The big bay nickered and stamped a bit more, but did not buck and did not throw his new rider. Dangerfield grabbed the reins, unwrapped them from the pommel, dug his heels into Solomon's belly, and pushed the horse forward. He walked him around the stable a few times, until both horse and rider reached an uneasy truce. He pulled back on the reins and sat the horse a few feet from Henry.

"Reckon you'll both get on all right," chuckled Henry. He strapped a bag of oats for Solomon and a canteen for Dangerfield behind the saddle. "You'd best be going now," said Henry. I told Jennings to expect you early today. Warrenton's a good 20 miles from here, and I reckon you'll need an hour or two of riding until the horse gets used to you. There's plenty of streams along the road. Don't push him hard, and let him have the oats about halfway along." Henry chuckled again. "Reckon you will both get on all right," he said again.

Dangerfield touched the brim of his hat and pointed Solomon down the rutted trail that led to Warrenton. Elsey emerged from the house, clutching the iron pot and the hickory broomstick. She stood silently next to Henry and touched his arm as they watched Dangerfield ride off. This time, it was Henry and Elsey who watched a vanishing rider until the dust had settled and no trace of horse or rider remained.

CHAPTER 5

It was almost dawn, and Turner was seated in front of his computer. His grandmother's last words haunted him, gripped him by the throat, and would not let go. Only now did he begin to realize that her ghost stories would never again be told, lost forever except in the fragmented memories of a handful of relatives. He had spent most of his life avoiding the old woman, and tolerating her stories only when absolutely necessary. Now, he relished her last 48 hours on earth more than the last 30 years.

He spent most of that morning looking for information about Dangerfield Newby. Everything his grandmother had told him about Dangerfield was true; his slave-master father, his marriage to another slave, his children, his emancipation, his struggle to save his family, his fateful decision to join John Brown, and his grisly end. Everything the old woman had told him was documented. He even found some web sites breathlessly proclaiming that Dangerfield's ghost still roamed the earth in an endless search for his family. A paranormal expert in New Orleans named Delilah Ann Miller had traveled to Harpers Ferry in search of Dangerfield's ghost. After a week of roaming back alleys and surrounding fields, Miller claimed to have taken a photograph of an ethereal man wearing baggy pants and a slouch hat, bearing a death scar on his throat, and clutching a tattered piece of paper and a leather coin purse. Everything the old woman had told him was true, and she had never gotten past the eighth grade, let alone touched a computer in her life.

Tracy walked into the study, yawning and holding a cup of coffee.

"What were you doing all night? A girl gets lonely in bed by herself."

"Research," explained Turner. "Do you believe in ghosts?"

"Ghosts? Nope. Only the Tooth Fairy and the Easter Bunny. Santa Claus too, but only on Christmas. This doesn't sound like medical research."

"It isn't. Look at this."

Tracy swept her hair aside and peered at the computer and chuckled as she read Delilah Ann Miller's scientific explanation of her encounter with Dangerfield's ghost. "She looks like she spends too much time in a lab somewhere," said Tracy as she let out a big yawn. "Is this why you stayed up all night?"

"I couldn't sleep, so I did some poking around, looking for stuff."

"Still thinking about that story your grandmother told you? I cannot believe the Great Man of Reason would even consider researching ghost stories."

"The ghost stories are the least of it. Everything she told me about Dangerfield Newby was true. His life, his marriage, his children, his death, all of it. I found credible sources to back up everything she told me."

"You sound surprised," said Tracy.

"It's not like I never believed her, but . . . ."

"You just could not be convinced that she saw ghosts, or talked to dead relatives."

"Oh, I believe she thinks she saw them and talked to them," said Turner. "I just don't think there was anything there."

"But if she believed it, isn't that enough?"

"Sure, and if some idiot believes aliens landed at Roswell, I should just nod, smile, and give him the benefit of the doubt." No, that isn't enough."

"Too bad, I was hoping the aliens would land and bring us intelligent life," said Tracy.

"You'll have to settle for me if you want intelligent life," replied Turner.

Tracy looked again at the image of Delilah Ann Miller. "What happened to Dangerfield's children after he died?"

"That part is unclear," said Turner. "Some think his wife was sold South, and eventually she landed in Ohio. No one knows for certain what happened to his kids. There are no records of them, and no information about where they went. They might have been sold South with their mother, but no one knows for certain."

Tracy absent-mindedly twirled her hair in her fingers and sipped her coffee.

"What are you thinking about," said Turner suspiciously.

"How do you know I am thinking about anything?"

"When you twist your hair like that, it always means you are cooking up some scheme. Last time you twisted your hair like that, we spent ten grand and a whole summer remodeling the basement for your in-home art studio."

Tracy put her coffee cup on the computer table, next to the picture of Turner's mother and Martin Luther King.

"Maybe you should take a couple weeks off and do some research on your own. Maybe go to Harpers Ferry, talk to some people, go to a courthouse and do some research. You know, see if you can find out what happened to Dangerfield's wife and kids."

"When would I do that," scoffed Turner.

"You have to make time," Tracy said sharply. "You never made time for your mom or dad. You never made time for your grandmother, and now you will never hear her stories again. You have to make time."

"So that's what this is about. I suppose you feel I don't make time for you either," said Turner.

"That's not what I said."

"You didn't have to. Look, work has been crazy, and I've been focused on getting this research grant. If this works out, and I get the grant, I'm next in line to be chief of surgery. Then we go somewhere, take some time off."

"You think you'll have more free time once you're chief of surgery?" scoffed Tracy. "I should start looking for an apartment now."

Turner waited for her to laugh, or smile, or something. She did not oblige.

"Maybe if I take a few weeks off to do research, you could come with me," offered Turner. "We could make it a research vacation. Spend a few days in Harpers Ferry, then maybe swing down to Florida for awhile. Can your sculptures wait a few weeks?"

Tracy picked up her coffee cup and allowed a smile to crease her face. "A vacation in West Virginia, researching dead people. You do know how to tempt a girl."

"It was your idea," said Turner. "Start packing. I'll get the tickets."

Tracy kissed him softly on the mouth, and gently padded upstairs. Turner was about to switch off the computer, but thought better of it. He looked up Delilah Ann Miller, and found her web site. Her home page showed her standing in front of an antebellum house in New Orleans at sundown, holding a flashlight and a notepad. She had jet-black hair, and she wore it short, closely cropped on each side, slightly longer in the middle. Large, round wire-rimmed glasses clung to the very end of her nose – it seemed like a slight breeze would have sent them crashing off her face. She wore a pleated navy blue pantsuit, and a white blouse. She was tall, and lean, and stern, and someone looking at her for the first time could not be blamed for thinking that her face had never known a smile. She could have passed for an accountant, or a librarian.

Turner studied her web site. "Delilah Ann Miller has studied paranormal activity for over 20 years. She has found spirits and souls in transition in cities around the world, but she focuses her work in the Southern United States, particularly her home city of New Orleans," her web site proclaimed. "She has spoken with troubled spirits and wandering souls from the Civil War and both World Wars, and many other times of historical interest. She has bridged the gap between this world and the next, and has facilitated direct communication between living relatives and spirits across the bridge, bringing closure to the living and the dead."

He found the page with the photograph of Dangerfield Newby. The photo was grainy and shadowy and poorly lit, like one of those photographs of Bigfoot or the Loch Ness Monster. The photo was taken from the front, and showed a figure of indeterminate height wearing a black hat pulled over his face, black pants, and boots. He held his right hand to his throat, and held a grayish object in his left hand, which dangled near his leg. He was bow-legged, and appeared to be lurching forward. "I took this photo in Hog Alley, in Harpers Ferry, West Virginia in August, 1999, at dusk," read a caption under the photograph. "I am convinced that the figure in this photograph is Dangerfield Newby, and the object in his hand is a leather pouch where he kept letters from his wife," it continued.

"Good grief," Turner muttered softly to himself. "This picture could have been taken anywhere, any time, and it could be anyone. There is no way to verify any of this stuff."

He sensed that he was wasting his time reading a web site from a con artist, but he found another page on her web site, and read on: "Delilah has also helped law enforcement officials solve cold murder cases by reaching across the bridge to the victims, and passing key pieces of information to law enforcement agents." The page showed a black-and-white newspaper photograph of Miller standing between two New Orleans police officers over a headline that read "NOPD Officers Crack 20 Year-Old Murder Case With Help From Local Ghost Chaser."

The accompanying story explained that Miller had helped police solve the case of a murdered prostitute found in a ditch in a remote wooded area on the outskirts of New Orleans. There were no witnesses, and police had been unable to locate anyone from the woman's family, or any of her friends. The case was unsolved for 20 years, until Miller read about it, and offered to help the police. Miller went with police to the ditch where the woman had been found 20 years earlier. She held a shoe the woman was wearing when found, and walked slowly back and forth in the ditch, clutching the shoe near her chest. After 30 minutes, Miller announced that she saw an image of a man wearing a blue uniform, maybe a jumpsuit, with numbers on the back. She saw a steel bed, white sheets, and a metal sink. Miller also said she heard a female voice telling her to look for a man named "L."

Police searched local prison and jail records, and discovered that a convicted rapist named Lenwood David Garvey had worked at a construction site 20 years ago near the spot where the woman was found. Garvey had been on work release: he worked during the day, and reported back to jail at night. Garvey was working at the construction site the day before the woman was found. Police searched the construction company's records, and discovered that although Garvey worked that day, his supervisor had reported him absent for the entire afternoon.

Police interviewed Garvey in prison, and he confessed to the crime: he had left work early that day, and driven back into the city to buy beer. He spotted the woman in an alley, picked her up, killed her, put her body in the trunk of his car, and drove to the wooded area, where he dumped her body into the ditch. He returned to jail that evening, and reported for work the following morning. Police had never thought to question him, because he was in jail that night, and at work the next morning.

"This case was stone cold until Delilah came along," said one of the detectives. "We could not have solved this without her. At first I was skeptical, but she gave us information that only the killer or the victim would have known."

Turner scratched his chin. He read the story again, then looked at the blurry picture of Dangerfield Newby clutching the object in his hand.

"Bullshit," he said softly to himself, and quietly turned off the computer.

CHAPTER 6

Three days later, they landed in Washington D.C., and drove to Harpers Ferry, West Virginia. Turner and Tracy strolled hand in hand down the historic streets, and soaked it all in. Turner read every sign, every historic marker, and every brochure he got from each place they visited. Tracy waited patiently at first, and then, as the day grew longer, she began tapping her foot and emitting deep sighs each time Turner would stop to digest yet another historical marker. Turner absorbed everything he could about the final resting place of the would-be relative who met his end and made his name in this place.

At 7:30 that evening, Turner and Tracy walked down Potomac Street to the Armory Pub, where they each paid five dollars for a tour of the ghosts and haunted sites of Harpers Ferry. The guide, a lanky and uncomfortable college student named Matthew, explained that this was the last tour of the day, and that the tour would conclude shortly after dark.

"This is a living history tour, not a paranormal experience tour," Matthew explained. "No one has ever seen a ghost on this tour, although you will hear of people who have seen ghosts in Harpers Ferry, and they will tell you what they saw and what they were doing." Tracy squeezed Turner's hand, but said nothing.

"You aren't scared, are you?" asked Turner.

"No, not really, just excited for you," said Tracy.

"Well, when the boogeyman comes, he'll come for me first. The black guy is always the first to get killed in the scary movies. The blonde chicks don't get killed 'til the end."

"Shut up and pay attention, you might learn something," hissed Tracy.

"Probably not, since I'll be the first one to get whacked."

Matthew cleared his throat and began the tour.

"Harpers Ferry is perhaps most famous as the site of John Brown's raid on the local armory, which took place in October 1859 when the city, then a small but vital commercial and military center, was located in Virginia. When Virginia seceded from the union in 1861, Harpers Ferry and other communities in the northwestern corner of Virginia objected, and voted to remain in the union. Two years later, West Virginia became a state, and Harpers Ferry then became part of West Virginia."

Matthew turned and gestured toward the confluence of the Shenandoah and Potomac rivers.

"Aside from the state boundaries, little has changed in Harpers Ferry – most of the town and the surrounding area is now controlled by the National Park Service, and many of the old buildings have been preserved and restored. Civil War re-enactors, park employees and history buffs often stroll through the town in period costumes, which adds to the town's lost-in-time feel," Matthew explained. "John Brown himself could stroll through the town without turning many heads. And although Brown and his men failed in their efforts to free American slaves, their unsuccessful rebellion planted the seeds for the Civil War and the eventual end of slavery."

Matthew led the group down Potomac Street for a half block, then turned right onto a paved walkway.

"This," Matthew announced grandly, "is Hog Alley, where Dangerfield Newby was killed. Dangerfield was a free black man and a member of John Brown's raiding party, and he was the first of Brown's men to be killed." Matthew was about to say something else, but he caught himself abruptly and stared at something at the end of the alley.

"Why do they call it Hog Alley?" asked someone from the group.

"It's not a pretty story," said Matthew, his voice cracking as he spoke. "After Dangerfield was killed, local townspeople cut off his ears as souvenirs. And then they rifled through his belongings, taking some of his personal effects, including letters from his wife. Remarkably, those letters survived. And then they fed his body to the hogs." Mathew paused. "Um, after the hogs finished eating, the town folk took what was left of his body and disposed of it." Matthew peered intently down the alley past one of the buildings at the end of the alley. He wiped his mop of black hair out of his eyes, pulled a handkerchief out of his pocket, and dabbed his sweaty forehead.

"Are you feeling alright?" asked Turner.

"Yeah, I'm okay, I just . . . . Nothing. Must be the heat," said Matthew.

"How did Dangerfield die?" asked another person on the tour.

"That is an equally unpleasant story," explained Matthew, regaining his voice.

"The townspeople had very little ammunition for their guns, since Brown and his men had captured the armory. Lacking ammunition, they fired anything they could find, including spikes, nails, even silverware that they melted down into balls. Dangerfield was hit in the throat by a six-inch spike fired from one of the guns. The spike cut his throat from ear to ear, and he died right where he fell." Matthew looked again at something at the end of the alley.

Turner looked down the alley, but he saw nothing.

"What about this ghost people keep talking about," asked Turner. Tracy shot him a sharp glance, but Turner was facing away from her.

Matthew coughed and cleared his throat. "As I said at the start of the tour, this is a living history tour, not a paranormal tour. As far as any ghost, well, I have never seen any ghost. But other people say they've seen a tall man wearing a black hat, and black leather boots, carrying a coin purse or satchel, right here in this alley. And they say he has a gash in his throat from one ear to the other."

"So, are we going to see him tonight?" asked Turner impishly. "We came all the way from Minnesota to see us some ghosts."

Several tour members chuckled. Tracy sidled up to him, squeezed his hand, and firmly dug her sharp fingernail into the palm of his hand. Turner flinched. "C'mon, I'm just having a little fun."

"I've never seen him, but tonight might be your night," said Matthew, his voice cracking again. "Let's get going, it will be dark soon, and we have other sights to see. He took another long look down the alley.

"In fact, let's take a different route this time," said Matthew weakly. "We'll go past Potomac Street, and head over to the railroad tracks, and I can tell you all about Screaming Jenny. Legend has it that Jenny lived in a shack near the railroad tracks. Locals say her dress caught fire one cold winter night as she leaned over her stove. She ran out of her shack, dress afire, and onto the railroad tracks, where she was run over by a passing train. Engineers still say that on a foggy night, you can see a screaming ball of fire heading from the hills toward the tracks. Her scream is unearthly. Some engineers won't even pass the bend until the fog clears."

Tracy leaned over and whispered in Turner's ear. "I didn't come all this way to spend the entire week hearing about men with slashed throats and women engulfed in flames. You owe me big time. Tomorrow, we are going shopping."

"C'mon, I thought you believed in this stuff."

"I do, but I don't need the gory details. I like the nice ghosts, like your kindly grandfather-type ghost who comes back from the dead and tells you where the family treasure is buried," replied Tracy. "Then he leaves, you find the treasure, and he smiles approvingly from heaven, but doesn't bother you anymore. Why can't you have any rich long-lost dead ghost relatives?"

"Where's the fun in that? I think you really are scared," said Turner.

"Not yet, but if I hear of one more slashing or self-immolation, I won't sleep for a week," replied Tracy. "Besides, the tour ends after dark, and I don't feel like walking back in the dark," said Tracy looking down the street.

"How about we duck out of the rest of the tour, and head back to the hotel," offered Turner. "Let's see if our room is haunted."

He kissed her softly on the mouth and they turned around and walked back to Potomac Street, leaving nervous Matthew and the rest of the tour group to their discoveries. As they crossed Hog Alley on the way back to the Armory Pub, something caught Turner's eye.

He walked slowly, with a slight limp, down Hog Alley with his back toward the couple. He wore a wide-brimmed black hat, black breeches, and leather boots.

He held something in his hand, but Turner could not see what it was. Turner watched him as he walked down the alley. Then he turned, briefly faced the couple, and continued walking straight down the alley. Turner touched Tracy on the shoulder.

"Babe, look, it's one of the reenactors," said Turner, laughing. "It's somebody pretending to be Dangerfield's ghost. His costume is spot-on. Look."

Tracy had been eyeing hand-made jewelry in a shop front three doors down from the Armory Pub. She turned and looked down the alley.

"Where? I don't see anything."

"Right down there, walking down Hog Alley, with his back turned toward us," said Turner. "Check out the costume. He's got the look down, even down to the boots and the hat. Man, these people take this stuff seriously."

She peered down the alley, holding her hand over her eyes as the last of the day's sun splintered across the alley. "I don't see anything," she said. "Are you trying to keep me from spending lots of money at this store? "Cause it won't work."

"No, really, don't you see him? There, he is facing us. Now, he just turned away from us and . . . no, there he goes, to the left. He has something in his hand. See? I wonder where they get those costumes."

Tracy looked again down the alley, for a long time, moving her head from side to side. "If this is supposed to be a joke, you're not funny. And I am not that easily distracted from jewelry. I saw a necklace that I think I could make if I had the right tools in my studio - -"

He gripped her arm and spun her toward the alley. "Right – there! Now he's still moving left, past the mill . . . ."

Tracy looked at his face, and gently pried his fingers from her arm. "Are you all right? I still don't see anything," she said."

He looked again, but now the reenactor was gone. "Well now I don't see him anymore," said Turner, disappointed.

"You sure you saw anything?"

"Maybe not," Turner said softly, continuing to peer down the alley. "Could be the heat."

"Yeah, it probably was the heat. And nothing takes my mind off heat like ice-cold jewelry,' said Tracy, as she took his hand and began walking away from the alley. "C'mon, this place is still open. Here's your chance to make up for taking me on the Magical Mystery Ghost Tour. Four or five necklaces and I might forgive you."

She turned to face him, and saw that he was still peering down the alley. "Did you find what you were looking for today?"

"Maybe so," he muttered absent-mindedly. "Maybe so."

CHAPTER 7

Turner lay awake the entire night in their hotel room, while Tracy slept beside him. He knew he had seen something, and he knew it was not the heat. Harpers Ferry was crawling with reenactors – it would not be too hard to find out which reenactor was playing Dangerfield's ghost.

Turner awoke early the next morning, and quietly dressed as Tracy slept. He scribbled a note on the hotel's stationery and left it on the bed beside Tracy: "Went into town to do some research. See you back here at noon for lunch." He dropped the note on the bed and quietly slipped out the door, leaving his slumbering wife behind.

Turner walked down Potomac Street back to the Armory Pub. He walked in, and looked around. A paunchy, middle-aged man was sweeping the floor. "We're not open yet," he said in a pleasant Tidewater drawl. "Come on back in about an hour or so."

"I'm actually here to see Matthew. Is he here yet?"

"He's in back." The man examined Turner. "Can I tell him what this is about?"

"I was here last night for a tour of the Harpers Ferry ghosts. Matthew was the tour guide, and I wanted to ask him a few questions."

The man stood the broom in a corner and walked toward the stairs that led to the basement." "Matthew, come on up for a minute, son. There is a gentleman here wants to talk to you." The man gave Turner one more long look, and then resumed his sweeping.

Matthew emerged from the basement with a pencil behind his ear. He was carrying a note pad, and he was still wearing the clothes he had on from the previous night. A hint of recognition crossed his face when he saw Turner.

"Can I help you?" said Matthew.

"I was on the tour last night" said Turner. "I thought you did a nice job, and I had a few questions for you."

"Sure, I remember you. The couple from Minnesota. You wanted to see some ghosts. Sorry I had to disappoint you."

"I noticed you looking at something last night during the tour. Did you see something you didn't want to share with the rest of the group?"

Matthew looked at him blankly.

"Last night, during the tour," repeated Turner. "I saw you staring at something at the end of the alley. Whatever it was, you looked at it for a long time."

"When during the tour?"

"Just before it got dark. You stared at something twice, for a long time."

"Right, right, now I remember," said Matthew. "I saw a stray dog down at the end of the alley. Normally, I take the groups down the length of the alley, but I was worried about the dog. It wasn't a dog I had seen before, and it looked a bit off-kilter, so I changed the course. Why are you asking?"

"A stray dog? That is what you saw?"

"Yes. Did you see the dog too?"

"No, I didn't see any dog. I thought I saw something else."

"What do you think you saw?"

Turner considered telling him what he saw, but quickly thought better of it.

"It's not important. Do you know any of the reenactors in the area?"

"I know a few," said Matthew. "Some of my buddies from school make a little money during the summer playing soldiers, and 19th century townsfolk. I used to date a girl who played Screaming Jenny. She got paid to sit in a shack near the railroad tracks and run out screaming when tour groups came past."

"Do you know if any of the reenactors play Dangerfield Newby?" asked Turner.

Matthew scratched his head. "No, I can't remember anybody ever playing Dangerfield Newby. It would be kind of creepy, knowing his story. Not many guys I can think of want to walk around with a fake gash from ear to ear."

Matthew examined Turner closely. "Are you interested in playing him? You kind of resemble him, from the pictures I have seen. We've never had a Dangerfield reenactor before. It might add a little zing to the story."

"I appreciate the offer, but I have a day job in Minnesota. So as far as you know, there are no Dangerfield reenactors roaming about Harpers Ferry?"

"None, and I would know if there were. My dad and I run the living history tour out of the bar here. There are two other tours in town, and I know the folks who run both of them. There have been a few reenactors playing soldiers, one Screaming Jenny, and the occasional John Brown, but no Dangerfield reenactors. I know that for certain. Why are you so interested?"

"I think his story is interesting. I may be related to him, and I'm just doing some poking around, doing some research."

Turner looked at his watch. "Listen, Matthew, thanks for your time. One last question – has anyone ever really seen Dangerfield's ghost?"

Matthew chuckled, and put his hand softly on Turner's shoulder. He leaned in closer to Turner. "I don't personally believe in ghosts," whispered Matthew. "There are some people in town who claim to have seen Dangerfield's ghost, and I know them. They are all either crazy or psychics, with significant overlap between those two groups."

Matthew looked toward the front door to make certain his father was no longer in earshot. "Look, we run a living history tour, not a paranormal tour," said Matthew softly. "We tell the tourists the ghost stories, because it sells tickets. I don't believe in ghosts. Not Dangerfield's ghost, or Screaming Jenny's ghost, or anybody's ghost, but ghosts sell more tickets than history. If you want, I can give you the names of the townsfolk who claim to have seen them both. Like I said, they're all crazy as loons."

Matthew stared at him, and allowed a smirk to cross his face. "You don't think you saw him last night, do you? Maybe you got your money's worth after all."

Turner returned the smile. "No, I didn't see anything last night. It must have been the heat."

"Sure, probably the heat. You want those names?"

"Sure, if you have them."

Matthew retrieved a pad from his shirt pocket and scribbled a few names and addresses on a piece of paper. He folded it in half, and handed it to Turner.

"Here you go. Like I said these folks are crazy as loons, but they like to talk about the 'haints' they claim to have seen here in town. A couple of 'em swear to have seen Dangerfield's ghost. They won't mind a friendly ear."

"Have you ever talked to any of these people?"

"Sure," said Matthew laughing. "Some of 'em come in town trying to sell their stories to newspapers and magazines. They come here and scare the hell out of my guests. I don't mind, because it's good for the tour business."

Turner examined the names and folded the note in his pocket. "How do you know they're crazy? Maybe they really did see something."

Matthew chuckled. "Seems awful curious that the same folks who claim to have seen Screaming Jenny also claim to have seen Dangerfield's ghost. Me personally, I've never seen any ghosts, and I've worked in this place and given the tours since I was 15. If anybody would have seen any ghosts, it would be me. The people who believe that stuff claim to have seen all the ghosts and spirits that supposedly haunt this town. The rest of us never see anything."

Turner considered his grandmother's fervent belief in ghosts and spirits, a belief she clung to while alive, and took with her to her grave. "Maybe you have to believe before you can see them," Turner said more to himself than anyone else.

Matthew snorted. "Count me among the nonbelievers. But these folks will be more than happy to have a sympathetic ear."

Turner extended his hand. "Thanks for your time, and the tour."

Turner left the pub and walked into the bright early morning sun. He walked down Hog Alley, turned to his right, and looked back at the pub. Then he continued walking down the alley, until he reached the end. On his left was the old mill. On his right, an old warehouse that now housed a coffee shop and a bookstore. He looked back up the alley toward the pub. "No way that thing was a dog," he muttered to himself. He thought about asking the owners of the coffee shop if they had seen a man wearing a black hat and boots carrying a coin purse or satchel around 8 p.m. last evening, but realized how crazy that would sound.

He took one last long look around, and went into the coffee shop for breakfast and a newspaper.

CHAPTER 8

Solomon moved briskly along the road to Warrenton, sometimes cantering, sometimes trotting. Henry had ridden to Jennings' plantation countless times, and Solomon knew every rut, every bend in the road, every stream crossing, and every rise on the way to Jennings' plantation. The big stallion wanted to run, and Dangerfield had to rein him constantly to keep him from breaking into a gallop. After an hour or so of riding, Dangerfield was comfortable with the reins, and knew when the big horse was about to run, and pulled back on the reins as necessary. The morning sun beat down on both of them, and Solomon was beginning to lather. Dangerfield bridled him and sat him next to a stream that ran alongside the path. He loosened the saddle belt, and led the stallion to the stream. Solomon dipped his mouth in the stream up to his nostrils, snorting and slurping in creek water. Dangerfield retrieved the feedbag and put a handful of oats in his hat. The stallion's muzzle barely fit inside the hat, and he inhaled the oats in two mouthfuls. Dangerfield gave him another handful, and another, never allowing the stallion to eat until he was full. After four handfuls, Solomon snorted and turned back to the creek. By looking at the angle of the sun, Dangerfield calculated he would be in Warrenton by late morning. He retrieved a biscuit and a piece of ham that Anna Mae had wrapped up for him, and sat next to the stream beside Solomon. He had no idea what to expect once he got to Jennings' place.

Solomon jerked his head suddenly and looked up. His ears pricked up and he turned his massive shaggy head toward the road leading to Warrenton. He snorted and stamped, lowering his head as if to improve his hearing.

"What is it old man?" said Dangerfield, standing up. Then Dangerfield heard the hoofbeats moving quickly toward them from Warrenton. Two horses, maybe three, sometimes cantering, sometimes galloping. The riders were in a hurry, and coming toward Dangerfield. Now Dangerfield could feel the approaching riders, feel the ground moving beneath them. He could hear the horses nickering over the sound of hoofbeats, and could hear the voices of men laughing.

The riders rounded a bend and came into full view. Solomon blocked the road, and Dangerfield stood beside him. Three horses galloped into view. The lead rider put up his hand and bridled his horse, and the other riders stopped behind them. Solomon lowered his head, and the lead rider, a tall white man with a thick black mustache, approached while the others stayed a few paces behind.

"Day, Marse," said Dangerfield, removing his hat.

The tall white man surveyed Dangerfield and Solomon for a few moments before speaking. "What is your business this morning," he inquired.

Dangerfield studied him quickly. He sat atop a smallish dun, maybe 13 hands high. He wore a black hat with the brim pulled low over his face, and a pale blue shirt tucked into black riding pants, which were tucked into tall cavalry riding boots. Aside from his thick black mustache, which curled up at the ends, he was clean-shaven. He had a jagged scar on the left side of his face that ran from just under his left eye to the corner of his mouth. He had a rifle strapped to the right side of his saddle, and a pistol on his belt. Behind him sat a single Negro man, shirtless, his hands tied tightly around his back. The Negro man had a thick rope tied around his waist, and a second rider following closely behind held the other end of the rope. The first rider's mount carried no saddlebags, just the two riders and the rifle.

"I'm headed to Warrenton, to see Marse Jennings. "Doin' some work for him this morning."

"Do you belong to Jennings?"

"No sir. I belong to Marse Henry Newby. He lives back yonder in Culpeper."

The man studied Dangerfield, and then eyed Solomon. "That's a splendid horse. Is it yours?"

"No sir, Solomon there belongs to Marse Henry."

"Does Henry Newby know you took his horse?"

"Yes sir, Henry told me to take him this morning. He lets me ride him now and again."

The tall man pulled at the corner of his mustache. "What business do you have with Dr. Jennings this morning?"

"Like I explained, Marse Henry sending me to work for Marse Jennings for a spell. When I finish, I go back home to Marse Henry."

"Does Dr. Jennings know you're coming?"

"Yes sir, he sent for me, so I suppose he must be expecting me."

The tall man looked behind him at the other riders, and then addressed Dangerfield.

"Have you seen any Negroes on the road this morning, on foot or horse?"

"No sir, I haven't. I haven't seen anyone else on the trail this morning."

The tall man looked him over, head to foot, and then looked at Solomon.

"Very well then. Good day." The tall man tipped his hat toward Dangerfield, spurred the dun, and it moved forward. As they passed, Dangerfield could see the lash marks on the Negro man's back, long red fingers dripping blood from his black skin. The lash marks covered his back from his shoulders to his waist, and stretched from rib to rib. Black flies covered his back, feasting on his wounded and open flesh. The man writhed as the flies bit him, but with his hands bound, he could do nothing to stop them.

The next rider approached. He was a smaller man, similarly dressed as the lead rider, but his mount carried two saddlebags. He too carried a pistol on his belt. He held the rope attached to the Negro man's waist.

The third rider wore the same uniform as the first two. His mount, a tall, stout bay, carried two saddlebags, and he also carried a pistol at his belt. But he did not have a rifle strapped to his saddle – instead, he carried a large brown whip, coiled but untied, the handle up and facing the rider for easy access. This rider studied Dangerfield carefully, and continued to watch him as he passed. This rider was young, no more than 16. He wore no hat, and his thin blond hair stretched past his shoulders halfway down his back. He had full lips, soft, almost feminine features, and as he passed Dangerfield, he rested his hand on the whip handle and smiled.

As the last horse passed, the lead rider called out, and the horses began trotting down the path. Dangerfield waited until the riders were out of sight and earshot before tightening up the saddle belt and mounting Solomon. Solomon nickered and moved forward. Well rested, the big stallion lunged forward and broke into a canter, then a full gallop. Dangerfield pulled back on the reins, then thought better of it, letting him gallop, keeping a loose hand on the reins. "Let's go, old man, get us away from here." Solomon was happy to oblige.

———◦((◦))◦———

They arrived at the Jennings' farm late that morning. Solomon was breathing hard, and well lathered – Dangerfield had indulged the big bay and let him gallop a bit more than he normally would have. As soon as he entered the gate, a young Negro boy came out to meet them, carrying a bucket and a brush. He looked quizzically at Dangerfield and Solomon. Dangerfield dismounted, and the boy took hold of Solomon's halter.

"Just a handful of oats and water, and brush him down well," said Dangerfield to the boy.

The boy stared at Dangerfield before speaking. "Are you here to see Marse Jennings?"

"Yes, I am. Marse Jennings is expecting me."

The boy led Solomon to the stable, said a few words to another stablehand, and then ran in to the main house.

Jennings emerged a few moments later, wearing the same clothes he had worn when he had visited Henry's farm. His black hat was dusty and torn.

"Day, Marse Jennings," said Dangerfield, removing his hat."

"Well, you made good time," said Jennings. "Has the boy taken care of your horse?"

"Yes sir. Oats, water, and a good brushing."

"Very well," said Jennings. "Henry says you'll help me two days a week, thirty dollars per week. Since today is already half over, I assume Henry couldn't properly object if you stay here an extra day this week, so I get my thirty dollars' worth. I have some fences in need of repair, a loose cattle gate, and I need to build a new corn crib. That and the usual chores – butcher hogs, repair sheds, that sort of thing. Henry tells me you can make saddles?

"Yes sir. I reckon I can make saddles, repair boots, and anything else might need to be done."

"Very well. I understand why Henry won't sell you. I might just change his mind someday. Let's have Harriet fix you some lunch, and you can get started on the fences."

The two men walked up to the main house. Jennings went in, and Dangerfield waited just outside the door. He surveyed his new employer's holdings – neat, well-built corn cribs, solid-looking sheds for livestock, a new smokehouse, and an enormous, open-air stable, home to at least twenty horses. A dozen or so men and boys tended the horses in the stable. Next to the stable stood a low, squat shed, built along a rushing creek and surrounded by a large group of women washing and hanging clothes. The laundry, like the rest of the buildings, was well built, and near enough to the main house so that the owner could observe the activities without having to leave his comfortable home. There were no leaning buildings, no broken windows, no punctured corn cribs spilling their contents, no one-hinged doors slamming in the wind. From all outward appearances, Jennings was doing far better than Henry, with more slaves, more cattle, and better buildings. Dangerfield began to understand Henry's hatred for Jennings, and Jennings' contempt for Henry – both men owned property, human and otherwise, but the similarities ended there.

After a few moments, a tall, willowy woman with large almond-shaped eyes and skin the color of dark coffee emerged from the house carrying a small plate of biscuits, chicken and corn. She wore a blue frock and her long black hair was pulled back and covered with a blue scarf. Her legs were long and in perfect proportion with the rest of her body. Dangerfield watched her closely as she set the plate on a small table next to the house. Jennings followed closely behind her and exited the house.

Jennings addressed the woman. "Harriet, after he's finished eating, show him the barn and the fence that needs repair. I'd like it started as soon as possible." Jennings turned and walked toward the stable.

"Yes, Marse," the young woman replied. She looked at Dangerfield. "You finish lunch, and then knock on the door to let me know you're done. I will show you what you need to see." She spoke in short, clipped phrases, and her speech was more refined than that of most servants, even house servants.

"Yes ma'am, I would like that."

She turned and entered the house. Dangerfield did not take his eyes off of her. She stopped, turned and looked at him. "What are you lookin' at?"

"You," said Dangerfield. "You remind me of someone back home. But you a far sight prettier than her."

Harriet studied him for a moment, shook her head and entered the house. "Knock on the door when you finish," she said before closing the door behind her.

Dangerfield watched her walk back into the house, and continued staring as he tucked into his lunch. He ate quickly, knowing that the faster he ate, the sooner he would see her again. He sopped his plate with a biscuit, ate the last bit of chicken, laid the plate on the table, and knocked on the door. He watched her walk toward the door wiping her hands on a towel. She looked up and he smiled as she approached.

"You eat fast, like a dog" she said as she exited the house and picked up his plate. She did not look at him, but started walking away from the house toward the stable. He followed her, and walked fast to keep up.

"I reckon I'm about hungry as a dog."

"You didn't take any food with you from Culpeper?"

"I did, but I ate all of it on the ride here."

"Your wife must not care 'bout you too much if she let you ride from Culpeper to Warrenton without enough food."

"Don't have a wife."

"You must have somebody who tries to take care of you."

"Marse Henry and Miss Elsey take pretty good care of all of us."

"Don't have a wife," Harriet muttered. "That explains why you look the way you do."

"I don't reckon there's anything wrong with the way I look."

"You look messy, dirty and hungry."

"I look like a man who just rode hard for twenty miles. Ain't nothing wrong with me, and I already got a father and a mother. Don't need anyone else issuing orders."

She chuckled, and kept walking, even faster now. Dangerfield was almost running to keep up as she spoke.

"Ain't never met a man yet who don't need a wife," she said.

"Well, I ain't never met a woman I wanted to have as a wife."

They walked in silence until they reached the stable, and the fence. The fence was sturdy where it joined the stable, but it sagged and buckled further away from the stable, and he could see several boards that the horses had kicked out. Two horses grazing near the fence looked up at them as they approached, eyed them impassively, and continued grazing. Harriet stopped at the first post.

"This is where he wants you to start. You see what the horses done to the fence. Marse ain't had time to mend them. She bent down to lift a board on the ground, and struggled for a few minutes to restore it to its intended position. As she did so, he could see the tops of her breasts, and her firm black nipples pushing against her thin blouse. He stared until she rose again, and looked him straight in the eye.

"You best get started," she said. "Marse keeps all his tools in the stable." She gave him a faint smile, and he could feel his stomach flutter. She turned and began walking back toward the house. He tried to think of something to say to keep her from leaving.

"Miss Harriet."

She stopped, but did not turn around immediately.

"Miss Harriet."

"Yes?"

"Marse Jennings – is he good to you?" I mean does he treat the servants kindly?"

Harriet turned slowly, and he could see her smile was gone.

"I reckon you won't have much of a problem, seein' as how Marse Jennings don't own you. You belong to someone else, so I reckon he won't do much to you."

"And what if he did own me? Would he treat me kindly?"

Harriet lowered her head, looked toward the house, and looked around before answering him in a soft whisper.

"Marse Jennings ain't so bad to the womenfolk. Least not those he thinks he can bed. Ain't so with the menfolk. He rides 'em hard, and cusses at 'em terribly. And don't think about running off. He don't spare the whip or the beatings. Marse Jennings says colored menfolk ain't no good 'til they broken. And he seems to enjoy breakin' 'em.

"Is he good to you?"

Harriet paused. "He ain't hard on me. Ma'am keeps an eye on him. She needs me in the house, so he leaves me alone. He don't bother me."

They stared at each other for a few moments, neither speaking. "You'd best get started," said Harriet.

He looked for the smile again, but her face was ashen.

She turned and walked toward the house and did not turn around to face him as she left. He did not take his eyes off of her until she had entered the house and closed the door.

"Don't have a wife," he muttered to himself as he walked toward the stable to gather the tools he needed. Dangerfield watched the afternoon sun and considered all he had seen that day. Jennings seemed to take good care of his slaves, at least as much as any other landowner. And if Harriet was any indication, someone was likely teaching them to read and write. And they all seemed well fed. But he sensed that something was wrong.

Dangerfield returned from the stable with his tools. He had just finished resetting the first corner post when a small boy came running toward him from the house, wild-eyed and screaming.

CHAPTER 9

Turner bought a cup of coffee and a morning newspaper and took a seat next to a window in the café. He knew he wasn't crazy, and he knew what he had not seen last night. "No way that thing was a dog," he muttered softly to himself. But not softly enough; a woman in the booth next to him looked over, smiled, and asked "Excuse me?"

"Oh, nothing, I was just talking to myself. Going over a few things in my mind."

The woman smiled again, noisily gathered her coffee, books and a newspaper, and moved to another booth across the café. "Maybe I am crazy," Turner thought silently to himself. He looked at his watch. It was now 9:30 a.m., and Tracy would be awake by now. He pulled out his cell phone and punched in her number. She answered on the first ring.

"Where the hell are you," she asked.

"Did you get my note? I got up early to do some research. I didn't want to wake you," he replied.

"You know I hate to wake up alone. Had you been here, you might have gotten lucky. Too bad for you."

"Can you meet for lunch at the hotel around noon? I can tell you what I found, and maybe I can get lucky later."

"My, aren't we presumptuous. Tell you what. You bring me that necklace I saw last night, and your luck will probably get better after lunch. I'll go for a run or something until you get back. Do you miss me yet?"

"Every minute I am away. I will meet you at noon at the hotel restaurant. I might even have a necklace for you."

"You will, if you want dessert."

Turner closed his phone, and pulled out the note from Matthew. Three names and addresses were scribbled on the paper: Lucas Miller, Ezekiel Frazier, and Sally Ann McKenzie. Turner examined the names and addresses, and checked the maps he bought earlier. He looked at his watch – he might have time to talk to all three and still make it back to the hotel by noon. All three lived just outside of town, in the hills overlooking Harpers Ferry, on the Maryland side. "No coincidence there," he thought to himself. "The crazies tend to keep to themselves." But Turner knew he had seen something the night before, and verification from a lunatic was better than no verification at all. He folded the note in his pocket, and walked out to his car.

Turner took the scenic route on his trip to the Maryland hills, and he arrived at Ezekiel Frazier's address about 10:30 a.m. The house sat on a small lot on a hill high above the confluence of the Potomac and Shenandoah rivers. Turner could hear the roar of the rivers as soon as he exited his car. He studied the house, and his suspicions about Mr. Frazier's sanity instantly grew stronger: blackened shingles buckled up from the roof; the warped gutters sagged and drooped; the front door hung at an angle, and someone had wedged a square of plywood where the door window once was; paint was peeling off the windows in fistfuls; and the knee-high grass in the front yard had gone to seed. Every window that wasn't broken was covered in black plastic. A pile of freshly cut logs lay against the south side of the house, and woodsmoke drifted from a chimney on the back of the house. Turner sucked in his breath, and stepped on the front porch. The uneven wooden slats creaked and groaned, until one of the slats snapped under his weight. Turner fell to one knee, quickly extracted his leg from the hole in the porch, and stood up.

Someone inside the house slowly pulled back the plastic that covered the front window, and quickly jerked it back.

"Mr. Frazier? Mr. Frazier, are you in there?" There was no response.

"Mr. Frazier, if you're in there, I would like to talk to you for a minute. I understand you know something about Dangerfield Newby. I am doing some family research, and I need to interview locals who know something about Dangerfield Newby."

Again, no response. Turner heard someone rustling inside, moving boxes or papers. More rustling, and then the sound of a lock opening. Turner shifted his feet uneasily, trying to avoid the hole in the porch. Then he heard a heavy metallic clanging sound, followed by a sharp thud, then more metal slamming against metal – the unmistakable sound of a shotgun being racked. The black plastic moved again, and Turner leapt off the porch. The broken front door slowly opened, and the home's inhabitant stepped out into the morning light.

Turner studied him cautiously. The person who stood on the front porch was no more than five feet tall, with a thick white beard and a great uprush of thick, uncombed white hair, which stood out against his coal-black skin. He wore a faded green flannel shirt that was at least two sizes too big, torn woolen trousers, and toeless slippers. He cradled an ancient side-by-side double-barreled shotgun in his arm, with the business end pointed in Turner's direction. He squinted in the morning sun, and shielded his eyes with one hand.

Turner took another step back. "Mr. Frazier? Are you Ezekiel Frazier?"

"Yes, I am," responded the elf-like black man. He spoke in an impeccable Carolina tidewater accent, and his voice was deep and melodious, unlike the high-pitched buzz-saw drawl so common to many Southerners. His appearance suggested a crazy local, but his smooth melodious voice and his accent instantly betrayed him as an educated and sophisticated stranger to this part of the country.

"Who are you, and why have you chosen to visit me," queried Frazier.

Turner briefly thought of telling Frazier that he wanted to discuss Dangerfield's ghost, but quickly thought better of it.

"I got your name from Matthew, the young man who runs the pub downtown," explained Turner. "I am doing some research on one of John Brown's raiders, and Matthew said you might be able to help me."

Still squinting in the morning sun, Frazier eyed Turner head to toe. "Research, you say. How nice of Matthew to send me a visitor," said Frazier flatly. "Where are you from, Mr. Turner?"

"Minnesota. Twin Cities area."

"What kind of research are you doing? Are you writing a book?"

"No sir, just family research. I am trying to find out if I might be related to Dangerfield Newby. He was one of John Brown's raiders."

Frazier scowled and gently tightened his grip on the shotgun. "Dangerfield Newby. So that's what this is about," growled Frazier in his mellifluous Tidewater drawl. Frazier took a step back into the doorway and slowly leveled the shotgun at Turner's midsection. "If someone sent you here to take me away, you can step off my porch now, or be carried off in a pine box. I don't cause any problems for anyone, I take care of myself, and I am not a threat to anyone."

Turner considered the irony of that last statement, but chose not to bring it up.

"No one sent me, and I'm not here to take you anywhere. I just want to talk." Turner eyed the twin shotgun barrels, which now seemed big enough to crawl into. "You can put that down now."

Frazier studied Turner again. He kept the shotgun leveled at Turner's gut. "What do you do for a living, Mr. Turner?"

"I'm a doctor. A surgeon."

"Are you a psychologist, or a psychiatrist?"

"No."

"Why not? Don't you want to understand the mysteries of the human mind?"

Turner studied his inquisitor, and instantly understood the reason for his questions. He paused and framed his answer carefully, knowing that his life depended on it.

"The human mind is too complex for anyone to truly understand or study, Mr. Frazier. If someone comes into my hospital with appendicitis, I can remove the appendix. If someone needs a spleen removed, I can remove it. But if someone comes in with mental health issues, I can't simply remove their brain. Besides, who are we to judge mental health? What might be profound mental illness to one man may just be a personal quirk or foible to another. I am not qualified to judge another person's mental health, Mr. Frazier, no matter how many letters I have after my name."

Frazier considered this response, and slowly lowered the shotgun.

"Please come in, Mr. Turner."

Frazier turned and stepped back into the inky blackness, with Turner close on his heels. Frazier closed the front door behind them.

The inside of Frazier's house was impenetrably dark. Frazier continued walking, and Turner could only follow the sound of his footsteps, hoping not to fall.

Frazier continued walking for a few moments more, and then switched on the lights. Turner could make out a single bulb dangling from the low ceiling, swaying slightly on a thin piece of wire. Frazier began to speak.

"Please accept my apologies for my earlier suspicions," drawled Frazier. "I suspect Matthew already told you something of my experiences with Dangerfield Newby's ghost. As you might imagine, my reputation has suffered, simply because I chose to tell the truth about what I have seen, and what I know to be true about those who straddle this world and the next. People may think of me whatever they wish, but I can assure you I am quite sane, and in control of my faculties."

Turner's eyes had adjusted to the dim light, and he surveyed the room. The inside of the house, like its exterior, did little to confirm the sanity of its inhabitant. Books were stacked in every corner of the room, in piles on tables, on the floor, and against the windows. Dirty clothes were scattered everywhere. A wooden rocking chair sat in the middle of the room, surrounded on every side by leaning stacks of books. A glass sat atop one of the stacks closest to the chair, and it appeared that the teetering stack of books had served as Frazier's end table for many years. Everything about the inside and outside of the house suggested that Frazier was nothing more than a crazy local. But his impeccable grammar and his cultivated Carolina tidewater accent suggested something deeper, something that was not easily explained. Turner knew he had to find out what made this man tick.

"How long have you lived here, Mr. Frazier?"

"17 years. I moved here from Charleston, South Carolina."

"That would explain your accent."

"You are a keen observer, Mr. Turner. Why do you think you are related to Dangerfield Newby?"

"I don't know for certain, but my grandmother said we are related somehow. I have never had a chance to look into it until now. What did you do in Charleston, Mr. Frazier?"

"I was a professor at Charleston College. I taught history and anthropology for 22 years until I was invited to leave by the tenure committee. It seems my teaching methods were too unorthodox for Charleston."

"What happened?" Turner enjoyed this opportunity to turn the tables on his inquisitor.

"I had been teaching anthropology and American history for many years," said Frazier. "One semester, I taught a class about Nat Turner's rebellion. The students seemed to enjoy it, and the topic was very interesting to me. One night, after a particularly fulfilling day of lectures, I had a vivid dream. Nat Turner was speaking to me, telling me everything about his decisions, his mindset, and how he convinced slaves to join him in overthrowing the institution of slavery. It was the most vivid dream I have ever had. I could see the scars on Nat Turner's back, see the pockmarks on his skin, see the sweat on his brow, smell the odor of his body, touch his rough black skin," explained Frazier, his eyes closed. "I could hear his voice, his inflections, and the way he paused between sentences. I could feel the heat of his breath. It was so vivid and real that I became convinced that it was not a dream. Nat Turner lived. He moved easily between this world and the next. And he had chosen me to convey the truth about his rebellion to the world, because the history books that we have do not tell the truth."

Turner took two small steps backward without realizing it, but continued listening.

"Nat Turner told me things about the rebellion that were not found in any history book," Frazier continued. "He told me of collaborators, conspirators, and informants who were not known to history. He told me the names of slaves whose role has never been fully known, and who are now lost forever. His descriptions were so clear, and so contextual, that they had to be true. I knew enough details about Turner's rebellion to know that what he was saying was true. It all fit, and all made sense. I concluded that Nat Turner had chosen me to tell the truth about what really happened. For whatever reason, I was chosen to tell Nat Turner's story. So I began to incorporate Nat Turner's statements into my lectures. I taught them the things Nat Turner told me. The students loved it, because it gave them insights into history that no one had ever had."

"You must have been a wonderful teacher."

"Yes, I was outstanding, consistently getting top reviews from students. But some of my colleagues began to question where I was getting this new information. All the scholars who had spent years studying Nat Turner's rebellion were eager to learn how I had obtained this new information, facts that had been unknown to the world."

"I see," said Turner. "And I suppose you could not just tell them."

"That is exactly what I did," said Frazier proudly. "I told them that my source was none other than Nat Turner himself, and that he had chosen me as his vehicle. I challenged them to disprove my theories, and to disprove the accuracy of what I was teaching. None of them could offer any facts to rebut what Nat Turner had told me. Yet they could not accept that Nat Turner spoke through me, or that I was teaching our students history based on facts conveyed through spirits. So they asked me to take a "sabbatical," which led to my being asked to leave because of my supposed unfitness to teach. I was blacklisted, and unable to land another teaching gig anywhere."

"I see," said Turner, continuing his retreat toward the front door. "And are you certain that it was Nat Turner's spirit who spoke to you?"

"Without a doubt, Mr. Turner, without a doubt," declared Frazier proudly. "Nat Turner spoke to me, and through me. I can still hear the inflections in his voice. Since then, I have seen other figures from history, including Dangerfield Newby. I have seen Dangerfield's ghost walking back and forth in Hog Alley."

Turner knew he should leave immediately, but he sensed the old man was no longer dangerous, just crazy. "What did Dangerfield's ghost look like?"

Frazier took a deep breath before speaking. "I believe you are mocking me, Mr. Turner. You may think me crazy, but I know what I saw."

"No sir, I am not mocking you," countered Dangerfield. "I really want to know what you think – what you saw."

Frazier closed his eyes, and threw his head back before speaking.

"The first time I saw Dangerfield's ghost was shortly after I landed here, after leaving Charleston. I was walking near the site of the old armory at dusk when I saw him. He walked slowly, with a slight limp, down Hog Alley with his back toward me. He wore a wide-brimmed black hat, black breeches, and leather boots. He held something small in his hand, perhaps a coin purse, maybe a small satchel. I could not tell what it was. He turned to face me just briefly, but continued walking on. In that moment, I knew that I was not the chosen one, not the one to tell his truth."

Turner's stomach became liquid, and his knees quivered. Frazier had described, down to the last detail, what Turner had seen the previous day. He was faint, and began to step backward.

"Thank you, Mr. Frazier, but I should be going now. I have taken enough of your time."

Frazier studied him in the dim light. "You may think me crazy, Mr. Turner, but consider this. Nat Turner was my downfall. It was his spirit that led to the end of my teaching career, and his truth that found its voice through me. And now, 17 years later, another Turner walks in my door, asking me about another spirit. Do you not see the irony that Nat Turner was my downfall, and that another Turner may be my salvation?"

"Your salvation? What are you talking about?"

"You are not here doing research on Dangerfield Newby," explained Frazier coldly. "You want to know if I have seen his ghost. There is only one reason for your presence here, Mr. Turner. You seek to confirm something you have already seen. I saw your face when I described Dangerfield's ghost. The pang of recognition, the fear coupled with the certainty of your observations. You are here seeking confirmation for what you already know to be true, but cannot acknowledge."

"With all due respect, Mr. Frazier, I don't believe in ghosts. I am a doctor, a scientist, I only believe what I can prove."

"With all due respect, Mr. Turner, I am an educator, with a Ph.D and enough letters after my name to fill a book. And I too used to believe only in what I could prove. But what better way to understand history than to have it explained by those who were already there? Nat Turner spoke to me, just as surely as you stand in my doorway."

Turner stumbled backwards onto the porch, facing Frazier as he moved. "Thank you, Mr. Frazier, I appreciate your time."

"One last thing before you go, Mr. Turner," said Frazier. "I knew instantly that Nat Turner had chosen me to tell his truth, that I would be his voice, his link between the past and present. I knew just as quickly that Dangerfield Newby had not chosen me, that I was not fit to be his voice. I am not the one to tell his truths. I knew instantly that I was not the chosen one, not the one to tell his truth. I can only hope that you achieve the same certainty. I can only hope that you have the courage to accept whatever destiny is presented to you."

Turner ran off the porch, stumbling on the broken floorboard as he ran. He fell face first in the knee-length grass and remained prone for what seemed like forever. He tried to get up, but the bile in his gut rose, and he vomited loudly in the grass. Finally, he rose and walked to his car, and drove back to his hotel to meet Tracy, still unable to process what had just happened.

———⸙———

Turner met Tracy in the hotel lobby, and she knew immediately something was wrong. "What happened to you? Did you find the ghost chasers you were looking for?"

"Sort of." He slumped into a chair in the lobby, still smelling like the damp, mildewy insides of Frazier's house. His shirt was stained with grass and vomit, and he had a small cut on his hand from falling off the porch.

"So what did you find?"

"I met a very interesting man. A former college professor. American history and anthropology.

"Did he have useful information?"

"Sort of." Turner rubbed the cut on his hand, and realized he had not eaten in hours.

"What happened? What did he say? I've never seen you like this."

Turner knew there was no easy way to explain what Frazier had told him, or why he went. Tracy hadn't seen what he saw the previous day, and he knew there was only one way to tell her.

"Do you remember last night, when we were on the ghost tour? And I told you I thought I saw a reenactor, a guy dressed up as Dangerfield Newby?"

"Yeah, I remember. I didn't see anything. Must have been the heat."

"No, it wasn't the heat," snapped Turner. "I saw something. I don't know what it was. But I saw something, and it wasn't a dog, and it wasn't the heat. I saw a man who looked like all the historical descriptions of Dangerfield Newby. The hat, the boots, the pouch, the whole thing. Same height, same general appearance. Babe, you have to believe me."

Tracy stared at him, unblinking. She reached out both of her hands, and held his hands, trembling and cold.

"Your hands are shaking. Maybe you need an aspirin or something," said Tracy.

"I don't need an aspirin. I know what I saw. I need you to believe me."

She gently squeezed both his hands, and then kissed them before speaking.

"Look, you know I believe in spirits and ghosts," said Tracy. "I get most of my artistic inspiration from things that are mystical, spiritual, and not of this world. Most of what I do comes from people or things that are not of this world, and not of the next. So you know I believe that the soul can live outside the body," she said.

She squeezed his hand, and let loose a wry smile.

"Of course, I'm an artist," she continued. "People expect me to believe that shit. You, not so much. You go back to the hospital and start talking about Casper the Friendly Ghost, and you can forget about being chief of surgery. I believe you saw something. We just have to figure out what you saw. Maybe it was a dog, maybe a reenactor maybe . . . it was something else. But first, tell me what you learned this morning. Tell me about this college professor."

"His name's Ezekiel Frazier. Short little brother, maybe five feet tall. Used to teach in Charleston, South Carolina."

"Did he know anything about Dangerfield Newby?"

"Get this. Frazier claims to have seen Dangerfield's ghost. He also thinks that Nat Turner spoke to him, and told him things about Nat Turner's rebellion that no one else could know. He claims that Nat Turner personally chose him to convey the truth about Turner's rebellion."

"Do you think he's crazy?"

"If you had asked me that question before yesterday, I would have said yes," sighed Turner. "Now, I don't know what to think. I feel as if everything I know, everything I believe in is fake. Reason, science, research, analysis – what good is it if some ghost can show up and destroy everything you thought you knew?"

"Maybe he's crazy. Or maybe he is just a vessel for someone else," offered Tracy. "I do believe that the living are sometimes asked to carry on the unfinished work of the dead. Do you remember that sculpture I did last year, the one I sold to that rich couple?"

"Yeah, I loved that one," replied Turner. "The sculpture of the woman holding the little boy's hand. The woman was blindfolded, but she was walking in front, leading the little boy. I loved the imagery of a blind adult leading a child."

"Do you know where I got the idea? It came to me in a dream. Originally, I wanted the boy to be blind, and the woman to have vision. I wanted it to convey the innocence of childhood, blindness to life's tragedies, and how adults can help children navigate through the world, providing children with vision. But eventually, children must see on their own."

"So why did you change it?"

"I was sleeping, and I had a dream. A female voice told me that adults are blind, that only children have clarity of vision. The voice told me that the blind can lead the blind, but only if we learn to trust those who cannot see. I remember everything about that dream – the woman's voice, her inflection, and the clarity of her speech. She had a Southern accent, but I couldn't place it. I got up the next morning, and changed the design right away. I made the woman blind, and gave the boy sight. But the woman is leading, because only a child with vision would trust a blind woman. To trust the blind is to have true clarity of vision."

"Wow, that's some deep stuff for a wacky artist," joked Turner.

"I had never thought about it that way, and I had certainly never had a thought that profound," replied Tracy. "But that night, it was as clear as if someone had written it down. A week later, the rich couple visited my studio. The wife saw the sculpture, and started crying. I asked her what was wrong, and she told me it reminded her of her mother, who was blind, and her younger brother. Her mother used to take the children for walks around the park, even though she was blind. She would lead the kids through the park, and the kids would walk behind her and warn her of obstacles. It never occurred to the children that their blind mom should not be in front. And you know the best part? She grew up in Kentucky. She spoke with the same Southern accent that I heard in my dream."

Turner said nothing, but knew instantly what Tracy was talking about. He sat for a moment, his head spinning and the small cut on his hand bleeding. "Babe, I need you to believe me. I know what I saw."

"I believe you saw something. We just have to figure out what it is. Maybe you can talk to Frazier again before we leave. C'mon, let's get you some food and some clean clothes."

Turner wiped his bleeding hand on a napkin. They left the hotel lobby and went back to their room to change before eating lunch.

CHAPTER 10

Two men walked along the side of the road, near the creek, so they could hide if they heard horses, dogs or men. The shorter man limped badly, and had a deep gash on his lower left leg. The other man supported his wounded companion, putting his arm under the wounded man's shoulder and helping him limp along the road. The sun would be up soon, and they would have to find shelter for the day – they would be quickly and easily found walking during daylight. Both men wore tattered and filthy breeches, and rough cotton shirts. Their bare feet were bloody and torn from the stones and twigs on the road. The taller man scanned the countryside for any kind of shelter, a hunting shack, a barn, an abandoned farm. As soon as the sun rose, the searchers would be on the road, splitting up, coming at them from both directions. Daylight without shelter would bring capture and even death.

It hadn't rained in weeks. The trees would normally be full, blocking out the sun, creating shadows and dark places to hide. But the lack of rain had stripped the leaves, and the naked trees and flat, parched landscape offered no shelter. In a normal year, the creek would sweep away anything in its path, noisy and foaming as it made its way to the river. But the creek was now just a trickle. Deer and raccoon had left their tracks deep in the creek bed, where the water would normally rage. In any other year, the two men could hide in the creek, and breathe through reeds, knowing the dogs could not find them in the water. But now the creek offered no shelter, only warm and muddy water barely suitable for a dog. There was no place to hide.

The trail ahead of them had been cleared of trees and brush on both sides, the clearings extending ten feet into the woods on either side of the trail. "Must be a turnaround for wagons," the taller man said. The shorter man grunted. There was no cover near the turnaround, and a man on horseback or in a carriage would easily spot them if they were in the turnaround. The taller man draped his companion's arm over his shoulder, and hoisted him over his back. The shorter man coughed up bloody spittle, and it ran down the taller man's back. The two men splashed across the shallow creek as the sun began to crest, ducking deeper into the woods to avoid the turnaround.

The tall man stopped to fill up his canteen in the creek, and took a long drink. He poured some muddy creekwater over his head, wiped his face, and poured creekwater over the shorter man's head. The muddy water mixed with blood from a cut on his head as it flowed over him. The tall man sank knee-deep in the mud under his companion's weight, and the two men returned to the trail, the taller man still carrying his wounded partner.

The taller man resumed walking when he felt the ground tremble beneath him. He stopped, and checked the wind. Now he heard them – horses, moving toward him. Four, maybe five horses, moving at a brisk pace. He heard the hoofbeats, checked the wind, and figured they were coming from ahead of him. He stepped off the trail, took a few steps back, and looked for a place to hide. But now he could hear hoofbeats coming from the other direction. Two or three horses approaching from the opposite direction, moving at a full gallop. Any minute now, the two groups of riders would meet on the trail, right where they were standing. He thought about running into the woods, but he knew he could not leave his brother behind. Besides, the dry weather had shriveled the brush and stripped the leaves from the trees. A man on horseback would see him running through the flat, parched and leafless woodland. The hoofbeats grew louder, and now he could hear men's voices shouting.

The creek was their only option. He carried his brother beside the creek until he found an undercut near a fallen tree. In a normal year, the water would be up past the tree and near the trail, but now the creek was low and the undercut was four feet above the water level. He wedged his brother into the undercut, and then backed in after him. Thick reeds and brush grew above the undercut, making both men completely invisible, even though they were just inches from the trail. The ground above them shook as the thundering hoofbeats grew closer. He could hear the horses nickering and blowing as the riders met in the trail. They were directly above him, and he could hear men's voices above the stamping and blowing horses. His heartbeat exploded in his ears, and his stomach turned to water as the two groups of men began to talk just inches above him.

"You see any sign of 'em?"

"Not yet. No tellin' if they came this way, or headed down to Warrenton."

"How soon before we can dogs on 'em?"

"Owner says he's got a couple of hounds. Says he can let us have 'em."

"They can't be too far. Not unless they stole a horse."

"We'd a seen 'em by now." They must be real close. They can't be movin' real fast, not with one of 'em shot in the leg, and maybe gut-shot." You see any footprints?"

"Not when it's this dry. Real hard to track when there ain't no rain." Won't be able to do much until we get dogs on 'em.

"There ain't no farms nearby. No place for 'em to seek shelter. I say we both keep moving in separate directions 'til we find 'em. When you get them hounds, start tracking back this way."

"What about the reward money?"

"We'll split it, same as always."

The two fugitives remained curled up in their creekside den, listening to every word spoken above them. Sweat beaded on the taller man's forehead as he silently considered their options. If the riders were leaving in opposite directions, both groups of riders would be moving away from them. And since the riders would move faster than them, they would have some time, maybe a few hours before the riders returned with dogs. And once the dogs were on scent, the chase would soon be over. The two men had left enough blood and scent on and near the road, so that the dogs would easily locate them. They had only two options: walk in the shallow creek, where they would leave no scent, but would be easily spotted; or take their chances in the barren woods, away from the trail, where they would not be seen, but where they could not move quickly, and would be easily caught. The taller man looked at his wounded brother, who was beginning to breathe heavily. The taller man spoke.

"You hang on now, George," he whispered softly. "I aim to get us out of here soon. We gon' have to walk through the woods, away from the trail. Dogs won't find us. You need to make it now, hear? Just keep quiet a little bit longer."

George turned and looked at his brother, and spoke in a weak, scratchy voice. "I'm going home now, Thomas. Can't go no farther. Going home." George began coughing loudly, and spitting up blood. He retched twice and then lurched out of the den, his head lolling out of the den facing the creek. Blood and vomit streamed from his mouth and into the shallow muddy water. The horsemen above had not yet left. Thomas heard voices directly above his head.

"What in blazes is that? I never heard no animal make a noise like that."

"Ain't no animal. We may not need them dogs after all."

Thomas heard riders quickly dismounting, and the dull metallic click of a revolver hammer being drawn.

"Fetch 'em out of there. Remember, the owner wants 'em back alive, if you can. Ain't no reward for dead ones."

Thomas pulled George's head back in the den, and considered their rapidly dwindling options. He heard the weeds above his head rustling, and then heard someone climbing down from the road above. He pulled a small sheath knife out of his breeches, and waited.

From inside the den, Thomas saw a cavalry boot descend no more than a foot in front of him, then another. The boots landed in the mud in front of the den, and then slowly turned around. Thomas saw a hand moving the weeds and brush in front of the den. He gripped the sheath knife in his right hand and prepared to lunge forward when he saw the barrel of a revolver poking through the weeds.

"You all come out of there now. Don't make me kill you both. Didn't come all this way for two dead runaways and no reward money. Come on out now."

Thomas looked at George, whose tongue now lolled out of his mouth. Only the whites of his eyes were visible, and blood ran from his mouth. There were at least four men above him, and he and his brother were trapped. Even if he got the first one with the knife, the others would finish him off. This way, maybe someone would take care of George, nurse him back to health. No reward for dead ones means the searchers should at least get George back alive. Double the reward money. Thomas put the knife back in his breeches and crawled out into the daylight.

The man standing in front of him was about his height, maybe a little shorter. He wore a wide-brimmed black riding hat, gray wool trousers, a sweat-stained blue cotton shirt, and new cavalry boots. His long brown hair flowed over his shoulders from underneath his hat. His thick mustache curled up at the ends, and a jagged scar ran like a vein from just under his left eye, down his cheek, and ended just before his mouth. He held the revolver loosely in his hand, casually flipping the barrel up and down while holding the grip. Thomas looked up and saw two other men on the trail, still mounted, pointing revolvers and long guns in his direction. The man with the scar spoke.

"Get the other one out of there. Pull him out slowly, and don't make me have to do it."

Thomas reached inside the den and grasped George by the hand. George's body was limp and heavy. Thomas pulled harder, and George fell out of the den and landed on his side in the mud.

"Can he stand up?"

Thomas shook his head. The man with the scar approached George and put his hand over George's mouth. He then touched his fingers lightly against George's neck, and stood up.

"This one ain't worth bringing back. He's still alive, but barely," the man with the scar announced to his comrades. "He won't make the trip back to his owner, and if we bring him back dead, the owner will say we killed him. Ain't no reward for dead ones, and I don't want the owner to think we killed him. Might not get the reward for this one if the owner thinks we killed the other one. Hate to carry these two all the way back for no reward. Won't get nothing if the owner thinks we killed one of 'em."

One of the riders spoke. "What do we do with him, then?"

The man with the scar pointed the revolver at Thomas. "Get up there with the others and get on that dun up there." He pointed at one of the other riders. "Tie him up and make sure he stays mounted. He'll ride with me. Hold the other end of the rope while we ride."

Thomas looked at his captors again and counted two mounted riders and the man with the jagged scar, each pointing a revolver or a long gun at his head. He walked slowly toward the trail, mounted the riderless dun, and waited. One of the riders dismounted, tied Thomas' hands tightly behind his back, and threw the rope toward his horse.

The man with the scar stood next to George in the muddy creek, touched his neck again, and stood up. He aimed the revolver at George's head, and pulled the trigger. George's head lurched back, and his whole body rose, then landed in the soft mud. Blood poured out of the hole in his head, and mixed with the muddy water. The man with the scar got up, and mounted his horse, the same horse now carrying Thomas. He sat in front and held the reins, while Thomas sat just inches behind him, his hands tied tightly behind his back. Thomas quivered with rage, but was powerless to act. Sweat from Thomas's head dripped onto the man's blue shirt. The men began riding.

"If the owner asks, tell him we found him dead near the creek," the man with the scar announced to his comrades. "Somebody had shot him, and we found this one close by. Ain't no reward for dead ones."

Thomas turned his back and looked at his brother for the last time. Blood flowed into the muddy creek. George lay face up, and mud clung to the whites of his eyes.

CHAPTER 11

Turner and Tracy went back to their hotel room. Turner took a shower, and stood in the bathroom looking at his reflection in the mirror. He saw the bags under his eyes, and his skin was gray and sallow. His hand throbbed and his stomach churned. He dressed the cut on his hand and looked at the confused soul staring back at him in the mirror. Nothing he had seen in the last two days made any sense to him. He knew what he saw that night, and it wasn't a dog. But it couldn't have been a man, and no one else saw anything. And nothing Frazier said made a damn bit of sense; Frazier was just crazy, plain and simple. Dead people don't come back to tell us things they couldn't tell us in life. Nat Turner didn't "choose" Frazier or anyone else to tell his story. Nat Turner lived, rebelled against slavery, and got killed for his efforts. End of story. And while historians and students can debate Nat Turner's rebellion for the next century, Nat Turner himself has nothing else to say on the subject. He's dead, and he always will be.

"You're a doctor, for God's sake," Turner thought to himself. "You can't believe this nonsense. But Frazier is a Ph.D. and he believes it. So what, Frazier is crazy. Lots of brilliant people are crazy. They go hand in hand. I will not abandon every principle of science and reason because I saw something that may have been a dog. And I'm not going to listen to some crazy person tell me about Nat Turner coming back to talk to him about history. That doesn't happen."

Tracy's voice rang out from the bedroom. "Babe, who are you talking to?"

"No one. I didn't say anything"

"Yes you did. Something about principles of science and reason and dogs. Are you re-creating Pavlov or something?"

"Shit, I guess I was talking to myself," he mumbled. Turner wrapped a towel around his waist and walked out into the room. It was early in the afternoon on a brilliant clear day, but Tracy had closed the blinds, and only a small amount of light filtered into the room. He walked out, and saw Tracy standing in front of the window, her body silhouetted against the low light trickling into the room. She was wearing a thick white hotel bathrobe, which she dropped as soon as she saw Turner. She grabbed his waist and tugged at the towel until it fell to the floor. He brushed his hands against her erect nipples, kissed the tops of her breasts, and felt her body shiver as he ran his hand along her naked thigh. It felt like years since he had touched her like this. She kissed him on the mouth, and led him to the bed, where they both collapsed. Turner explored every inch of this body he had known for years, and he knew just where and just how to touch her.

When they finished, Tracy let out a guttural sigh, and Turner felt the weight of the last two days lifting from his chest, a lightness and confidence he had not felt since he got here. Tracy rolled over and kissed him on the neck, and they both fell into a deep and well-deserved sleep.

He didn't know how long they had been sleeping when he heard the noise. A hollow thud just outside the hotel door, followed by slow, shuffling footsteps walking away from their room. Turner leapt out of bed, and noticed the hotel room door was slightly ajar. He pushed the door open and stepped out into the hallway.

Turner saw a man standing at the top of the stairs, looking back toward Turner's room. His battered hat was pulled low over his face, and his baggy trousers were dirty and torn. He wore black, dusty riding boots. The hallway smelled like sweat, leather and gunpowder. He was staring at a piece of yellow paper, caressing it in his hands, turning it over and over. Turner watched him reading whatever was on the paper. He did not look up.

Turner wanted to speak, but his voice had left him. He inhaled and yelled with all his might, but only a whisper escaped.

"Who are you, and why were you in my room," croaked Turner.

The man looked up and pushed his hat back. He peered at Turner, but did not move, did not run. He was calm, serene, as if he broke into hotel rooms every day. He turned to face Turner and lifted his head, and Turner fell back against the door frame when he saw the deep gash in the man's throat. Blood ran down his neck, and into his coat, and when the man lifted his head, Turner could see the whitish flesh in the man's throat, and his severed vocal cords. His throat had been cut almost to the cervical vertebrae. The two men looked at each other for a few moments, neither man able to speak.

The man in the hat folded the yellow piece of paper, put it in his coat pocket, and walked down the stairs. Turner willed his legs to move, but when he reached the top of the stairs, the man was gone. Disappeared into thin air. Turner looked back, and saw the blood trail leading from his room to the top of the stairs, where it ended in a pool where the man had stood moments before. He watched his legs move down the stairs until he could see the first floor. He could see no trace of the man, or any blood.

He stumbled back to his room. He did not feel his legs move, and it felt like he was gliding, not walking. He saw his hand reach out to open his hotel room door, and as he did, Tracy pulled the door open. She was wearing the thick white hotel bathrobe.

"What the hell are you doing? Where have you been?"

Turner opened his mouth, but he could not understand what came out. Someone else was talking, someone else was explaining the man with the hat, the yellow letter, the riding boots, the gash in the throat, the blood on the floor. But it wasn't him talking. It was someone else using his voice and his body. He felt like he had a pillow over his head as the words tumbled out.

Tracy said something in response, and the fog lifted.

"Look down," she whispered.

He did, and saw that he was stark naked.

"Get in here now, before we get kicked out." Tracy pulled him into the room just as the door across the hall opened. An elderly woman came out of her room, gasped, and closed the door when she saw Turner's naked backside walking into his room. Tracy hustled him into the room, and shut the door behind them. She slammed the security bar closed, and locked the door knob. She looked out of the peephole, and watched the elderly woman nervously exiting her room. She waited until the woman was gone before speaking.

"What the hell is going on," Tracy hissed. "Why are you crawling around naked in the hallway?"

Turner felt his voice returning. He told her about the noise, the man in the hall, and the blood trail. Everything tumbled out at once, but now it was his voice, not someone else's.

Tracy looked at him unblinking before she spoke.

"The door was locked. I closed it myself and locked the security bar when we got back from lunch. I wanted to surprise you, and I sure as hell wasn't going to leave the door unlocked if I knew we were going to have sex." Her voice quavered.

"As for the blood, look at your hand. Your cut from this morning opened up. The blood you saw in the hall is yours." Turner examined the blood dripping from the cut on his hand, staining the carpet as he stood there.

Turner looked at her. "I saw something," he croaked. "I know what I saw. I saw him, I smelled him, I saw the paper. I saw something. It was him."

"You had a dream," she snapped. "You've been working too hard, and you're tired. You had a dream, plain and simple. I have crazy dreams after I get laid. Go back to sleep and we'll talk later. Take a few of my sleeping pills. Your cut just opened up, and you bled on the floor. There is a perfectly rational explanation for what you saw."

Tracy pulled him to the bed and handed him two small white pills. "I use these when I really need to sleep. Take them, and let's figure this out when you wake up."

Turner looked at the pills. "What are these?"

Tracy caressed his shoulders, and kissed him on the mouth. "Just trust me, and take them. My husband is a doctor."

Turner took the pills, and drifted back to sleep. Tracy waited until he started snoring. Then she quietly got dressed, slipped out of the room, and closed and locked the door behind her.

CHAPTER 12

The boy ran screaming from Jennings' house, with an older Negro woman right behind him, waving a stick and shouting. The boy should have easily outrun her, but his progress was hindered by the boots he wore, at least three sizes too big and almost up to his knees. The woman was right on his heels, waving at him with the stick and screaming something about him being a thief. The boy saw Dangerfield and ran toward him, begging for help. Dangerfield saw that it was the same boy who had met him at the gate and tended his horse when he arrived. The boy ran behind Dangerfield and clutched the back of his pants, grateful for any barriers between himself and the woman's rage. The woman approached, breathing heavily and sweating.

"You let that little thief go, you hear? Tried to steal Marse Jennings' boots, he did."

"Didn't try to steal 'em," gasped the boy. "Just wanted to see what they felt like. Never had on nice boots like these." Wasn't goin' to take 'em."

"Well, you about to feel the side of this switch." The woman grabbed the boy by his shirt collar, pulled him away from Dangerfield, and began beating him on the shoulders with the stick. The boy cowered, and fell to his knees, putting his hands above his head. The woman kept swinging, harder, until Dangerfield grabbed her forearm and stopped her in mid-swing.

"I think you taught him his lesson for today, Missus. That's enough."

The woman spat at him, red-eyed with anger. "Marse Jennings won't have no thieves in the house. If he'll take Marse's boots from the house, Lord knows what else he done took already." The boy was still on his knees, bleeding from his shoulders and whimpering.

"Boy says he didn't intend to steal anything," said Dangerfield. "And I don't see how he would have gotten very far in them boots, big as they are. He could fit both feet in one of them boots. Wouldn't last long in the stable floppin' around like that. I think he learned enough for one day."

Dangerfield pulled the boy up from his knees and brushed him off. "You go on back to the stable and see if you can't find some rags to stop the bleeding," said Dangerfield. "Give them boots back to Missus here and see if she can't return 'em before Marse Jennings finds out." He turned and faced the woman.

"What will Jennings do if he thinks the boy tried to steal his boots?" asked Dangerfield.

"Marse will beat him something fierce," the woman replied. "He'll beat him twice as bad as I just did, and twice as long. I was hopin that if I beat him with the switch first, Marse would let it be. He'd be in real trouble if Marse got hold of him first. I was just trying to save him from something worse."

"So you thought by beating him now, you could save him from a worse beating later?" Dangerfield thought it unlikely that Jennings could have beaten the boy any worse than the woman just did, and it frightened him to think that Jennings would be that savage toward a young stable boy. Then he remembered what Harriet had told him about how Jennings treated his male slaves.

"Tell you what, Missus," offered Dangerfield. "Let's send the boy back to the stable. You take these boots back to the house before Jennings finds out. Seein' as how you have already delivered his punishment, I don't see any need to say anything else to anybody. Have Miss Harriet bring some clean rags from the house down to the stable. I think you already done everything Marse Jennings would have asked of you."

The woman stared at him, then picked up the boots and walked toward the house. "Don't let me catch that boy near the house any time today," she growled.

The woman huffed back to the house holding the boots. Dangerfield lifted the boy by his arm, and brought him to his feet. "Get up off your knees. Can you walk?"

"Yes" he whimpered.

"Then get back to the stable before Jennings finds out. Miss Harriet will fetch some cloth from the house. You'll be fine."

The boy looked at him, coughed, and walked slowly back to the stable. Dangerfield called out: "What's your name, boy?"

The boy turned around. "They call me Jericho."

"Jericho, did you steal them boots?"

"No. Just wanted to try them on. Ain't never had nice boots on before."

Dangerfield looked down at the boy's bare, leathery feet, his legs, spindly, gray and bow-legged, and his ragged, threadbare breeches. It was impossible to determine his age – he could have been eight or eighteen.

"You go on back to the stable," said Dangerfield. "I will see to it that you get some boots."

Dangerfield watched the boy amble back to the stable. The door to the house opened, and Harriet rushed out carrying clean rags and a bucket of food. She was wearing the same blue frock, but she had cinched it tighter around her waist. She had changed her scarf and her long black hair was now covered with a shiny new yellow scarf. It had not been ten minutes since he had last seen her, but she had found the time to change her clothes — she looked more beautiful than the last time he saw her. Dangerfield watched her walk, and felt a thump in his gut.

Harriet caught up with Jericho just as he reached the stable door. She took his arm, applied the cloth to his wounds, and gave him the bucket of food. She kissed him on the cheek, and sent him inside the stable, out of view of the house.

She saw Dangerfield and walked toward him.

"Thank you for sparing Jericho," Harriet said. "Lilly would have beaten him half to death."

"She says she was tryin' to save the boy. She says Jennings would have beaten him worse for stealing them boots," replied Dangerfield.

Harriet's face darkened. "She's right. Marse Jennings don't tolerate no thieves in the house. He would have beaten him somethin' fierce."

"Can't imagine he could have done worse than Lilly," said Dangerfield. "Besides, boy says he wasn't stealing 'em, just tryin' 'em on. And it looks like he could use some boots."

"Jericho wasn't stealing anything," replied Harriet. "Marse Jennings don't wear them boots no more. No reason he can't wear 'em if no one else is."

"You seem to have a strong interest in the boy," offered Dangerfield.

Harriet paused and tightened the cinch around her waist before speaking. "He's my son. Nine years old."

Dangerfield felt the thump in his gut again, and his throat tightened. "He's a beautiful boy. You lucky you get to be so close to him."

Dangerfield examined her: long legs, dark hair pulled tight under the yellow scarf. She was the most beautiful woman he had ever seen. He assumed Jennings was Jericho's father — no sensible man could resist a woman like that, and any man who owned her wouldn't have to — he could have her any time he wanted. And Jennings was most likely very protective of any house servant who looked like Harriet. He struggled to find something to say, but could find no words. Harriet spoke.

"Jericho's father died last year," said Harriet as her voice cracked. "He was one of Marse Jennings' stablehands. He was crushed by a bull when it broke loose in the barn. Jericho don't speak much about it, but he ain't the same boy any more. He's my only child. Marse feels sorry for him, so he don't beat him as much as he would another. But Mistress says Marse needs money again, and might have to sell some of the stablehands. A young boy with years of hard work ahead of him might fetch a fair sum."

"You think Jennings would sell him away from you?"

"He's done it before," replied Harriet. "One of the house girls had a little boy, five or six. Jennings ran up his accounts in town, and couldn't pay 'em back. He sold the boy and kept the house girl. Marse Jennings don't easily sell his house girls.

He'll sell young boys first. Says young boys ain't worth much 'til they at least thirteen, but you have to feed 'em and clothe 'em the whole time 'til then. Says he'll let someone else deal with 'em 'til they get old enough, and he'll get his money right now. Says he'd rather buy an older stablehand that's already broke than deal with a young boy that needs to be fed and clothed, but can't do much. He don't seem to mind keepin' the girls."

"Jennings must have a reason for sharing all his business with you."

"He don't," replied Harriet. "Mistress shares all of Marse's business with the house girls. And Marse sometimes leaves his books open where we can see 'em. The house girls know a fair amount of Marse's business, and those who can read know even more." Harriet released an exhausted sigh, and then sat on the ground sobbing.

Dangerfield sat on the ground next to her, and put his hand on her shoulder.

"I told the boy I'd find him some boots. I'll bring 'em next time I come."

Harriet looked him in the eyes, and gently touched his arm. She was still crying. "You don't have to do nothin' for me. But we'd both be obliged."

"I promise you I'll bring 'em next time I come." He lifted his hand from her shoulder, and stood up to leave, but she grabbed his hand and put it back on her shoulder. She would not let him move. He sat back down. She held his hand, and the two of them sat wordlessly together on the ground, she still crying, and he grateful that he could sit next to her just a little while longer.

CHAPTER 13

Tracy found a quiet booth in the Armory Pub on Potomac Street. She ordered a tall Guinness, and pulled her cell phone out of her purse. Over the last month, she had been worried about her husband – he wasn't sleeping, he talked to himself more than usual, and he had been having bizarre, sometimes frightening dreams. She had convinced herself it was nothing to worry about – doctors worked long hours, and if he wanted to become chief of surgery, he had to put in even more time, and take the most difficult assignments. She knew when she met him that Turner was intense, moody and brilliant, and he carried on long conversations with himself about recent events. She knew this when she married him. But she had never seen anything like this. He had crazy dreams, but he had never gotten up in the middle of a dream and walked around – she had heard of sleepwalking, but thought it happened only in movies.

She looked around to see if anyone was in earshot, and then punched in the number she needed. If she screwed this up, she knew her husband's career was done.

Dr. Damon Lee had been Turner's partner and friend in medical school. The two men met during the first week of medical school, and quickly became fast friends. Turner and Lee were more like brothers than friends – extremely competitive, and downright contemptuous of those they considered their intellectual inferiors. But both men were committed to medicine, and helping people. During med school, Turner and Lee staffed a free on-campus clinic for the homeless. They did this for two years, supervised by a licensed doctor, but with virtually no help from any other students. At the end of the two years, Turner and Lee posted a sign on the clinic door, announcing that they would no longer be working at the clinic, but providing the cell phone number of another student who would be taking over – a student they both despised because he was lazy and unmotivated, and had never even set foot in the homeless clinic. It was this blend of whip-smart intellect, acerbic sense of humor, and inner drive that first attracted Tracy to Turner, and cemented Turner and Lee's friendship. The two men remained close even after Turner pursued a surgical residency, and Lee pursued a career as a psychiatrist.

But Tracy disliked most of Turner's other med school classmates – most of them were selfish, and obsessed with making enough money to pay their med school loans and buy enormous suburban houses. After Turner began his residency, things got even worse. Turner would drag her to parties hosted by the doctors-in-training. They spoke of their patients as a necessary evil, instead of the reason for their existence. When she told the residents she was a sculpture artist, the female residents hated her, and the male residents hit on her, even when Turner was in the room with her.

Damon Lee was the only resident who seemed interested in her work, and not just her looks. She had always assumed he was gay until one night after a party, Lee pulled her aside and drunkenly suggested that she should leave Turner for him. She laughed him off, and told him to go home. He did, and apologized profusely the next day. "Please don't tell Michael what I did," he pleaded. "It would ruin everything." Tracy never did tell Turner exactly what Damon had said, but she never let Damon forget his drunken transgression. She would call him when she needed a prescription or anti-depressants, and didn't feel like going to her regular doctor. As years went by, Damon's drunken pass was forgiven if not forgotten, and she now genuinely considered him a close friend. But she still occasionally called in a favor. And now she needed a huge favor.

He answered the phone on the second ring.

"Dr. Damon Lee speaking."

"Hey, Damon. It's Tracy Turner."

"Hey, beautiful, how are you? Where are you calling from? I thought you and your no-good husband were on vacation."

"We are. In beautiful, historic Harpers Ferry, West Virginia."

"My, your husband does know how to treat a beautiful woman. He could have taken you anywhere in the world, and he takes you to Harpers Ferry, West Virginia. Were all the hotels in Disneyworld full?"

"I'm not being sarcastic, Damon. Harpers Ferry is beautiful. Michael is doing some family research, and I wanted to be here with him."

"My apologies. Next year, you two can visit some other historic podunk village. I hear Deadwood is lovely this time of year. But I digress. What can I do for you?"

"I'm actually calling on behalf of my cousin. I have to be discreet, because I don't want Michael to know my unpleasant family business."

"Where is Michael now?"

"He's sightseeing. I told him I needed a nap, and he left me in the hotel room. He thinks I am sleeping."

"I don't know if I can be a party to this intrigue and deceit," laughed Damon. "You know, Michael and I shared a cadaver in med school. Once you've tag-teamed a liver dissection, there aren't too many secrets you can keep from each other. He tried to convince me to go into surgery, but I couldn't do it – too many sick people. I like psychiatry – probe their minds and give 'em some antipsychotics. Most days, I don't even have to use a scalpel."

"This is a medical issue," said Tracy quietly. "And I am calling you for medical advice."

Damon paused before speaking. "This is about your cousin?"

"Yes. I've been worried about her. She has been under a lot of stress with her job. She hasn't been sleeping much. I saw her last week, and her husband told me that she has been having vivid, bizarre dreams. Crazy stuff. And she has started sleepwalking. She'll wander around the house, and not remember waking up. She walks around and does stuff in her sleep. Her husband has to chase her down and put her back to bed, and she doesn't remember a thing."

"I can't provide a diagnosis over the phone," said Damon evenly. "Tell her you are worried about her, and that you want her to see a doctor. I'll examine her myself."

"She'll freak out if I send her to a psychiatrist, and she hates doctors. Can you at least tell me what would cause someone to start sleepwalking?"

"Does she use drugs or sleeping pills?"

"No."

"Did she use drugs when she was younger? LSD, PCP, anything like that?"

"No. She may have smoked a little pot when she was in her 20's, but she never touched the hard stuff."

"How do you know?"

"We have been close for a long time. We spent a lot of time together in our teens and twenties. I know her as well as anyone can."

"Interesting that you would have that close a relationship with a cousin," offered Damon. "Most siblings aren't that close. Someone should study both of you."

"Spare me your psychiatrist's probing questions. You know my family was messed up. My cousin was the only one who accepted me for who I was. Everyone else tried to change me, but she didn't. I am as close to her as anyone."

Tracy paused. She was too deep into this lie to back off now, but she knew Damon would ask enough questions to give her an answer."

"Is there a history of epilepsy in your family? Seizures, even one, even if it was caused by a fever?"

"Not that I know of."

"Did your cousin sleepwalk as a child?"

"No."

"And you are confident your cousin has never used hard drugs?"

"I am certain."

"Have you ever had a seizure, even once, as a child?"

"No, I haven't. Why are you asking about me?"

"It goes to your family history. If you ever had seizures, that may establish a family history that could explain your cousin's behavior."

"I'm not asking on my behalf. This is about my cousin," insisted Tracy.

"I know, I know, this is about your cousin, not you. I've heard that before," scoffed Damon.

Tracy smiled, confident that she had thrown him off course. Damon paused before answering.

"Basically, there are four main causes of sleepwalking in adults who have no history of sleepwalking as children," explained Damon calmly. "The first one is a reaction to sleeping pills, drugs or alcohol. You tell me your cousin doesn't have drug history, and booze by itself almost never causes sleepwalking. Of course, it is possible to drink enough alcohol so that your hippocampus temporarily shuts down, in which case it is possible to do all sorts of things without being conscious of doing them. But a hippocampus blackout is usually preceded by extreme intoxication, and that is not what you have described to me. So I think we can rule that one out for now."

The second one is a medical condition like epilepsy, or seizures. No family history of seizures, with you or your cousin, so I think we can rule that one out for now. It's not impossible for a healthy adult to have seizures later in life, but it doesn't happen often. So let's leave that one out for now."

"The third is the most common," continued Damon. "Extreme stress or hardship that causes a disruption of the sleep cycle can cause sleepwalking in adults with no prior history. You said your cousin has been under a lot of stress, and not sleeping well. That can cause sleepwalking events, especially if the stress causes the disruption of the sleep cycle. Basically, no sleep plus a lot of stress can lead to sleepwalking. Has your cousin done anything to endanger herself or her family?"

"No. Her husband said he found her walking around the house stark naked, and headed out the front door. He had to pick her up and bring her back to bed."

"Lucky man," quipped Lee. "Based on what you have described, I think stress is the most likely culprit. Tell your cousin to take a week off, sleep more, and lay off the booze before bed. If that doesn't work, have her see a doctor. Okay?"

"You said there were four things. What is the fourth?"

"Well, sometimes sleepwalking occurs because the patient has, uh, an organic disorder of the mind, or some other neurological disorder."

"Organic disorder of the mind?" What does that mean?"

"It can mean many things, Tracy. The beginnings of Alzheimer's, or some other degenerative brain disorder. It could, in rare cases, be an indicator of a more problematic brain disorder.

"Problematic brain disorder? Skip the psychobabble and tell me what you mean.""

"Well, Tracy, in rare cases sleepwalking is merely a symptom of some form of dementia or psychosis. I hesitated to tell you about that one, because it scares people. But it is a possibility, although in this case it sounds like a very unlikely possibility."

"So if it isn't stress, she's going crazy? Is that what you're telling me," said Tracy hesitantly.

"Psychiatrists don't use the 'c' word, Tracy. It's vulgar. And it makes crazy people suspicious."

"Funny. So you think too much stress and not enough sleep?"

"That is my informed diagnosis, having never met your cousin, having very little medical or family history to go on, and the information I do have comes secondhand."

"Thanks, Damon. I owe you one."

"Tell your cousin to take it easy and see someone if it doesn't stop in a couple weeks. Speaking of stress, how is your hubby handling things? Talk is swirling that he's on a very, very short list of people who might be the next chief of surgery. Is he okay?"

"You know him. Like a rock, inside and out. He's fine."

"And how are you? Are you sleeping enough?"

"No. But I am an artist, so I don't have a real job. Which means I have no stress to complain about."

"I envy your carefree, artistic life. Have fun in West Virginia, and say hi to some coal miners for me. And say hi to Mike."

"Will do, Damon. Thanks."

Tracy closed her cell phone and rubbed her temples. She twisted her blonde hair around her finger without realizing it, until she felt her hair pull tight against her scalp. She should have been pleased that she had gotten a free diagnosis from a psychiatrist without jeopardizing her husband's career. But she doubted that Turner's stark-naked stroll down the hotel hall was caused by stress. He was a doctor – he had been under stress for his entire adult career. Stress defined him, made him who he was. And as long as she had known him, he had never once sleepwalked, or seen visions. Bullheaded as he was, he had one of the strongest minds she had ever known – clear, concise, brilliant, with no hesitation or weakness. And as far as she knew, his family had no history of seizures, or mental illness. It had to be stress – there was no other explanation.

But she remembered the look in her husband's eye when he told her he saw someone who looked like Dangerfield Newby – he was certain he had seen something, and someone. No hesitation or weakness. Tracy slowly allowed herself to consider the possibility that her brilliant, intense, moody husband had an "organic disorder of the mind" – something she could not help him overcome. The only other possibility – improbable as it was – is that Turner had seen something on the bridge that night, and that there was absolutely nothing wrong with his mind. She paid for her Guinness and headed quickly back to the hotel.

Turner was completely naked, and standing in the middle of the street. His head hurt, and his stomach ached. The cut on his hand throbbed, and dripped blood onto the street. He did not know how long he had been there, or how he had gotten there. He remembered Tracy pulling him inside the hotel room, scolding him, and putting him to sleep. She had given him some kind of pill, but he did not know what it was. "How stupid do I have to be to take a pill without knowing what it is," he thought. He did not know how long he had been sleeping, but it must have been a long time, because it was now dusk. The streets were wet, and a light, steady rain fell on his face.

There was no sign of Tracy. Turner did not recognize the streets, or the street names. He did not know how to get back to the hotel, or who to ask for directions. He could not recognize a single landmark or building. The street lights flickered on and cast weak yellow shadows through the dense fog. His bare feet were cold on the wet pavement. There was no one else on the street, or the sidewalk.

He had begun walking on the sidewalk toward the top of a hill when he heard the roar of a car traveling at high speed. He ducked behind a thick elm tree and saw a car racing over the top of the hill toward him. The car was at least 50 years old – enormous round headlights perched at the end of a long metal nose, with a shiny metal grill sandwiched between. The hood bulged up in the middle, and the bulge extended all the way to the windshield, which angled back sharply toward the driver. The pale yellow sedan looked familiar – Turner thought he must have seen a picture of it somewhere. He peered out from behind the tree and saw the driver – a well-dressed black man, wearing a fedora and a dark-colored suit and a tie. The man looked behind him as he drove, and Turner then saw another car, a sleek black sedan, also at least 50 years old, close behind. There were four white men in the black sedan, and the driver peered intently at the car in front of him. The other men in the car were yelling something, but Turner could not hear what they were saying. The second car appeared to be gaining ground on the first.

Turner watched the two cars speeding down the hill. The street dead-ended at the bottom of the hill. A thick grove of trees grew a few feet from the end of the road, and beyond that, a dense forest, impenetrable in the waning light. The first car approached the dead end with the second car right on its bumper. There was no room to turn around. The first car suddenly accelerated, then braked hard just feet from the grove of trees. The driver spun the wheel hard to the left at the same time as he braked, and the big yellow car spun around on the wet street, its rear end swinging around perfectly just as the driver accelerated again. The black man in the fedora pointed the yellow car forward and back up the hill, and sped off just inches to the right of the second car, which was still accelerating toward the dead end. Turner smelled the acrid burning rubber and heard the whine of the engines from his hiding spot behind the tree.

The driver of the second car tried executing the same maneuver as the first car, but he was too late; the car braked hard, skidded sideways, and rolled over once before landing on its wheels and slamming into a tree at the edge of the grove. Turner saw the front seat passenger eject out of his window and heard a thud as the passenger landed somewhere in the woods. Smoke roiled from the hood of the wrecked car, and Turner's eyes stung from the burning rubber, oil and gasoline.

The driver of the first car stopped midway up the hill, just in front of Turner's hiding spot, and got out. He was tall, with dark brown skin and a thin mustache. His hat was pulled low over his eyes, and his well-cut suit flowed as he walked down the hill toward the wreck. He approached the wreck, peered inside, and pulled open the rear door, grabbing one of the men in the back seat. He pulled a small revolver out of his suit pocket, and shot the rear seat passenger once in the head. He then walked around to the other side, shot the other rear seat passenger, and then casually strolled toward the front of the car. He pulled open the front door and shot the driver once in the head.

He looked up the hill, saw no one, and walked into the woods toward the ejected passenger. He disappeared into the woods, and after a few moments, Turner heard a single gunshot. The man emerged from the woods, slid the gun into his suitcoat, and walked up the hill toward his still-idling yellow car. He walked past Turner, got in, and roared up the hill.

Just as the yellow car reached the crest of the hill, a green coupe sped over the top of the hill. The pale yellow car turned hard to the right, but the coupe slammed into the driver's side of the yellow car. The two cars skidded down the hill, the nose of the coupe drilled deeply into the driver's side of the yellow sedan, and both cars screeching down the hill directly toward Turner's tree. Turner tried to back up, but his legs would not move, and his arms froze. The cars slammed into Turner's tree, the coupe nearly cutting the yellow sedan in half. Turner saw the yellow sedan crumple as the nose of the coupe drove forward directly into the driver before slamming against the tree. The driver of the yellow sedan sat upright, blood gurgling from his mouth, the steering wheel wedged into his rib cage. His fedora hung from the broken glass on the passenger side of the car. His head hung at an odd angle, and his eyes bulged. The steering wheel had bent and was partially wrapped around his body. He looked familiar, yet Turner could not imagine where he would have seen him, or why he was driving the old car. Turner almost choked on the smell of gasoline, burning rubber, and fresh blood.

Turner heard groans coming from the coupe, and heard someone struggling to open a door. His legs and arms began to move, and he regained his sense of place. He ran naked into the woods before anyone could see him.

CHAPTER 14

Elsey sat at the kitchen table making Henry's dinner. She took a small cup of cornmeal, and rolled it into a ball. She took out a spoonful of grease from a jar in the cupboard and spread the grease with her fingers on her favorite cast iron pot. The top of the oven was not hot enough, so she threw more wood in the belly until the heavy flat plate on top of the oven was hot to the touch. She shook a few drops of water on the oven top and listened to the water sizzle. Then she put the cast iron pot on the oven until the grease began to pop. She flattened the cornmeal in her hands and laid it flat in the pot, turning it with a wooden spoon when she thought it was done enough on each side. When the cornbread was done, she plucked it from the pot and put it on one of the good plates. She leaned her head out of the kitchen window and called to him.

"Henry, bring that ham in here while the stove still hot."

Henry walked out of the smokehouse carrying a metal bucket filled with ham hocks and cuts from a hog he had butchered and smoked two weeks ago. He walked into the kitchen and handed the pot to Elsey.

"Alright, missus, I got what I could carry. How long until we eat?"

"Soon's I get this ham into the pot. Cornbread's over there." Elsey sliced chunks off the ham hocks and laid them in the pot, the grease sizzling and popping in the small warm kitchen. Elsey worked quickly, slicing meat and pulling the chunks from the cast iron pot after just a few minutes. Her wiry black fingers gripped the knife firmly. She turned her back to Henry as she worked. Henry looked at her from behind.

"You ain't said much today," said Henry.

"Ain't got much to say today. If you feel like talkin' go on ahead." She spoke without turning to look at him, and without stopping her work."

"You aint' had much to say to me for the last few days."

"If I need to tell you something, you'll know soon enough."

Henry paused and looked out the window.

"Don't worry about him," Henry said. "You know the boy can take care of himself. Jennings won't harm him. I won't allow it."

"Don't tell me what you will and won't allow on someone else's farm," snapped Elsey. "Fact is, he's at least a two hour ride from here. You ain't got no say in what is and ain't allowed at Jennings's farm."

"I had no choice. Besides, I didn't sell him. I let Jennings have him two days a week, thirty dollars per week. Rest of the week he's back here with us. He's still here with us."

Elsey continued slicing ham, and did not bother to respond, or even turn to face him.

"What would you have me do, missus? You know the problem as well as I do."

Elsey spoke without turning. "I don't see how my circumstance got anything to do with that boy. If Jennings don't like our situation, he should take it up with you. Or me."

Henry chuckled. "You know Jennings won't take it up with me, not as long as he can use it to his advantage. And he's scared to death of you. Thinks you'll kill him in his sleep if he takes you back. I don't blame him. You almost killed him the other day, hammering that pot with the broomstick. He looked like a damn bird, legs flapping about."

Elsey tried to conceal her laugh, but Henry could see her body shaking. He spoke. "You know how to handle a cook pot in more ways than one, missus. I won't let Jennings take you back."

Elsey whirled around to face him so quickly that he instinctively stepped back and raised his hands in defense.

"I don't ever want to go back to Jennings," hissed Elsey. "But since he owns me and you don't, I reckon he can come and take me back any time he pleases. And since you seem unable to fix things, I reckon you and me both have to live with the fact that he might take me back. So don't you tell me what you will and won't allow. 'Til things change between you and Jennings, we all got to live with that fact." She finished preparing the meal and set two steaming plates of ham and cornbread on the table.

Henry slumped in his chair, and slowly poked at his ham and cornbread. Elsey stood and peered out of the window for a few moments before turning to face Henry.

"Why don't you call Anna Mae and Gabriel in here for dinner," she said. "Reckon there's enough room in the kitchen for all of us. I'd like to see all of us together more often than I do. Gabriel hardly comes in the house anymore, and now Dangerfield ain't around much more either. Be good for all of us to sit together for a time."

Henry looked at her figure standing in the early evening sun. "Missus, you never expressed much concern about all of us spending time together before now. You worried something might happen to us?"

Elsey turned again, and Henry flinched. But this time, Elsey had allowed a smile to crease her dark, time-worn face. She picked up the pot and scooped more ham and cornbread on Henry's plate. "No, I ain't worried about no one I can see in my home. Nothing will happen to any of the rest of them. I won't allow it."

She put the pot down on the stove, and the sound of iron hitting iron rang throughout the house. Henry got up, called the others in the house, and sat down to finish his meal.

———❖———

Against all of his better judgment, Dangerfield finally left Harriet and returned to work on the fence. He worked on the fence from afternoon until dusk, resetting posts, driving nails, straightening boards. His only company after Harriet left was a dun-colored mare and her colt, and a shaggy old gelding. The colt would approach him cautiously and then bolt when he moved or stood up. When he was finished with his work, he held out his hand and remained still until the colt approached him and touched its muzzle to his outstretched hand. He scratched its muzzle until the mare nickered, and the colt skittered back to its mother. The old gelding ignored him completely. He gathered the tools Jennings had given him, and was returning them to the stable. He had not gotten halfway there when he saw Harriet approaching him carrying a tin of food covered by a white cloth.

"Marse told me to bring you some food. You must be about wore out."

He took the food and removed the white cloth from the tin. Harriet had brought him four thick slices of ham, steaming cornbread, and a small pail filled with coffee. He took the plate and sat down on the ground and began eating.

"I didn't figure Jennings to feed his help this much," said Dangerfield between mouthfuls of ham.

"Jennings – Marse – told me to feed you. He didn't say how much. I made this myself. Figured you must be about wore out." She sat down next to him so that her knee touched his and watched him eat. Dangerfield quickly consumed the ham and cornbread, then drained the pail filled with coffee in two large gulps. Harriet watched him finish eating, then took the tin from him and set it in the grass next to her.

"Marse Henry don't feed you back home?"

"Yes, but apparently not enough. Thank you for the food."

"Too late for you to ride back to Marse Henry's, I reckon. Where are you going to sleep tonight?"

"Jennings didn't discuss that with me. I imagine in the stable."

"Jericho's father had a place in the stable," offered Harriet quickly. "Hidden, up in the hay loft, above the tack. I'll show you."

Harriet picked up the tin pail and the cloth. They both stood up and started walking toward the house and barns. It was almost dark when they returned. They walked into the stable, and the horses nickered and shuffled. The big doors on either end of the stable were still open, allowing the last dying rays of daylight to enter.

Harriet pointed to a rough-looking wooden ladder that led to the loft.

"Up there," she said. "Be mindful, that ladder rocks back and forth."

Dangerfield wondered how she knew about the rickety ladder, then remembered what she said about Jericho's father. He put his hand on the first rung and turned to face her.

"I am obliged, Miss Harriet. Sleep well." He turned and began climbing the ladder, but she put her hand on his shoulder.

"Let me show you where it is. You won't find it in the dark. It's been a while since I've been up here, not since . . . ." Her voice trailed off. He climbed down and stepped to one side. She began climbing the ladder. He waited until she was at the top, and climbed up to meet her. They stood together in the dark hayloft, not saying anything, until he reached out his hand and touched her breast. He felt her quiver, and felt her nipple swell and harden. She took his hand, and led him into the darkness, the two of them stumbling forward into a strange place neither of them knew.

CHAPTER 15

Turner jumped out of the bed and fell to the floor, feet still moving, still naked, still running through the woods. Only he wasn't in the woods, he was in his hotel room. And he wasn't naked, he was wearing the pajamas Tracy had given him for his birthday last year. He looked around the room. The curtains were still drawn, and his and Tracy's suitcases were pushed against the wall, just as they were when they returned after lunch. The room was dark, and his head hurt, and the cut on his hand throbbed. He heard a noise in the bathroom, and then Tracy emerged wearing her bathrobe.

"You're finally up," she said. I thought you would sleep all night."

Turner rubbed his head. "What time is it?"

"6:30 p.m. You have been asleep for almost five hours. You needed it." She climbed in bed next to him, stroked his chest, and gently kissed him on the mouth. "Are you feeling better?"

"Sort of. He looked around to make certain he was in the same hotel room in the same city. He checked the nightstand, and was relieved to see his wallet, keys, a tourist's guide to Harpers Ferry, and a notepad bearing the hotel letterhead. It had all been a dream, a bizarre dream, but nothing real. He was still in Harpers Ferry. He lay down again.

"What are you looking for," Tracy said. "You want to go out for dinner?"

"No, let's stay here awhile. Were you here the whole time I was sleeping?"

"I, uh, left for a few minutes to get some things from the hotel lobby," said Tracy weakly. "I wasn't gone very long. I wanted to make certain I was here when you woke up."

"What kind of sleeping pill did you give me?"

"Just a little something I take when I can't sleep." She propped herself up on her elbow and stared at him as he lay on the bed. "I need to know if you are feeling better. You didn't have any bad dreams, did you?"

He paused before answering. "No. No bad dreams. I slept fine."

Tracy curled her body tightly against his. She put her head on his chest and gently stroked his chin. "Why don't we stay here for awhile? We can get dinner later."

"Yeah, let's do that. I'm not feeling as good as I thought," said Turner.

They lay in bed together until Turner heard Tracy snoring softly. He felt her body rise and fall as she slept. Turner tried to make sense of his dream, tried to figure out what had happened to him. None of it made sense. There were no ghosts. It must have been the heat, or a dog, or maybe a homeless person he saw the day before. That had to be it. That was the explanation for what he saw yesterday.

But what about the cars, and the crash, and the man with the gun, and the shooting, and him being naked in the middle of the street and running through the woods? None of that made any sense. Then he remembered that Tracy had given him sleeping pills. Maybe that had something to do with his weird dream. Sleeping pills can cause all kinds of weird reactions. She gave him something to knock him out, and he had a weird dream. That was it. There was a simple explanation. Nothing to worry about.

He had put his mind at ease and was just about to drift off to sleep when he heard, clearly and unmistakably, Ezekiel Frazier's deep, mellifluous voice: "I can only hope that you have the courage to accept whatever destiny is presented to you."

Turner lay awake for a long time, remembering what the crazy old man had said. He looked at Tracy, curled up next to him in the expensive sheets and hotel bathrobe, her body slowly rising and falling with each breath. He could hear people talking and laughing on the street below, complete strangers, people going to dinner or sightsee, people who were oblivious to the darkness that was beginning to surround him. And then he knew that he would have to see Frazier again. He needed to rid himself of this madness once and forever, before the blackness surrounded him and took everything he had ever known. He lay awake for what seemed like hours before finally surrendering to sleep with Tracy curled up alongside him.

CHAPTER 16

Dangerfield awoke early the next morning, partly out of habit, and partly because he did not know what Jennings would do if he found out his newest hired field hand had bedded one of his house girls. Dusty shafts of morning light penetrated the hayloft where Dangerfield and Harriet had made their bed. He rolled over and studied Harriet as she slept. Dark brown coffee-colored skin. Her long dark hair, freed from the scarf she always wore, covered her shoulders. She was wrapped up in an old horse blanket, and beneath that, she was completely naked. Below them, the animals in the stable began to stir.

Dangerfield caressed her back, not wanting to awaken her, but knowing they both had to leave. She grunted, moved his hand away, and went back to sleep. He looked around at their makeshift bedroom. His shirt and breeches were crumpled in a corner; one boot lay in a pile of hay, and the other had been thrown in a corner. Harriet's dress, scarf and petticoats were neatly folded and lay on top of an old feed box that doubled as a dresser. Someone had spread a heavy layer of spring hay across the wooden slats that made the floor of the loft; two heavy horse blankets stretched across the hay, and several more blankets were neatly rolled up beside the feed box. Two coarse cotton pillows rested near the blankets. The area was small, just big enough for two people – the barn made the back wall, and in front were stacks of hay, tools, an old saddle, and assorted other tack, all of which obscured the little den from below. Someone had taken great pains to create this small den in a horse stable. The dusty light fell on Harriet through a crack in the wall, and she finally stirred.

"Get up," he whispered softly. "Lord knows what will happen if Jennings finds us."

She grunted and turned to face him. "Marse won't find us. He goes to the milkhouse first thing in the morning. Stay there at least two hours. Don't usually come to the stable until late in the morning." She rolled away from him and stood up to get dressed. He watched her as she dropped the horse blanket and stood naked before him for a glorious moment before putting on her petticoats.

"I reckon you don't normally sleep here," he said. "Jennings will know you didn't sleep in the house last night."

"Marse lets me sleep in the field cabins from time to time," she replied. "Jericho still needs me." She continued dressing as she spoke. "Marse will just figure I slept in the cabins with Jericho. If I tell Ma'am that Jericho needs me, she don't usually mind."

"Who minds Jericho if you ain't around?"

"A few of the field hands have taken a shine to Jericho. They watch out for him, take care of him when he's in the field and I am in the house. And the house girls also look out for him when I can't be with him."

"So Jericho don't stay with you?"

She turned to face him. "I told you Marse ain't fond of young field hands. But he'd rather have 'em in the field than in the house, distracting the house girls. And this way, I know where he is. I may not see him during the day, but I know where he is." She paused. "At least I know for the time being.' Marse ain't sold him yet, but I suspect he might." She finished dressing and turned around.

"Marse won't suspect anything if he don't see me in the house for a night or two," said Harriet, yawning. "He'll just reckon I slept in the cabins. But I reckon you'd better be up and about soon."

Dangerfield didn't want to leave. "You told me Jericho's about nine" said Dangerfield tentatively. "Boy seems a bit young to spend so much time away from his mother, if you don't mind me sayin' it."

Harriet leveled her eyes before speaking.

"You take it up with Marse Jennings if you think you ought," she said coldly. "When the boys turn nine or so, Jennings moves 'em out to the fields to work with the field hands. If they work and he needs 'em, he might consider keeping 'em. If they don't work, or Marse has run up his accounts in town, he sells 'em. Sometimes he sells 'em when they ain't but five or six. And as I explained, I always know where he is, and who is taking care of him." Harriet paused before speaking.

"I am obliged for your help earlier with Jericho and Lilly," she said firmly. "You'd best be on your way now. My, but you slow in the morning. Ain't even dressed yet." She smiled, wrapped her scarf around her head, and began climbing down the ladder. Dangerfield rushed to his feet and reached the ladder just as she touched the ground and turned to walk away."

"Miss Harriet, where do you suppose I should sleep this evening?"

Harriet looked up and smiled. "You take it up with Marse Jennings if you think you ought. I'll bring some breakfast round by the fence. You'd best be up."

She turned and walked out of the stable. He watched the sway of her hips and the way her scarf bobbed up and down when she walked. He could have followed her all day. But the sun was starting to bake the stable roof, and he knew Jennings would be looking for him soon. He pulled on his breeches, found his boots, and shook the hay out of his shirt before putting it on. He took a look around, and wondered how many times Harriet had been up here. She had mentioned Jericho's father, and how he had been killed by a bull. Had she been with others since he died? Were there others before him? Dangerfield barely knew her, and yet he already could not stand the thought of her up here in this dusty bedroom with another man, even if he was now dead, even if he was the only one to share the stable with her.

He started down the ladder, and was at the bottom when he heard footsteps entering the stable. He turned and watched Jennings stride through the door.

"Day, Marse."

"Yes. I trust you found a place to sleep last night? No one saw you in the cabins last night."

"Didn't know I was to stay in the cabins. You didn't say where I was to sleep."

"I assumed you would stay in the cabins with the others. Where did you sleep?"

Dangerfield searched the stable for a passable explanation that would not reveal the location of Harriet's hideaway.

"In the tack room over yonder. Found a few horse blankets and jes' curled up in 'em."

"Tack room, eh? Couldn't have been very comfortable. Next time you sleep in one of the slave cabins. Bring a blanket with you, and make room on the floor."

"Yes, Marse. "Just on my way to finish that fence. Got dark before I could finish setting all the posts."

"Well, you finish what you can this morning. Reckon Henry will want you back, so you'd best be on your way by afternoon. Henry will want you back before nightfall."

Dangerfield's throat tightened when he heard Henry's name. He had not thought of Henry or Elsey or Gabriel or any of his family after he met Harriet. He had been here only one day and one night, but now it felt as though his previous life had fallen away, disappeared down a well. It seemed like months since he had seen his family or slept in his own bed, but it had been only one day and one night.

"Yes, Marse. Finish what I can, and get on back before nightfall."

"Very well." Jennings turned to leave, then turned back. "Has Harriet brought you breakfast, yet? I haven't seen her this morning."

"No, Marse, she ain't."

"Well, go on up to the house and get some breakfast, then finish the fence."

"Yes, Marse."

Jennings turned and walked out of the stable, and headed toward the slave cabins. Dangerfield left the stable and walked in the other direction toward the house. When he arrived, Harriet was waiting at the door, holding a plate of biscuits and ham. She eyed him warily.

"Morning, Miss Harriet."

"Morning'" she said as though she had not seen him in weeks. "You'd best eat quickly. Marse will want you to finish that fence before you leave."

"Yes, Miss Harriet, I do intend to finish the fence before I leave, but thank you for the kindly reminder." He smiled at her, but she did not return the smile. She set the plate on the ground and returned to the house. He watched the sway of her hips as she walked and closed the door behind her. He finished the food and his stomach turned at the thought of leaving her behind to return home. But he also knew that Elsey wanted him back, and had probably not slept at all last night, worried sick about him.

Everything he knew about the world was with Henry, Elsey, Gabriel, and Anna Mae. He knew that Henry "owned" him, but until now, he did not clearly understand what that meant. After just one day at Jennings' plantation, he was beginning to under-stand what it meant, and what it meant to other slavers. He briefly considered asking Jennings if he could stay another day and night to finish the fence, but he thought of Elsey and knew he had to return home. He set the plate on the ground and turned toward the pasture.

He worked until the early afternoon. There was only one post left to set, but he knew he needed to start riding soon if he wanted to be home in time for supper. He looked up, determined it was about 2 pm, and estimated that it would take him another hour to set the post and level the boards. If he left around 3 p.m., he would be home by late afternoon, well before dusk. He turned his spade into the earth, and quickly finished his work. Jennings approached just as he was gathering his tools.

"Day, Marse."

"You work quickly. I thought it would take you another day to finish up."

"Yes, Marse. You and Miss Harriet both said that fence need to be done today, before I leave."

Jennings arched his eyes. "Harriet seems to have some interest in your work. "Don't reckon she's ever fixed a fence."

"I suspect not, Marse. She was likely just repeating what she heard you say."

"That must be it." Jennings eyed the fence posts, which were plumb, and the boards, which were dead-level to the naked eye. "You do good work. It's hard to get fence posts plumb like that. I can see why Henry won't part with you."

"Yes, Marse."

Jennings pulled a small gold watch from his waist pocket. "It's 2:30. You'd best be on your way if you want to make it back to Henry's place before supper. I'll have Jericho fetch your horse and your saddle. Meet me at the house."

"Yes, Marse."

Dangerfield gathered his tools and returned them to the stable. The walk back to the house seemed like it took forever. When he got to the house, Solomon had been saddled, bridled, and brushed. Jericho held his reins. The boy looked up at him wistfully.

"Thank you kindly, Jericho. Reckon I'll see you again in a few days. Take good care of Miss Harriet."

Jericho smiled, and watched him as he mounted Solomon. The big horse nickered, and swung his shaggy head from side to side, eager to run.

Dangerfield gently pushed his bootheel into Solomon's flank, and the big horse lurched forward. Jennings stood by the door with his arms crossed, looking past him at something ahead on the trail. Harriet stood inside the door, looking at him. He tipped his hat toward her, and she smiled, the first time he had seen her really smile since he arrived. She went back inside the house, and he turned toward home.

He had gone only 50 yards or so toward home when he realized what Jennings had been looking at. Three men on horseback were riding hard toward Jennings' plantation. The horsemen drew closer and Dangerfield recognized them – the slave catchers he had met on the trail. He sat Solomon and waited for the men to approach. The lead rider with the thick mustache and scar held up his hand, and the two trailing riders slowed their horses. The lead rider drew his mount beside Solomon. This time, he was alone. Solomon was at least two hands taller than the smallish dun. Dangerfield did not dismount, but instead peered down at his inquisitor.

"I see you made it safely to Dr. Jennings' farm," said the man with the scar.

"Yes, Marse, had a safe ride."

"That is a fine mount. Reckon Henry Newby wants him back."

"Yes, Marse. On my way back to Henry's place now. He's expectin' me."

"Did you finish your business with Dr. Jennings?"

"Yes, Marse."

"Is Dr. Jennings home? I have business with him."

"Marse Jennings is in the house."

"Very well then. Good day."

He twisted the end of his thick mustache, touched the brim of his hat, and rode on. The second rider passed Dangerfield without looking at him. The third rider, the young boy with long thin hair, spurred his horse. He held the handle of his whip as he passed, and he stared at Dangerfield and Solomon. He gave a thin, toothless smile, and then he rode on toward Jennings's plantation.

Dangerfield rode about 50 feet then turned and watched the men as they approached Jennings' plantation. Jennings walked out of the house and approached the first rider. Out of the corner of his eye, Dangerfield saw Jericho run out of the back of the house, toward the slave cabins. There was no sign of Harriet. Jericho ran until he was out of sight.

Dangerfield turned around and nudged Solomon forward, toward home.

CHAPTER 17

Turner awoke at 6 the next morning. He had slept through the night with no dinner, and he was famished and confused. Tracy's side of the bed was empty. Her bathrobe lay on the chair. Her suitcase was open.

He stumbled into the bathroom, but she wasn't there. "She must have gone to get some breakfast," he thought to himself. He splashed water on his face and studied his reflection in the mirror. He had been sleeping over 11 hours, but it had done him no good – deep wrinkles creased his face, and the skin around his eyes sagged. The cut on his hand still hurt, and his head ached. He could think of nothing except Frazier's voice, and how clearly it spoke to him last night. He could hear Frazier's Tidewater accent, his crisp and precise inflections, the pauses between sentences. Frazier's voice could not have been clearer if he had been whispering in his ear.

"I've gotta figure this out," Turner said out loud to the face in the mirror. "This can't be happening to me." As he spoke these words out loud, to no one, he realized that he did not know what was happening to him – he did not know what "this" was.

The door opened, and Tracy entered carrying two large white bags.

"Hey, Rip Van Winkle, I thought you'd never get up." She set the bags on the table next to the bed. "You made me miss dinner last night, and I got up at 5:30 this morning so hungry I could eat the furniture. I got us some bagels, cheese and fruit from the restaurant downstairs." She opened one of the bags, took out a bagel and sat on the bed looking at him as he stood in the bathroom, still studying his reflection in the mirror.

"Did you sleep well last night?"

Turner paused before answering. "Sort of. Yesterday was a long day, and things caught up with me."

"Did you have any dreams?"

"No, none that I can remember." It was true – he had slept for over 11 hours, but had no dreams. This was good.

"No, I had no dreams at all last night. I just need to eat."

He sat on the bed next to Tracy, opened one of the bags and tore into the bagel. He started to feel better immediately. He just needed to eat, and everything would be back to normal. Tracy put her hand on his knee and stared at him.

"I was worried about you. You were really restless last night."

"Really? Did I do anything stupid?" He finished the bagel in three bites, and tore into the cheese and fruit. He felt better already, and started to think he didn't need to see Frazier after all. Whatever had happened to him over the last two days would pass soon enough. No need to panic, he was strong enough to beat this.

"No, you didn't do anything stupid, but you were moving and talking. Loudly. You woke me up twice. I thought about sleeping on the floor."

Turner stopped chewing. "What was I saying?"

"Something about a car crash and a man with a gun. I was half asleep myself, so I couldn't hear everything. But if you don't remember any dream, it couldn't have been that important."

Turner felt a thump in his stomach as he heard her talk. He put the cheese and fruit back into the bag.

She stood up and gave him a long kiss on the mouth. "I'm glad you're feeling better. Let me hop into the shower and we can enjoy our final day in Harpers Ferry. It's been fun, but a girl gets tired of ghosts and gun battles. I need to get back to the studio. Think about what you want to see today. We'll do whatever you want."

She took off her clothes, grabbed her bathrobe from the chair, and walked past him toward the bathroom. He sat on the bed and watched her beautiful naked backside until she closed the bathroom door. On any other day, he would have pulled her back to the bed and skipped sightseeing. But now, he sat slumped on the bed. He had not told Tracy about the dream he had about the car crash and the man with the gun. She could not have known anything about that dream unless he said something. But he did not remember any dreams from the last night. Nothing at all. Could he have relived that dream without remembering it?

He felt the room grow smaller, until the walls were within inches of his face — with an outstretched arm, he could have punched his fist through the wall into the hallway. It was early in the morning and the curtains were partially open, but the room grew darker until he could not see the fingers on his hand. He felt the room closing around him, until he could feel his breath bounce off the wall and back into his face. He closed his eyes and tried to think of anything that would keep the blackness from overcoming him. He thought again about what Frazier had told him, and when he opened his eyes, the room had returned to its original dimensions, and the early morning sun shone through the curtains. He knew he had to see Frazier once again, to get some answers, to find out what was happening to him. Frazier had perfectly described the image of Dangerfield Newby that Turner had seen two days ago. Perhaps he had other insights that Turner had been unwilling to accept.

Tracy emerged from the bathroom ten minutes later, with a white towel draped on her head. Turner was still sitting on the bed.

"You better get dressed," she said. "We didn't come all this way to spend our last day in the hotel. Did you decide what you want to see?"

"Let's eat a real breakfast first. Then we'll hit the armory one more time." He paused. "After that, I want to see Ezekiel Frazier again."

Tracy rubbed the towel on her hair.

"He's the guy you saw yesterday who claims to have seen Dangerfield's ghost, right? The one who thinks that Nat Turner spoke to him, and told him things about Nat Turner's rebellion that no one else could know. The one who claims that Nat Turner personally chose him to convey the truth about Turner's rebellion? I thought you concluded he was crazy."

"He might be. But I told you I saw something the other day. And I know it wasn't a dog, or the heat."

Tracy looked at him evenly. "Did you see anything last night? Did you see the reenactor again?"

"No. But some strange things have been happening to me. I thought it might have been the sleeping pills you gave me, but now I am not so sure. If I can talk to Frazier again, that might help me answer some questions."

"What do you hope Frazier will tell you that you don't already know," replied Tracy. "I've never known you to trust anyone's instincts except your own."

Her words hit home, and he knew she was right.

"I still need to see him," said Turner. "I want to find out if there is any hope for him, or me."

"Why do you care so much about him? You don't even know him."

"Actually, I feel like I know him better than I know a lot of people."

Tracy twirled her wet hair tight against her fingers and looked at him again. "Do you want me to go with you to see him?"

"No, I think I should do this myself. Let's walk around town for the morning, and I will stop by his house this afternoon. Are you going to be okay for a few hours this afternoon?"

"Sure. I'll start packing while you are gone."

Turner looked at her with a pained expression on his face.

"I don't mean pack to leave you," said Tracy quickly. "I mean pack to leave here. Maybe I should go with you. This Frazier guy sounds interesting."

"No. I have brought you far enough into this. I'm sure it's just fatigue. It will pass once we get back home. But I do want to see Frazier again."

"If that will make you feel better, that's what you need to do." Tracy kissed him again and looked into his eyes. "I'm sure it's just fatigue," she added. "But if isn't, we'll get you through this. Whatever it is, I will help you. C'mon, get dressed." She turned to leave, but Turner gently grabbed her hand.

"What do you mean 'if it isn't'"?

"Nothing," said Tracy. "Get dressed so we can get started."

"You must have an idea of what is going on with me if you think it might not be fatigue. If it isn't fatigue, what do you think it is, Tracy?"

"Well, fatigue and certain organic disorders of the mind often present similar symptoms." Tracy instantly regretted her explanation.

"'Certain organic disorders of the mind.' Sounds like my wife has been checking up on me."

"Of course not. I've heard enough shop talk to be dangerous. My husband's a doctor. Now get dressed or I'll find someone else to have breakfast with." Turner smiled and Tracy knew she had disarmed him, at least for now.

Turner quickly got dressed and they left the room for breakfast. After breakfast and another tour of the armory, Turner left Tracy in the hotel lobby before going to see Frazier one last time. Turner kissed her hard, and Tracy looked at him.

"You sure you don't want me to go with you? Frazier sounds like quite a character."

"No, I need to do this alone. I think I can handle this."

"I know you can. You are the strongest man I know. Good luck."

Turner watched her walk back to the hotel, and he felt more confused than ever before. They agreed to meet at the hotel at 2:30 p.m., pack up, and drive to the airport.

Turner's head was racing as he drove up the winding road on the way to Frazier's house. It was easy to dismiss Ezekiel Frazier as a crackpot, but as he drove toward his house, he realized he had a lot in common with Frazier. They were both educated, driven, brilliant black men in competitive professions. Turner and Damon Lee had been the only black students in their med school class, and Turner suspected that Frazier had been a similar novelty on the faculty at his college. Turner had never doubted his own abilities, but he also knew, deep down, that he owed a tremendous debt to those who came before him, those who had endured and survived far greater hardships than he would ever know. Black men like Frazier, and his own father. Turner knew he could never repay that debt, which in his mind relieved him of the obligation to try.

He needed to know what made Frazier tick, what motivated him. If only he could find out more about Frazier's past, he would discover some hidden secret, something in his past that caused him to snap, something that caused him to abandon a successful career in academia and live in squalor in West Virginia. And if he could prove that Frazier was crazy, he could dismiss Frazier's talk about visions and spirits and channeling Nat Turner's spirit. Frazier was plumb crazy – Turner was just exhausted. That was all it was. It all had to make sense, and once he found out what made Frazier go crazy, and got some sleep, everything would make sense, and go back to normal.

He arrived at Frazier's house just after 10:30 a.m. He parked on the road and walked toward the house. The black plastic still covered the broken windows, and pieces of plastic flapped in the morning breeze. Smoke curled from the chimney, which was pitched forward, cracked and missing several layers of bricks. He stepped on the creaking front porch, which sagged under his weight. The hole in the porch from his previous visit was still there – Frazier hadn't even bothered to put another board in place. He walked around the hole, and saw the front door was ajar. He peered into the inky hovel and was about to knock on the door, when he heard a familiar voice behind him.

"Get away from my house now, and leave me alone. You have no business here, and I've done nothing wrong."

Turner spun around and saw Frazier waving an ax that was almost as long as he was tall. He wore the same pants as yesterday, and a filthy checked lumberjack shirt that was at least three sizes too big. His great white uprush of hair was matted on one side, as though he had slept on that side and simply not bothered to comb his hair. At least three days of bright white whiskers poked through his coal-black skin. He squinted in the sun as he peered at his visitor.

"Mr. Frazier, it's Michael Turner. I paid you a visit yesterday. We talked about Nat Turner and Dangerfield Newby."

Frazier squinted, then smiled and lowered his ax. "Yes of course, Mr. Turner, the doctor from "Minnesooooota," he said, drawing out the long 'o.' "Please forgive me, I was chopping firewood. I wasn't expecting visitors, and you have caught me off guard."

Turner chuckled at the tiny ax-wielding man with the Tidewater accent and precise diction. He decided to break the ice immediately.

"With all due respect, Mr. Frazier, I suspect you don't get many visitors. Perhaps if you didn't greet people with a shotgun or an ax, more of your neighbors might stop by."

Frazier smiled, and returned the gentle barb. "Perhaps you misunderstand my intentions, Mr. Turner. If I wanted visitors, I would host a weekly tea party. By greeting would-be visitors with a shotgun or an ax, word of my reputation spreads, and I am spared the bother of company. But, despite my best efforts, you have returned, which tells me either you left something here yesterday, or you enjoyed my company. I hope it's the former, but I fear and suspect it may be the latter."

"Fair enough, Mr. Frazier. It's the latter. I hope you have a few minutes to talk. I am interested in your work involving Nat Turner."

Frazier eyed him coolly, then propped the ax against the side of the house. "Very well, Mr. Turner. I suspect your interests lay elsewhere, but since you have so, ahem, graciously paid me a visit, let us discuss Nat Turner. Please, come inside."

Frazier escorted him into the house. Although the interior was still musty and poorly lit, the late morning sunlight illuminated the first few feet of the doorway.

Nothing had been moved since Turner was last in the house; the books were still stacked in every corner of the room, in piles on tables, on the floor, and against the windows. Dirty clothes were strewn about everywhere. Dusty drinking glasses sat on a low, slanting coffee table. Turner gingerly lifted one of the glasses, revealing a dark circular spot where the glass had sat, perhaps for a week, perhaps for a month or longer. Frazier motioned toward the wooden rocking chair, and Turner sat uneasily, the chair creaking under his weight. From his chair, Turner could see a single bare light bulb flickering in the kitchen. There were two lamps in the sitting room, unlit. "At least he has electricity," Turner thought to himself.

"Would you like some coffee, Mr. Turner? I made it fresh two days ago." Turner suspected he was not kidding. Frazier took two of the dusty glasses into the kitchen and returned moments later, both glasses filled with a dark liquid. Turner took one of the glasses and took a long tentative sip of room temperature coffee laced with something else. He coughed, and Frazier smiled. "I took the liberty of adding a dollop of whiskey to our morning beverage, Mr. Turner. It makes the coffee last longer." Frazier retrieved a metal folding chair from within the kitchen and sat across from Turner.

"Tell me what you want from me, Mr. Turner."

"I want to hear more about the first time you knew Nat Turner was speaking to you. Didn't you try to resist what you were hearing?"

"Yes, of course," said Frazier, crossing his tiny legs. "No one wants to believe, even for a moment, that he is crazy. The risk to my career was obvious. But the dream, Mr. Turner, oh, the dream! It was so vivid, it was as though the two of us were talking just as you and I are talking today. It was a conversation, and Nat told me things no one could know, facts that have been lost to history. As I told you previously, I could hear his voice, his inflections, and the way he paused between sentences. I could feel the heat of his breath."

"But you had already spent years studying Nat Turner's rebellion. What could he have told you that you did not already know?"

"I will spare you the full history lesson, Mr. Turner. But let me give you a bit of background first. I'm sure you know Nat Turner's rebellion took place over two days in August, 1831. Fifty-six whites and many, many more blacks were killed during and after the rebellion. You may recall that much from your history lessons."

Turner nodded.

"But did you know what prompted Nat Turner to begin the insurrection? Visions from God, Mr. Turner. After the rebellion and before he was executed, Nat Turner told his lawyer that he had visions from God, direct and clear instructions from The Almighty One to strike a fatal blow against the sin of slavery. He told his lawyer that while he was working in his master's fields, he heard a loud noise in the sky, and God appeared before him. God told him that evil walked the earth, and that he, Nat Turner, should take up the yoke that Christ had laid down and fight the serpent of slavery. God told him that 'the time was fast approaching when the first should be last and the last should be first.' God told him to slay the Serpent. Nat Turner interpreted these visions to mean that he had been called to rebel against slave owners. And that is what he did."

"That is all very interesting," said Turner coolly. "But you must have known that information before you ever saw Nat Turner in any vision."

"Yes, yes of course," replied Frazier. "What I just told you is well known – Nat's lawyer published this information shortly after Nat was executed, in his book called *The Confessions of Nat Turner*. William Styron later wrote a novel of the same name. But the original story comes from Nat's lawyer, not the Styron book."

"Yes, I've heard of it, and the Styron book," said Turner. "But that still doesn't explain why Turner – Nat – chose you. And you still haven't told me anything I couldn't have found in his lawyer's book."

Frazier smiled. "You are curious, Mr. Turner, the kind of curiosity that goes far beyond a simple desire to know. You seek something I may not be able to give you. But allow me to finish. The first time I saw Nat he told me about his visions. He also told me details about one of the people he killed during the raid."

"What did he tell you?"

"Although he undoubtedly killed many people during the raid, Nat confessed to killing only one person, a woman named Margret Whitehead," explained Frazier. "He smashed her head in with a fence post. In my dream, Nat told me he killed her because she was the Serpent. Initially, he had planned to spare her life. But as he looked at her, lying on the ground, he saw her face and body transform. She changed from a frightened woman into a writhing, hissing snake, coiled and ready to strike. He saw the transformation with his own eyes – this woman was no longer human – she had literally become the Serpent. He saw the venom dripping from her fangs. Nat struck her down the way you would strike down any snake."

"That was when Nat realized that his vision was real, and that his orders were true," continued Frazier. "God told him to strike down the Serpent, and here before him was a real, hissing, writhing serpent. The message could not have been clearer. Nat told his lawyer that he killed Margret Whitehead, but he never told him why. Only I knew that she had become the Serpent, the living embodiment of Nat's vision from God. Only I knew what Nat Turner had seen. And to this day, Mr. Turner, I am the only one on this earth who knows what Nat Turner saw."

Beads of sweat pooled on Frazier's head. He stood up quickly, and walked toward the kitchen, holding his glass of rancid coffee. "Pardon me, Mr. Turner, I get excited when I consider the opportunity I have been given, and what has been taken from me because of that opportunity. Would you like some more coffee?"

"Only if you put more whiskey in it."

Frazier returned with two more glasses of days-old whiskey-laced coffee. The two men sat in silence for a few moments, drinking. Turner took another long pull of coffee and whiskey before speaking.

"So Nat tells you why he killed Margret Whitehead. You are now the only one who knows this information. Forgive me for being blunt, Mr. Frazier, but did you consider that none of this happened? Did you consider seeking counseling, or mental health treatment?"

Frazier finished his drink and looked evenly at Turner. "I know what you think, Mr. Turner. Nat was crazy, and so am I. But Nat told me something else that I could not escape. Just before he left me that first time, he told me that even those who do not believe can receive visions. Nat Turner never asked to receive his visions from God. He was chosen – he did not seek. Nat never wanted to be the messenger. And he told me that I had been chosen to reveal the truth about his actions – I was chosen. I certainly did not seek."

Turner shifted in his chair and looked at his watch. The two men sat in silence for several moments before Frazier spoke.

"Do you believe in God, Mr. Turner?"

"No, I don't. I believe in science, and reason, and evolution. I think there is an explanation for everything that happens. I believe in facts, not fairy tales. God is a fairy tale."

"That's good," exclaimed Frazier. "I don't believe in God either. Even after my experience with Nat, I don't believe in God. But clearly some do. And though I don't believe in God, I believe it is possible that humans can experience events that don't have an easy scientific explanation. You must believe the same, Mr. Turner, or else you would not be here. Tell me what you saw."

"What makes you think I saw anything?"

"The way you looked yesterday. Matthew told you that I had seen Dangerfield Newby. And although you have been a patient guest, your interest is clearly not Nat Turner. You want to know what I saw, and what Dangerfield looks like. As I told you yesterday, I have seen his ghost walking back and forth in Hog Alley. I told you what he looks like – the hat, pants, black boots, and the small coin purse. I am not chosen to tell his story, and he has never spoken to me. I don't know what he wants from us. Perhaps you do. So tell me what you saw."

Turner cleared his throat, and the words rushed out in a jumble. "I saw what you saw, Mr. Frazier. I saw him walking in Hog Alley. He looked just like you described – the black hat, the boots, the coin purse. I saw the gash on his neck, and the blood. I saw just what you saw only – only I saw him more than once. I saw him in Hog Alley, and then I saw him again in my hotel room. At least I think it was him, I can't tell. But I know I saw something, more than once."

Frazier eyed him coolly. "Did he say anything?"

"No. He said nothing."

"But you have seen him more than once?"

"Yes," said Turner softly. "I am certain of what I saw."

Frazier turned away. "I can't tell you what you want to know, Mr. Turner. I can't tell you whether you have been chosen to tell Dangerfield's story, or even whether he has a story. Perhaps you have been chosen to tell another story, someone else's story, whose identity has yet to be revealed. Perhaps you have not been chosen for anything. But I can't tell you what that story is. You must have the courage to accept your fate. Nat Turner and I were chosen — we did not seek. You must decide for yourself whether you have been chosen, and if so, what your path should be. I will tell you this — I saw Dangerfield, but he never spoke to me, not like Nat spoke to me."

Frazier stood up and walked toward the door. "I am afraid I told you all I know, Mr. Turner. Choose your path carefully, and don't be afraid of what others may say. I may have lost everything by speaking the truth, but I have gained something far more valuable to me."

Turner thanked him, and exited the house, squinting in the bright sunlight. When he returned to the hotel, he and Tracy packed their things, left the hotel, and made the long drive to the airport, where they caught the 6:30 p.m. flight back home.

CHAPTER 18

Henry awoke at first light, but when he walked into the kitchen, Elsey was already there, preparing breakfast. She had lit several candles and placed them on the table as she put wood into the stove. Henry stood behind her, watching her work.

"Mornin, missus."

Elsey put more wood into the stove belly, and set a large pot on the stove to boil. She addressed Henry without turning around.

"Henry, I need you to fetch some of those ham hocks from the smokehouse. And I also need a dozen fresh eggs this morning. I reckon we'll have enough corn meal left from yesterday to fry bread for all of us." She spread a handful of grease around her favorite cast iron pan, and set the pan on the kitchen table while she waited for the water to boil.

"What are we having today, Missus?"

"Boiled eggs, ham and corn bread, and maybe apples if somebody can fetch 'em from the storehouse."

Henry stood in the doorway watching her work. "Boiled eggs, ham and corn bread, eh? All this for breakfast, and it ain't even my birthday."

"It ain't just for breakfast, and it ain't just for you Henry. I reckon we'll eat together and all of us have a proper supper when he gets back later today. I'll make something for breakfast and have everything ready for supper when he gets back today." She turned to face him. "He is coming back home today, right? You and Jennings worked that out before he left, right?"

"Yes, Missus, he's coming home today. "He'll be home awhile before he has to go back to Jennings' place. He'll always come home. I told you I won't sell Dangerfield, Gabriel, or Anna Mae to Jennings or anyone else. I promised you, Missus, and I don't break my word. He'll be back today."

"Well, Henry, you promised Jennings you'd sell me back to him once you two work out your differences. I reckon you plan on keeping that promise, and if you do, Jennings owns me free and clear just like he used to."

"That ain't the same kind of promise, Elsey, and you know it. We been over this. You know Jennings had me over a barrel back then. I told him what I had to tell him to make certain you could stay here. Things are different between me and

Jennings now. He can't take you back, and I ain't legally obligated to sell you to him. I promised him what I promised him, but he don't own you."

Elsey turned to face him, and caressed the handle of the frying pan.

"I know what you told him, Henry," said Elsey in a low, menacing growl. "But I know how things change between men. The promises of men don't mean much when it comes to money and women. I know one thing, I'll kill both of you and hang at noon before I ever call that man Marse again. "I won't ever let him touch me again, Henry."

"He ain't Marse to you or anyone else long as I'm around." He turned to leave the kitchen, but then spun back around to face her.

"You're a hard woman, Elsey, a real hard woman. Ain't I been good to you? You and all of our children? We all live here together, under one roof, as close to a real family as the law will allow. I ain't never hurt you or the children, and I won't start now. He'll be back, and he will always come back from Jennings' place. I won't let Jennings keep him. I promised you, Elsey."

She turned back toward the stove and dipped her finger in the pot. "You better fetch those eggs, Henry. Water's set to boil soon. Henry turned, but Elsey grabbed his arm before he could leave.

"You ain't never given me any reason not to trust you Henry. As far as I know, you kept your word to me. I reckon I can't ask for anything more. Now get them eggs and apples if you want all of us to eat together this evening like a proper family."

Henry's face brightened, and he kissed Elsey on the cheek. He turned and strode out the door toward the smokehouse.

——— ((◦)) ———

Elsey was gathering firewood near the smokehouse when she heard hoofbeats on the trail leading to the house. She stood and watched until Solomon's huge shaggy head appeared. Against Henry's advice, Dangerfield rode him at full gallop around the final bend toward the house, his dark mane flying in the wind, massive hooves kicking up clouds of dust as horse and rider made a triumphant and riotous return home. Henry and Gabriel heard the commotion, and emerged from the smokehouse. Anna Mae emerged from the house and smiled as she saw him approach. Dangerfield bridled Solomon to a clattering stop, the big horse blowing and nickering, and wrestling the bit in his mouth. He slowly dismounted.

Henry tried to calm Solomon, slowly brushing his mane with his hand. "You ought not to run him hard like that at the end of a ride."

Dangerfield brushed the dust off his coat, and stretched his legs. "Didn't intend to run him that hard. He came around the bend and knew we were close to home, and he took off running. Did all I could do to stay in the saddle."

Gabriel and Anna Mae ran up from the fields. Elsey walked slowly from the house, and brushed past the others. She hugged him hard, holding his body against hers.

"I missed you, boy. Felt like you was gone for a month."

"I was only gone about two days, Miss Elsey. You knew I'd come back." Dangerfield looked at Henry and smiled.

Anna Mae and Gabriel walked up and hugged him. "I hope you all didn't make too much trouble while I was gone," said Dangerfield.

"No," said Gabriel, laughing, "but we left all of your work for you to do when you got home. Elsey made a big meal, so you ought to have plenty of reason to earn your keep now that you home for a spell."

"All of you go on inside and get ready for supper," barked Elsey. "I didn't spend all day cooking just to listen to idle chatter."

Henry, Dangerfield and Gabriel walked Solomon toward his stable, while Elsey and Anna Mae went into the house and prepared for supper.

Although he had been gone for only two days, everyone in his family felt the need to tell him what had happened while he was gone – not much had happened, but everyone had something to say. Anna Mae told him about the new chicks in the barn, and how hard it was to gather eggs when the hens were near. Gabriel talked about the new foal, and how it was now up and running, almost able to keep up with the mare. Elsey said she had been thinking of what to cook for his return from the moment he rode off – she made a list of things to gather even as she could see him leaving. Henry ticked off a list of things that needed to be done now that he was back – repair the hole in the smokehouse wall, fix the fence nearest the milkhouse, put new shoes on the gelding. He and Gabriel could do most of these things, you understand, but some things required three men, and now that Dangerfield was home, everything would be back to normal, at least for a few days. Everything was going to be just the way it was before.

He should have been happy to be back home. Although he had ridden hard for over two hours, he had no appetite – he poked listlessly at his supper while everyone else devoured the boiled eggs, ham, corn bread, and fresh apples. Everyone else talked effortlessly, cheerfully, but he did not care what they were saying. He could not stop thinking about Harriet, and Jericho, and the men he encountered on the trail. He saw Jericho running from the back of the house, away from the men, and he could not stop thinking about him. Was Jennings planning to sell Jericho? Was he going to sell Harriet? Now that he was back in the warm embrace of the only family he had ever known, he could not stop thinking about a woman and child he had known for only two days.

He continued poking at his food, half listening to the conversation around him. He looked up to see Elsey staring at him.

"You ain't hardly touched your food," said Elsey. "Can't usually stop you from eating everything you can find. You must be tired from your ride."

"I reckon I'll be fine, Miss Elsey. I just need to rest a bit." He forced himself to eat one of the boiled eggs, and a few pieces of ham before excusing himself.

"Reckon I'll give Solomon his oats and water before I brush him. Henry, since it appears we have a lot of work to do, I might take a look at that fence behind the milkhouse. You and Gabriel welcome to join me after you finish your supper."

He pushed himself away from the table and walked toward the door. He turned and faced his family, still seated, still eating. "It sure is good to be home," he said before leaving the house.

Solomon was munching contentedly on clover and alfalfa when Dangerfield approached. He lifted his head and nickered when he saw his rider.

Dangerfield retrieved a brush and a bag of oats from the stable and began brushing Solomon's mane. Solomon shook his head and continued eating.

"Well, old man, looks like the two of us going to spend a lot of time together from now on. Lot of riding between here and Jennings' place. I hope to go back every chance I get. Reckon you the only one I can talk to about it now." Solomon pressed his nose into the oat bag, and stomped his feet while he ate.

Lost in his conversation with Solomon, Dangerfield did not hear Henry's footsteps.

"You got more to say to old Solomon than you do to us," said Henry. "Elsey's worried about you. Sent me down here to see if you were sick."

"I ain't sick, Marse Henry. Just a bit wore out from the ride, and not too hungry. Thought I might brush Solomon and clear my head a bit."

"No need to call me Marse when it's just us family. It's Henry or Pa unless Jennings or someone else is around. It's just the two of us now."

Henry found another brush in the stable, and began brushing Solomon. The two men brushed the big horse on opposite sides without talking to each other – the only sound was Solomon slowly grinding his oats and clover. Henry spoke after a few minutes.

"Did Jennings say anything to you while you was at his place?"

"Nothing in particular. Why?"

"Just curious. Did he say anything to you about me or Elsey?"

"No. Was he supposed to tell me something about you or Elsey?"

"No. It's just that people talk sometimes. I ain't asking for any reason. Just curious."

"He didn't say much of anything to me. Just told me what needed to be fixed, and where to find the tools."

"Did he say anything about our arrangement?"

"Not much. He just said I should stay another day, since I didn't work a full day the first day. Said you wouldn't mind if I stayed an extra day."

"Reckon I can't quibble with him on that. Did you mind staying an extra day?"

"Whatever arrangement you worked out with Jennings is between you and him. I ain't got much say in what arrangements you make with him."

"Well, you know I don't intend to sell you, or anyone else to Jennings. Jennings can ask all he wants, but I don't intend to sell you, or anybody in this family to Jennings or anyone else. If he asks, you can tell him I said it," said Henry sharply.

"I imagine you already told him that. Besides, you'd have Elsey to contend with."

Henry laughed. "Ain't much to contend with there. Reckon Elsey'd split my skull with that pan if I even thought about selling any of you."

Both men laughed, and continued brushing Solomon. They worked in silence for a few moments before Dangerfield spoke.

"What arrangements do you have with Jennings?"

"He can have you two days a week, thirty dollars per week, just like we discussed when he paid us a visit."

"What other arrangements do you have with him?"

Henry paused before speaking. "Jennings and I have done business for years. Sometimes I do business with him because I want to, sometimes because I have to. I have other arrangements with Jennings, but none that concern you. Two days a week, he pays me thirty dollars per week for your help. That's what we worked out. That ain't changing."

Henry continued brushing Solomon while Dangerfield trimmed his hooves with a knife he retrieved from his coat. Dangerfield cleared his throat, and spoke.

"Thing is, I might need to spend more than two days a week at Jennings' place. Awful lot of work to do there, and we need to give him his money's worth."

Henry dropped his brush on the ground. "We need to give him his money's worth? I reckon Jennings has got more than a fair bargain for your time. He'd spend close to a thousand dollars of his own money to buy a healthy man that knows how to butcher hogs and make saddles. What did Jennings tell you? Does he want to change our deal? Hell if I'm changing what we agreed to. Two days a week, he pays me thirty dollars per week. Hell if I'm changing it," spat Henry.

"Jennings didn't tell me anything," replied Dangerfield quickly. "Didn't say anything about changin' the deal. Just that there's an awful lot of work to do there, and . . . well, just an awful lot of work, that's all."

"You, me and Gabriel got an awful lot of work to do around here. Damned if I let Jennings try to change what we agreed on."

"I told you, it ain't Jennings. There's somethin' else."

"What?"

Dangerfield finished trimming Solomon's front hoof and moved to the back before speaking.

"Jennings has this woman, she works in the house. He's got a few women work in the house, but there's this one woman in particular. Jennings told her to show me around. She . . . well, I reckon I never met a woman quite like her."

"A woman, huh?" Henry picked up his brush and continued brushing Solomon. "So that's it. Seems like you've taken a shine to this woman."

"I reckon you could say that," said Dangerfield, remembering their night in the hayloft.

"Does Jennings know about you and this woman?"

"No."

"That's probably for the best. She have a name?

"Harriet. Her name's Harriet. And there's something else."

"Lord Almighty, what else could there be?"

"Harriet's got a little boy named Jericho. Nine years old. Nice little boy. Harriet worries about him."

"So the mother worries about her son. Why is it your business?"

"I suppose it ain't, at least not yet."

"Not yet," said Henry softly. Henry held the brush in his hand for awhile before speaking.

"When I sent you off to Jennings, I tried to consider all the bad things that could happen. I tried to consider every possibility, so if it did happen, I could explain it to Elsey. I thought about you getting hurt or killed while you was at his place. I thought about Jennings trying to sell you, or trying to convince you to stay with him. I could explain everything to Elsey. And I had a plan if Jennings tried to change things. I thought of every possibility. But I never thought it would be a woman. Lord Almighty."

"Thing is, I reckon I'm going to spend more than two days a week at Jennings' place," interjected Dangerfield. "Maybe three, maybe even four."

"How do you propose to tell Elsey?"

"Hadn't thought about that."

"Well, you'd better start thinkin' about it. You'll be here for another three days, at least. Consider what you want to tell Elsey, and when. Don't leave her wondering."

The two men finished brushing and trimming Solomon, then put the tools back in the stable and returned to the house. Solomon lifted his shaggy head and watched them return to the house. He lowered his head and resumed eating.

BOOK II

CHAPTER 19

Turner tried to sleep on the flight back to Minnesota, but sleep did not come. He thought about what Frazier had told him, and what he had seen in his short time in Harpers Ferry. Four days ago, he was invincible – a highly regarded doctor, the next chief of surgery, the king of his world. Now, he had gruesome visions of ghosts, and inexplicable dreams about car crashes. None of it made sense. He knew at least that he had seen Dangerfield Newby's ghost. But who were the people in the car crash? What did this have to do with Dangerfield? He rubbed his temples and looked around the airplane. Most of the passengers in first class were people like him – busy, successful professionals, traveling around the country, vacationing, working, living the American dream. How many of them had visions like he did? How many of the bright shining people around him were secretly struggling with unknown demons? How many of them saw ghosts, and vivid car crashes?

Turner surveyed the thin, smiling, beautiful denizens of first class, tapping on their laptops, listening to their iPods, reading the financial pages. And for the first time in a long time, he did not feel like one of them. He was an outsider, the other. Just like his father, just like Frazier, just like the others who had come before him.

He looked at Tracy seated next to him. She was reading an art magazine. He tapped her on the shoulder.

"What are you reading, Leonardo?"

"A really interesting article on tribalism in modern sculpture," said Tracy. "How everything is now turning back to the earliest forms of sculpture – simple, minimalist, forms and shapes. Artists experiment with new stuff, but we always go back to the original stuff."

"So no matter how hard we try, we cannot escape our past, huh? I always thought art gave us an escape from our past. Turns out you guys want to tie everybody to what has already been," said Turner.

Tracy laughed. "Methinks the doctor doth protest too much. We are all bound by our past, our history. Besides, I've never known you to take such a keen interest in the history of tribalism in modern sculpture. We should go to Harpers Ferry more often."

"This last trip should tide me over for a while." Turner paused. "I can't stop thinking about what happened to me – to us – on this trip."

Tracy folded her magazine and turned to face him. "I've been thinking about it too." She twirled her hair around her fingers and looked out the window. "I think we both need to be honest with each other about what you saw – what you think you saw – in town. I'll fess up first, I haven't been honest with you. And you haven't told me everything about what you saw."

Turner felt his gut tighten. "Why don't you go first? Then you tell me what you want to know from me."

"No," said Tracy. "I ask the questions first. Then you'll understand why I did what I did."

"Christ, did you kill someone back there?"

"Nope. I may have saved someone," countered Tracy. "Let me talk, and then I will explain."

"Okay, boss."

"I need to know about this dream you had, about the car crash. You said something about a car crash and a man with a gun. You woke me up, you were talking so loud. I appreciate you telling me about the Dangerfield reenactor. There are a few explanations for that. It may have been the heat, a dog, a reenactor, or something else. I think there's an explanation for that. But you have never talked about any car crash, or any men with guns. Tell me exactly what you saw."

Turner shifted in his seat, and looked around the first-class cabin, hoping not to see anyone he knew.

"Okay," he said uneasily. "I was standing naked in the street. Completely naked. Except I don't know where I was. It was foggy, and there were these old-time street lamps lighting the street. I have never seen anything like them. My hand still hurt, and I had a headache, and I had no idea where the hell I was. I tried walking back, but there was no place to go. I didn't know where I was."

"What about the car crash?"

"Well, I was standing there next to this tree trying to figure out what was going on. Then I saw two cars come flying over this hill. The first car was this big yellow car, and the second car was a shiny black car. But get this – both cars were old-time cars, maybe 1930's or 1940's. The big yellow one had this long sleek nose, and the black one looked just like it, except shorter. They were both driving really fast, and the black car was chasing the yellow car. They passed right by me. I could hear the engines and smell the exhaust. I was right there, but I wasn't. I can't explain it."

Now Tracy looked around the cabin, twisting her hair. "Jesus Christ," she said softly. "Did you see who was driving the cars?"

"The guy driving the yellow car was a black man, very well dressed. He was wearing a fedora and a sharp gray suit. He had a thin mustache. Kind of a dark-skinned brother, real good looking. He looked familiar too, like I had seen him someplace. But I don't know who he is. Or was. I could see his face clearly. It was like I was standing right next to his window, but he was driving right past. He almost ran me over."

"What about the other car?"

"Four white guys chasing the yellow car. The guy driving had short dark hair. No hat. He was kind of swarthy, and he looked like he hadn't shaved in a few days. White shirt, unbuttoned at the neck. I couldn't see what the other three guys were wearing. They were shouting something, but I couldn't make out what they were saying. It was weird, babe – like I was right there, but they didn't see me. They just drove right past. The cars were within a few feet of me, but I wasn't scared. It was like I was watching a movie."

"Did they look at you?"

"Nope. None of them looked at me. It was as if I wasn't there, like I was invisible."

Tracy closed her eyes and twisted her hair until it was tight against her fingers. "What happened next?"

"Well, the yellow car comes to a dead-end, spins around, and comes back up the hill. The black car tried the same thing, but crashed into the woods at the end of the road. One guy went flying out of the car, into the woods. The other guys were trapped in the car. The black man in the fedora stops his car, walks back down the hill, and shoots all four of them. One after the other, bang, bang, bang, bang. Slides his gun back into his suit, and walks back to his big yellow car."

"Did he say anything?"

"Not a word. Just shot all four of them, and walked back to his car."

"How did this dream end?"

"Well, fedora man gets back in his car, and drives back up the hill. But another car, a green one, big, comes flying over the hill and hits the yellow car broadside. The green car almost cut the yellow car in half. Both cars slammed into the tree where I was standing. I could have been killed. But I wasn't really there, I was just watching. Fedora man was almost cut in half. I saw the steering wheel slammed up into his ribs. His head was at a weird angle, like his neck was broken. Blood gurgling out of his mouth, and him just sitting there, slumped against the door. His hat laying on the seat. I saw pieces of broken glass in his forehead. One of his eyes had popped out."

"Oh my God."

"Then, I heard someone in the other car moan, and then my legs began moving. I ran as fast as I could into the woods. And then I woke up, back at the hotel."

Tracy did not open her eyes, but reached for her purse underneath her seat. She pulled out a small bottle and handed it to Turner. She was pale, and she was sweating even though the cabin was frigid. She handed the bottle to Turner.

"What is this?"

"These are the sleeping pills I gave you before you had the dream. Remember? I gave you some pills to help you sleep. You needed to rest."

"You think the sleeping pills caused this?"

"Read the bottle."

Turner held the bottle up closer to the airline seat light and read softly, but out loud:

WARNINGS AND PRECAUTIONS

- Need to evaluate for co-morbid diagnoses: Revaluate if insomnia persists after 7 to 10 days of use.
- Abnormal thinking, behavioral changes, complex behaviors: May include "sleep-driving" and hallucinations. Immediately evaluate any new onset behavioral changes.
- A variety of abnormal thinking and behavior changes have been reported to occur in association with the use of certain sedative/hypnotics. Some of these changes may be characterized by decreased inhibition (e.g. aggressiveness and extroversion that seemed out of character), similar to effects produced by alcohol and other CNS depressants. Visual and auditory hallucinations have been reported as well as behavioral changes such as bizarre behavior, agitation and depersonalization.

"Sleep driving and hallucinations? Abnormal thinking and behavior changes? Where the hell did you get this stuff," hissed Turner.

"Never mind that for now," replied Tracy. "Now it's my turn for complete disclosure. I gave you this stuff because I needed you to sleep for a long time. While you were sleeping, I left the room and called Damon. I wanted to talk to an expert."

"You told Damon about what I saw?"

"Give me more credit than that. I told Damon my cousin was having some problems, and I wanted him to do an armchair, long-distance diagnosis. I played it off like my cousin was having the problem and Damon, perceptive doctor that he is, assumed that I was calling on my own behalf. Your name never came up, not once. He doesn't know a thing. C'mon, I am smarter than that."

"What did Damon say?"

"Just what you would expect him to. Stress, and lay off drugs and booze."

"I assume Damon also explained that these symptoms could be the product of dementia, or some other . . . ."

Tracy cut him off. "Organic disorder of the mind. Yes he did. And if you do have some organic disorder of the mind, I should be the first to know."

"Well, Dr. Tracy, give me the diagnosis. Am I crazy?"

"Well, there are a lot of explanations for what you saw that night in Harpers Ferry," explained Tracy. "Sometimes, the mind plays tricks on us. And there are some things that simply cannot be explained. The human soul cannot be neatly analyzed, much as you hate to hear that. The soul can see what the eyes cannot."

"Everything has a logical explanation," Turner countered. "That dream with the car, for example. You gave me a sedative that is known to cause hallucinations. What I saw with the yellow car and the man with the fedora was a hallucination, plain and simple. It wasn't real. I won't take that stuff anymore, and the problem is solved."

"Well, Doctor, explain what you saw in town and in the hotel."

"Stress-related disturbance caused by exposure to suggestive elements in the atmosphere," replied Turner. "Sort of like if you are looking at buying a red car, suddenly every car you see is a red car. Well, if I am in Harpers Ferry and everybody is talking about Dangerfield's ghost and Screaming Jenny, pretty soon everybody believes in ghosts. The suggestion influences how the mind interprets external inputs. It all makes sense to me now. There are perfectly rational explanations for everything that happened to me."

Tracy looked out the airplane window as the plane began to descend into Minneapolis. She twisted her hair, closed her eyes, and sank her lithe frame into the seat. "Convincing explanation, Doctor. But there is more here than you may know."

"What do you mean?"

"I think I know who was driving that yellow car you saw in your dream. I know who that man in the fedora is. We need to pay a visit to your cousin Vernita when we get back."

CHAPTER 20

After Dangerfield and his father finished brushing Solomon, Dangerfield ate dinner with his family, helped Gabriel repair fences, and later that night, slept in his own bed. It had been only a short time since he had last slept in his bed, but it no longer felt like his. Harriet wasn't in this bed. He remembered her earthy smell, and her coffee-colored skin, and the way her body quivered when he touched her. He thought about Jericho, and the man with the scar, and the other slave traders talking with Jennings. He lay in bed wide awake.

And then his insides turned to water, and he sat up straight in his bed. He saw Jericho running from the house. He watched Jericho run toward the stream behind Jennings' house, and then saw him jump into the roiling current, legs churning, water splashing. He saw Jericho run until the water was up to his neck, and then his upturned nose, and then the current took his forlorn and ageless body downstream. He watched Jericho's head sink under the swirling foam, and then pop up like a cork, and slide back soundlessly into the black water. He could feel the boy's heart pounding within his own chest, his lungs exploding under the water. Then, he was calm, and air once again filled his lungs. Dangerfield stood up and looked out at the night sky. His heart was pounding and his lungs filled with air, but the feeling was gone. He went back to bed, but sleep would not find him this night.

As soon as dawn broke, he sprang from his bed, dressed in his riding gear, and went toward the stable. Solomon nickered and stamped when he heard the sound of Dangerfield's boots. Dangerfield retrieved a thick blanket and Henry's best saddle from the tack room, and slung the saddle up over the big horse's withers before tightening it around his back and belly. He fastened the bridle around Solomon's head, wiped the bit with cloth, and pushed it against Solomon's teeth. He threw the reins over Solomon's head, and looped them over the pommel before heading toward the house.

Anna Mae and Elsey were up making breakfast. Anna Mae was filling a pot with water she had retrieved from the creek when she heard his footsteps. Elsey froze when she saw Dangerfield standing in the door.

"My, you up early. Breakfast not quite ready yet. Henry ain't up yet."

"Mornin' Miss Elsey." Dangerfield rocked back and forth on his bootheels. "I need to speak with Henry right away. Don't reckon he'll mind if I wake him."

"What's all this?"

Dangerfield knew he needed to tell Elsey everything, but he didn't know where to start. Anna Mae stared at him, and put the pot she was holding on the table.

"Miss Elsey, there's something I ought to tell you. Henry and I discussed it last night, but it didn't seem like the right time to talk. I need to go back to Jennings' place today. This morning. Right now."

Anna Mae directed Elsey to sit down in the kitchen chair. Elsey eyed him evenly. "I knew it would come to this," she said. "Knew Jennings would do everything he could to tear us apart. Been telling that to Henry ever since that devil rode in here last week. I knew it."

"No, Miss Elsey, this ain't nothing to do with Jennings. He didn't ask me to stay any longer, and he ain't tried to change the arrangement he has with Henry. This ain't about Jennings, at least not directly. There's something else."

"Something else," demanded Elsey. "Something else at Jennings' place more important than us?"

He looked at Anna Mae and back at Elsey. Both women were seated side by side at the kitchen table, hands on their laps, staring at him directly, without blinking.

"Well, boy, tell us what's on your mind," Elsey said softly.

Dangerfield held his hat in his hands, and tugged at the brim.

"Jennings has an awful lot of work to do at his place. Henry told him I'd be there two times a week. Thing is, there's so much needs to be done. I ought to be there more than two days. Maybe three or four days."

He paused and looked at his mother and sister, both seated at the kitchen table, staring at him. Neither woman spoke for a long time.

"Three or four more days away from your family," Elsey whispered.

"Thing is, Miss Elsey, you still have Gabriel here. Gabriel and Henry do just fine together. And when I do come back, the three of us can get everything done around here that needs to get done." Dangerfield spat the words out quickly, hoping to get some glimpse of approval from Elsey or Anna Mae. Elsey looked down at her black, wrinkled hands, and wiped them on her apron. Anna Mae smiled and then her eyes sparkled with some unspoken knowledge, a secret no one else knew. She opened her mouth to speak, but Elsey interrupted her.

"So you leavin' us to go work for Jennings three or four days a week because he has work to do. Is that all? I reckon there's somethin' else."

"He don't need to tell us, Miss Elsey," declared Anna Mae. "Reckon I know. Reckon this has something to do with one of Jennings' house girls. You went over to work for Jennings and now you cotton to one of his girls. Ain't that right?"

Dangerfield tugged at the brim of his hat. Elsey spoke first.

"When were you going to tell us about this Harriet?" Elsey's eyes sparkled, and she looked at Anna Mae and smiled.

"How did you know?"

"Didn't take much to figure out this was more than work," replied Elsey. Henry told Jennings he could have you two days a week. No man in his right mind would work for Jennings four days a week without pay unless there's somethin' else. Besides, Henry told me about you and this Harriet last night."

Elsey stood up slowly, and wiped her hands on her apron. "Why don't you fetch some corn from the storehouse, some ham hocks, and a few eggs. Anna Mae and I will fix breakfast. Whatever it is you got to do at Jennings' place can wait until we all eat together. Hurry before Henry gets up."

Dangerfield shuffled toward the door, and then turned.

"Henry told you about Harriet?"

"Henry tells me most of what I need to know," said Elsey as she split a piece of stovewood. "Rest, I figure out for myself. Besides, men ain't too hard to figure out. Now go and get us some food."

Dangerfield left the house and retrieved the ham hocks, corn and eggs.

When he returned, Henry was standing in the kitchen, talking to Anna Mae and Elsey. Henry's hair was rumpled, his rough woolen shirt was partially untucked, and one of his suspender buttons was unfastened.

"Day, Henry."

"Elsey tells me you aim to go back to Jennings' place this morning, right now. Somethin' you care to tell us?"

"Ain't much I can tell Henry, I just . . . I just need to go back and check on Harriet and Jericho. Can't explain why."

"You was just there yesterday. You think something happened to 'em?"

"I don't . . . I can't explain. I just need to go back today."

"How long you aim to stay?"

"Not long. Maybe just a day. Stay overnight, and come back home at first light."

Henry and Elsey looked at each other. Henry stroked his chin and stared out the kitchen window.

"What do you intend to tell Jennings? Reckon he'll fall off his chair when he sees you riding in this afternoon," said Henry.

"Hadn't thought about what I will tell him. Maybe just tell him I intend to finish the fence."

"This ain't about no fence," spat Henry. "It's about Harriet and that boy. Much as I hate him, I'll say one thing for him, Jennings ain't dumb. You better figure out what you want to tell him, and what you want him to know."

"Reckon I'll have a few hours to think about what I might tell him."

Elsey clapped her hands. "Everyone set down, and eat. Let's have the boy tell us about this Harriet woman. A little food might clear his mind."

At breakfast, he told his family what he knew about Harriet, Jericho, Jericho's dead father, and Harriet's fear that Jennings might sell Jericho. Henry said very little, loudly devouring his eggs, corn and ham. Gabriel wanted to know what Harriet looked like, and whether Jennings had other house girls like her. Anna Mae wanted to know about Jericho, Jericho's dead father, and how Jennings treated his house servants. Dangerfield told them what he knew, leaving out the night in the hayloft. Elsey did not utter a word.

Dangerfield ate quickly, and stood to leave, stuffing a large piece of ham in his mouth as he got up.

"Thank you all kindly for breakfast. I need to start out."

Elsey and Anna Mae stood to clear the dishes. Gabriel stood and clapped his brother on the back. "When you get back, tell me if Jennings has other house girls. Maybe the two of us ride up there sometime."

The words had barely left his mouth when Elsey and Henry glared at Gabriel. "Reckon you've enough to do here, especially with him gone," said Henry. "Don't think you will be leaving any time soon."

Elsey turned to face Gabriel. "Since your older brother intends to be gone, you need to fill in for him. I need a week's worth of stovewood and kindling for the kitchen. When you finish that, you and Henry got three hogs to butcher and clean. Chicken house needs to be fixed, and so does the corn crib. Reckon that'll keep you busy enough."

"Yes, Miss Elsey." Gabriel quietly retrieved his hat and slouched out of the house toward the barn.

Elsey turned toward Dangerfield. "I need to talk with you before you leave. Henry, Anna Mae, y'all let us have the kitchen."

Henry and Anna Mae left the kitchen and walked out of the house through the front door. Elsey watched them through the window before turning to Dangerfield.

"Reckon something must have happened when you was at Jennings to make you light out again like this first thing in the morning. Tell me what that devil did to make you want to go back. Does he beat this Harriet girl? Is that why you need to go back?"

"Not that I saw, Miss Elsey."

"What about Jericho? Does Jennings beat him?"

"Not that I saw, although Harriet worries Jennings might sell the boy someday."

"Someday. But you never saw him beat Harriet or Jericho?"

"No, Miss Elsey, not that I saw, although the boy doesn't suffer for lack of beatings. The other house servants beat him something fierce. Jennings has a house servant named Lilly, and she just about beat Jericho half to death."

Elsey stared directly at him. "Tell me why on God's earth you need to go back now. What happened? There must be a reason."

Dangerfield looked out the window. Henry and Anna Mae were examining a patch of coneflowers near the smokehouse.

"Miss Elsey, I don't know how to explain it. I just need to go back," stammered Dangerfield. "I . . . something happened to Jericho. I saw him fall into the creek behind Jennings' barn. He couldn't swim, and he went under the water, and . . . that's all I saw. He fell in the water and he couldn't get out and . . . ."

"You saw this in a dream?"

"Yes, Miss Elsey. There may not be anything to make of it, but it just looked so real, it felt real, almost like I could . . . well I can't explain it. Almost like I could . . ."

"Reach out and touch the water, and pull him out if you had been there," Elsey whispered. "You had a vision."

Dangerfield stared at his mother, who was wiping her forehead with a kerchief.

"You'd best be going. You won't be worth much around here 'till you sort this out on your own. Go on."

He turned to leave, but Elsey stopped him. "Before you go, you need to know that Jennings is the devil. That man is evil as anything that walks God's earth. He'll ruin us first chance he gets. Been tryin' since before you was born. Keep that in mind before you get more involved with one of his house girls."

She wiped her forehead again and stuffed her kerchief in her apron. "You'd best be goin'."

Dangerfield walked out to the stable, finished saddling Solomon, packed his saddlebags, and began riding toward Jennings' farm.

⟫⟪⟫⟪⟫

The sun was almost directly overhead. He had been riding much slower than normal to give himself time to think. He guessed he had been riding for over two hours – he would be at Jennings' farm soon. Solomon picked his way over the trail, moving left and right to avoid rocks, fallen tree limbs and ruts in the trail. Dangerfield did not notice anything on the trail. He rode with his hat pulled low against the sun, and his thoughts on what he would find at Jennings' farm.

Despite having had over two hours to consider what he would tell Jennings, he had no explanation for why he was there. "Jennings won't mind havin' extra help, even if he don't expect it," he thought to himself. "I'll tell him I hadn't quite finished the fence, and I want to start clean on my next job. Man won't ask too many questions about havin' extra help." He was rehearsing what he would say to Jennings when Solomon nickered and pulled hard to the right, toward the sound of running water. Dangerfield reined him hard to the left, but Solomon kept pulling toward the creek. Dangerfield was about to lean into his flank when he noticed the bulging saddlebag he had packed – Solomon's oats. Dangerfield then realized that he had ridden Solomon for over two hours without a break for oats or water. He loosened his grip on the reins and let Solomon pull toward the creek. He dismounted, and led the big horse by the bridle to the creek's edge.

"Well, old man, I reckon you got a right to be angry. Reckon you wanted oats and water about an hour ago. Sorry I ain't been better company." He pulled the sack of oats out of the saddlebag and set it on the ground. Solomon lifted his head from the creek, and shoved his muzzle into the feedbag, dripping creek water into the sack. The rumble in his gut told him he ought to eat the lunch Anna Mae had packed for him. He sat on the ground next to Solomon.

"We both ought to eat now, before we get to Jennings' place," he said. No tellin' what we can expect when we get there." He pulled out his knife and sliced chunks of ham off the hock Anna Mae had given him. He took a swig of water from his canteen and wiped his mouth with his sleeve. "Day, Marse Jennings," he said softly to himself. "Yes, I know you wasn't expecting me till a few days from now. I know you said you had some work to do on the hog shed, and I looked at it before I left. Hog shed looks like it needs more attention than I thought. Reckon it's better to finish that fence so I have a full day to work on that shed next time I'm here. Reckon I'll get started now"

Solomon lifted his head from the feed bag and snorted. Bits of oats and foam sprayed from his muzzle, and he shook his head before sinking his muzzle back into the feedbag.

"Reckon he won't believe that, eh, old man? I better come up with another story." Dangerfield stood and was about to fold up Solomon's feedbag when he noticed something on the shore of the creek. Torn pieces of cloth were scattered along the creek side. He looked up, and saw buzzards circling overhead.

"Let's go, old man. Ain't nothing good for us here." He folded up Solomon's feedbag, mounted, and rode on.

Jennings was walking from the stable toward the house when Dangerfield came riding hard over the hill. Dangerfield considered having Solomon walk the final yards to Jennings's house, but thought better of it – best to make an entrance. Solomon galloped over the hill, then slowed down into a canter. Jennings stopped and stood with his hands on his hips. Solomon walked to within five feet of where Jennings stood.

Lilly, the old house maid, was standing just inside the front door. She walked out of the house and stood a few feet from Jennings, holding Jericho by the arm. The boy was shirtless and shoeless, wearing nothing but a pair of filthy woolen breeches. Dangerfield remembered that he had promised to bring the boy a pair of boots. "Next time," he thought to himself. Jericho squirmed and tried to escape Lilly's grip, but the boy's thin frail arm fit completely inside the old woman's hand, and she did not let him go. Dangerfield did not dismount.

"Day, Marse Jennings," he said, removing his hat.

"Wasn't expecting you back so soon. Did you forget something important when you left?"

"No Marse, I didn't forget anything. There was just a few things I wanted to finish on that fence before we – I – get started on the hog shed."

"Fence looks pretty finished to me," countered Jennings. "It was finished when you left here. And nothing in that hog shed that couldn't wait until you were supposed to be here," said Jennings. "Mind you, I won't complain about extra help. But I hope Henry doesn't expect me to pay him extra if he sent you here without first asking me."

"No, Marse. Henry didn't send me, and he don't expect you to pay him extra. You pay him the same as before."

"Did you discuss this with Henry before you came? I'd be surprised if Henry discussed his finances with his slaves, even if they are his flesh and blood."

"Henry don't expect you to pay him extra."

"You'd best come down and explain this."

Dangerfield dismounted, and stood facing Jennings. Harriet came running up from the slave cabins, and stopped when she saw Dangerfield. He felt a thump in his stomach.

"Day, Miss Harriet," said Dangerfield. Harriet smiled at him but said nothing, pressing her hands over her dress, and adjusting her kerchief. Lilly stared at her, and tightened her grip on Jericho.

"Marse and I got to take care of this business, Harriet," said Lilly. "We got to put a stop to it, for his own good. You'd best stay out of it."

"Lilly, you know he is a good boy," said Harriet. "Just stubborn, that's all."

"Stubborn don't explain him tryin' to run like that," Lilly said. "Almost drowned. I almost drowned myself pullin' him out of the creek. 'Sides, where would he go? How would he eat? Where would he live? We got to do this for his own good, Harriet. Next time he runs, whoever finds him needs to know where to bring him back. It won't kill him. Didn't kill the other men."

"He ain't one of the men, Lilly," pleaded Harriet. "He's just nine. My little boy. Please."

Jennings said nothing while Lilly and Harriet discussed Jericho's fate. Harriet faced Jennings. Dangerfield stood next to Solomon, helpless to intervene.

"Marse, please," cried Harriet. "Just spare him this time, and it won't happen again. I will watch him real careful."

Jennings looked at the two women, and smiled.

"Well, Harriet, I'm afraid Lilly is right," said Jennings. "I didn't act when Jericho stole a pair of my boots, but this . . . ."

"He didn't steal them boots, and you know it," exclaimed Harriet. "He was tryin' em on, tryin' to be a man. He wants to be a man, but he don't know how. Men wear boots, and he wants to be a man. He just don't know how, that's all. Please, Marse, he's just a boy. He's too young for this. Please."

"Lilly says he stole them, and she has no reason to lie," replied Jennings. "Besides, Harriet, you ought to be lucky I am not selling him. Not this time. Lilly, go stoke the fire outside the stable, and bring me the iron. I'll heat it myself."

Jennings turned to Dangerfield. "You came just when we were dealing with a minor problem," explained Jennings. "Harriet's boy Jericho tried to run away late last night. He fell in the creek and damn near drowned himself. Lilly was up and heard him splashing and yelling and carrying on. Ran out of the house in her bed clothes and pulled him out. Almost drowned herself. Boy's damn lucky. Lilly, go stoke that fire." Lilly turned and left.

Dangerfield spoke. "He's lucky it was a full moon last night. That current gets real fast right around those rocks. If Lilly hadn't pulled him out, he would have been sucked under the current, or maybe smashed by those rocks just 'round the bend. Real deep pool just after those rocks, even if it ain't rained for a few days. Not easy to swim out, especially for a young'un."

Harriet, Jericho, and Jennings stared at him. Harriet's jaw dropped open.

Jennings examined him and arched his eyebrows. "Didn't expect you to have time to study the creek last time you was here. Thought you spent all your time in the field, or in the stable. Wouldn't expect you to know much about the creek, unless you paid a visit to the slave cabins."

"No Marse, I slept in the stable last time I was here. I just know something about that creek, that's all." Dangerfield closed his eyes, and saw again Jericho's fragile body being pulled under the water, and his reed-thin arm grasping for anything before being pulled under the current.

"You know something about this creek?" demanded Jennings. "You been fishing here without me knowing?"

"No, Marse, I ain't been fishin. I just know something about this creek. It's kind of hard to explain."

"Well, sometime you and Henry should explain it to me." Just then, Lilly walked up from the stable, holding a branding iron. "That fire real nice and hot now, Marse."

"Lilly, take the boy down to the stable. Harriet, you come too." Jennings looked at Dangerfield and chuckled. "I reckon Henry doesn't discipline any of you. Lets you do whatever you please. Well, things run different around here. You'll see."

The group reached the stable and the fire Lilly had started. Woodsmoke curled up around them. Burning oak logs popped and hissed, and sparks flew up around them before landing on the grass and dying. Jennings gripped the handle of the iron and held the brand close to the fire while he addressed the group. "You see, discipline not only maintains order, it promotes responsible behavior," pronounced Jennings. "Now I know Harriet does her best with this boy. But the other young bucks behave. Never steal, and never try to run off. Best thing for this boy is to stay here and learn how to be a proper field hand. Even if I sell him, he will at least have some skills. If I let him stay here without teaching him anything, that reflects poorly on me. This is better for him. Lilly, bring him here."

Lilly pushed the boy toward Jennings without releasing her grip on his arm. His entire arm fit within her gnarled hand, and his skin was bruised where Lilly held him. The boy squirmed and wriggled, and when he realized he could not escape Lilly's grasp, he screamed. He turned toward Dangerfield, white-eyed with fear, and he screamed until his voice was hoarse. Harriet reached for him and grabbed his other arm, and tried to pull him away, but Lilly pushed her away. Jennings grabbed the arm where Lilly had held him, and Lilly released her grip. Jennings spun the boy around, and shoved the red-hot brand on his narrow back. The brand barely fit between his shoulder blades. The brand hissed, and smoke curled up from the boy's naked back. Dangerfield smelled the burning human flesh, and his head began to spin. Harriet's knees buckled, and she fell against Dangerfield. The boy screamed again, but nothing came out.

Jennings spun the boy around to face him with one hand, while holding the iron in the fire with the other hand. Spit rolled out of the corner of the boy's mouth, and his knees buckled. The boy began to fall backwards, but Lilly stood behind him and propped him up. Jennings shoved the brand onto the boy's skinny chest, searing the flesh across both nipples. Harriet slumped further against Dangerfield. Jennings removed the brand, but did not release Jericho. Jennings put the brand in the fire again, waiting to deliver another blow.

Dangerfield watched his own hand reach out and pull the iron out of Jennings' hand. He watched from far away as someone who looked like him threw the iron across the yard, where it arced then landed in the grass with a soft hiss. The boy was lying on his stomach, quivering. Lilly stared at Jennings, and then at Dangerfield. Harriet wrapped both hands around Dangerfield's arm, trying to hold herself up. Jennings looked at Lilly, and then at Dangerfield.

"Well, Lilly I think that's enough for today," said Jennings softly. "I think the boy's learned his lesson. Take him in the house and dress his wounds. He will be fine."

Harriet ran toward Jericho before Lilly could reach him. She pushed Lilly away and lifted her son in her arms, and carried him into the house, Lilly following behind. Jennings looked off into the distance before turning to face Dangerfield.

Dangerfield was a full head taller than him, with long, rangy arms, and at least 50 pounds heavier. Both men stared at each other.

"Henry lets you all do whatever you please," growled Jennings. "Remind me to tell Henry the benefits of discipline. Things run different around here. Now go get started on that hog shed, if that's the reason you came."

Dangerfield walked toward the stable to retrieve his tools.

CHAPTER 21

Turner emptied his suitcase on his bed and stared at the contents. He sat on his side of their king bed and poked through his belongings, looking at the brochures and glossy magazines they had picked up on their trip. Harpers Ferry seemed a lifetime removed from his house, this moment back home in Minnesota. Tracy left her unopened suitcase on the bed. She kicked off the pumps she had worn on the plane, and pulled a pair of white sneakers from her closet.

"Are you ready to go? Call Vernita and tell her we're coming over," said Tracy.

"Tell me why you think Vernita is the key to this mystery," countered Turner. "What does she know about my dream that I don't?"

"I don't think she knows anything," said Tracy. "It's something I saw once when we went to visit your grandmother. A photo she had in her house. Vernita may know something about the photo. Maybe it's nothing. It will make more sense if you see for yourself."

"We just got home. It's already 9:30. Vernita may be in bed already. Let's stay here and rest. We can call her tomorrow. Besides, Vernita doesn't exactly welcome visitors. Especially me."

"Well, this might just be the spark you two need for a reconciliation," said Tracy. "Let's go. Don't you want to find out what this is about?"

"Of course. I just don't think . . . ."

"What? You don't think what?"

Turner looked around his bedroom. The king-size bed with the soft, $1,000 sheets. His walk-in closet with his tailored, hand-made suits and Bruno Magli loafers. The master bathroom with the Italian marble vanity. The teak bookshelf that Tracy saw while they were on vacation in Tuscany, and had ordered on the spot without a moment's thought about money. Tracy never asked how much it cost to ship it home. She never had to. They had earned all of it.

Turner rubbed his temples. "I don't want to wind up like Frazier. Losing everything."

"What's wrong with Frazier?" I didn't meet him, but you said he was brilliant."

"He is brilliant. He also lives in a run-down shack."

"You think that might happen to you?"

"It happened to him. It happens to a lot of people."

"It won't happen to you. You are the strongest man I know. We just need to figure out what you saw. There's got to be an explanation." She sat next to him on the bed and placed her hand on his thigh. "Besides," she said, whispering into his ear, "I would never let you live anywhere unless I could do all the decorating. And I don't do shacks." She stood. "Let's go."

Turner pulled her toward him. "Tracy, you don't understand. Please."

"What? Tell me what I don't understand."

Turner closed his eyes and spoke slowly. "I don't have anywhere else to go. I can't ask anyone else for help. You remember that research you did on mental illness? Stress, sleeping pills, and various symptoms?"

"I didn't do much," said Tracy weakly. "Just some noodling around on the Internet."

"Don't you think I knew about that research before you ever started looking? I know all about what stress can do to the mind. I know every recognized medical symptom of stress. Stress doesn't explain what's been happening. I deal with worse stuff every day. I'm a surgeon. I have dealt with stress for years. And a vacation sure as hell won't stress me out any more than work. It's got to be something else."

"Well, maybe it's the pills I gave you."

"That might explain what I saw *after* you gave me the pills. It doesn't explain what I saw that first night in Harpers Ferry. I know I saw something. It wasn't a dog. And whatever it was, I saw it *before* you gave me the pills. I know what I saw."

Tracy sat next to him on the bed and examined his face. "What do you want from me? What can I do?"

"There is nothing you can do, love. But I need you to know I can't talk to anyone else about this. Anyone."

"Why don't you ask Damon? He's your best friend from med school. You don't have to disclose details about the ghost or . . . anything you saw. Just tell him you are dealing with a lot, and you need an informal consult. God knows if I could get free advice from a psychiatrist, I'd be there every week."

Turner stood abruptly. "Damon is the last person who needs to know. Dammit, if word gets out I saw a shrink, I'm done. You can forget about chief of surgery. They will put me on admin leave for six months, and then I will be eased into a "consulting physician" role. After that, I am eased out of medicine completely. I trust Damon, but word gets out. Hell no. I have to do this alone. Have to get to the bottom of it myself."

Tracy stretched out on the bed. "You can't do this alone. Some things are bigger than you, bigger than both of us. For God's sake, let me help you." She sat up and reached for her purse, fumbling through the contents. Unsatisfied, she threw her purse against the wall, spilling the contents about the room. "God, I never should have quit smoking."

Turner chuckled, and opened the bottom drawer on his nightstand. He pulled out an unopened box of Marlboro Lights and flipped it toward her. "Just this once," he said.

She expertly tore off the plastic wrapping. "Dr. Turner, I thought you were helping me quit," she said as she pounded the box against her palm."

"I am helping you quit. Most people can't go cold turkey. Besides, this is an emergency."

Tracy found her lighter and without stepping outside, lit her cigarette and took a long pull. She tilted her head back, closed her eyes, and then slowly exhaled smoke through both nostrils.

She let out a soft moan. "God I needed this."

Turner watched blue smoke curling about his bedroom. "I guess you did," he said.

"Look, Trace, I can't talk to anyone about this. You understand. I need you to help me so I – we – can figure out if something is wrong with me. I don't have anyone else to talk to. Not Damon, not anyone. I have to trust you."

She took another long pull and exhaled from the side of her mouth. Nicotine cleared her mind and bolstered her confidence.

"Is chief of surgery that important to you? More important than your happiness? Can't you let your guard down just once and get help from someone?"

"Chief of surgery is the only thing I've wanted for the last six years. Besides you, it's the only thing I care about. Nothing else matters." He reached into his nightstand again and pulled out a dark blue ceramic ashtray. "Why don't you put that out so we can go. I think maybe you had a good idea about visiting Vernita."

————))(((((————

They arrived at Vernita's apartment in East St. Paul a little past 10:30 p.m. A group of teens milled about the entrance, blowing hazy blue cigarette smoke into the air and laughing. As Turner and Tracy approached the security door, Turner realized the kids were not smoking cigarettes. The group eyed the couple and slowly dispersed as Turner walked up the steps and pressed Vernita's buzzer. Moths flitted about the only light in the doorway that wasn't broken. The teens grumbled and shuffled a few feet from the door. Tracy stood a few feet away, gazing at the knot of young men. Turner buzzed twice more before Vernita's voice crackled over the intercom.

"Who is it?"

"It's me, Vernita, Michael. Sorry for the short notice."

"Come on up. Try to be quiet, the baby's just got to sleep."

The security door buzzed, and Turner and Tracy quickly entered, pulling the door closed behind them. The young men resumed their positions near the door, laughing and blowing smoke into the night sky.

Vernita lived on the third floor of a tired brick walk-up built in the late 1960's. Although it was now past 10:30 p.m., the hallways buzzed with activity – apartment doors were open, and music blared from an apartment with the front door propped open with a beer bottle. More young men walked out of the open door, laughing and singing as they headed for the stairs. Empty beer cans littered the hall, and the couple had to step out of the way of a man stretched out in the hallway, two doors down from Vernita's apartment. Tracy wrinkled her nose and spoke.

"My first apartment in college smelled like this. I always thought no other place in the world had that smell."

"I think we all lived in apartments like this when we were young," sniffed Turner. "Most of us got out as soon as we could. I don't know why Vernita stays here."

"I suspect your cousin would leave if she could. We all had to start somewhere, Mike. Besides, I think Vernita can help you – us. We need her now."

Turner knocked. Vernita pulled open the door, and peered through the crack.

"It's me V. Sorry again for the late notice. Can you let us in?"

Vernita closed the door, undid the security chain, and waved the couple inside. She swiftly closed the door behind her and re-fastened the security chain, and slid the deadbolt closed.

"Quite the party going on outside," said Turner. "Is it always like this at night?"

"Ain't no party you or me want to attend. Nothing but the normal nocturnal commercial activity that goes on in this building. People coming and going, buying and selling at all hours of the night."

"Do they bother you or the kids?"

"No – Frank has an understanding with them. They leave us alone, and Frank don't split their heads open."

"Where is Frank?"

"At work. He started night shifts at the plant. Gets extra money for working night shift. We actually started saving a bit for a new place. Frank keeps working nights, we might save enough to leave this little urban paradise. It's hard not having him around at night, but we need the money."

"Is the baby okay?"

"Just got her to sleep. She's colicky. Been trying for two hours to get her to sleep. The boys been asleep for hours." She turned her head toward a closed bedroom door. "But you two didn't come here for chit-chat or the atmosphere. What is it that couldn't wait til tomorrow?"

Tracy spoke. "We have been trying to solve a mystery that came up while we were in Harpers Ferry, and we need your help. We didn't know about the baby. We can come back later."

Vernita chuckled. "You need my help? You two? Can't imagine I got anything you two might need or want."

"It's about a picture I saw once when we were visiting your grandmother," Tracy said. "That picture could be very important."

"Picture?" huffed Vernita. "You came over this late at night to ask about a picture?"

"I remember you and your grandmother talking about the picture when Michael and I came to visit. It was very important to your grandmother. It was one of your uncles, or maybe a great-uncle, I can't remember. He was posed in front of his car."

"What did he look like?"

"Quite handsome, like most of the men in your family."

Vernita smiled despite herself. "What was he doing in the picture?"

"I remember he was standing in front of a car, smiling or something. Your grandmother loved that picture. He was wearing a hat. I know I've seen it."

"You two wait here," said Vernita wearily.

Vernita carefully opened the bedroom door and went inside. She returned a few minutes later with a brown box sealed with tape. She removed the tape, rummaged through the box and came out with a small picture frame wrapped in newspaper.

"This what you want?"

Turner peeled off the newspaper and saw a slim, light-skinned black man looking at him. The man wore a fedora, and stood in front of a light-colored car. The photo was a grainy black and white, but Turner instantly recognized the car – enormous round headlights perched at the end of a long metal nose, the shiny metal grill sandwiched between, the bulging hood that extended all the way to the windshield. It was the car he had seen in his dream, the one that smashed into the tree just inches from where he stood. The smiling man in the fedora was the driver.

Turner felt his knees buckle, and he sat in one of Vernita's vinyl kitchen chairs.

"Where did you get this," Turner croaked.

"Gran had so much stuff to sort through. After she died, Frank and I agreed to keep some of her things here, at least until we could have a family meeting to sort it all out. Gran loved that picture. Billy was a handsome devil, wasn't he?"

"Who is this man?" said Turner.

"Great Uncle Billy," said Vernita. "You know Gran was always talking about him. Her little brother, her favorite brother. Billy was always in trouble, either with the law, the ladies, and quite often both. Gran was never the same after he died. She kept this photo to remind her of better times. She missed Billy more than she wanted us to know."

Turner felt his insides turn liquid. Tracy rubbed his shoulders.

"I remember now, Gran said he died in a car crash," said Turner weakly. "Did she ever say how it happened?"

"Don't think she knew," replied Vernita. "Police told her the car slid off the road in a rainstorm, and hit a tree. Don't think anyone knows for certain, but Gran suspects Billy may have had a few drinks. He liked the whiskey almost as much as he liked women."

Turner could hear his grandmother's voice now, telling the story of Great Uncle Billy, the car crash, and how she would see his ghost on rainy nights, the steering wheel of his wrecked car wrapped around his neck. And now he had seen the wreck himself. But what he had seen wasn't the story everyone thought they knew.

"You remember those stories she used to tell, don't you," said Vernita. "About the crash, and Billy's ghost, and all that nonsense? We listened to humor her. I never thought you paid much attention."

"I remember it now," whispered Turner. "I remember it like it happened yesterday."

The baby squealed and let loose a wheezy cough from inside the bedroom.

"Shit, not again," muttered Vernita. "That baby keeps everyone up all night."

"Let me try to put her back to sleep," said Tracy. "You two keep talking." Without waiting for an answer, Tracy opened the bedroom door and picked up the screaming infant. She carried the baby out of the room, and walked slowly back and forth, cooing softly.

Vernita sat down next to Turner, and watched as he examined the photograph.

"I still don't understand why this couldn't wait until tomorrow. What is it about this photo that got both of you so riled up?"

Turner paused, trying to concoct an answer that would make any sense.

"I'm sorry to bother you, V. Tracy and I saw something while we were in Harpers Ferry, and . . . I think we might have discovered some distant relatives, and it reminded me of you and Gran talking about Uncle Billy, and so . . . I, we, we, uh, just thought we would stop by when we got back. I am sorry that we came over so late."

Vernita stared at him without blinking. "You had to go to West Virginia to be reminded of distant relatives, and then you came over here – your real relatives, who live in the same town – at 10:30 at night to ask about some photograph that you probably ain't thought about in years. You two may be rich and successful, but both of you strange as a three-dollar bill."

Tracy had walked the baby back to sleep, and she quietly opened the bedroom door, placed the baby in her crib, and closed the door behind her.

Vernita jerked a thumb toward Tracy. "Your wife's pretty good with babies. I might hire her as my daytime nanny."

Tracy laughed. "Call me anytime you need me, V."

"I have to be at the hospital early tomorrow," Turner said. "Teaching day for the residents, and I get to demonstrate surgical procedures. We'd better go. I'm sorry again for bothering you, V. Thank you. Can I keep this picture?"

"Seems to mean a lot to you, so go ahead and keep it."

Turner examined the man in the picture for a few minutes before tucking the picture in his coat pocket. Vernita turned the deadbolt and unfastened the security chain before she gestured toward the door.

"Michael," she said as the couple walked out into the hallway. "Stop by and visit more often. I could use a little help, especially at night, when Frank ain't here. Unless your hospital schedule won't allow it."

Turner smiled and hugged his cousin. "I'll come by more often, I promise. Thanks for letting me keep this."

Turner arose at 4:30 the next morning, but he would have been better off not sleeping at all. It seemed like he awoke every half hour to look at the picture. No mistake. The fedora, the slim, light-skinned man, the car with the bulging hood. It was exactly what he had seen in his dream in Harpers Ferry. He did not remember ever seeing this picture before. But Tracy had seen it and remembered it, so he must have seen it. He had probably walked past the picture dozens of times while visiting his grandparents' house, but had never bothered to stop, never bothered to ask questions.

This was not surprising. For most of his adult life, he never bothered to ask questions about any of his relatives, viewing them at best as minor annoyances, sources of meaningless small talk to be endured until he could excuse himself for something more important. As he lay in bed watching the clock, Turner played his grandmother's dying words over and over in his mind.

"You was always special, boy," she said. "You may not know it, but you was always special. Still are. Just know what it means."

He still had no idea what she meant.

He dressed in the dark, careful not to awaken Tracy. He was almost out of the bedroom when she turned toward him, still half asleep.

"Good luck today. What procedure are the newbies learning today?"

"Nothing too complicated. Removing a benign breast tumor. Patient has no signs of metastasis, but the lump bothers her. Should be a routine procedure."

Tracy yawned. "Does she mind having an audience watching you remove a lump from her breast?"

"It's a teaching hospital. She consented to the residents watching. Besides, she will be under. Won't see a thing."

"Lucky gal. Does she get paid for putting on this show?"

"Not exactly."

Tracy stretched out and propped her chin on the palm of her hand, gazing at her husband as he adjusted his tie in the mirror.

"Have you thought any more about talking to Damon? Just as friends, in private?"

"I have, and the answer is still no. You have to believe me, Tracy, I can't talk to anyone until I have an idea what is going on. I have to do this myself. I need to know I can trust you, until I can get this figured out."

He knelt by the bed and kissed her on the forehead. "Go back to sleep. I will be fine."

She looked at him, unsmiling, as he closed the door behind him. "Yes we will," she said to herself as he walked down the stairs. "Yes, we will."

He arrived at the hospital at 6 am, and pulled into his reserved parking space. No matter how many times he saw it, he read the sign and smiled – "This Spot Reserved At All Times, Dr. Michael E. Turner. All Others Towed." Something as silly as his own spot, with his name on it. He remembered what it was like to drive to the hospital only to search for a spot. He never wanted to do that again.

He waved his security card before the guard, who glanced up from his newspaper just long enough to see Turner's face. "Morning, Dr. Turner," he said, turning his face back toward his newspaper.

"Morning, Ed," he said while glancing at his watch.

He ran up the two flights of stairs to his corner office at the end of the hall and opened the door. The early morning sun splashed in through the floor to ceiling windows. He checked a few e-mails, then reviewed the morning's procedure. 47-year-old white woman, family history of breast cancer. Lump first discovered ten months ago. Oncology did a full battery of standard procedures before concluding the lump was benign. No signs of metastasis, or other lumps. White blood cell count had been stable. She could have left it as is, but the lump bothered her. Should be a simple excision, easy to explain to the surgical residents. The tricky part was removing the lump while preserving most of the breast. He had performed a similar procedure last year, with spectacular results – the patient wrote him a thank you note explaining how happy she was. According to Hillman's notes, four new surgical residents were scheduled to observe this morning's procedure. He felt a surge of confidence wash over him as he exited his office. In his element, invincible, doing what came naturally to him.

Hillman was waiting for him when he scrubbed in.

"Morning, Mike. Sorry to get you up for something as simple as this. We have four new residents in surgery, and I wanted them to watch you. I could have had anyone do this, but I figured you could do this procedure while explaining everything to the residents. Something simple like this, you can cut and teach at the same time."

"Not a problem, Roger. You're the chief, so you can assign it to anyone you want. Besides, I have been out of town for a few days, so I need to earn my keep."

Hillman watched him as he scrubbed his hands and fingernails, then turned as an assistant helped him into his scrubs.

"You know, Mike, one of the things I won't miss about being chief of surgery is dealing with the residents. When I first started, I enjoyed it. Now, they all seem about 20, and they already know everything about surgery. I used to enjoy teaching, but I don't have the passion for it." He paused. "Come to think of it, I can't stand the administrative stuff, either."

Turner chuckled as the assistant finished helping him. "So other than teaching residents and dealing with administrative headaches, you still enjoy the job. Roger, I'd say you are retiring just in time. It's our loss. You've been a great leader."

Hillman walked beside him as Turner walked toward the OR.

"Mike, I know you have considered throwing your hat in the ring to be the next chief. How serious are you?"

"Well, Roger, you haven't left yet, so I don't want to presume anything. I know there are other people who want the job. Prandra is a great surgeon. I know he wants it."

"Prandra is a great surgeon, and a first-rate asshole," scoffed Hillman. "Besides, he can't teach. His students know less than when they started after he gets done with them. I still have 11 months before I leave, so I have some say in who replaces me."

"I appreciate your insights, Roger. Now may not be the time to discuss this, so maybe you and I can have lunch after this procedure."

"You read my mind, Mike. Let's plan on lunch after you finish this morning. I want to know how serious you are about being chief. You don't mind if I watch you work this morning, do you?"

"Looks like my audience will be a little bigger than planned."

"You won't notice me. Pretend I'm not here."

Turner entered the OR and addressed the four new surgical residents."

"Good morning, ladies and gentlemen. Today's procedure should be very simple. We are removing a large, but benign breast tumor. Our patient has had a biopsy, which confirmed that this tumor is benign. As all of you know, this type of tumor is not dangerous, and generally does not spread outside the breast."

"However, there are some benign breast tumors that pose a greater risk than others," Turner explained. For example, papillomas and tumors that show atypical hyperplasia are indicators of a higher risk of breast cancer. This patient's tumor is a classic papilloma. In addition, this patient has a family history of breast cancer. Combining those factors, the patient felt strongly that the lump should be removed. Today, we will do that. I will explain each step as we proceed."

He looked toward Hillman, who was watching the procedure from the observation room, and listening on the intercom. Hillman took a few notes, and looked up and smiled at Turner.

Turner addressed his first assistant. "May we begin?"

"As we make the first incision, we first note the size of the tumor, and determine how to remove it without removing too much of the surrounding tissue." He looked up to make certain the residents were paying attention, and saw a man's figure walking behind Hillman in the observation room. Slightly taller than Hillman, the figure wore a black hat, and walked with a slight limp. Turner froze as he watched the man stop, stand next to Hillman, and turn to face the OR. As he did so, Turner saw the deep bloody gash at his throat. Underneath his hat, Turner could see that the man's ears had been brutally torn off. The figure looked at Turner, then left the OR. Hillman did not notice.

CHAPTER 22

Dangerfield worked alone for the rest of the day. Harriet did not visit, and he saw no sign of Jennings. He worked on the hog shed until late in the evening, then he stopped to admire his work. He had replaced the crooked and rotting side boards with wood left over from a fence that Jennings had moved. He left one inch between each board. He had replaced the door, which had nearly rotted off its hinges, with a door from a milkhouse that Jennings had torn down to make room for a bigger one. He opened and closed the door. The bolt fit neatly into the latch, and the bottom of the door brushed slightly against the threshhold. The hinges made no sound. He was about to set one more nail into the board above the door when the rumble in his gut reminded him he had not eaten since the morning's ride. He went to retrieve his saddlebag when he saw Jennings walking toward him.

"Evenin, Marse. Just about done with this shed. Two more hours and I should have it done. Reckon I can finish it tomorrow morning."

Jennings walked around the shed. He leaned against the side boards and pushed the anchor posts. He put his fingers in the space between the boards. He pulled the door open, then pushed it closed with his finger. He pulled the bolt from the latch, and then put it back. He closed the door and then spat on the ground.

"Looks about done to me," said Jennings. "It's a hog shed, not a church."

"I know, Marse, but I want to set a few more boards and fix that hole in the roof. Take me about two hours to finish up here, then we can start something else."

Jennings kicked the bottom of the door with the toe of his boot. "Well, Henry was right about your work. Henry says you are pretty good with harnesses. You ever made any harnesses?"

"Yes, Marse. Made plenty."

"Well, tomorrow, we can start on some harnesses. Ones I got now about wore out." The sun was now just below the ridgeline.

"Where are you going to sleep this evening?"

"Hadn't thought about that, Marse. Last time I was here, I slept in the stable, and you told me to sleep in the cabins with the others. Reckon they'll make room if you tell 'em to."

"I know I told you to sleep in the cabins, but I changed my mind. I don't want you anywhere near those cabins. You sleep in the stable until I figure out what to do with you."

"Yes, Marse." Dangerfield turned toward the stable. Jennings spoke.

"One other thing. You stay away from that boy, Jericho, you hear? I take care of that boy just fine. He's better off here than if I sold him South. And you'd best keep your distance from Harriet, if you got any sense. That boy keeps acting up, I might sell him and Harriet South."

Dangerfield's insides turned to foam, and he tasted bitter acid in his mouth.

"You intend to sell Miss Harriet?" he croaked.

Jennings eyed him evenly. "It is none of your business if I sell that boy, Harriet, my hogs, or any of my property. I hope Henry don't let you mind his business that way."

"No, Marse, he don't. Just asking.'"

"You'd best be off. Sleep in the stable. And mind what I said. Stay away from Harriet and that boy, you hear?"

"Yes Marse."

It was almost dark when he arrived at the stable. He looked in the tack room for the blankets he slept in last time, but he could not find them. Then he remembered the secret den he shared with Harriet. The last of the sun's dying light filtered through the walls of the stable, and guided him toward the loft. He started climbing the ladder. Halfway up, his foot slipped off the rung and he almost fell. He regained his balance and resumed climbing when he heard something moving above him. Then he heard a match striking flint, and saw Harriet's face illuminated by a candle.

"I told you last time that ladder rocks back and forth. Got to mind your step. You must not have been listening."

"Well, Miss Harriet, I was in a hurry last time. Didn't have time to worry about my feet." He scrambled up the ladder and held Harriet's face in his hands. He kissed her lips, and remembered her taste. She put the candle on the feed box that doubled as a dresser, and stepped away from him. She was wrapped in a woolen horse blanket. She let it fall to the floor, revealing her magnificent naked form. She led him by the hand toward the makeshift bed. He kicked off his boots and tugged at his shirt as she pulled him toward the floor. Once inside, he tasted her again, the earthy, salty, coffee-colored flesh. She sighed, and wrapped her hands around the small of his back. They lay coiled together for a long time in silence. Harriet finally spoke.

"I'm obliged for what you did for Jericho today. Marse might have burned him to death if you weren't there."

"I didn't think about it. Just did it. How is the boy?"

"He'll live. He ain't the first to suffer the brand. But he's just a boy."

"Where is he now?"

"In the cabins. Lilly bandaged his scars, and took him in the house. Marse said he could stay in the house, just for the day. I stayed by his side all day. Lilly said I should leave him be, but Marse was outside, so I stayed with him. I put cold water on him and fed him until he fell asleep. Then I took him out of the house, away from Lilly. He is sleeping in the cabins."

"Who's looking after him?"

"I told you, some of the field hands have taken a shine to him. They look after him from time to time. He's sound asleep in the cabins. He'll be fine until I get back."

"Well, Miss Harriet, I do appreciate your company, but you ought to be with him now. Case he needs you."

"I know, but when I saw what you did for him I couldn't . . . I didn't know how long you was here, or when you was going to leave. I didn't know if I would see you again."

"I thought you might bring me supper like you did last time."

"I had a mind to, but I couldn't leave Jericho's side. I had to stay with him until I knew he was better." She turned on her side to face him. "'Sides, I thought it best to leave you be, after what you did to Marse. Didn't know what was going to come of you. Don't hardly see anyone ever stand up to Marse like that. Marse would have beat one of his own something fierce."

She pulled him closer.

"Ain't you afraid of him?"

"Like I said, I didn't think about it. I just did it."

She looked at him, her face backlit by the flickering candlelight.

"Are you afraid of Henry?"

"No."

"Does Henry beat y'all?"

"No, Henry never beats us. Not since we were young, and even then only when we acted out. Henry hasn't beaten any of us since we been grown. Now Elsey . . . ."

"What do you call him? Marse? Henry? Pappy?"

"Henry at home, Marse when we go out in public, or when company comes over. Henry makes it clear that we call him Henry or Pa at home, and Marse only when we have to."

He turned to face her.

"What do you call Jennings?" asked Dangerfield.

"Always Marse, or Sir," said Harriet. "Plenty of other things when he ain't around."

"Does he beat you?"

"He ain't so bad with the house girls. He beats the field hands something fierce. You saw that. That's why I fret so over Jericho."

"Reckon he has his way with all of the house girls," said Dangerfield. "They can't say no." He gently traced his finger around her nipples, watching the dark flesh quicken in the candlelight.

She touched the side of his face, and kissed him.

"He's tried it out with me a few times, if that's your question. Never got past my petticoats. But he has tried it out a few times. Truth is, he was scared to death of Zeke. Jennings knew Zeke would kill him, so he never tried real hard with me."

"Zeke?"

"Hezekiah. Jericho's father. I told you about him. Everyone called him Zeke."

"You told me just a little bit."

"Ain't too much to tell," explained Harriet. "Marse took Zeke as trade for a bad debt. A farmer out past Culpeper owed Marse more than he could pay him. Marse took Zeke as payment in full for the debt. Zeke and I took a shine to each other right away. We had Jericho about a year later. Thing is, Zeke never feared Marse. Marse used to beat him somethin' fierce, but he never broke him. The lash never took. Jennings knew Zeke would kill him if he hurt me or Jericho. Zeke told Jennings to his face that he would kill him and wait for the hangman if he tried anything with me. Jennings was scared to death of Zeke, which explains why he never tried anything with me."

"Surprised Jennings would keep him around if he feared him so."

"Jennings couldn't sell him," said Harriet laughing. "Zeke was wild. Strong. Not afraid of anybody. Weren't no man could break him. That's the reason the farmer was so keen on getting rid of him. Man told Jennings he could have Zeke for free if he would just forgive the debt. Marse didn't know what he was getting. He mighta picked another one if he'd known."

She turned away from him. He watched her body quiver and heave. He said nothing for a long while.

"What happened to Zeke?"

"Don't know for certain. One of the hands who was there said Zeke and Marse were moving the bull in from the meadow. Jennings had Zeke get in the stall to turn the bull around. Jennings clapped the bull with a hot iron while Zeke was in with him. Bull went crazy, and crushed Zeke against the boards. The hands brought him out and laid him in the field so I could see him. His eyes were still open, 'bout popped out of his head. His neck was twisted, and his tongue was hangin' out like a dog. Marse buried him other side of the fence yonder."

He caressed her back while she sobbed.

"I still see him sometimes. Walks back and forth along the fence line. Like he still keeping watch over us. Tryin' to make us safe. I ain't felt safe in awhile."

She turned to face him, and he wiped her tears with his thumb. She wrapped her arms around his waist, pulled him closer, and closed her eyes. He held her for a long while before speaking. "You'd best be getting back, Harriet. I'll climb down with the candle and light your way."

But she did not hear him, because she was already fast asleep. He watched the curve of her body rise and fall. He listened to her breath for much of the night, and then he blew out the candle and waited for the dawn.

He awoke to the sound of the stable door opening, and footsteps approaching the tack room. He heard the door to the tack room open, close, and then footsteps approaching the ladder. The footsteps stopped just below the ladder. Then silence. Early morning sun filtered through the holes in the side of the stable. He knew it was light, but he could not tell if the visitor could see into the loft. He looked at Harriet. She was still sound asleep, her body slowly rising and falling. The footsteps moved to the left, and then right, but still just below the ladder. He thought of waking Harriet, but then considered the outcome if she made any noise upon awakening. He scanned the loft, and quickly determined there were no feasible escape options.

The ladder moved, and he could hear a tentative foot testing the first rung. He could see the top of the ladder move in response to the foot on the rung, and it was then that he noticed the top of the ladder was not secured to the floor of the loft – somehow, the ladder had become untethered from the loft. He remembered last night's climb, and realized he must have dislodged the ladder when he almost fell while climbing up to meet Harriet. Another footstep on the ladder, and then another. With each step, the top of the ladder swayed. And then he saw his only option. He nudged the top of the ladder away from the loft with his foot. He watched as it slowly fell to his left, then picked up speed. When he was confident of the result, he put his hand over Harriet's mouth and whispered "Keep quiet and don't move." The ladder crashed to the floor, and he heard a dull thud and a groan as a heavy body fell to the floor. The stable erupted as the horses stamped and whinnied, kicking at their stalls and snorting. "Stay here, and don't move," he hissed. "Someone tried to come up."

He peered through a crack in the floorboard, and saw Jennings struggling to free himself from the ladder. Jennings pulled himself to his feet, then hobbled to the end of the stable, and opened the big door. Sunlight streamed in, and the horses continued their symphony. Jennings walked outside and went behind the stable.

"Get dressed as quickly as you can," hissed Dangerfield. "Gather up your things and leave as soon as I get down. You'll have to jump." Dangerfield pulled on his pants and boots, and partially buttoned his shirt. He leaned over the edge and calculated the jump to be about ten feet. He swung his legs over the edge, then turned around and gripped the floorboard. He lowered his body down until his arms were fully extended, and jumped the remaining few feet. "Get dressed and climb down like you saw me as soon as I leave. I'll keep Jennings busy."

He then ran out the front door of the stable, hoping to intercept Jennings as he circled. Jennings had made it less than halfway around.

"Day, Marse. I heard a ruckus in the stable, and came a'runnin. What happened?"

"Where in blazes did you come from?"

"I was back by the fence. Had to piss if you must know."

"Where did you sleep last night?"

"In the stable, like you told me. What was all that noise?"

"I fell off a ladder. You come with me and show me where you slept."

"Yes, Marse." They walked slowly around the stable, taking the longest way possible. Dangerfield walked slowly, as if he had just gotten up.

"Seems peculiar for you to be climbing ladders in the stable, Marse. You could have had me look for you."

"Never mind that. Just show me where you slept."

They walked in through the side door, directly across from the loft. "Right over there. In that hay." He pointed to a makeshift nest of loose hay that some of the field hands used for midday rest. Blankets were tossed over the hay, which had been spread out in some places, and remained in piles in other places.

"I thought you slept in the tack room."

"I did last time. Couldn't find no blankets, so I slept in that pile of hay. Somethin' wrong, Marse?"

"Where's Harriet?"

"I don't know."

"I think you do. Where is she?"

"Did you check the cabins?"

"That's the first place I checked. I found that boy sound asleep, and Harriet nowhere near. Only one thing I can think of that would take her away from that boy's side."

"You think she's up there?"

"Help me put that ladder back up there."

Dangerfield picked up the ladder and examined it. "Top looks like it broke, Marse. Might be why you fell."

"Put it back up there, and hold the bottom while I climb up."

Dangerfield picked up the ladder, and slowly lifted it toward the loft, pushing it into place. He gripped the rails, and watched Jennings ascend. He considered pulling the ladder away as Jennings reached the top, but realized the fall would not kill him. Jennings reached the top, and looked around for a few moments. Jennings said nothing while he searched. Dangerfield could hear his heart beat.

Jennings descended the ladder clutching something in his hand.

"You find anything, Marse?"

"I didn't find her, but I found something."

He turned and tossed the object at Dangerfield. It was one of Harriet's petticoats.

"I found this behind that feed box up there. All crumpled up. Hasn't been up there long. Looks like someone wore it recently."

Dangerfield held the petticoat. He could smell Harriet. He said nothing.

"Go back to the house and get your things. I'll have one of the hands bring your horse up. Ask Harriet to pack us some food, since she seems to have an interest in feeding you. You and I will ride to Henry's farm this morning, right now. I don't want you staying here while I am gone – won't get much work out of you anyway, not as long as she's here."

"Why are we going back to Henry's farm, Marse?"

"Circumstances have changed. Henry and I need to discuss the terms of our arrangement. Circumstances have changed, and Henry needs to know what you've done."

Dangerfield walked slowly back to the house. As he approached, he saw Harriet and Jericho standing in the front door, the boy clinging to his mother's waist.

"Day, Miss Harriet. Day Jericho." Marse Jennings would like you to pack us both some food. Says we both riding to Henry's place today."

"When are you leaving?"

"Right now. Marse says we have to leave right now. Both of us going.'"

Jericho squirmed and tried to hide in his mother's dress. "When you comin' back?"

"Don't know. Likely discuss that with Henry."

"Marse say why you have to leave?" asked Harriet.

"Didn't have to. Found one of your petticoats behind the feed box."

She hung her head and started to cry. "Lord have mercy on us."

"Ain't your fault," said Dangerfield. "I should have had you stay in the loft. I could have kept Jennings from going up there. Walked him behind the stable. I should have thought of something different. It ain't your fault. "

"You ain't comin' back."

"Hush. I will come back. Henry and Jennings will work something out. I'm comin' back, just don't know when." He pulled Jericho out from his mother's dress. "Besides, I told him I'd bring him some boots. I have to come back just to bring him those boots."

Jericho looked up at him. His back and chest were covered in bandages, but he had already recovered some of a young boy's energy.

"You come back and bring me them boots, hear?" The boy smiled and looked up at his mother.

"Come on, Jericho. Get back in the house," said Harriet.

Dangerfield waited for Harriet to shoo the boy away so he could speak to her in private, but she had already closed the door behind her.

The two men rode in silence back to Henry's farm. Solomon was bigger and stronger than Jennings' mount, a small and stubborn dun-colored mare. Dangerfield bridled Solomon to keep him from riding too far ahead of Jennings. They stopped alongside a creek to feed and water the horses, and eat the lunches Harriet packed them. The men ate beside their horses, neither speaking to the other.

They arrived at Henry's farm late in the afternoon. Solomon recognized the path up the hill toward home, and Dangerfield could no longer bridle him. Dangerfield leaned back, pulled slightly on the reins, and let the big horse run toward home. Solomon clattered into the yard, blowing and stamping, as if he recognized the beauty of a night in his own stall. Jennings and his tired little mare rode up a few moments later.

Elsey was in the yard with an armful of eggs when she saw Dangerfield ride up. Her smile evaporated when she saw Jennings ride up behind him. Dangerfield did not dismount.

"Day, Miss Elsey." He tipped his hat. Elsey did not respond.

Jennings approached. "Good day, Elsey. I need to speak to Henry right away. Is he home?"

Elsey eyed the two men sitting atop their mounts. "I'll fetch him, Marse Jennings."

Henry came out and looked at both men, who had dismounted. Elsey stood next to him.

"Wasn't expecting to see you back so soon, boy. Dr. Jennings, I wasn't expecting to see you at all."

"Henry, we have important business to discuss, and it concerns this one right here," said Jennings pointing at Dangerfield. "He's taken up with one of my house girls, despite my specific instructions telling him not to."

Henry pulled at his chin.

"How do you know this, Jennings? Did you see them together?"

"Just about. I found the place they sleep together. Found the girl's petticoats in a hayloft in the stable."

"But did you see them together?" countered Henry. "I don't mean to speak ill of you or your house girls, but you've got more than one. And unless you've seen them together, it could have been any one of your house girls, with any one of your field hands."

Henry paused, then smiled. "And I don't reckon you take your house girls to the stable, Dr. Jennings. I assume you have a nicer place for that."

Jennings glared at Henry.

"Well then, Henry, I will have you ask him directly," said Jennings. "You ask him, and see if he lies to your face."

"Well, let's have it, boy. Is this true?" said Henry, already knowing the answer.

Dangerfield removed his hat. "Yes, Marse Henry, it is true. I have taken quite a shine to Miss Harriet, and we have spent some time together. Can't lie about any of it."

Jennings smirked, and turned toward Henry. "Well, Henry, I think this changes things quite a bit."

"How? You pay me for his work. He does the work. 'Less you tell me he ain't working, I don't see how this changes anything. He does everything you ask of him, doesn't he?"

"Yes, Henry, he does. I will admit, his work is excellent. I don't have anyone like him. The fence, the hog shed – his work has been fine. But I can't have this Henry, I won't allow it."

"Won't allow what, Dr. Jennings? Slaves having babies? Human instincts? Reckon you're too late to stop that."

"That's not what I meant, and you know it." Jennings approached Henry and stood inches from his face.

"Henry, you and Elsey let your half-breed mongrels run around your place like freemen," sneered Jennings. "I know you taught 'em to read and write, and I know you share your business with 'em. I could turn you in just for teaching 'em to read and write. Putting ideas in their heads. Last time he was at my farm, that one stopped me from branding one of my own bucks. Took the brand from my hand and threw it away from me. My own slave, and that one of yours," said Jennings pointing at Dangerfield, "stopped me from branding him. Only reason I didn't beat him senseless was because he's yours, and we have an arrangement. Been one of mine, I would have beaten some sense into him. Someone needs to, since you don't seem up to the job."

"That's enough Jennings. I don't mind your affairs, you don't mind mine."

"No, Henry, it isn't enough. You want to treat him like a freeman at your place, that's your business. But he certainly isn't a freeman anywhere else, not in Virginia. You and Elsey ain't doin' him any favors, putting ideas in his head. You want to treat him like a freeman, someone somewhere will remind him he isn't. You need to put some sense into him, one way or the other. If you don't, I will. Next time it happens, Henry, I will take the lash to him, I don't care if he's your son, and I don't care about our arrangement. You ain't doing him any favors, letting him think he's a freeman. They're better off my way, long as they stay in Virginia."

Jennings turned toward Elsey and smirked. "And as for that one, Henry, you don't seem to have any arrangement at all. You treat her like a regular wife, like a princess instead of the piece of ass she is."

Jennings turned to walk away, but Henry grabbed him by the shoulder. Jennings turned to face him, and Henry drove his fist into Jennings' nose, sending a spray of snot and blood across his face. Jennings fell back and quickly recovered his balance, but Henry was already there, and drove another fist into his mouth. Jennings' head snapped back, and Dangerfield heard his jaw crack as spit and teeth flew out of his mouth. Jennings fell to the ground. Blood gushed from his lip, and a frothy mix of blood and snot poured from his nose. He struggled to get up, but Henry was on top of him. Henry grabbed him by the coat collar, lifted him up, and drove one more blow into his stomach. Jennings fell and coughed hard, expelling blood. Henry picked up Jennings by his collar.

"Jennings, you lay a hand on that boy, and you'll pay," snarled Henry. "We have our arrangements, and I intend to honor them. You will do the same. As far as Elsey, if I ever hear you speak her name again, I will kill you. You and I both know our arrangements, and you should know I have less to lose than you."

Henry stepped back, and examined the bleeding gash on his knuckle. "Now, if you are ready to talk sense, Jennings, hear what I have to say. The boy does good work, by your own word. You need him, and I could use the money you pay me, I won't lie about that. Now if the boy and this Harriet woman have taken a shine to each other, I would agree that any children will belong to you. I could fight you for ownership of those children since he belongs to me, but in the interest of peace between our families, any children those two have are yours completely, free and clear. You own the children outright, he continues to work for you, you continue to pay me, and you let Dangerfield and Harriet to their own business. That's a fair arrangement, Jennings."

Henry shuddered, and sat down. "Elsey, please fetch Dr. Jennings some cloths and cold water for his face. Jennings, you clean yourself up, and get off my land. You leave now, you will be back home before lunch. The boy stays here for a few days while you consider my offer. You think it over, and let me know if you accept. If so, I will send him back in a week or so, and we pretend this never happened. You think it over on your ride home. And remember what I said, Jennings. I hear you speak Elsey's name again, and I kill you where you stand."

Elsey returned with the cloths and cold water. Jennings took them, and wobbled to his feet.

"I won't forget this Henry." He gingerly climbed atop his mount and started toward home.

CHAPTER 23

Turner looked up at Hillman, but the figure was gone. Hillman was taking notes, and looked up at Turner. He stopped taking notes, and tapped his pen impatiently on his notepad.

"Dr. Turner, I am ready to proceed whenever you are," said his first assistant. The four residents looked at him without saying a word.

"Yes of course," said Turner. "I wanted to make certain everyone was keeping up. As I was saying, we make the first incision, we consider the size of the tumor, and determine how to remove it without removing too much of the surrounding tissue. Of course, we will have to remove some of the surrounding healthy tissue to make certain we get all of the tumor."

He pushed the scalpel along the incision marks that his first assistant had prepared. His hand trembled, and the scalpel slipped out of his hand. He retrieved the scalpel, tightened his grip, and continued cutting, sliding the scalpel deep into the tissue and along the marks. His hand trembled again, and a bead of sweat escaped his headgear and dropped down his nose before falling into his mask. His first assistant leaned in close to dab his forehead.

"What the hell is wrong with you," she hissed as she leaned in. "Are you sick or something? Do you want me to finish?"

"No, I'm fine," he croaked. "Let me finish." He looked into the observation room at Hillman, who had put his note pad down, and had his hands behind his back. He was rocking back and forth on his heels. Two of the residents were whispering to each other, while the other two stared at their feet.

"This procedure, ladies and gentlemen, is a simple lumpectomy, also known as a wide local excision. Our goal is to preserve as much of the healthy breast as possible. If that is not possible, the remaining option is of course a mastectomy." As he spoke, Turner regained his footing. He decided to keep talking instead of cutting to buy himself some time.

"In our case, the patient's tumor was visible on the ultrasound," explained Turner. "We know what it looks like. However, the patient's treating physician could not feel the tumor during the last pre-surgery physical exam. When that happens, we use a pre-surgery procedure known as wire localization. This helps me locate the tumor so it can be excised."

He cut deeper into the tissue along the incision marks until he felt the needle.

"I have now reached the needle, which the radiologist inserted to mark the location of the tumor. If you will look on the screen, you will see that the needle marks the beginning of the mass." He cut open and peeled back the flesh near the needle. The residents peered up at the OR screen, and saw the needle poking into a solid gray mass.

"We will now remove the mass." His muscle memory took over, and his hands gripped the scalpel. He moved the instrument around the gray lump and around the needle. He cut under the lump and around it, taking a thin layer of pink healthy flesh around its entirety. After about 45 minutes, he lifted the mass and displayed it to the residents.

"This, ladies and gentlemen, is the culprit. My first assistant, Dr. Martinez will take this down to pathology, where they will examine it to confirm that it is benign. Although the biopsy determined it was benign, given this patient's history, we don't want to take chances."

He placed the mass into a metal tray, and handed it to Martinez. "Dr. Martinez, please do the honors." The residents clapped politely.

Martinez walked past him and picked up the tray. "Nice work," she whispered into his ear. "I was worried about you for a minute."

"So was I."

He exited the OR and walked into the scrub room. His head throbbed.

Hillman walked in after him, tapping his note pad. "Nice work in there, Mike."

"Thank you. I haven't had an audience in a while. Kind of a rocky start."

"I'll say it was. I think the residents were worried one of them might have to finish." He stared at Turner. "Did something happen in there Mike? You were really pale for a minute. I could see the sweat on your head from the observation room. Did something happen? Did you see something in that tumor?"

"No, nothing happened. I just . . . nothing happened. Just nerves."

"Nerves? You must have done over a hundred excisions. Did you know the patient? Ex-girlfriend or something?"

"No, Roger, of course not."

"Sorry, bad joke," said Hillman. "Look, I think I am to blame for the rocky start. I shouldn't have told you what I was thinking about you being chief of surgery. And me taking notes after what I told you probably didn't help. And not to mention me observing the procedure on such short notice. I gave you a lot of expectations, and then basically had the job interview right away, with no notice. I'm sorry."

"That's not it Roger. No apologies necessary. I deal with this every day. Nothing happened. Just nerves."

"Well, you finished nicely. I liked how you explained the wire procedure. You talked more than you cut, that was good. I suspect a few of the residents knew what a wire procedure is, but it never hurts to over-explain. The residents learned something, even if you almost fumbled at the beginning."

Hillman stared at him, then looked around to ensure they were alone. "Look, Mike, I meant what I said earlier. I know everyone on the nominating committee. And as the outgoing chief of surgery, I have some say in who takes my place. This is confidential, but if you decide to go for it, it's between you and Prandra for next chief. And you know how I feel about Prandra."

"Roger, you know I think Prandra is a good surgeon."

"He is. A world-class surgeon and a first-rate asshole."

"I appreciate what you told me, Roger."

"Listen, don't tell anyone what I told you. Do you want to reschedule our lunch? I think you could use some time to think. Let's have lunch next week. That will give you some time to figure out what you want to do."

"Yeah, let's reschedule. I could use a little time."

Turner cleaned up and drove home. When he walked through the front door, Tracy was lying on the couch, feet up, reading a magazine.

"Hey," he said listlessly.

"Hey yourself. How did the surgery go?"

"Fine. I removed the tumor completely. I suspect it was benign, but we sent it to pathology just to be sure. I had four surgical residents and Hillman watching me. Hillman took notes like it was his first day in med school. Martinez was great, as always. Oh, and I saw Dangerfield's ghost in the operating room. Walked right behind Hillman during surgery. Probably bled all over the observation room."

"Very funny," said Tracy, not looking up from her magazine.

"I'm not kidding. I saw him again," said Turner. "I was about to make the first incision, and I saw him. Gash at his throat, ears torn off, just like I saw him in Harpers Ferry. He had the hat, the limp, the same stare. It was him." He sat down on the couch and rubbed his temples.

"Jesus Christ, honey, I'm so sorry," said Tracy.

She moved next to him, and rubbed his shoulders. He held his head in his hands.

"I need help, babe. I don't know what else to do. I've considered everything, every possibility. The sleeping medication you gave me. Stress. Mental suggestion caused by external environmental factors. The sleeping medication might explain the dream with the men in the cars, but it doesn't explain how I saw Dangerfield back at Harpers Ferry. It doesn't explain the photograph at Vernita's house. And it sure as hell doesn't explain what happened today. In the OR. The only place where I can control everything." He closed his eyes and rubbed his temples.

"I'm lost, babe," he continued. "Medicine is my world, OR is my second home. And right now, I am stuck. If I can't figure this out . . . ."

He leaned back on the couch and closed his eyes. "If I believed in God, I might pray, or seek divine intervention. But I don't, so I have to accept the fact that I am sick. I'm losing my mind. No other explanation. Whatever it is, the only explanation left is some kind of . . . ."

"Organic disorder of the mind," interjected Tracy. "I remember."

"And as you remember, organic disorders of the mind are usually linked to degenerative brain disorders like Alzheimer's, psychosis, or dementia," said Turner. "And I have no family history of Alzheimer's."

Tracy sat next to him on the couch, rubbing his shoulders, while he held his head in his hands. Neither spoke for a long time. Then Tracy slid off the couch and retrieved a pack of cigarettes from her purse. She lit one, took a long pull, and exhaled deeply. Turner noticed the blue ashtray next to the couch was overflowing with cigarette butts.

"How many of those have you had this morning?"

"More than one and less than 50. Here." She flipped the pack toward him. "Helps me clear my mind. Try one."

He retrieved a cigarette from the pack, and fumbled with Tracy's lighter before finally getting it lit. He took a long pull.

"I haven't smoked since med school," said Turner. "I guess this is truly the end." Tracy stood next to an open window, blowing smoke out of the house. "I feel responsible for you starting up again," said Turner. "You were doing so well before all this . . . ."

Tracy took another long pull, then crushed her cigarette in the ashtray. "Don't worry about me," she said. "You're the one with the problem right now." She pulled another cigarette from the pack, lit it, and took a deep pull. She stared out the window, softly blowing smoke.

"Have you thought about visiting Damon?"

"I told you I can't. I can't see anyone about this. I'm stuck."

She exhaled deeply, blowing dual plumes of smoke from her nostrils. Neither of them spoke for several minutes. "Well, if you won't get help from Damon or someone else, I know what you have to do," said Tracy. "You have to go back."

"Back where? To Harpers Ferry?"

"No. Back to where you were when you first saw your Uncle Billy."

"What the hell are you talking about?"

She did not answer, and walked into their bedroom. She returned with the picture of the slim man in the fedora standing in front of his car.

"The answer is right there, doctor." She handed him the picture. "Your grandmother loved her little brother, your great-uncle Billy. She went to her grave thinking he slid off the road in a rainstorm. But you saw something else. You saw how he died. You saw the chase, and the crash, and the other car that hit him. The police told your grandmother he just slid off the road, and she died thinking that was true. But something else happened. You know he didn't slide off the road in a rainstorm. You have to decide if you are strong enough to find out for yourself."

"You aren't making any sense," said Turner.

"You aren't willing to see and listen." She took another long pull. "Remember what that crazy guy told you back in Harpers Ferry?"

"You mean Frazier?"

"Yeah, him. He told you Nat Turner's ghost paid him visits. That Nat Turner picked him to reveal to the world Nat's untold secrets. Like he was some kind of portal between Nat Turner's unknown past and the real world."

"Frazier said all that, but he was crazy," said Turner. "Are you suggesting I go back to Frazier?"

"I think Frazier has already told you what you need to know," replied Tracy. "And here is what we both know. You saw your great-uncle in a car crash. Your grandmother kept his picture, so you know it was him. You saw the guy in this photograph in your dream. You know it was him. You know how he died. And now you know who he was." She tapped the photograph with her index finger. "Your grandmother's little brother. You owe it to her to find out."

She took the photograph from his hand and looked at it. "Your answer is somewhere in this picture," she said. "There, and in that big beautiful brain of yours. Your grandmother would want to know the truth, even if it isn't what she wants to believe."

She took another long pull from the cigarette, leaned her head back, and exhaled from both nostrils.

"Frazier told you something," continued Tracy. "Something about how he knew Nat Turner had picked him. You told me what he said."

"He told me that I need to have the courage to accept whatever destiny is presented to me," said Turner. "I didn't know what he was talking about."

"I think you do now. You know what you saw. I believe you saw something. First Dangerfield, then your great-uncle's gory death. Maybe I didn't believe it before, but I believe it now. You know who you saw. He's right here, in this picture. The only thing you don't know is why it happened. Someone wants you to find out."

"God, Trace, please tell me you don't believe in this stuff," pleaded Turner. "Ghosts, spirits, Nat Turner speaking from the grave through the voice of an insane professor. For God's sake woman, please tell me you don't believe this stuff. None of it makes any sense. It's all just gibberish."

"Do you have a better explanation, doctor? You just told me you're stuck, and you won't seek professional help. I'm asking you to consider the possibility that the answer is somewhere you don't want to go, a place where your intellect and reason won't help you."

"For God's sake woman, tell me you are not serious."

"For a man who doesn't believe in God, you seem to invoke his name often."

She wrapped her arms around his waist and pulled him close to her. "Look, I believe you saw something in Harpers Ferry. I believe you saw something in that dream in the hotel. I believe you saw something in the OR today. Just allow yourself to see, and it will all make sense. You said Frazier is crazy, but he believed he was chosen to tell Nat Turner's story. Maybe you have been chosen to find some other truth. About Dangerfield, or maybe something else."

"Chosen by whom?"

"Your grandmother always said you were special," said Tracy. "Maybe it doesn't matter. All I know is you have tried to solve this problem the way a doctor would – logic, reason, intellect, science, medicine – and it hasn't helped. You've tried it your way, and it hasn't worked. I'm just asking you to consider trying something else."

"What do you suggest, doctor Tracy?"

Tracy retrieved her purse and pulled out the bottle of sleeping pills. "Last time I gave you these, you had one hell of a dream. Let's see if it works again."

She shook out two of the white pills and held out her hand.

"I can't," said Turner. "I mean, this doesn't make sense . . . what am I supposed to be looking for?"

"I don't know," countered Tracy. "You don't either. But I think this is your last hope. Your last chance to figure out what is happening to you – to us. You have to trust me. If you won't get help from someone else, you have to trust me." She held out her hand again.

"You're asking me to abandon everything I know for some black magic, hocus pocus," said Turner hoarsely. "I haven't been chosen for anything, I haven't been chosen to tell anybody's goddamn story. I don't know what is going on, but I can't simply abandon medicine and start practicing some goddamn black magic voodoo. This is crazy, Trace, you can't ask me to do this."

"Well, your only other option is to call Damon or get some professional help from someone else," said Tracy. "You won't get professional help, so this is your only chance. This might prove you aren't crazy. Maybe there is an explanation. But that explanation is something you don't want to believe, in a place you don't want to go. Maybe you are more special than you want to admit."

She held out her hand again.

"Babe, I can't, I just . . . none of this makes sense."

"You have to trust me," implored Tracy. "I need you to trust me. You need to do this for your family. For me. Nothing else has worked."

Turner took the pills from her hand, popped them in his mouth, and stood up. Tracy wrapped her arms around his neck, and kissed him on the mouth. "Let's get you to bed, these things work fast." They walked together toward the bedroom, arms wrapped around each other's waists. They both undressed and slid into bed naked together. Tracy kissed him until he fell asleep, leaving him with her soft lips as his last memory before slumber.

———◦《◎》◦———

Turner awoke with a pounding headache. He was naked and lying in front of a red barn. Beside the barn was a large, pale yellow sedan. It had enormous round headlights perched at the end of a long metal nose, with a shiny metal grill sandwiched between. The hood bulged up in the middle, and the bulge extended all the way to the windshield. He recognized that car from somewhere.

He tried to figure out where he was at. Tracy was nowhere to be found. He stumbled to his feet and walked toward the car. On the passenger seat, he saw a man's fedora. He had also seen that before. He opened the passenger door, and picked up the fedora. Underneath the fedora he saw a small revolver resting on the seat. The cylinder was open. Three of the chambers were empty, and three were loaded. He put the gun back on the seat, and placed the fedora back over the gun. He tried to get his bearings, but did not recognize his surroundings.

Turner heard a door slam. He turned toward the sound, and saw a slim man exiting a house, walking toward the car. He wore a dark-colored suit, white shirt, and tie. He had dark skin and a thin, sculpted mustache. This man moved quickly, with a long-limbed, jumpy and confident gait. Turner recognized the man from somewhere. Turner tried to move, but his legs were frozen, and did not obey his commands. Finally, he was able to move his legs enough to stand in front of the car. The man approached the passenger side of the vehicle and opened the door. He did not seem to notice Turner. The man put on his fedora, and examined his revolver. He looked around the car, under the car, and back toward the house. He walked around the barn, then returned to the car. He reached into his pocket, retrieved three bullets, and inserted the bullets into the empty chambers. He snapped the cylinder shut, and put the gun into his suitcoat.

Turner tried to speak, but nothing came out. Air entered his lungs, but neither words nor air escaped. The man took another look at the barn and then walked toward the house. Turner yelled as loud as he could.

"Hey. Hey. Come back, I need you to help me."

The man turned and looked behind him. He looked directly at Turner, then turned around and walked into the house, closing the door behind him. Turner walked up to the house, and looked in through an open window. He saw the man in the dark suit talking to another man, who was seated at a large table. The seated man was much older. He had caramel-colored skin and a ragged gray beard. His face was sallow, and one eye was swollen shut. He held a pearl-handled cane in one hand, and twirled it slowly as he spoke. Turner did not recognize the seated man. Turner was only a few inches from both men, but they did not see him.

"You got everything ready," said the older man.

"Yea boss, I got everything ready. It's all in the trunk."

"How much they want?"

"Said they wanted three barrels for now. If they like it, maybe more."

"Where the barrels at?"

"In the barn. When they come in to pick 'em up, I'll take care of it."

"How many comin' by?"

"Two, maybe three. Met two of 'em last week."

"How do you know they ain't bringing more?"

"I can handle six," said the young man in the dark suit. He retrieved the revolver from his suitcoat and snapped opened the cylinder, displaying the six chambers, each loaded with a bullet. "Got the trigger nice and loose."

The old man squinted with his good eye at the revolver, and counted each round in the cylinder. "You best hope they ain't carryin."

"Won't matter. Takes two men to lift each barrel into a car. Got three barrels. While they got they hands busy lifting the barrels, I take 'em out one by one."

The old man grunted, and slowly stood up. "I don't like it. Somethin' ain't right. You need someone else good with a gun. Can't do this by yourself."

"You used to be pretty good with a gun. You can back me up," said the younger man."

"Hell no. Too old. My hands shake. Can't do it. You need someone else, someone younger," said the old man.

The old man tapped his cane softly. "Ain't no one else around, except the girls. Lorraine and Sally are upstairs. Lorraine knows how to shoot."

"No. Can't get the girls involved, boss. Keep them out of it," said the younger man. "I don't want to give them crackers any more reason to come after the girls. Keep the girls upstairs. No reason for anyone to know they at home."

"Well, you better hope this works." Turner watched the old man sit down, and heard him sigh.

Turner stepped away from the window and walked into the yard, trying to figure out where he was. He whirled when he heard a car approaching the house. A dusty black pickup truck with a bulging hood and cracked windshield pulled up slowly next to the house. Turner heard gravel crunching under the tires as the truck eased to a stop in front of the house. Two white men sat in the front seat. They wore hats pulled down low over their eyes. One of the white men exited the truck and approached the front door, while the other man remained in the front seat.

Turner watched the younger black man in the dark suit stand up inside the house. He pulled the revolver from his suitcoat, checked the cylinder, then put it back into his coat. He pulled his fedora low over his eyes, straightened the brim, stepped outside, and greeted the visitor a few steps outside the front door.

"Mornin,' Boss."

"Good morning, William. Your grandfather around?"

"In the house, Boss."

"Tell him to come out here."

"He ain't feelin' good today, Boss. Let him stay in the house. I got what you asked for right in the barn. Come on with me. Bring your partner along, take both of you to carry them barrels back to your truck."

"I want to see your grandfather before we inspect anything you have in the barn. Anybody else in the house?"

"No boss. Just Pap and me."

"Where are your sisters?"

"Out, Boss. Don't know where."

"Just as well. I expect Lorraine might not want to see me."

"Probably not."

"Listen, I know what you and your family think. I never touched Lorraine. I have too much to lose in town. And even if I did touch your sister, no one will take the word of a colored girl against mine. It's her word against mine, and I think you know how that will turn out. Best thing for you and your family is to forget anything happened. Sheriff has already said he doesn't know what happened."

"I wasn't there Boss."

"No, you weren't. Let me speak to your grandfather for a few minutes, then we can finish our business in the barn."

Turner watched the visitor enter the house and speak with the old man in the kitchen. The old man never stood while the visitor spoke to him. The old man twirled his cane slowly in his hand. After a few minutes, the visitor emerged from the house, and walked within two feet of Turner. Turner could smell the man's aftershave, and the cigarette smoke that clung to his clothes. The man took no notice of Turner.

"All right, William, let's see what you have for me." He pulled a pack of cigarettes from his suitcoat, and lit one. He took a long pull and exhaled twin plumes from his nostrils.

"Alright, Boss. How much help you got today?"

"Just me and Frank. Why are you asking?"

"Said you wanted three barrels. Takes two men to move each barrel. Might have to make three trips."

"Don't worry about us, William. Frank will move the truck closer to the barn." He motioned toward the truck. The man inside the truck drove the truck beside the yellow sedan, and parked it a few feet from the barn. He exited the truck, and rolled up his sleeves. Frank wore a tattered black sportscoat, unbuttonable over his sizable paunch. Turner walked over and stood within inches of Frank, who took no notice of him. Turner smelled the sweat from his body, and watched as Frank pulled a handkerchief from his pocket and dabbed his forehead. Turner was close enough to pull out the handkerchief.

"William, we want to taste the merchandise before we pay you," said the first visitor. "Tap one of the barrels and let us have a taste."

"Sure thing, Boss." The black man in the fedora walked into the barn and returned a moment later with two jars filled with amber liquid.

"Here it is, Boss. Same brew we sold y'all last time."

The two white men slowly sniffed the contents of the jars. Frank took a sip, coughed and spit out some of the brew. The other man downed his in one gulp. He looked at Frank and laughed. "Handles his liquor like a woman," scoffed the first man.

"Alright William, this will do. Frank, you and me will get those barrels and put them in the back."

The two white men walked into the barn and returned, both rolling a large oak barrel. The man in the fedora watched them intently. As the two men approached the truck, Frank and the first man grabbed the ends of the barrel. As they lifted then dropped the barrel into the bed of the truck, the black man in the fedora pulled the revolver from his suitcoat, and shot the first man in the forehead. His head snapped backward, and blood and brain matter sprayed across the back window of the truck as the man slumped against the truck, blood gurgling from the hole in his head.

Frank looked at his dead partner, and Turner saw a dark spot appear in the front of his trousers. Frank turned to run, but the man in the fedora pulled the hammer back, and shot Frank in the back of his head. The bullet passed through his skull and shattered the mirror on the passenger side of the truck. Frank lurched forward and fell against the side of the truck before sliding down and hitting the broken mirror, leaving a smear of blood and brains on the side of the truck.

Turner watched the man in the fedora walk up to the first man, put the revolver in his ear, and shoot. He then approached Frank, put the barrel between his slack jaws, and pulled the trigger. He wiped the gun on his sleeve, and put it in his suitcoat.

The man in the fedora removed his suitcoat and reached down to pick up the first dead man. Turner heard the front door open and saw a tall, dark young woman standing in the door. She wore a simple blue dress, and her black curly hair shook as she trembled in the doorway. Turner recognized her from somewhere. He tried to move, to run, but his legs were frozen.

"Lord Almighty, Billy, what have you done? Good God, Billy . . . ."

"Get back in the house, Lorraine. You should have stayed upstairs."

"Billy, you don't know what you just done. You don't know. Oh God, Billy, Oh God, why?"

"We took care of it, Lorraine. Knew the sheriff wouldn't so we did. We fixed it, Lorraine. He won't bother you no more. We'll put 'em both in the back and drive the truck into the pond. Tie blocks on the bodies first so they don't float up. Won't nobody look here, 'cause no respectable white man comes to the colored part of town, 'specially for the business they was in. Now go on back into the house."

The woman slumped in the doorway and began sobbing.

"Go on back, Lorraine."

The woman stood and wiped her eyes. "God, Billy, you a dead man now. You as good as dead."

Turner examined her figure, and tried to remember where he had seen her. The almond-shaped eyes, and smooth, obsidian skin, vaguely familiar. The jet-black curly hair. And her name was familiar. He must have seen a picture of her somewhere.

And then his knees buckled and his gut thumped when he realized that the sobbing young woman in the doorway was his grandmother. Turner inhaled and tried to scream, but nothing came out.

CHAPTER 24

Henry sat slumped in his kitchen, with a wet cloth wrapped around his bleeding hand. He rubbed his forehead with his good hand. Elsey brought him another wet cloth and a mug of cider. Dangerfield, Gabriel and Anna Mae stood in the corner, neither speaking.

"Never thought I'd see the day you best Jennings like that," said Elsey.

"He had it coming. Been had it coming for years. I never had cause until now."

Elsey looked at him, and rubbed a hand over his wrinkled, leathery face.

"You mean what you told him?"

"What part?"

"Everything. Everything you told him. About killing him if he speaks my name again."

"I meant it, or else I would not have said it. I suspect I may come to regret saying it."

Elsey stood up and walked toward the stove, where she checked the supply of stovewood. "I don't regret you sayin' it. Don't think you regret it neither. No one in this family regrets you sayin' it, at least not that part."

"What are you getting at, Elsey?"

Elsey wiped her hands on her apron and spoke to her children. "Anna Mae, go out and fetch some more eggs, some apples, and two of the young hens. Gabriel, go fetch some stovewood, and a ham from the smokehouse. Henry gets his favorite supper tonight. Dangerfield, you stay here."

Gabriel was about to speak out, but the look on Elsey's face convinced him that any protest would be both useless and painful. Anna Mae knew better, and quickly grabbed the box she used to gather eggs, and a sharp knife to butcher the hens. Elsey watched as they left the kitchen and walked toward the sheds. She brought Henry another cup of cider.

"Don't know why you had to promise Jennings he could have the boy's children," said Elsey. "Those are his children, they don't belong to Jennings."

"I didn't aim to promise him anything," replied Henry. "It just came out. I had to tell him something. It just came out."

"It ain't right, Henry. You two tradin' that boy's children like they was cattle, and they ain't even been born yet."

Henry stood, holding his bleeding hand.

"What would you have me do, Elsey? Like I said, I didn't aim to promise him anything, it just came out. Case you ain't noticed, plenty of people are willing to barter slaves like cattle every day. We don't engage in that business any more, but you can't expect me to pretend it doesn't happen."

"Well, Henry, we do now. You just did. You should have asked the boy first before you promised his children to someone else."

"And just how would I have done that? 'Excuse us, good Dr. Jennings, while we discuss who will own my son's unborn children.' It just came out, Elsey. I didn't even think about it before it was out. It just came out. I didn't mean to say it."

Dangerfield watched the man who owned him and the woman who birthed him discussing his future, and the future of his children he did not yet know. He wanted to speak, but realized he had no opinion he could articulate – he could think of nothing to say that would matter. He watched things happening to him, powerless to change his fate or even offer an opinion of the events at hand. Elsey turned toward him.

"Well, boy, how many times you been with this Harriet?"

"Well Miss Elsey, I don't feel right discussing Harriet like this. She's . . . ."

"Ain't nothing you can tell me I don't already know about making babies. I don't want Jennings owning those babies. Means he's still controlling this family. How many times you been with this girl?"

Dangerfield fiddled with his hat and stared at the floor. "We been together two times, Miss Elsey."

"Don't take more than once," said Elsey. "Henry, you reckon Jennings will take you up on what you said? You think he wants them babies? Maybe he might forget what you said."

Henry removed the bloody cloth from his hand and threw it on the floor. "Jennings won't forget. I promised him any babies the boy has with this Harriet belong to Jennings. He'll hold me to my word."

Gabriel and Anna Mae returned with the apples, eggs, freshly-killed chickens, and a fresh ham. Elsey walked toward the stove and retrieved a pot for the chickens.

"Don't know what it takes to be free of him, Henry. All these years, Jennings been controlling this family. Threatens to take me back any minute. You finally stand up to him, give him what he deserves, and now he owns this family's babies. Our babies."

Henry rubbed his hand against his head, eyes closed. "Let it go, Missus. Ain't no babies to speak of yet."

Elsey did not reply to Henry, but turned her attention to the pot. "Gabriel, go fetch up some water for the kettle." Elsey slammed her empty pot on the stove, and pushed three pieces of fatwood into the cold belly. She lit a match, placed it under the fatwood, and kicked the stove door closed, so hard it rattled the kitchen window. No one spoke. Dangerfield knew from experience that the conversation about his unborn children was almost over. If he did not speak now, he never would.

"Henry," he said, his voice cracking. "If you mean what you said to Jennings about me and Harriet, reckon you ought to make it formal."

Henry looked up. "What do you mean, boy?"

"I mean make it formal. If you mean what you said to Jennings about my children belonging to him, you ought to set it down in writing. If you aim to buy us some peace, it ought to be in writing."

Henry stared at him, slack-jawed. Elsey dropped a spoon on the floor.

"Son, I think you mean well, but you don't understand the nature of the agreements I have with Jennings. Tried my best to shield all of you and Elsey from this business. Some things you just don't know, and you all are better off not knowing about," said Henry.

"Don't care about your business with Jennings," retorted Dangerfield. "Only thing I care about is Harriet, and that boy Jericho. If you promise Jennings he can have those babies, he won't sell Harriet, not if he knows he's getting more property he could sell later. And if he doesn't sell Harriet, I can be with her. Jennings won't sell newborns. Prefers to hold on to them, least 'til he can figure out their value. You keep your word, Jennings don't sell Harriet, and I can be with her. We can worry about babies when they come."

Elsey slumped into her chair. "Lord help us," she whispered.

Henry rubbed his forehead with his good hand.

"Son, I don't think you know . . . ."

"Seems like there ain't much else to discuss, Henry," said Dangerfield. "You already promised Jennings my children. My children. I know you keep your word. I know you want what's best for all of us. And if this buys you and Elsey some peace, and fixes me and Harriet for a spell, you ought to set it in writing. I can take it to Jennings next time I go."

Elsey wept softly in her chair. Dangerfield sat next to her.

"Elsey – Ma – I don't aim to hurt you, or the family," said Dangerfield. "But you and Henry been discussing my business. I ought to have a say in what happens. We all want peace, and if this buys us some peace, we ought to do it." He turned toward Henry.

"Reckon it's time to set it in writing, Henry," said Dangerfield firmly.

Henry stood up, stiffly, and looked at his family. Dangerfield thought he had aged ten years in the last five minutes.

"Goddamn this wretched business. Flesh traders," said Henry. "Now I'm in the business of selling babies. We ain't no better than Jennings. Damn this business."

Henry walked upstairs, and returned with a leather bound book. He sat in his chair and scratched away in the book with a quill pen. He stopped for a few moments, looked at Elsey, then continued scrawling in the book. He signed his name, and carefully cut the page out of the book with his knife. He folded the paper in thirds, and gingerly placed it in a small leather pouch. He turned to face Dangerfield.

"This ought to satisfy Jennings, and anyone else who needs it later," said Henry. "Keep this in the pouch, and you can bring it to him in a couple of weeks, after he calms down."

Dangerfield closed the pouch. "Reckon I'll leave tomorrow at first light. No point in waiting."

"You ain't going nowhere tomorrow," interjected Henry. "I told Jennings I'd send you back in two weeks. I think you ought wait at least two weeks."

Dangerfield looked directly in his father's eyes. "I will wait one week. I leave one week from today. I'll bring the pouch and your letter."

"I think you ought to wait longer. Jennings would sooner eat breakfast with the devil himself than see you."

"I'd rather see the devil than see Jennings, but I need to see Harriet more. I have to see her. Just have to." He looked at Elsey, and was about to speak, but Elsey cut him off.

"You leave in one week if you feel you need to," said Elsey. "Reckon we all ought to eat now. Get some work done tomorrow. You and Gabriel and Henry put up them fences, and fix that hole in the corn crib. You get some work done here, and then you go on back to Harriet. You don't need to explain anything else."

She turned to Gabriel. "Hurry up and fetch that water, boy. Stove's gittin' hot."

Elsey and Anna Mae prepared Henry's favorite meal of smoked ham, roasted chicken, boiled eggs and fresh apples. They ate together. No one uttered a word.

Six days later, on the day before Dangerfield was to return to the Jennings farm, Gabriel, Dangerfield and Henry rose early. They devoured Elsey's breakfast, and set out to work. They worked quickly, with a sense of urgency unique to each man. They set to work putting up a new fence between the corn crib and the pasture. Dangerfield dug the post holes and set the posts, Gabriel leveled the boards, and Henry nailed them in place. They exchanged no words except those necessary to finish the fence – "higher," "that ain't level," "straighten the post."

At noon, Anna Mae brought a lunch of boiled eggs, ham, tins of coffee, and fresh berries. They ate in silence, sitting on the ground, backs against the posts, sweat dripping from their foreheads. They finished the fence by late afternoon, and set to work on the hole in the corn crib. Dangerfield ripped out the rotten boards, Gabriel sawed new boards to size, and Henry nailed them in place. In just a few moments they found a cadence, the pace of each man's work tied to another, a rhythm born from years of working together in grueling physical labor. Gabriel had a new board ready soon after Dangerfield had torn out the old one, and Henry had the new board nailed in place while Dangerfield pulled and Gabriel sawed.

They finished repairing the hole just as the sun fell below the hills to the west of the farm. They sat on the ground reflecting on the day's work, with their backs against the corn crib, their shirts open and damp with sweat. There was no need to speak – each man knew, in his own way, the importance of the next day. From inside the house, Elsey rang her bell, which meant it was time to come in. Henry rose stiffly.

"Well, boys, you both earned your keep today. Stay out here for a spell if you want, but don't keep Elsey waiting too long. And come in before it gets dark." Henry walked toward the house, stoop-shouldered and bent, while his slave sons watched. Gabriel turned toward his brother.

"Well, brother, I reckon we won't see much of you from now on. It ain't goodbye, but it may as well be."

"I ain't leaving. You know the arrangement. I stay at Jennings two or three days a week, and then come back home. 'Sides, I can't leave you in charge."

"You seem awful taken with this Harriet," said Gabriel. "Once you get over there, not much reason to come back."

"Didn't expect you to know so much about women, since you ain't never left home," replied Dangerfield. "What other advice you got for me?"

"I may not know much about women, but I know my own kin," replied Gabriel. "You ain't been the same since you first went over to Jennings. Almost like you can't wait to leave us, can't wait to get back to him."

"I could go mighty long without seein' Jennings."

"What about that boy of hers? Don't suppose you thought about bein' a father to another man's son."

"Harriet don't expect me to be Jericho's father. She never asked."

"Reckon she didn't have to."

Dangerfield stood and stretched a kink out of his back. "Well, brother, you wait 'til you find you a woman. You'll see. You'll feel like you fell off a cliff, except you don't want to get up. Nothing else matters, except her."

"I hope to find a woman, I just don't want whatever you got," said Gabriel. "Like a fever."

Gabriel stood up and clapped his brother on the back. "Make certain you say goodbye before you leave."

"No need. You'll see me in a few days."

"I know. But make certain you say goodbye, at least to Miss Elsey."

Dangerfield and his brother walked back toward their house, both awaiting the coming day.

Dangerfield was up at dawn. He bridled and saddled Solomon, and packed his side bags with oats and some loose green hay. Rain fell lightly on the roof of the stable. Dangerfield walked Solomon out into the yard. Solomon nickered and shook his head when he felt the rain. Rain would add at least another hour to the trip – Solomon had never been good on muddy trails. Once, when Henry was his rider, Solomon had lost his footing when descending a steep hill. The big horse slid sideways, pinning Henry against an oak tree, which kept horse and rider upright. Henry hadn't ridden him in the rain since.

Dangerfield went into the house to wake Gabriel. Elsey was already up, sitting next to the window, reading the Bible in the gray early morning light.

"Day, Miss Elsey."

"Morning, boy. I don't suppose you changed your mind 'bout goin' back."

"No, Miss Elsey, I ain't changed my mind," said Dangerfield. "I stayed a full week, like I said I would."

Elsey closed her Bible. "I didn't reckon you had. Thought I'd ask."

Dangerfield worked the brim of his hat, and looked down at his shoes. Elsey spoke.

"Well boy, you'd best be goin' if that's your intention. I'll tell everyone you said goodbye. No need to wake everyone up."

"I'll leave directly, but I need two things before I go. I need that letter that Henry wrote last week. And I need to take a pair of Gabriel's old boots.

"Why on earth do you need Gabriel's old boots?"

"I promised Jericho I'd bring him some boots. Gabriel's old boots might be close to fitting."

Elsey rubbed her eyes. "Go on and wake your brother. The letter is on the table."

Dangerfield went to where his brother was sleeping and shook him awake.

"I'm leaving. Thought I'd take a pair of your old boots."

Gabriel rubbed his eyes and yawned. "What do you aim to do with a pair of worn out boots?"

"I promised Harriet's boy I'd bring him some boots."

Gabriel sat up. "Reckon old man Jennings has enough money to buy boots. Don't see why it's your duty. This Harriet got you wrapped up pretty tight." Gabriel retrieved a pair of tan leather boots from under his bed. The leather soles had separated, and there were holes in each of the bottoms.

"These should do. I can fix 'em up later," said Dangerfield.

He walked back into the kitchen. Henry and Elsey were both waiting for him. Henry spoke.

"Letter's in that pouch," said Henry sternly. "Keep it dry and mind the rain. Put it in one of the bags and cover it with something. And don't ride Solomon hard. He don't like the rain."

"I remember."

Elsey picked up her Bible and turned toward the window. Henry looked at her and turned toward Dangerfield.

"When do you expect to be back?"

"Reckon I'll stay three days then come back, unless Jennings says otherwise. No more than four days."

Elsey kept her face to the window. Dangerfield could see her shoulders heaving. He started toward her, but Henry raised his hand and stopped him.

"Go on, unless you changed your mind," said Henry.

Dangerfield turned and walked out of the house. He put the leather pouch inside one of Gabriel's old boots, folded the top of the boot down, and put both boots inside one of Solomon's saddlebags. He mounted Solomon, touched his bootheel against the horse's flank, and started him down the trail.

Less than an hour into the trip, the rain came harder. It came in on a north wind, blowing sideways, battering horse and rider. Dangerfield pulled his hat down over his eyes. Fierce droplets pelted his cheeks. He could hear the rain slapping Solomon's flank, and watched it bounce off his hide when the wind blew it sideways. With each fresh gust, Dangerfield turned Solomon so his hindquarters faced into the rain, and waited until the wind died before turning him around. They continued in this fashion for over two hours, Dangerfield never allowing Solomon anything faster than a walk.

They stopped at a bend in the trail, blocked by a freshly fallen tree, about half as thick as a man's body. Dangerfield turned Solomon away from the rain, and retrieved a handful of oats and some loose hay from the saddlebag. He fed Solomon, and checked the leather pouch inside Gabriel's boot. Still dry. He returned the boot to the saddlebag, and fished out a small ax. He hacked off the biggest branches he could, and then tried to move the tree. It was still attached at the roots, and would not budge. He walked around the tree and began hacking at the roots. The rain had let up, and he took off his hat. He heard something move in front of him.

Two round black faces peered out at him from behind a thick stump. A boy and a girl, the boy about 15 or so, the girl slightly older. The boy was shirtless and barefoot. The girl wore a plain white cotton frock, filthy and torn. She too was barefoot. The girl stepped gingerly away from the tree stump. The boy kept his distance, eying Dangerfield warily. The girl spoke.

"Where you get that horse, mister?"

"Horse belongs to Marse Henry Newby, in Culpeper. What are you all doing out here in the rain?"

"Marse Henry Newby own you?"

"Yes. What are you doing in the rain?"

"Andy and me are lost. Tryin' to get home."

"Where's home?"

The girl jerked her thumb up the trail toward Jennings' farm. The boy edged closer, never taking his eyes off Dangerfield.

"Lost, huh? If you live that way yonder, you two going in the exact opposite direction from home. You live at Marse Jennings' place?"

"Don't know any Marse Jennings. We just live up that way."

"Like I said, if you live that way, you going in the wrong direction. You two ain't lost."

The boy spoke. "Ain't lost. Just trying to get somewhere else. Maybe you can take us someplace."

Solomon snorted and tossed his shaggy mane. Dangerfield looked up at the parting clouds, and the emerging sun.

"Can't take you anyplace. Got places to go myself. You two ought not to be out in daylight. Easy to find you. Men with dogs and horses find you right quick if you out on the trail like this during the day.

"They don't know we left," said the boy. "'Sides, dogs can't track real well in hard rain. Hard rain washes away any footprints. Makes it hard to smell us. That's why we left when we did."

"Won't rain forever. Look up. And when the rain stops and the sun comes out, you two get caught real quick." Dangerfield looked around, listening for baying hounds or approaching horses.

"Where you two aiming to go?"

The boy spoke. "Don't know yet. Just need to go"

The girl was now hiding behind the boy. Dangerfield spoke.

"She your sister?"

"No, she ain't my sister."

Dangerfield cocked his head, listening again for hounds or horses. The rain had stopped completely, and the sun was out in full.

"Listen, you both need to stay off the trail until nightfall," said Dangerfield quietly. He pointed to his left. "That way yonder is a old Indian trail. Goes straight into the woods. Follow the Indian trail through the woods till you come to a hill. Climb the hill and on the other side, there's an old cabin in a clearing. My brother and I used to go there when we was younger. Don't nobody live there. Stay in the cabin 'til just before nightfall. Then, get back on the trail and go wherever you think you need to go."

"Where should we go," said the boy. "You could take us someplace, or at least tell us someplace to go."

"I told you, I can't take you anywhere. I don't know where you should go, I just know you ought not to be out here in daylight."

Dangerfield retrieved a small sack and opened it, revealing two thick pieces of ham, two apples and some hard bread. "Take this food, and get on to that cabin I told you about." He looked at the boy, and fished around in the other saddlebag. He pulled out Gabriel's boots and set them on the ground while he looked for something else. He pulled out a small straight-blade knife and handed it to the boy.

"Take this too. Might need it."

"I could use them boots, if you ain't usin' 'em," said the boy.

"Can't give you the boots. They belong to someone else. Take the knife, and the food, and get off the trail."

The boy pulled out and carefully examined the food, and looked at the girl. He put the food back in the sack, dropped the knife in on top, and twirled the sack closed.

"Obliged, Mister," said the boy as he took the girl's hand and headed off into the woods. The girl turned and looked at Dangerfield for a moment, before they both disappeared into the woods. Dangerfield put the boots back in the saddlebag, and finished cutting the fallen tree.

It was late afternoon when he arrived at Jennings farm. The rain had stopped, but Dangerfield was still soaked from the morning's hard rain. Solomon stamped when he recognized the final bend in the trail that led to Jennings' farm. He bridled Solomon to a halt and looked around before dismounting. No one was out in the yard. He saw no movement from inside the house. He dismounted, and retrieved the leather pouch from Gabriel's boot. He took the pouch and knocked on the front door.

Lilly opened the door and stared at him.

"Day, Miss Lilly. I need to speak to Marse Jennings, if he's home."

Lilly closed the door slightly, but continued looking at him.

"I don't think Marse Jennings is expecting you."

"No, Miss Lilly, he ain't, but I do need to speak to him. Henry – Marse Henry sent me here to talk to Marse Jennings. If he ain't home, I can wait outside."

"Marse Henry Newby sent you here?"

"Yes, Miss Lilly."

"And you ain't here to see Harriet or that boy?"

"No, Miss Lilly."

"Wait here."

Lilly left the door open and went into the house. After a few minutes, Jennings appeared, still bearing traces of his fight with Henry. His jaw was purple and swollen, and his broken, engorged lip jutted out from his face. His left eye was still swollen almost shut, and his left cheek bulged out of his face.

"Lilly, go on back in the house," Jennings said thickly. "I will handle this."

Lilly stepped back inside the door, but did not retreat into the house, staring intently at the two men.

Jennings stepped out of the house and stared at Dangerfield. Dangerfield, a full head taller than Jennings, tried to avoid looking at him directly.

"What in blazes are you doing here?"

"Day, Marse Jennings. Marse Henry sent me here with a message from him. Here." Dangerfield handed him the pouch.

"What is this?"

"Don't know. Marse Henry said it has something to do with some business you have with him. There's a letter in the pouch."

Jennings retrieved the letter from the pouch and looked at it. "Thanks to Henry, my left eye is almost swollen shut. Read what Henry has to say."

Dangerfield took the letter and looked at it for a few moments.

"I can't read as well as some others, Marse Jennings. Reckon you'll have to read it yourself."

Jennings snatched the letter out of his hand. "Like hell you can't read. I know Henry taught all of you how to read, and Elsey too. Thinks he's running a negro schoolhouse. Fine, I'll read it myself, and then you get the hell out of here."

Jennings began reading the letter out loud:

I Henry Newby, of Culpeper County, Virginia, being of sound mind, and being a landowner in possession of over 200 acres of land, as well as several slaves, both adults and infants, declare the following: That I am the lawful owner of one adult male slave, of mixed negro and white parentage, said slave named Dangerfield Newby, and having the approximate age of 28; that said Dangerfield Newby may have taken up with an adult female slave of unknown parentage named Harriet, said adult female slave being owned by Augustine and Carola Jennings, of Warrenton, Fauquier County, Virginia; that Henry Newby, being of sound mind and body, does hereby give up any ownership rights to any offspring that may be born to Dangerfield Newby and Harriet; that Augustine and Carola Jennings shall have full ownership of any such children that may be born to Dangerfield and Harriet; and that in exchange for giving up any ownership rights, Henry Newby asks in exchange only that Dangerfield and Harriet be allowed to raise their family in peace, subject to the ownership rights mentioned above.

Signed this 27th day of May, 1848.
Henry Newby

Jennings looked at the letter for a few moments, then folded it and put it in his shirt pocket.

"You tell Henry he's a damn fool, and he's wasted his time. Under Virginia law, the owner of the mother owns all the offspring. So any children that Harriet has, with you or anyone else, legally belong to me, regardless of what anyone else wants. I own her, which means I own her children. Don't matter who the father is, now or ever. That's what the law says, and I don't need Henry's agreement. I own any children Harriet has, under any circumstance. Is that the only reason Henry sent you?"

"Marse Jennings, I think Marse Henry wanted to buy peace. I think he's sorry 'bout what happened."

"How do you know he's sorry?"

"I don't. That's just what I think."

"How long were you planning on staying this time?"

"I can turn around and leave right now if you want, Marse. Else I can stay for a few days if you got work needs to be done."

"Always work that needs to be done." Jennings took out the letter and read the last part again:

> *Henry Newby asks in exchange only that Dangerfield and Harriet be allowed to raise their family in peace, subject to the ownership rights mentioned above.*

Jennings folded the letter and put it back in his pocket. "Damn fool," he muttered to himself, but his face had softened. He turned to say something to Dangerfield, but started coughing. He coughed uncontrollably, until he coughed up blood, thick dark blood mixed with secretions from his lungs, which ran past his split lip and down his chin. He braced himself against the door.

Dangerfield reached into his pocket and pulled out a handkerchief.

"Here, Marse. Take this."

Jennings coughed again into the cloth, spitting up more dark red mucus blood into the handkerchief.

"Well, if you're offering to stay, I could use the help. Truth is, I've been laid up sick the last two days, and haven't left the house. Don't know what's happening in the fields. Haven't been outside for two days."

"I can stay for a few days, Marse."

"Good. Lilly, please take Dangerfield down to the cabins and show him where he is to stay."

Jennings erupted in another fit of coughing, spraying more blood into the handkerchief. Lilly helped him inside, then left the house, closing the door behind her. Without saying a word, Lilly began walking toward the slave cabins. Dangerfield followed.

"Marse Jennings wants you to stay in the cabins this time, not the stable."

"Reckon I'll stay wherever he wants me."

"I'd tell you to stay clear of Harriet and that boy, but I reckon it won't do any good. Don't matter anyway."

"What do you mean, Miss Lilly?"

"Harriet been real tired the last day or so. Can't hardly get up."

Dangerfield quickened his pace toward the cabins.

"You think she got whatever sickness taken hold of Marse Jennings?"

"Doubt it. Marse Jennings been spittin' up blood. Harriet been just tired. Can't hardly get up to do her work.

"She been to see a doctor?"

Lilly stopped and looked at him. "Doctor? She don't need no doctor, not for what she got. Simple woman sickness, all it is. I seen it often enough to know what it is. Had it myself enough times."

Dangerfield stopped walking. "Woman sickness? "Fraid I don't know what that is, Miss Lilly."

Lilly looked at him, shook her head and kept walking. "I strongly suspect she carrying a baby, that's what it is. Most likely yours, if talk is true. Marse Jennings wants her to stay in the cabins 'stead of the house 'til she feels better, so she can mind that boy. Also, he don't want her layin' around in the house, tired."

They reached the first of the cabins. Lilly threw open the door. Harriet was lying on her back on a low wooden bunk. Jericho sat on the bunk next to her.

Harriet sat up when the door opened. She saw him in the doorway, and struggled to get up. Jericho ran to him. The burn from his branding was beginning to heal – the black burn marks on his chest and back had scabbed over completely.

"Momma, I tol' you he'd come back. Tol' you he would, cause he said he'd bring me some boots. You bring me some boots this time?"

"Yes, Jericho, I brought you some boots. You been minding your mother, and stayin' out of trouble?"

"No," said Harriet, "he ain't been doing either one, but his mother forgives him anyway." Harriet stood face to face with him, looking him in the eyes, saying nothing. Jericho hopped up and down, his frail body hardly moving the floorboards in the cabin.

"The boy was right. You knew I'd come back."

Lilly spoke. "You stay here 'til I ask Marse what he wants you to do. "I'll be back shortly. S'pose it ain't no harm in you staying here."

Lilly turned and walked back toward the house, leaving Dangerfield, Harriet and bouncing Jericho alone in the cabin.

CHAPTER 25

Turner watched the sobbing young woman slumped in the doorway. He was looking at a young version of his grandmother, and his great-uncle Billy, who had just shot two men. Turner did not know where he was. He tried to run, but his legs were frozen, and he could not move.

The dead man named Frank slumped against the side of the truck, his body resting against the side mirror, his head slumped forward. Billy put his hands under Frank's arms and hauled him towards the back of the truck. Frank's heels made tracks in the gravel. A small rivulet of blood ran from the hole in his forehead. Billy propped the dead man against the open tailgate, then grabbed his legs and flipped his body into the bed of the truck. He then pulled the first man off the ground, propped him against the tailgate, and flipped him into the bed of the truck. He closed the tailgate, and walked toward the barn.

Billy walked within inches of Turner, but did not see him. Turner could smell his great-uncle's aftershave, mixed with sweat and cigarette smoke. Billy's shirt was wet with blood, and stained with grayish brain matter. Turner could feel his own mouth moving, but no breath escaped. Billy walked into the barn, and returned with two large coils of rope. He threw the rope into the bed of the truck, then walked back into the barn. Turner tried moving his arm, but it was numb. As Billy walked past, Turner felt the rush of air, and smelled the after-shave, sweat, and cigarette smoke. Billy returned with two long wooden planks under one arm, a hammer and can of nails. Turner heard a noise from the house. The old man was standing next to Turner's grandmother, who was still seated and weeping.

"Get up, Lorraine. You'd best get in the house."

Lorraine stumbled to her feet. "You both as good as dead now. They won't stop looking for 'em. They'll find you both out quick."

"Go back in the house, Lorraine," the old man croaked. "You and Sally stay with your cousins in Tennessee for a few weeks. I'll drive you tonight. Go on upstairs and pack enough for a few weeks. Me and Billy got some housekeepin' to do."

The old man grabbed her arm, and she stumbled into the house, her body still trembling.

Billy continued his work, undisturbed by his sister's weeping. He threw the planks, the hammer and nails into the bed of the truck. He started the truck, and waited for the old man to get in. The old man emerged from the house without Lorraine, and slowly climbed into the passenger side of the truck. The truck bounced down the gravel road past the barn. Turner heard the gravel crunching under the tires and watched plumes of dust trail behind.

Turner felt something spreading through his body. He felt lighter and lighter until his body rose above the earth, above the barn, above the house. He floated above the truck as it drove through a field behind the barn. Turner could see the two bodies in the back, jouncing and rolling against each other with each bump in the truck's path. Frank and the other man were now entwined, and each bump and rut tightened their deathly embrace.

Turner watched from above as the truck rolled to a stop next to a large pond. Billy exited, and walked toward the back of the truck. He straightened out each of the bodies, and laid them next to each other in the bed. Then he shoved a plank under each of the bodies, wiggling the bodies back and forth until each body rested cleanly on its makeshift cooling board. Billy took the ropes and wrapped them over and under each of the bodies, making certain that the ropes went underneath the planks. He then tied the ends of the ropes to the loading rails on the side of the bed, and nailed the rope ends to the planks.

Turner watched the old man exit the truck and walk slowly along the water's edge. He found a heavy rock and brought it back to the truck. Billy placed the rock on the accelerator while the old man stepped away from the truck. Turner heard the engine whine and rev. Billy opened the driver's door, jammed the truck into first gear, and jumped out of the way. The truck heaved forward into the water, whining and revving, sending a spray of mud and water into the air. Turner watched as the truck disappeared into the pond, first the nose, then the bed. The truck seemed to float for a few moments until roiling brown water began to cover the bed. Turner watched the ghostly white faces of Frank and his companion slowly disappear under the water. Within minutes, only turbid bubbles remained where the truck had been. Billy and the old man watched their work for a few moments, then began walking toward the house.

Turner felt even lighter. He soared above the pond until he could no longer see the bubbles. Billy and the old man were just specks against a muted green and brown landscape. He soared over the house, and could see in the distance a small town he did not recognize. He flew higher and higher, unable to control his movements. Now he swooped down. He flew next to the house and passed Lorraine's window, and he could see her packing her bags, still crying. He flew past another window on the other side of the house, and saw the old man sitting on the bed, holding his cane. A suitcase was open on the old man's bed, but nothing was in it.

Now something took him higher, above the house, above the barn, into the clouds, and toward the sun. He tried to scream, and now air filled his lungs. He released a roar from deep within his body, and he could feel his upward movement slowing, then finally stopping. He was suspended high above the countryside.

Then he began falling, uncontrollably. Faster and faster, and now he could see the ground coming up to meet him. He moved his legs and flapped his arms, but to no good purpose; he felt the rush of air on his face, and now he could see individual blades of grass reaching out to meet him. He heard the wind in his ears and felt the air pushing his cheeks tight against his face. The wind pushed his eyelids open, and he could see a bare patch of earth right where he expected to hit the ground. He reached out an arm to break his fall, but too late – everything went black.

***

Tracy picked up her phone and found Damon's number on her speed dial. She hadn't discussed her plans with Turner before he went to sleep. She would tell him when he woke up. Tracy poked her head in their room to make certain he was still sleeping. She heard him snoring loudly. Satisfied, she closed the door and quietly walked to their backyard patio. She closed the patio door and pressed Damon's number.

"Dr. Lee. How can I help you?"

"Damon, it's Tracy Turner."

"Hey gorgeous, how you been? Last time I talked to you Mike had you in some exotic location – Kentucky, Tennessee, Arkansas – "

"West Virginia, Damon. Harpers Ferry, West Virginia. Mike was doing some family research."

"Right, right, of course. West Virginia. No doubt exploring the link between coal mining and tooth decay." He laughed at his own joke.

"Very funny. I wonder how an elitist snob like you can practice psychiatry. Don't you have to understand everyone, regardless of background?"

"Understand, yes. Enjoy, no. I'm a city boy through and through. Wouldn't last a minute in red-state America. But you didn't call to hear my political opinions. What can I do for you?"

"Remember the advice you gave me about my cousin?"

"Sure. Your cousin, female, had been experiencing sleepwalking. No family history of epilepsy or seizures. No heavy drug use in her past. No PCP or LSD. Not a heavy drinker. Possibly under a lot of stress at work. I told you to tell her to lay off booze for a week, and get plenty of sleep. How is she doing?"

"Well, the sleepwalking has stopped, but now she's having really weird dreams. She's scared."

"Go on."

"She's been having these dreams where she sees things from the past. Crazy, violent dreams. Car crashes. People dying. Violent, crazy dreams. But the dreams take place a long time ago. Almost like she's having a flashback to a time before she was born."

"I see. And your cousin told you all this?"

"I told you, we are quite close."

"Closer than most married couples. Certainly closer than most siblings."

"What are you suggesting?"

"Nothing. Has, um, your cousin's situation changed at all since our last conversation? Any increase in alcohol use, or sudden interest in drugs?"

"No."

"What about her husband? Is he abusive? Does he use drugs or alcohol?"

"Not abusive. He's a light drinker."

Damon paused before responding.

"So you know for certain your cousin's husband isn't abusive? This seems like a lot of information for a cousin to share."

They both remained silent for a long time before Damon spoke.

"Is your cousin sleeping?"

"Far as I know." Tracy remembered the sleeping pills she had given Turner on their trip to Harpers Ferry. "She does take some sleeping pills once in awhile."

"Sleeping pills? You didn't mention that last time we talked. What kind of sleeping pills?"

"I don't know."

"Do you have the pill bottle with you?"

"No, it's in my purse – I mean I don't have any pill bottle. It's my cousin, remember?"

Damon sighed into the phone.

"Look Tracy, we've been friends for a long time. We have a lot of history. You and Mike are my closest friends. If you're struggling with something, please tell me. You have my doctor's professional oath to keep it confidential. I won't even tell Mike, even though I think you should tell him. I won't tell anyone. I can refer you to someone, and you call them when you are ready. Okay?"

"Damon, I told you, this is not about me."

"Not about you, but you have the pill bottle in your purse. I see. Okay, fine, let's keep it about your cousin, then."

"So would the pills cause these crazy dreams?"

"Quite possibly, yes. Do you remember the four things we talked about last time?"

"Sure. Drug use, family history, extreme stress, or an organic disorder of the mind."

"Very good. Let's add another one to the list. Sleeping pills. Certain sleeping pills in combination with stress, or even by themselves, can cause hallucinations, and other complex behavioral changes, either sleeping or when awake."

"So my cousin could be normal?"

"I won't go that far. But there's no law against taking sleeping pills. And sleeping pills are known to cause a lot of different types of behavioral changes. So for now, I'd say there are two possible causes of your cousin's dreams – sleeping pills, or she's bat-shit crazy. That's my informed medical opinion, based only on second-hand descriptions from what is almost certainly a biased source. Tell her to lay off the pills for two weeks."

"Thanks, D. I owe you one."

"Yes, you do. How's Mike doing? Rumors are flying that Hillman has already anointed him as next chief of surgery."

"He's fine. He's not taking anything for granted."

"Of course not. One last thing before you go. If you call again on behalf of your 'cousin,' I am going to recommend an in-person visit. No more advice over the phone. You or your cousin can see me, or someone else, but go somewhere. Of course if this is about your cousin, and she's cute, she can see me. If she isn't, I'll send her to someone else."

"Very funny. Thanks again."

"Have Mike call me when he's free. I haven't seen you guys in awhile."

"Will do."

She ended the call and walked back into the house. Then she heard a loud thud and a scream from inside her bedroom, and she ran toward the noise.

⸻ ◆ ⸻

Turner hit the ground hard, screaming, his arms and legs flailing. He remembered reading somewhere that if you are falling in a dream and hit the ground, it means you have died. He was surprised that heaven looked like the floor of his bedroom. His slippers were under the bed. So were Tracy's white sneakers. He pulled himself up and saw Tracy's nightgown, folded neatly on her side of the bed. Her side of the bed was empty.

The room was dark except for a small shaft of light that slipped through a part in the curtain. He looked around for Billy, and the old man with the pearl-handled cane, and his grandmother, Lorraine. They were not there. He was back in his own bedroom.

Tracy ran in and flipped on the light.

"Jesus Christ, honey, are you all right?"

Turner rubbed his eyes and looked around . "Yeah, I guess I'm fine. Unless I'm dead and this is heaven, which wouldn't be so bad either."

"It's not heaven, so you will have to settle for me. What happened?"

"I'm not sure. I had another dream. At least I think it was a dream. I can't . . . I don't know what it was. I don't know if it was a dream, it was so real." He walked toward the closet and put on his bathrobe, and sat on the bed. Tracy sat next to him.

"What happened?"

"Remember the dream I had, where I saw the car crash?"

"Yes. You think the man in the car was your great-uncle Billy."

"I don't think, I know. I know it was him. We saw the photo at Vernita's house. It was the same guy. Same hat, same big yellow car, same mustache, same smile. The man I saw in the crash was the man in Vernita's photo. I know it's him."

"So did you see him again?"

"Yes, but it was before the crash. He was at a farmhouse, someplace I don't recognize. And there was this old man with him. The old man was stooped over, gray beard, and he had a pearl-handled cane. Trace, it wasn't a dream, I could smell Billy's after-shave. I could smell his sweat, and the cigarettes he smoked. I could see the wool fibers in his jacket. It was real, as real as you and me on this bed right now."

"Wow. Are you okay?"

"Yeah, I'm fine. But you won't believe what happened. The three of us are at this old farmhouse . . ."

"The three of you?"

"Yeah, me, Billy, and the old man with the cane. Except I'm naked and I can't move, just like the last time. And they can't see me, even though I'm right in front of them. Like I'm invisible."

"Who was the old man?"

"Billy and Lorraine's grandfather. So I guess that makes him my great-great-grandfather. Anyway, the three of us are standing there and I can hear Billy and the old man discussing some situation. And then this old pickup truck comes into the driveway. Two white guys driving it."

"Who were they?"

"Don't know. Didn't recognize either of them. So they get out and start talking with Billy and the old man. And I could hear every word. Like you and I are talking now. The two white guys want to buy some liquor or something. So Billy takes them back to this old barn. They start loading these big barrels of something into the truck. And then Billy pulls out this gun and shoots both of them. The old man was sitting in the house."

"My God."

"I could hear the gunshots and smell the gunpowder. Billy shot both of them dead. Then the old man comes out. And then this woman comes out. Beautiful black woman with curly hair, she's maybe 20 or 21. She sees the two dead men and starts crying. And old man tells her 'Lorraine, get back in the house.'"

"Wasn't your grandmother's name Lorraine?"

"Exactly. It was her, Trace. It was my grandmother, except she was young. I saw her face, the curly hair, everything. It was her when she was very young."

"What did she do?"

"She's just sobbing, can't stand up. And the old man tells her to go pack, and he's taking her to Tennessee."

"So why did Billy shoot these two people?"

"Don't know. But I heard one of the men say something about no one believing a colored woman against a white man. Said no one would take her word against his, and the best thing for the family to do was forget anything happened."

"And so Billy shot them both."

"Shot them both in the head. Brains everywhere."

"Jesus. Is that why you woke up screaming?"

"No, that's not the end. Billy and the old man take the bodies, tie them to the truck, and send the truck into a pond. Truck sinks into the pond, and takes the bodies with it. Then I started flying, like a bird. I could see everything for miles around. Houses, buildings, roads, railroad tracks. Almost like I had some heightened sense of vision. And then I started falling. And I'm screaming and falling. I hit the ground, and I woke up on our bedroom floor. That's when you came in."

Tracy stood up and pulled a pack of cigarettes from the bottom drawer of their dresser. She lit one and took a long pull. She threw her head back and blew smoke from both nostrils.

"God, honey I'm so sorry. This is all my fault. I never should have given you those pills in the first place. "It's my fault, I – "

"Don't apologize. Don't be sorry. I think I understand what's going on now."

"You do? 'Cause I sure as hell don't."

"I do. Remember Frazier? From Harpers Ferry?"

"Sure. The crazy man who had visions."

"Yeah, him. He told me not to be afraid of my destiny. I think I finally know what he meant."

"What are you talking about?"

"Trace, this stuff is happening to me for a reason. I don't know why, but there has to be a reason for it. Seeing Dangerfield in Harpers Ferry, the dream with Uncle Billy in the car crash, Dangerfield again in the OR, and now this. There's got to be some connection between everything."

"How? How can any of this be connected?"

"Damned if I know yet. But my grandmother wanted me to know about my history, my past. She wanted me to know about Dangerfield Newby, and the sacrifice he made for his family. I never much cared for any of that sentimental stuff, but maybe I should."

"I still don't see any connection between Dangerfield, your grandmother, and these dreams with your great-uncle."

"I don't either. But I know my grandmother loved her little brother. At the family reunions, she was forever talking about Billy this and Billy that. I wish I had paid more attention. And she died thinking his car ran off the road in a storm. But I know how he really died."

"How can you be sure that you know anything? It was just a dream."

"I saw it. It wasn't a dream. I was there. Lorraine was there, and so was Billy. Physically. I saw things, I heard things, I smelled things, I touched things. It was real, Trace. I know it's weird, but I was there, just like I'm here now."

"So what are you going to do next?"

"I don't know yet. But I have to find out more about Billy, and my grandmother. I have to learn more about my family. Something weird happened, and I don't think my grandmother knew what really happened. Maybe that will help me figure out this connection between Dangerfield and these dreams about Billy."

"Why do you want to know? Why do you care now? What the hell are you even looking for?"

"I . . . I can't explain it. I don't know why. I never cared much before so . . . ."

Tracy stubbed her cigarette into the ashtray, and lit another one. She opened the bedroom window and blew smoke outside.

"Are you sure you don't want to talk to a professional?" said Tracy evenly.

"Don't need to. There's enough evidence for me. All this makes sense now. My grandmother's picture is real. Dangerfield was real. Uncle Billy was real. Billy's car was real. I just have to put it all together, draw up the connections."

He walked up to Tracy and put his arms around her waist. He kissed the back of her neck, and lightly touched the button on her jeans.

"Are you with me on this? I know what I have to do, but I can't do it without you."

She turned to face him. Her face was streaked with tears. "Yes," she said. "Wherever it is you're going, I'm going there with you."

"Good," he said. "First thing tomorrow, we go back to Vernita's to look for more evidence."

CHAPTER 26

illy left the cabin and walked to the main house, leaving Dangerfield, Harriet and Jericho alone. Dangerfield touched Harriet's neck. Jericho continued hopping about the cabin, unable to control the first joy he had felt in days.

"Lilly says you been tired."

"Ain't nothing. Goes away after a few hours."

"Lilly says you got woman sickness. Says you carryin' a baby. Is that true?"

"Lilly ought to mind her own business. She got enough to do."

Jericho ran toward her, and wrapped himself around her leg. The charred skin on his burn stretched as he wrapped his rail-thin arms around his mother.

"Mama, you got a baby? How long 'fore he comes out? What you gonna call him? How old will I be when he comes out?"

"Jericho, this ain't your business, not yet," said Harriet.

Dangerfield knelt down so he was face to face with Jericho. "I brought you them boots, just like I promised. You will find 'em in my saddlebag. Go on and find my horse, and fetch them boots out of the saddlebag. Bring 'em down so I can see if they fit."

Jericho raced out of the cabin toward the stable. Dangerfield watched him leave, then spoke to Harriet.

"Are you carryin' a baby?"

"Don't know for certain yet. Too early to tell. Feels like it did when I was first carryin' Jericho. Get real tired for a few hours, then it goes away. And my breasts are real sore."

"When do you know for sure?"

"When my belly starts to get big. With Jericho, I could feel him kick sometimes. Lilly says sometimes you feel 'em kick, and some don't kick ever."

"How does Lilly know so much about babies?"

"Lilly's had four babies since Marse Jennings bought her. All boys. Talk is that Marse was father to two of 'em. One of the field hands was father to the other two. Lilly ain't never told me directly about the fathers, that's just what the talk is."

"Where are Lilly's boys?

"Marse sold 'em. The two that was his, he sold to someone in town. Two that wasn't, he sold 'em South."

"Jennings sold his own kin?"

"Talk is, Marse ran up his accounts in town, and needed the money. He sold his own to someone in town so he could see 'em once in a while. The two that wasn't his, he had no use for 'em, so he sold 'em South."

"Reckon that explains why Lilly's mean as rattlesnake. Four boys, and she never got to keep any of 'em," said Dangerfield.

"You ought not to judge Lilly," replied Harriet. "When she was carryin' those babies, she was real nice to me. Told me what was happening to her. Told me all about babies. Said it was better to hear it from a woman before being with a man. Told me everything I needed to know before Jericho was born."

"Why is Lilly so close with Marse after what he done to her?"

"Reckon she figures that's the best way to make it here. Everybody here got their own ideas on how not to get sold South."

Harriet stumbled, and put her hand on Dangerfield's shoulder.

"I don't feel right," she said. "Let me rest for a bit."

Dangerfield helped her as she struggled to lie down. He put his hand behind her head and eased her into her bunk.

"Just let me stay here for a bit. Be all right in a few minutes." She closed her eyes and began breathing heavily.

Jericho burst through the doorway holding the boots Dangerfield had brought him.

"See you found 'em. Let's go outside and try 'em on. Your momma needs to rest. Let's get them boots on."

They walked outside. Dangerfield pulled the rough wooden plank door closed behind him. Jericho pulled on Gabriel's old boots and took a few steps. The soles were loose. The boy's feet flopped as he walked, and the soles slapped against the ground.

"They feel just right," he shrieked. He flopped about for a few more steps.

"Stuff some rags into 'em," said Dangerfield. "Make 'em fit better."

Dangerfield looked up and saw Lilly returning from the house. She watched Jericho clomping about in his oversize man's riding boots, and shook her head. "Boy ain't got no sense," she muttered to herself before turning to Dangerfield.

"Marse Jennings want you up at the house right away. I'll go with you." She turned and began walking toward the house without waiting for an answer.

"Miss Lilly, you sure Marse don't mind me sleeping in the cabins tonight?"

"Don't matter to him or me. Don't see any harm if you sleep in the cabins with Harriet and that boy. You already done your business with her."

"What do you aim to say, Miss Lilly?"

"I mean she already carryin' your baby. Ain't much else you can do."

Dangerfield paused before speaking.

"Miss Lilly, you seem awful hard on Jericho, if you don't mind me sayin' it."

"Don't see how that is your business," snapped Lilly. "Sides, I know what happens to boys here. You'd best not get too attached to that boy. If you don't mind me sayin' it."

Dangerfield paused again before continuing his efforts to make a new ally against Jennings.

"Marse was coughing real hard when we saw him."

"Been like that since he got back from Henry's place. Been coughing up blood. Ain't left the house since he got back."

"What do you reckon it is?"

"Don't know. He ain't the first one to get it."

They arrived at the house. "Wait here," she said.

Through the open window, Dangerfield could hear Lilly speaking in low tones. He could not hear Jennings. Jennings coughed, and Dangerfield could hear him emptying the contents of his lungs on the floor. Lilly said something else to Jennings before returning.

"Marse wants you to move the old bull out from his stall into the pasture with the heifers. Says he wants it done now."

"I'll do it now, Miss Lilly."

"Wait. Marse says he wants to go with you. Says he needs to show you some things. Wait here for him." Lilly went back into the house and closed the door behind her.

"Don't see how that old fool can be of much help," Dangerfield thought to himself as he waited.

Then his gut froze when he remembered that Hezekiah had been crushed by a bull, and that Jennings had deliberately frightened the animal moments before the accident. Dangerfield sat on the ground, his knees shaking.

Jennings emerged from the house. Dangerfield wobbled to his feet. Jennings began to speak, but his lungs did not cooperate. He coughed again, sending a dark red spray of blood and mucus onto the ground.

"Here, Marse," said Dangerfield, offering another handkerchief.

Jennings spat into the handkerchief, and gave it back to Dangerfield.

"Lilly told you what I want?"

"Yes, Marse. Reckon I can move the bull out with the heifers myself. Might be best if you stay in. You don't seem well."

"That old bull is prickly. I think it best if I go with you. He might be calmer if I go with you."

Dangerfield could not imagine how Jennings, with all his coughing and spluttering, would calm the animal. Jennings spoke as they walked.

"Still don't know Henry's intentions in sending you here," said Jennings. "Henry of all people must know that I already own Harriet, her boy, and any other children she might have, with you or anyone else. His offer to let me keep them was a waste of his time."

"I don't know, Marse. Henry don't share his business with me. I think he just wanted to make peace with you."

"Like hell he did. I think I know why Henry sent you. He wants to buy Elsey from me free and clear. He thinks letting me keep Harriet's children is a fair exchange. Damn fool. I'll be damned if I sell her back at any price."

Dangerfield paused, trying to absorb Jennings' words.

"I don't know anything about that, Marse."

"Like hell you don't. Henry shares everything with you like you were white men. Well, you can share this news with Henry. When you go back, you tell him I intend to take Elsey back by the end of this month. You tell that to Henry, and see what he says."

Dangerfield could feel his stomach boiling.

"Well, Marse, reckon you can tell him that yourself," Dangerfield said weakly. "I don't mind his business."

Dangerfield's head spun, and he could not walk straight. He wanted to run, but there was nowhere to go. He could not imagine Elsey living anywhere else, and certainly not with Jennings. Dangerfield tried to imagine the two women he loved most in this world living under the bootheel of the man he hated more than anyone. He contemplated family meals without Elsey, just him and Gabriel and Henry and Anna Mae, sitting together looking at Elsey's empty chair. He thought about Elsey and Harriet both living within easy reach of Jennings' lustful hands.

"I don't think I need to speak with Henry again," Jennings sneered. "I expect Henry to get my message one way or another, if you can't." Jennings laughed softly. "Henry don't share his business with me," Jennings muttered to himself.

Dangerfield felt his anger taking solid form within him, as though he had swallowed a burning stone that could not be expelled.

The men walked past the meadow where several cows and heifers grazed. One of the heifers looked up as the men walked past. She stopped chewing for a moment and swung her head to follow the men as they walked toward the barn. She followed with her eyes for a few moments before placidly resuming her day's work, chewing and grazing.

As soon as they entered the barn, Dangerfield heard the old bull rumble in his stall. From ten feet away, Dangerfield could see the bull's crest rising above the boards. The bull snorted and stamped his hooves when he heard footsteps.

The bull had one end of the barn all to himself. His stall was about fifteen feet long and just as wide. Thick oak boards surrounded the sides and each end of the stall, with about four inches between each board. Stout black fenceposts anchored the boards. A heavy wooden gate allowed the animal to exit in only one direction, out of the barn and toward the pasture. Guiding the animal out of the barn was as simple as walking into the pasture, opening the gate, standing behind it, and letting the bull out. Once released, he could only move out of the stall, into the pasture.

Dangerfield approached the rear of the stall, and peered through the slats. The bull was brockle faced, with a large brass ring through his nose. One of his eyes was milky, and the tip of his left ear was missing. Thick, curly hair covered his head and face. Deep scars discolored his flank. Dangerfield reached his hand through the slats, and gently scratched the bull's nose. The animal released a contented grunt, and licked Dangerfield's hand.

"Old Bull seems alright today, Marse. Don't reckon this should take two of us."

"One of us needs to turn him around, and one needs to open the gate," said Jennings. At the sound of Jennings' voice, the bull rumbled, and swung his massive head from side to side, slamming his head against the boards. Jennings walked slowly toward the stall, and the bull roared, ramming his head against the boards. He leaned his flank against the side of the stall, and the oak boards groaned against his weight.

"Might be best to wait just a bit, Marse. You got him upset."

"I want him out today," said Jennings. "Got a few people in town willing to pay a fine price for his calves. I want him out with those heifers now. You get in his stall, and I'll open the gate from outside."

Dangerfield felt the hair on his neck rising.

"Don't think either of us needs to be in that stall, Marse. Why don't I just go around into the pasture and open the gate. Soon's he runs out, I come back in, close the gate behind me, and climb out back. Ain't no need for anyone to get in there with him."

"Henry might let you half-breeds argue with him, but I don't. Now get in the stall and wait for me to open the gate. If you don't, you can go on back to Henry right now, and I can find someone else to replace you. Reckon it won't be long before Harriet takes up with someone else. You ain't her first, and you won't be her last. That is, if I don't sell her first."

"Yes, Marse." Dangerfield scratched Old Bull's mangled left ear, and the animal shook his head and grunted softly. He climbed the boards, and jumped into the stall.

"You behave now, and don't make me pull on that ring," Dangerfield said softly. He continued talking in a low, soft voice while he scratched the bull's nose. Old Bull closed his eyes and wheezed, as if he might fall asleep any minute.

Jennings coughed hard, and leaned against the stall. The bull rumbled again, and rammed his head against the board where Jennings was leaning, knocking the old man down. Dangerfield jumped to one side, while the bull thrashed, kicking his hooves against the side boards. Dangerfield ran to the gate and tried to open it. The inside latch was stuck, and would not move. He tried to climb out, but the bull whirled, and was now facing him.

Red-eyed and snorting, Old Bull charged toward Dangerfield, who was half way up the stall.

"Easy, ol'man, you don't want to hurt me," Dangerfield said as he continued climbing. Old Bull lowered his head and rammed the board, missing Dangerfield's foot by a hair. Dangerfield heard the board creak and groan, and then saw it splinter and crack as Old Bull continued his assault. Dangerfield's foot slipped and he fell a few feet back into the stall.

"Marse, you best get outside and let him out now!" screamed Dangerfield. He looked through the slats, and saw Jennings across the barn, slowly picking himself off the ground. Jennings walked slowly toward the stall while Old Bull thrashed. Jennings put one foot on the stall board and looked at Dangerfield frantically trying to escape.

"I got half a mind to leave you in there," sneered Jennings from outside the stall. "You seem to know so much, let's see you climb out. I told Henry I had a long memory. He'll never know how long."

Old Bull heard Jennings' voice and whirled again to face Jennings. As he turned, his flank slammed into the side board and pinned Dangerfield's leg against the board. For an instant, Dangerfield could feel the animal's heat, and the unforgiving wood against his leg.

Old Bull pushed away from Dangerfield and leaped toward Jennings. Jennings calmly took just a few steps back from the stall and crossed his arms, confident he was safe from the animal's attack. Old Bull lowered his head and leveled his shoulders at the boards separating him from Jennings. One of two middle boards creaked and then shattered, sending wood fragments and nails flying across the barn. Old Bull's head and part of his shoulders broke through the opening.

Jennings jumped back, but not soon enough – the bull's head hit him square in the chest, his arms still crossed. Jennings flew across the barn, landing in a heap against two branding irons propped up against the wall. Dangerfield climbed to the top of the stall, and felt arrows of pain shooting through his leg. He looked down and saw no blood, and he could still move his leg. He reached the top of the stall and was about to jump down, but something stopped him.

Old Bull continued his assault on the oak boards. He rammed his head through the opening, and pressed his full weight against the remaining boards. The second middle board bowed and popped out intact, nails flying. The animal's massive crest pushed against the top board until it began to creak under the pressure. The fence posts that held the boards leaned. Only the top board separated Old Bull from his freedom. He swung his head from side to side, blood flying from his nose and face. He lowered his shoulders and drove his crest against the top board, until it bowed, cracking and splintering, before exploding outward.

Jennings tried to get up, but he was consumed with coughing. He struggled to get to his feet, but he had landed awkwardly. He looked up to see Old Bull thrashing and kicking the side boards. Nothing separated him from Jennings. Blood dripped from the enraged animal's mouth and face, and the ring in his nose was partially torn out. Jennings struggled to his feet and yelled.

"You get him away from me, you hear?" screamed Jennings. Hearing Jennings' voice, Old Bull lowered his shoulders and swung his head so his good eye faced Jennings.

"Don't say anything else, Marse!" cried Dangerfield. He jumped down from the stall, forgetting about his injured leg until he landed. Lightning tore through his leg, and his knee buckled. He stood up, and was relieved he could still move his leg. He realized he would not reach Jennings in time.

Old Bull turned his head, and spotted Jennings across the barn. He rumbled out of his broken stall and across the barn, shoulders down, cocking his head so his good eye was locked in on his quarry. Jennings picked up one of the brands, and pointed it toward the charging animal. Old Bull reached his target in seconds. Jennings thrust the iron at the bull's nose, but missed, hitting him in the chest just as the animal reached him. His head hit Jennings square in the chest, knocking him off his feet. He flew into the wall of the barn and bounced back into an open area. Jennings struggled to get up, but failed. Blood flowed from his mouth, and he coughed again, a deep, viscous cough that seemed to come from every organ of his body.

Old Bull charged again, and drove his head into Jennings as he lay on his back. Dangerfield watched as the animal pushed his haunches forward, driving his entire weight through his shoulders and into the supine man's chest. Jennings' ribs snapped one by one, like kindling being cracked over a man's knee. Old Bull kept pushing until a fountain of blood erupted from Jennings' mouth, shooting up into the animal's face and eyes.

Old Bull shook his head, spraying a foamy mix of animal and human blood. He snorted and then calmly turned back and went into what remained of his stall. Dangerfield limped out of the barn, and toward the house.

Harriet was hanging linens when she saw him limping toward her. She rushed out to meet him,

"Lord Almighty, what happened to you?"

"Ain't me you need to worry about. I need you and Miss Lilly to come to the barn right now. Marse Jennings is hurt bad."

"What happened?"

"Old Bull. Marse had me go into his pen to turn him around. Old Bull got upset, and pinned me against the board."

"Oh God, he did you just like he did Hez . . . ."

"'Except Old Bull had somethin' for Marse, too. Old Bull broke out his pen, and charged Marse. Marse couldn't get away. Old Bull crushed him 'fore I could do anything."

Dangerfield put his arm around Harriet, and tried putting his weight on the injured leg. He winced, and collapsed against her.

"Oh, God, your leg, you hurt real bad . . . ."

"Don't fret over me. Get Lilly and we all need to get down to the barn."

Harriet ran into the house, and Dangerfield sat on the ground, feeling his leg throb.

Harriet and Lilly broke from the house, both running at full speed. Harriet stopped and helped Dangerfield to his feet. Lilly did not look at him as she raced past.

When Harriet and Dangerfield arrived, Lilly was kneeling, holding Jennings' head in her hands. She was sobbing softly, rocking back and forth on her heels, holding her master's bloody head in her hands. Dangerfield and Harriet hobbled up.

Jennings' face was streaked with blood and phlegm. His eyes were open and cloudless. He looked peaceful, like a man gazing out the window after a satisfying meal.

"Miss Lilly, we ought to have someone fetch a doctor," said Dangerfield.

"Ain't no need," said Lilly. "Doctor can't help him now." Lilly pulled out a kerchief and gently brushed the blood off Jennings' face. She smoothed his matted hair against his head, wiped off the blood and gazed into his unblinking eyes. She let out a deep sigh, and pulled his eyelids closed before letting his head come to rest on the ground. Behind them, Old Bull snorted.

"Miss Lilly, we ought to leave, and be quiet about it. "Ain't nothing to keep Old Bull in his stall."

Old Bull had his head facing the gate into the pasture. He rubbed his head on the latch and snorted, trying to get outside.

"Old Bull won't hurt us," said Lilly. "Go on and let him out."

Dangerfield hobbled outside the barn into the pasture, and released the outside latch. The door swung open, and Old Bull trotted out, swinging his head back and forth, looking for heifers. He spotted a clutch of heifers and cows in the distance and rumbled off, grunting as he ran. Dangerfield closed the door behind him and hobbled back into the barn.

Lilly had her head buried in Harriet's shoulder. Her shoulders heaved, but she made no noise.

"I'm sorry, Miss Lilly," said Dangerfield. "Did all I could."

Lilly looked up. "I reckon you did," she said. "Old fool had no reason to be here anyway. Everyone knew Old Bull might get him someday. I told him to let you alone. Never listened to me like he should have."

Dangerfield took off his hat and scratched his head before speaking. "Miss Lilly, I reckon I can't figure why you so upset. Marse Jennings didn't treat you well. Things might be better for you all."

"Better for us all? Is Henry Newby going to buy us? Is Henry Newby going to be our new master?"

"I suspect not, Miss Lilly," said Dangerfield. "I just mean to say Marse Jennings weren't kind to any of you. Beat that young Jericho something fierce. I never saw him act kind to anybody or anything."

"You wasn't here all that much," said Lilly. "'Sides, you say things might be better. You don't know what it's like for us here. Henry Newby treats you and your kin like family. Well, this right here is the only family we know. This is all we got."

Lilly looked down at Jennings' figure. "I ain't sayin' I loved the man, or even liked him. But what we had here with him is all I ever knew. I had two of his babies. And whoever comes next might be even worse. No tellin' where all of us might be tomorrow."

"Alright, Miss Lilly. Why don't we leave you in peace now. Me and Harriet, we'll go on and find someone to take Marse back to the house. Leave you with him for a bit."

Dangerfield put his arm around Harriet, and they hobbled out of the barn. Lilly stayed behind, gazing at her dead master.

≈«()»≈

Dangerfield stayed at Jennings' farm for another four days, until the day after the funeral. His leg was stiff, but not broken. After four days, he could put his full weight on it, and the limp had almost gone away.

Henry had ridden in for the funeral. After the service and burial in the Jennings family plot, Henry and the other white guests returned to the main house. Dangerfield and the other Jennings' family slaves stayed behind in the fields and barns.

Henry paid his respects to Jennings' widow, Carola. He spoke with her for a few moments as she stood in the doorway of the main house. Henry tipped his hat, and said a few words. When he left, Dangerfield was standing under the big oak tree in the front yard.

"Terrible thing about Jennings," said Henry. "Never much liked the man, and I reckon I still don't, but he's leaving a family behind."

Dangerfield did not respond.

"When you are ready, you can tell me what happened. Jennings' girl Lilly says you tried to save Jennings?"

"I did, Marse. Reckon not fast enough."

"It's just Henry or Pa right now, between the two of us. We don't need to worry about Jennings any more. Nobody can hear us." Dangerfield rocked back and forth on his heels, refusing to look Henry in the eye."

"One thing I can't figure out," said Henry, "is why in God's name were you in that pen with a dangerous old bull. Best thing would have been to open up the gate from outside and let the bull on to his business with the heifers. Ain't no reason for anyone to be in that pen with an animal like that. You of everyone ought to know that."

"Reckon you're right, Henry. Made a bad mistake. Shouldn't have happened."

Henry looked out at the stable, and then picked up a stone off the ground. He threw it as far as he could, bouncing the stone off the stable wall.

"If I didn't know any better, I'd almost wager Jennings told you to go in there, and you tried to tell him what a bad idea that was."

"That would be a good wager, Henry."

Henry picked up another stone, and threw it at the stable. This time, the stone bounced off the roof before landing in the grass.

"And knowing you and knowing what kind of man Jennings was," continued Henry, "I'd wager you went in there to do your job, and Jennings did something stupid to get that bull all riled up. You tried to save yourself, but the bull had other ideas. He went after Jennings, and you tried to save him, but the bull got there 'fore you did."

Dangerfield looked down at his boots, and did not respond.

Henry picked up another stone, and this time aimed it squarely at the stable window. He grunted as he threw the stone with all his might. The glass shattered, and the stone rattled off the posts inside the stable.

"I just want to know one thing," said Henry. "Did Jennings tell you to get in that pen with that bull?"

Dangerfield looked his father in the eye. "Yes, Henry, he did. Jennings told me to get in that pen with the bull, just like you said. Told me some other things, too."

"What else did he tell you?"

"Said he was going to take Miss Elsey back at the end of the month. Told me to tell you he was taking her back, and there weren't nothing you could do about it. Said he might sell Harriet too."

Henry did not respond. He picked up another stone, and aimed it at the broken stable window. More shards of glass flew.

"Henry, I think you need to tell me what business you had with Jennings," said Dangerfield. "He made it sound like he could take Elsey any time he wanted."

Henry picked up another rock and aimed it at the stable, but stopped himself. He rolled it in his hand for a few minutes before dropping it.

"Truth is, Jennings owned Elsey," said Henry softly. "Owned her free and clear. Could have taken her back any time he wanted. But he also owed me quite a bit of money, going back for many, many years. We had a gentlemen's agreement. He left Elsey with me, and I wouldn't collect on the large debt he owed me. It all worked fine, until you started working for him."

"What do you mean?"

"Jennings owned Elsey free and clear," explained Henry. "That means he also owned all of her children, even if he wasn't their father. Not only could he take Elsey any time he wanted, he could take any of Elsey's children, unless he sold them to a lawful buyer. I could have found enough money to buy Elsey. But I never had enough to buy Elsey, you, Anna Mae, and Gabriel."

Dangerfield tried to absorb what Henry had just told him.

"You mean . . . ."

"What I mean is Jennings could have come over any time and left with Elsey, you, Gabriel, and Anna Mae, or any combination he wanted."

"So why didn't he?"

"I suspect he knew I would demand he repay me the money he owes me. He also knew if he tried to take Elsey back, I would kill him. Jennings was a coward, but he wasn't stupid. All the slaves in the world don't help none once you die."

"Henry, why didn't you tell us this before?"

"What would you have done if I had told you? You planning on buying Elsey yourself? You planning on buying Anna Mae and Gabriel too? Ain't nothing you could have done if you'd known. Most likely thing to happen is you'd try to kill Jennings yourself. Then I'd lose you for certain."

Henry picked up another stone and threw it at the stable.

"Jennings didn't have enough to repay me," said Henry as he watched the stone clatter off the stable wall. "But if he took all of you back and sold you, he probably would have had enough to pay me free and clear. I could have lost all of you, Jennings would have paid me what he owes me, and that would have been the end of it. I figured if you worked for him, that might make it better for us."

Dangerfield turned his back away from his father, and looked back at the house.

"Look son, this is all damn wretched business. All this bartering back and forth, dealing in flesh, swapping slaves, trading souls — look, I ain't any better than Jennings. I just did what I could to keep all of us together. Figured if I let you work for him, he'd get the benefit of having you around, without having to take you back. Maybe buy some peace for Elsey. I did the best I could."

Dangerfield picked up a stone, and threw it at the stable.

"I won't speak ill of the dead, but what happened to Jennings is the best thing that could have happened to us, at least for now," said Henry.

"What happens to Harriet, and Lilly, and everyone else here," said Dangerfield.

"Carola still owns all of 'em. Reckon she won't sell 'em – she certainly can't take care the place by herself. She needs the help more than Jennings did."

Dangerfield looked around and imagined life at the Jennings farm without Jennings.

"Why don't you come on home for a spell," said Henry. "Ain't nothing needs to be done around here that can't wait. Elsey misses you."

"Tell Miss Elsey I'll be home in three or four more days. I got some obligations 'round here that I need to take care of."

"What obligations?"

"Harriet's carrying a baby. My baby."

Henry sucked air through his teeth.

"Ain't much you can do for her. Why don't you come home?"

"I will, but Harriet and Lilly are mighty upset about Jennings. Bad as he was, he's all they ever knew. They need me. Jericho needs me too."

The two men said nothing, just stood next to each other. Finally, Henry spoke.

"All right, then, come home soon as you can. Take care of Harriet, and that boy, and then come home to your family."

"I aim to take care of my family, Henry. Just like you do," said Dangerfield.

Dangerfield tossed a stone toward the stable. "Something I been meaning to ask you, Henry," said Dangerfield. "When Jennings offered to buy me for $750, were you thinking about selling me?"

"Hell no," said Henry. "You ain't for sale at any price. That was just Jennings talking."

"Then why did you let him talk about buying me?"

"That was just Jennings talking, son," said Henry softly. "He was always trying to remind me of our arrangements. I never once considered selling you. Jennings could have offered the moon and I would have said no."

Henry hugged his son, clapping him on the back. Then he walked to the stable, saddled his horse, and rode home. Dangerfield watched him as clattered down the trail away from the Jennings farm.

CHAPTER 27

Turner sprang out of bed early the next morning. He made coffee, then returned to the bedroom and dressed as quietly as he could while Tracy slept. She was sprawled across the huge bed, snoring loudly. He tapped her shoulder. No response. He walked into the living room and called Vernita. It was 6 am, but she would be up. She answered on the second ring.

"H'lo," said Vernita.

"Hey, V, it's Mike. Hope I didn't wake you."

"I wish you had. Baby been up all night. I didn't get much sleep. Just got her down when you called. What do you want?"

"Sorry to disturb you. Is Frank home?"

"Frank gets home from work at 10. Why?"

"I was hoping I could come over this morning. I need to look through those boxes that Gran left. See if I can find any more pictures like the one you gave me."

"I gave you that old picture of Billy and his car. What else are you looking for?"

"I don't know just yet. But I saw Gran had quite a few boxes. I just want to look through them, see if there is anything interesting there. Family heirlooms, family history, stuff we should be saving."

"I looked through some of that stuff after Gran died," said Vernita. "Don't think there's much in the way of heirlooms. Just a bunch of pictures, some clothes, and old newspaper articles. Junk, mostly. I was planning on throwing most of it away."

"Don't throw anything away. We should look through everything first."

"Fine, I won't throw anything away," Vernita said as she yawned into the phone. "Is there some reason you have to look at this stuff this morning? Can't this wait?"

"I'm on call at the hospital starting at noon, going until midnight. I'm doing 12 hour shifts this week. If we could come over this morning, I would really appreciate it."

Vernita yawned again. "Fine, come over this morning. What time?"

"We'll be over in one hour. We'll bring breakfast. Tracy can keep an eye on the baby while I look through Gran's boxes. You can get some sleep, or run errands while we're over. Sound good?"

"If you bring food and watch the baby, you can come over any time you want."

"Alright, V. See you soon. Thanks."

He hung up and walked into the bedroom. Tracy was awake, but still sprawled across the bed.

"Hey sunshine," he said. "How'd you sleep?"

"Not well," said Tracy. "I don't know what happened. What about you? Did you have any dreams?"

"Nope, slept like a rock all night. Don't think I woke up once. I haven't slept like that since the day after the last med school exams."

"Glad one of us got some sleep. I might have to take some of those pills I gave you." She sat up, yawned mightily, and fell back on the bed.

"We're going to Vernita's this morning to look through my grandmother's things. See if I can find some more pictures, more clues. I told Vernita we'd be there in an hour. We'll pick up some food on our way. I'll get you some coffee."

"'We're going to Vernita's?' Why do you need me?"

"Baby didn't sleep last night. I told Vernita you'd keep an eye on the baby so she can sleep, or run errands. I should have asked, but you were asleep."

"Don't think I will be much good watching any baby. Maybe we can do this later."

"I don't want to do this alone. Besides, you got me this far. You're the one who remembered Uncle Billy's picture. You're the one who paid attention on all those trips to visit my family. I need you to tie things together. I need your intuition."

"Fine, I'll go. I suspect I might regret what I started." She stood up, stretched, and let her nightgown fall on the bed. She walked toward the bathroom. Turner admired her naked body and the curve of her hips as she walked past.

"You owe me," she said as she stepped into the shower.

"Always will," he said.

They arrived at Vernita's apartment an hour later, armed with coffee, bagels, cream cheese, and sausages. Vernita opened the door, still wearing her nightgown.

"Never thought I'd be this happy to see you two at 7 in the morning," she said, yawning. "What did you bring?"

"Light breakfast for all of us." Turner took two strides into the apartment and dropped the food on the only uncluttered corner of the kitchen table he could find. The rest of the table contained old newspapers, an empty box of diapers, crumpled tissues, baby wipes, a pack of matches, and what looked like two weeks' worth of mail. He noticed several unopened envelopes with dire warnings of "Final Notice," "Overdue," and "Notice of Termination of Service." He pretended he had not seen them.

"How's the baby?"

"Still asleep for now. Just got her back to sleep in her crib when you called." Vernita, her face creased and haggard, studied Tracy, who was freshly showered, perfumed, and made up.

"So Mike volunteered you to watch the baby," said Vernita warily. "You don't mind keeping an eye on her while I get dressed, maybe read in bed this morning? I might even go back to sleep."

"No, Vernita, not at all. Least we can do for imposing on you so early," said Tracy.

Vernita laughed. "I don't think this was your idea, but thank you anyway." She put a bagel and two sausages on a plate, and walked toward her bedroom.

"Plates and cups are in the cupboard," said Vernita as she walked toward her bedroom. "Gran's boxes are in the extra bedroom next to the baby's room. Stay as long as you need to. Try not to wake the baby."

Vernita stared sleepy-eyed at Turner as he rummaged through her cupboards looking for plates. "Still don't know what you think you looking for," she said. "Why are you interested in this stuff now? You never had time for Gran or any of us when she was alive. You never had time for me. And now I can't get rid of you two. What is it you want now? Why are you here?"

"I don't know what I'm looking for either, V," replied Turner wearily. "Not yet. Maybe I won't find it. I just don't want us to throw out anything that was important to Gran."

Turner paused. "I remember once Gran was trying to talk to me at a family gathering," he said softly. "Said she had something important to tell me. I had med school duties the next day, and I was tired and did not want to hear any more damn stories. So I told her I had to leave and get some sleep. She did not say another word, just turned around and left. I will never know what she had to say that day. Maybe I am just trying to make up for not being around before. I don't know what I am looking for, V."

"You don't know what you looking for, but you think it might be in these boxes," sighed Vernita wearily. She retreated into her bedroom and closed the door behind her. Tracy eased into a chair outside the baby's room.

Turner wolfed down a bagel and sausage and walked quietly into the small spare bedroom. The musty remnants of his grandmother's life were jammed into old cardboard boxes, and newer packing crates. Three black plastic bags were stuffed into a corner. Someone had taken an inventory of the boxes and crates, and written the results in crude, uneven black marker on each box – "clothes," "pictures," "momentos," "newspapers," "shoes," "housewares, "misc." Turner did not know what he was looking for, but the box marked "pictures" seemed like a good place to start.

He pulled out an 8 by 10 frame, wrapped in old newspaper. He tore off the newspaper, and saw Lorraine, his grandmother, looking back at him in grainy black and white. She was standing next to an older black man with white hair. The man held a cane, and he was slightly stooped. He wore a dark suit, carefully knotted tie, and a waistcoat. They were standing in front of a white house. Turner recognized the old man from his dream – he was Uncle Billy's accomplice.

Turner carefully removed the picture from the frame. On the back, someone had written "Big Sis and Grandpa Red, Summer, 1931."

Turner could not remember seeing any pictures of his great-great grandfather, but he remembered the timbre of his voice and the way he twirled his cane as he sat. He remembered how he groaned as he stood up. Now, he knew the man's name, or at least his nickname.

He pulled out another picture, and unwrapped it. Looking back at him was his great-uncle Billy, without the suit and fedora, standing in front of a large light-colored car. A cigarette dangled from his lips, and his arm was around the waist of a young fair-skinned blonde woman. She was laughing at something unseen. He recognized the car instantly.

He removed the picture from the frame, and read the handwriting on the back; "Billy and Ann, Summer, 1931, trying not to get Caught." The handwriting on both pictures was the same. He did not recognize the woman in the photo.

He put the photo down and reached for the box marked "newspapers." Inside, he found several heavy cardboard file folders, fastened and tightly secured with string. He pulled out one of the file folders, untied the string and slowly extracted a specimen.

He found himself holding a gossamer but still legible copy of the August 4, 1932 edition of The Jeffersonian, which billed itself as "Jefferson County's Home Newspaper." "Established June 1907 – An Independent County Newspaper," bragged the masthead. He wondered how many newspapers existed in Jefferson County, Kentucky in August 1932.

"August Milk Price Higher After Milk Price War Ends," read one front-page headline. "Farm Families to Picnic at Fair Grounds – Next Thursday to be Big Day for Homemakers and 4-H Clubs," read another. He carefully turned the page and chuckled at what the good citizens of Jefferson County considered newsworthy in 1932. "Polish Beauty Queen Reveals Her Secret – She Eats Nothing but Eggs!" proclaimed one banner. "Doctors Save Local Man's Eye after Gruesome Shop Accident" read another. "Why did she keep this stuff," Turner muttered to himself. And then he looked at the page three headline, and his throat tightened.

"Disappearance of Two Local Men Baffles Authorities," read the headline on page three. "Prominent Banker and Local Business Owner Not Seen since June." Underneath the headline was a picture of a stern-looking man, hair parted on the left, wearing a dark suit and white shirt, staring into the distance. Next to him was a picture of another man, stocky, double-chinned, rumpled, wearing a light-colored jacket and dark tie.

Charles "Elmer" Harris, a Vice-President of Citizens and Farmers Bank and long-time Louisville resident, was last seen on June 3 of this year. Harris was an active supporter of Prohibition, and had been a member of the Kentucky Committee of 1,000 Supporting the 18th Amendment. He frequently offered his opinions on the topic in this paper in the "Facts About Prohibition" column.

Also last seen on June 3 of this year was Frank C. Miller, owner of Miller Shoe and Leather, and also a Louisville resident. Miller was also a prominent supporter of Prohibition. Miller once said in these pages that "the legalized liquor traffic had become disgusting to Christians and other decent citizens across Kentucky, and elsewhere." Miller was an active member of the Kentucky Temperance League, and also a contributor to the "Facts About Prohibition" column.

Both men were prominent in the community, respected, and had no known enemies. Miller donated time and money to the Orphans Home in Newburg. Harris tutored young delinquent Negro children, who otherwise would have become a menace to society. Although neither man had known enemies, authorities suspect their strong support of Prohibition and frequent condemnations of the liquor trade may have angered bootleggers and other criminal elements. Both men were married. Trustworthy citizens with information about either man are asked to contact the Jefferson County Sheriff's office, or the Louisville police department.

Turner examined the picture of Charles Harris, and his insides froze when he realized who it was. It was one of the men he had seen in his dream, the first one Billy had shot. Turner remembered the gunshot, and the sound of the man's brains splattering against the back window of the truck. And Frank C. Miller was his partner, the fat man in the tattered sportscoat. Turner remembered watching him piss his pants just before Billy splattered his brains against the truck.

Turner put the newspaper down, and looked around the room. "So that's what they were doing," he thought to himself. Turner closed his eyes and remembered the contorted bodies tied to the back of the truck, their pallid faces looking toward heaven as the murky water slowly claimed them.

He gently folded the newspaper and set it aside. There were more file folders, each tied with string. He pulled out the next folder and quickly extracted another newspaper.

Another edition of The Jeffersonian, this one from September 4, 1933. "Kentucky Citizens Prepare for End of Prohibition," read the headline. "Local Churches and Temperance Activists Fear an Increase in Drunken and Lawless Behavior after Repeal," read another.

Turned felt the pages crinkle as he turned them. His shaking hands made it difficult to read the page 2 headline.

"Baffled Authorities Close Case of Two Missing Men."

"No Clues in Disappearance of Prominent Banker and Local Business Owner Not Seen since June of Last Year."

The Jefferson County Sheriff's Office has closed its investigation into the disappearance of two missing men, Charles "Elmer" Harris, a Vice-President of Citizens and Farmers Bank and long-time Louisville resident, and Frank C. Miller, owner of Miller Shoe and Leather, also a Louisville resident. Both men were last seen on or about June 3, 1932. Despite pleas from the Sheriff's office and the Louisville Police, no new information has been provided about the missing men. The last information received came from an unnamed Negro resident, who claims he saw the two men driving a black truck toward the south end of the county. Authorities were unable to confirm this information, and have since learned that the individual providing the information is known to be a heavy drinker, and sporadically employed. "With no new leads from credible sources, we have no choice but to close the investigation for now," said Jefferson County Sheriff Lloyd Freeman. "Should additional information from trustworthy citizens become available, we will renew our search immediately" said Freeman.

Although Freeman would not speculate on the fate of the two men, it is well known that both men were prominent supporters of Prohibition. Some have suggested that their public condemnation of liquor angered traffickers and other criminal elements.

Trustworthy, sober white citizens with information about the whereabouts of either man are urged to contact the Jefferson County Sheriff's Office or the Louisville Police.

Turner folded the newspaper and walked out of the room. Tracy was holding the baby while walking around the room, singing softly.

"I can see where your cousin needs some help" she whispered softly. "I put my plate in the sink, and the sound woke her up. I think I can get her back to sleep. I don't want to wake Vernita. She looked beat." Tracy rocked the baby and cooed in her ear.

"You find anything interesting in there?"

Turner sighed. "You remember that dream I had where I saw my grandmother?"

"Sure," whispered Tracy. "You thought you saw a young version of your grandmother in a house or something."

"That's part of it. Do you remember anything else I told you about that dream?"

"Yeah. There was an old man in a house, and someone you think was your great uncle Billy. And two white dudes in a truck, and something about something that happened with your grandmother."

"Do you remember anything else," asked Turner.

"Mike, can't you see I'm busy?" hissed Tracy. "I've almost got the baby back to sleep. I got up at dawn to come with you on this trip. Vernita is sleeping. Please keep your voice down so you don't wake her or the baby. And why are you quizzing me on your dream?"

"I know this is weird, but please help me. Do you remember anything else about the dream? What happened to those two men?"

Tracy rocked the baby and turned in a circle, cooing in the baby's ear. "Yes," she whispered. "You saw your great uncle Billy shoot both of them. Then he and the old man put them in a truck and drove the truck into a lake or river or something. Is that what you want to know?"

"So you remember me telling you all that, right? Before we came here today?"

"Of course. You told me right after you had that dream."

"Okay. When you get the baby back to sleep, come in the extra room."

Tracy walked toward the baby's room, and gently laid her in her crib. She stepped out and pulled the door closed. "Okay," she whispered, "I think she is finally asleep. What is this about?"

Turner walked toward Vernita's room and put his ear to the door. Vernita snored softly.

"Come in here, I have something I want to show you."

He picked up the first newspaper and handed it to Tracy. "Read the headline on page 3. Careful, the paper is very delicate."

Tracy yawned, and began reading out loud, softly to herself. "Prominent Banker and Local Business Owner . . . ." Her voice trailed off. As she read, she twisted her hair around her finger. Her eyes widened as she read. She looked at the pictures of the men, then back to the story.

"Are these the two guys you saw . . . ."

"Yes. These are the two men I saw in my dream. I am dead certain. I saw them before we came here. Before I ever saw this article."

"Are you sure? Lots of guys in the 1930's looked like these two."

"Tracy, I was there. I saw them. I smelled them, their cigarettes, their sweat, their aftershave. The fat guy was sweating. I saw him wipe his brow with a handkerchief. I watched them talking to Billy and the old man. I was only a foot away. I saw both of their brains splattered against a truck. It was them. I was there."

Tracy put down the newspaper and listened for the baby. "Listen, honey, I know this stuff has been hard on you. Why don't you go back home and sleep until your shift starts. It's only 8:30 now. You don't start until noon. Go home, get some sleep, and we can talk later. I'll stay here with the baby until Vernita gets up. I'll be fine."

Turner crossed his arms and closed the door behind them.

"You don't believe me, do you? You're the one always talking about destiny and fate, and spirits and souls. You gave me those sleeping pills. You allowed me to see something I could never see. You can't leave me now."

"Keep your voice down. It's not like I don't believe you, honey, it's just . . . ."

"Just what?"

"Just that you can't tell anyone else about this," snapped Tracy. "Okay, let's say I believe you. You saw these two guys in a dream. They were alive. They disappeared. In 1932. So what? What do you think is going to come of this? You think you can find them?"

"No, but I can find out why I keep having these dreams. I was meant to find this out, discover some family secret. I think Frazier was right – I finally have the courage to confront my destiny."

"What destiny? What do you think is going to happen if you go down this path?"

"I don't know. But a wise woman I know and love once told me that 'the soul can see what the eyes cannot.'"

"Oh, for Christ's sake, stop it."

"Look you told me that," said Turner. "I never believed you, just figured it was some artisty crap. Now I think I can see."

Tracy rubbed her temples. "Okay, look. There is nothing else we can do now. We have to stay here until Vernita gets up, or Frank gets back. I think you found enough newspaper articles for now."

"Let me show you one more thing," said Turner. He picked up the second article, and handed it to her. Tracy began reading out loud in a soft voice

"Baffled Authorities Close Case . . . ." She read softly, first out loud then silently. She gently folded the paper and put it down.

"So they never found the two guys," said Tracy.

"Not unless some trustworthy, sober white citizen told the Sheriff where to find the bodies."

"Okay, what do you want to do next?"

"I need to take another one of those pills. See what happens next. I don't know what this is about, but I do know I am not crazy. I see things very clearly now. I will take another of those pills after I get home, and see if I can unravel this mystery."

"No, honey, no more pills," said Tracy. "Not until we talk to someone."

"Who could I talk to?"

"Damon. I don't want you taking any more pills until we find out what's going on. We are going to talk to Damon, and get his advice."

"I can't tell Damon what's going on. You said so yourself," said Turner.

"You won't tell him what's going on," Tracy retorted. "You will do research on your patient's problem before coming to a conclusion, just as you always do. Except now, you are the patient. You are the doctor and the patient. I'm the nurse."

"How can I talk to Damon about this without letting him know it's me?"

"Just tell him you are doing research as part of your application to be chief of surgery. Damon knows you, and he knows Hillman. Tell him you want to bounce a few ideas off him about neurosurgery. Get him talking, and see what you can learn. I want to make certain these pills won't damage you or your career."

"Listen, I can handle this without help. I have the vision. I just need the tools. Why don't we . . . ."

"No. Nothing else happens until you talk to Damon. I can go with you if you want. That might make it easier."

Turner looked at his wife and sighed. "Alright, we'll do it your way. I'll see if Damon can meet for coffee tomorrow morning before my shift."

Turner carefully put the newspapers and the photos back in the folders and boxes where he had found them. He put his ear next to Vernita's bedroom door. She was now snoring vigorously – brief periods of silence interrupted by violent snorts and gasps. Turner retrieved a pen and paper from the kitchen table, and wrote a short note to Vernita asking her not to throw anything away.

"Go on home and get ready for your shift," said Tracy. "I'll stay here with the baby until Vernita wakes up."

Turner kissed his wife and softly exited the apartment.

At work, he charged through his rounds. The prospect of having a new problem to solve, a new mystery to work with, energized him, even though he knew he was the patient. He had grappled with some of the most complex, baffling surgical procedures known to medicine, but had never had a reason to unravel the slumbering mysteries inside his skull. Until now, he had no reason to think about those mysteries – his mind was his greatest weapon, both sword and shield. He used it like a delicate precision tool to untangle medical problems, and like a sledgehammer to crush people and ideas he deemed unworthy. Until now, he had no reason to doubt the power or accuracy of his mind.

He passed Roger Hillman's office in between appointments. Hillman's door was partially open, and Turner could see him peering at his computer screen. Turner poked his head in the office.

"Afternoon, Roger. How's everything going?"

"Not bad Mike, not bad for an old lame duck. Say, you have time for coffee this week? Maybe one day this week before your rounds begin. I need to discuss a few things with you."

"Sure, Roger. Anything you want to talk about now?"

"Can't talk about anything now. Stop by Friday morning at 9:30 or so, before your shift starts. You're doing twelves this week, right?"

"Yep. Noon to midnight. I'll see you Friday at 9:30, Roger."

"Good. See you then." Hillman tapped his pen on the keyboard. "Say Mike, uh . . . well, never mind, I won't bother you now. See you Friday at 9:30."

"Everything okay, Roger?"

"Yeah, sure. See you Friday. I have a call now, so could you close the door?"

Turner pulled Hillman's door closed, and finished his morning rounds. On his break, he called Damon. Damon answered on the first ring.

"Mike, what's happening? Been meaning to call you."

"I'm good, Damon. Say, can you meet me for coffee tomorrow morning at 9:30? I'm doing twelves this week starting at noon, and I need to run something past you."

"Yeah, tomorrow at 9:30 it is. Where do you want to meet?"

"Someplace not at the hospital. Let's meet at the coffee shop around the corner from your apartment."

"Everything alright?"

"Of course. I just don't want to talk at the hospital."

"I think I understand. See you tomorrow."

Turner hung up his phone. "I'm hoping you don't understand," he muttered to himself.

Damon was waiting for him when he arrived at the coffee shop the next morning. Damon was wearing a slim-fitting gray suit, narrow-striped blue shirt, and a purple tie. Turner was unshaven, and wore his hospital scrubs. The men ordered their coffees. Damon gave the server, a tall, thin brunette with her hair in a ponytail, a long admiring glance as she walked away.

"You're all dressed up," said Turner.

"I have an initial consult at 10:30. Woman claims that Jesus lives in her closet. She's afraid to get dressed or change clothes for fear of disturbing the Savior. Her daughter made the appointment."

"What do you prescribe for someone like that," said Turner.

"Sometimes nothing. If she gets through her day without hurting herself or anyone else, I might not prescribe anything."

The server brought their coffees back, and Damon took a long sip from his mug.

"I once had a 62-year old male patient who claimed his dead mother lived in his broom closet," said Damon as he put his mug on the table. "Police checked the place out, found nothing unusual. The guy worked a regular job, paid his bills, didn't bother anyone. His son made the appointment. In every other respect, this guy was normal. No history of harming anyone. So I told his son to move everything out of the broom closet to make more room for the dead mother. The patient never came back, and I didn't prescribe any drugs."

"So you didn't do anything else?"

"Any medication would have done more harm than good. Better to have an imaginary dead mom in the broom closet than a zombified patient who needs $5,000 worth of anti-psychotics every month. So as long as Jesus stays in the closet and this lady poses no threat to herself or others, I might just ask the daughter to move the lady's clothes to another closet. Problem solved."

Turner took a sip from his coffee.

"Listen, Damon, I know you've been talking to Tracy about one of her cousins."

Damon arched an eyebrow. "She did say something about one of her cousins having hallucinations. Female, in her 30's, moderate drinker, no history of drug abuse or extensive use of hallucinogens. In good health generally. Vivid, detailed dreams about car crashes and such. I assume Tracy has told you about all of this, or else you would not have brought it up."

"Yes, well I'm worried about her."

"Tracy or her cousin?"

"Her cousin, of course. Listen, as a psychiatrist, would you say that vivid hallucinations are a sign of mental illness? I mean, is she crazy?"

Damon took another long sip of coffee and leaned back in his chair. He swiped at a cotton fluff on his shirt.

"Mike, my professional opinion is that all of us hallucinate all the time, sometimes every day. Most of the time, it's perfectly normal. Do you remember our med school neurology professor?

"Dr. Schwartzmann. I loved him."

"Most brilliant man I know. He's the reason I became a psychiatrist instead of a thoracic surgeon. Anyway, remember the case histories of those Civil War soldiers, the amputees?"

"Sure," replied Turner. "Their limbs had been amputated, but they still felt sensations in the missing limbs."

"Not just sensations, Mike, actual pain. These men had their legs amputated at the knee. Yet after the amputation, they reported pain in their toes. Their toes, Mike. They could still feel acute pain in their toes. Some could even identify which toe hurt, even though there was no toe, no foot, no calf, no limb. There were simply no nerve endings to feel any sensation below the knee, let alone a non-existent digit."

"Okay, but what does phantom proprioception have to do with hallucinations?"

"Those men who felt pain in their toes weren't crazy, Mike. They weren't insane. Their brains were simply playing tricks on them. They were otherwise perfectly normal in every respect."

"So hallucinations are normal?"

"Sometimes. Look, if it's possible for the brain to trick an amputee into feeling pain in a non-existent digit, why is it abnormal for the brain to trick someone into thinking they are having a conversation with someone who isn't there?"

"Alright, I take your point, but I see a big difference between remnant nerve sensations and vivid recollections of things that never happened."

Damon laughed, and signaled for another coffee. "Mike Turner, brilliant surgeon, ever the rationalist. You surgeons are all materialists – everything has a physical explanation. Problem is, the brain is infinitely more complicated than any other body part. There are no great mysteries left in the small intestine, Mike.

But the brain, Mike, that is a vast unexplored wilderness. I am an explorer in that wilderness. There is no mystery in a spleen. But a woman who thinks Jesus lives in her closet, now that is a true wonder."

Both men laughed. Turner ordered another coffee.

"Damon, I'm surprised. I thought you were a materialist. Could it be that the great psychiatrist has a spiritual side?"

"I used to be a pure materialist, like you," replied Damon. "Everything had an explanation, a biological or chemical answer. Now, I consider myself a dualist. I think we can explain 90 percent of human behavior using genetics, formulas, chemicals, reactions, and hormones. The other ten percent is a mystery to us. Any honest neuroscientist will tell you that."

Damon took another sip of his coffee.

"Have you ever read anything by Oliver Sacks," asked Damon.

"Love him," replied Turner. "He's my second favorite neuroscientist, after you."

"Sacks once described an incident that took place in the 1960's," continued Damon. "A couple he knew spent the afternoon at his house. They had tea, and a lengthy conversation. They left his house after a lovely afternoon. Except it didn't happen. They were never there, Mike. The whole thing was a vivid, tactile, hallucination. It simply never happened. And Oliver Sacks was many things, but lunatic was not one of those things."

"Fair enough, but couldn't some of those things be caused by mind-altering drugs?"

"Of course. But the Civil War soldiers hadn't taken mind-altering drugs. The lady with Jesus in her closet hasn't taken drugs. Most of the dreams we have every day aren't caused by drugs. Sometimes it's something else, Mike."

"So hallucinations aren't necessarily a sign of impending mental deterioration?"

"I didn't say that. Look, every human on this planet is a few loose connections from the nuthouse. Some of those loose connections are more dangerous than others."

Neither man spoke. Turner swirled his coffee in his cup. Damon looked for the server, and cleared his throat.

"Look Mike, this isn't about Tracy's cousin, is it?"

"No."

"Is Tracy okay?"

"Yeah, she's fine."

"Are you okay?"

"Of course I'm fine, Damon. Remember what you said about me after our first-year med-school exams? 'Your brain is a steel trap, Turner. Nothing gets in or out.'"

Damon laughed. "If you weren't okay, would you tell me?"

"Yes, I would. I trust you."

"Good. Listen, Hillman and I were talking about you yesterday."

"Oh? What did Hillman want?"

"Not much. He just asked me how you were doing, and whether we had talked about you making a move for chief of surgery."

"Why was Hillman asking you?"

"He knows we're close. That's all."

"I'm meeting with Roger on Friday. I plan on throwing my hat in the ring for chief."

"Good. Roger will be happy to hear that."

Turner stood up. "Thanks for taking the time, Damon. I've got some work to do before my shift, and you have to deal with Jesus in the closet."

"Tell Tracy I said hi. Tell her I don't want any more calls about her cousin."

"Will do."

Turner strode out of the coffee shop. Damon Lee watched his friend walk away before pulling out his cell phone and punching in a number. He looked furtively around the coffee shop while he waited for the phone to ring.

CHAPTER 28

After Henry returned home, Dangerfield stayed at the Jennings farm. At night he slept in Harriet's cabin, sleeping alone in her bed.

Harriet spent most nights in a cabin she shared with Jericho and two other women. She slept in the main house only when Jennings or Carola were sick and needed more help than Lilly could provide alone. But Carola, consumed with grief over the death of her husband, needed constant attention, and Lilly could not take care of her alone. Lilly tended to the newly-widowed Carola during the day, while Harriet and four other slave women cooked, washed and cleaned the house. At night, Harriet remained in the house and kept watch over Carola, bringing her tea and sitting with her while she cried herself to sleep. When she had a few minutes during the day, Harriet would return to her cabin, check on Jericho, and sleep for an hour or so before resuming her duties in the house.

Dangerfield spoke to her just a few times in the first few days after Jennings was buried. Once, he saw her talking with Jericho in the cabin as he returned from the fields. He kissed her, and wrapped his arms around her waist. She lingered but only briefly, saying she had to get back to the house to attend to her mistress.

Another time, he had returned to the cabin in the late afternoon to find Harriet sound asleep in her bed. He crawled in beside her, and she turned toward him, half asleep. She opened her eyes, and smiled at him. "I knew you'd come back," she said dreamily. "Told Lilly she was wrong." He moved his hand up and felt her swollen breast quiver, but then he heard voices outside the cabin. He asked her about the baby, but she had turned, and was already asleep. He got up, smiled at her, and left. He recalled these two encounters during the next few days, when he did not see her at all.

Lilly, Harriet and the other women waited on the stream of guests who came to pay their respects and offer condolences to the new widow. After a week, the visitors had stopped coming, and an uneasy, fearful calm returned to the main house. None of the house slaves knew for certain what would become of them, but they all had theories, based on bits of overheard conversation between Carola and her visitors. Some thought Carola might scatter the family and sell them all to pay the debts Jennings had incurred. Others suspected Carola would simply hire an overseer and things would continue as they were. Some suspected that Carola, still pretty and much younger than her dead husband, would quickly remarry, giving them a new master to deal with.

Harriet initially thought that Carola would sell all the house girls except Lilly, and keep the field slaves to work the farm. After spending a week in the house, Harriet rejected that theory – Carola required constant attention, day and night. If anything, she needed even more house servants now that Jennings was dead. After the first week, no one had been sold. No slave auctioneers had come to the house to inspect teeth, measure hips, squeeze breasts or count the number of whip marks before bidding on new inventory. No screaming children had been torn from their mother's arms and loaded into a wagon bound for a new master, while the powerless father watched. The house servants began to allow themselves the quiet possibility that nothing would change, that life as they knew it would go on just as it had, only better, without Jennings.

The field slaves entertained no such thoughts. With no master to direct their work, and no one to punish the miscreants, some quickly began plotting their escape. Lilly, who had often served as an unofficial overseer, was preoccupied with Carola, and rarely left the house. Four days after Jennings was buried, Dangerfield was coming in from repairing fences when he overheard two stable hands, Micah and Andrew, discussing how they would escape to Canada. Micah, coal-black and thin as a five-penny nail, had met a white man in Warrenton three months ago while Micah was delivering one of Jennings' old mares to a buyer. The man claimed to know people who could get them to Canada.

"How you plan on getting to Warrenton with no master?" asked Dangerfield.

"Got a plan," replied Micah. "Folks in town know Marse send me into town from time to time to sell some of his horses. Folks know Marse dead. I jes' tell 'em Mistress asked me and Andrew to take two horses into town and sell 'em. We tie 'em up in town, leave 'em, and make our way to the man who takes us to Canada."

"What about him," said Dangerfield, pointing a finger at Andrew, who was about five inches shorter than Micah. Andrew's skin was the color of weak tea. He was freckle-faced and round-bellied, and appeared to be as wide around as he was tall. His tattered and thin shirt did not cover his ample midsection, allowing a thick slab of belly fat to roll over the top of his breeches.

"Got that figured too," said Micah. "Man can't ride two horses at once. Mistress want make sure them horses get into town. Take two men to ride two horses."

"Folks in town won't take kindly to seeing two of our kind on horseback, free or slave," said Dangerfield. "Might be better to ride one and have the other one tied up. 'Sides, ain't no one going to believe that Mistress sent that one to ride a horse," said Dangerfield, pointing at the corpulent Andrew.

"No time for that," said Andrew, patting his belly. "We ride 'em both in. Mistress won't know, and Lilly ain't been around. Time anyone gets wind, we ought to be North."

Micah hitched up his dirty breeches around his bony waist and eyed Dangerfield.

"You ain't plannin' on tellin' Mistress Carola, are you?" said Micah. "Bout us leavin'?"

"Don't aim to tell Mistress Carola, or anyone else 'bout your plans. "I've never spoken one word to Mistress Carola in all the time I been here. All my business was with Jennings. Fact is, I ain't never been in the house."

"Well, now that Old Man Whipcord is dead, I don't suppose you plan on stayin' either," said Micah.

"I aim to stay for a bit," said Dangerfield. "I promised Harriet and Jericho I'd stick around."

"Well, what you plan on doin' when Mistress sells Harriet and that boy," said Andrew. "You ought leave now, and take Harriet and that boy with you," he said as he slapped at a black fly that landed on his fat belly.

"Hadn't considered that," said Dangerfield. 'Sides, I still have family nearby. Don't want to leave them, neither."

"Family, huh," scoffed Micah. "Henry Newby treat you like family?"

"Far as I know," said Dangerfield. "Ain't never had any other family."

"You a damn fool if you ain't considered leavin' for Canada," huffed Micah, tightening the waist of his breeches." "I bet Henry Newby sell you in a heartbeat if the price is right. I know Jennings woulda sold us off in a minute if somebody made him a proper offer. Hell, he sold his own children."

"So I heard," said Dangerfield. "Sold two of his boys he had by Lilly."

"Sold 'em without even tellin' Lilly," said Micah. "Had traders ride out to the cabins and take 'em while Lilly was in the house. She came back to the cabins and her boys had been sold. Henry Newby do the same thing to you, if you ain't careful. Ain't a white slaver alive puts his family over money. Not one. Every white man got a price. You ain't family to him."

"Reckon I spent more time with Henry than you," said Dangerfield. "'Sides, I made promises, and I aim to keep 'em. Henry won't sell me."

"He didn't have no problem rentin' you out, but you don't think he'll sell you?" taunted Micah. "You are a damn fool. If Henry can get more from selling than renting, he would sell you real quick. You ought to take Harriet and that boy to Canada. If the boy's too much trouble, jes' take Harriet."

Dangerfield pondered what Micah had said, then shook his head. "Even if I was to leave, I wouldn't leave Jericho behind," said Dangerfield. "No tellin' what would happen to him."

"And you stayin' won't help him neither," said Andrew. "You can't prevent Mistress or anyone else from sellin' him. You ought to come with us tomorrow.

Man in Warrenton says he knows houses where we can hide, and they take us North bit by bit, house by house. We'll be in Canada in two months."

"Well, I ain't going anywhere, least not yet. Henry and Elsey'd worry, and I don't know where I would go, especially with Harriet in her condition."

"Suit yourself," said Micah. "Me and Andrew, we aim to be gone this time tomorrow." Micah turned to walk away, and then turned again to face Dangerfield. "You ought to come with us. Take Harriet with you, and the boy, if it suits you. All of us be in Canada in two months."

"I heard they let coloreds buy houses in Canada, jes' like white people," said Andrew. "'Magine that, all of us in a house, like free men."

Dangerfield pondered for a moment.

"How you know any of this is true?" said Dangerfield.

"White man I know in Warrenton told me," said Micah. "They got houses where they hide us until we get to Canada."

"What if you get caught?" said Dangerfield.

"Won't be no different than it is now. We get caught, they jes' send us back here," said Andrew, slapping at another fly on his belly.

"Wouldn't bet on that," said Dangerfield. "You get caught, first they whip you, then they brand you, and then Mistress Carola will sell you South. Mistress Carola won't just let you back like nothing happened."

"Don't matter," said Micah. "We all better off someplace else, whip or no whip."

Andrew and Micah returned to the stable. Dangerfield watched them leave, then headed for Harriet's cabin.

⸺⸺•((◦))•⸺⸺

While Harriet was occupied in the main house, Dangerfield took Jericho into the fields with him. Dangerfield's leg had healed, and he now walked with only a slight limp. Dangerfield showed the boy how set fence posts so they were plumb, and taught him how to drive nails without bending them. Jericho was an eager, if not distracted assistant. Once, while setting posts, Dangerfield had asked the boy to hold the post upright so Dangerfield could make it plumb. When Jericho did not respond, Dangerfield looked up and saw him sitting in the grass ten feet away, holding a thick black snake. The snake writhed and curled around the boy's skinny arms, slithering over his wrists before Jericho, laughing and giggling, could scoop it up and then hold it by its tail. Other times, Dangerfield spotted the boy simply staring into the distance, beyond the fences and confines of the Jennings farm.

One morning while setting fences, Dangerfield asked Jericho to hand him a nail. When Jericho did not respond, Dangerfield turned and saw Jericho staring into the sky.

"What you lookin' at, boy?"

"Clouds," said Jericho.

"Why?" said Dangerfield. "Ain't nothing to look at. We got work to do."

"Clouds go where they want," said Jericho. "Clouds is free. Go where they want, and don't have to mind nobody," said Jericho dreamily.

"Boy, stop that nonsense, and hand me them nails so we can finish before dark." Jericho clumsily handed him a nail, but continued looking skyward. "Clouds is free," Dangerfield muttered to himself.

After finishing the fences, Dangerfield and Jericho went to work in the barn repairing the stall Old Bull had destroyed. Dangerfield had not set foot in the barn since the day Old Bull killed Jennings.

Wood fragments were scattered everywhere. Two splintered oak boards lay just outside the entrance to the stall, with the nails facing up. The side slats were bowed out, and Dangerfield ran his hand over the spot where Old Bull had tried to crush him against the boards. Someone had nailed up two thin boards at the end of the stall to keep Old Bull from wandering around the barn when he returned from the pasture. The branding irons were still on the ground. A large dark spot on the ground spread from the barn wall out to the middle of the floor. Dangerfield saw long strands of hair and a thick glob of dark reddish material in the center of the spot. He closed his eyes, turned around, and went to retrieve a spade from the other side of the barn.

"Here boy," he said to Jericho, "why don't you get some dirt from the pasture and cover up that spot over here. Fetch a bucket, and don't stop till that spot is all covered."

"What is this," said Jericho.

"Just a spot. Fetch the dirt and cover it up. Mind them boards and nails."

Jericho returned with the bucket of dirt and began spreading it over the dark spot while Dangerfield picked up the broken boards. Jericho silently scattered the dirt for a few minutes before speaking.

"How long you gon' stay with us?"

"Long as there's work to be done. Why?"

"Ain't no work has to be done. Ain't no master to make us work."

"Plenty of work to be done," said Dangerfield. "Look at this barn. Someone has to feed them horses. Cows need to be milked. Corn needs to be planted. Corn needs to be picked. What you plan on doing if you don't work?"

"You don't own the barn, the horses, or the cows," said Jericho evenly. "Ain't none of this yours. So why you tend after 'em if they ain't yours?"

Jericho stared coolly at Dangerfield. "Ain't nothin' in this barn belong to me. Ain't nothin' belongs to you. Nothin' keeps you here. Nothin's for me here neither."

"Well, boy, you got any ideas on what to do now that Marse is dead?"

"I aim to leave, like I tried doin' before."

"And from what I hear, you got caught both times, and whipped good to show for it," said Dangerfield.

"Ain't no one to whip me now."

"Lilly is still here. From what I've seen, she don't spare the whip. 'Specially on you."

"Lilly won't whip me. Not with Marse dead, and not with you here."

"That may be, but I can't help you if you run away. You give any thought to what happens to you outside that fence?"

"I just know I won't get whipped no more."

"Maybe not by Marse or Lilly," replied Dangerfield. "No tellin' what might happen if you get caught by someone else. They'd catch you and sell you someplace else. You want to leave your momma like that?"

"I'd take her with me. Momma thought about runnin' more than once."

Dangerfield paused before speaking.

"Don't think your momma going anywhere for awhile. Not in her condition."

"You mean 'cause of the baby, she can't run?"

"I mean 'cause of the baby, and she got no reason to run now."

Jericho spread more dirt on the ground. He flipped a small stone with the end of the shovel.

"Momma's afraid you won't come back next time you go back home to Marse Henry," said Jericho excitedly. "She think you might go home and leave her here."

"She tell you that? When?"

"Last time you went back to Marse Henry," said Jericho. "She said she didn't think you was comin' back."

Dangerfield picked up one of the oak boards and tossed it softly against the barn wall.

"Did I tell you I would bring you some boots to wear?"

"Yes."

"Did I bring 'em?"

"I s'pose," said Jericho, casting his eyes on the ground.

"Did I tell you and your momma I'd come back?"

Jericho did not respond.

"I aim to keep my word. And if I say I'm coming back, I will, unless I'm dead or dying. Ain't no need for you or your momma to worry about that."

Jericho kept looking at the dark spot on the ground.

"Lilly told momma you weren't comin' back," said Jericho, not lifting his eyes. "Lilly said a man can't have two homes. She said since you already got a home with Marse Henry, you werent' comin' back here. Lilly told momma to forget 'bout you. I heard her talkin' after you left last time."

Dangerfield picked up another board and hurled it against the wall. It bounced back several feet, and caromed off the corner of Old Bull's stall, almost hitting Jericho where he stood. Jericho jumped back.

Dangerfield knelt next to the boy.

"I just told you, I keep my promises," said Dangerfield in a low whisper. "If I don't come back, it means I'm dead or 'bout to be. I know where home is. Tell your momma what I said, if you see her 'fore I do."

Jericho looked up and smiled.

"Now, as far as you runnin' off again, get that notion out of your head. I know where my home is, and so do you. You ain't goin' nowhere without your momma, and she ain't leavin,' so you'd best stay here. You won't last two days on your own. You given any thought to how you'd eat if you ran away?"

"Didn't think about it."

"I know you didn't. Now, finish up covering that spot, so we can go on up to the house."

Jericho resumed his work, then turned when he heard his mother's voice.

"Jericho, I been looking all over for you," said Harriet from the doorway of the barn. "You weren't in the cabin this afternoon when I went to check on you. Been looking for you everywhere. Was afraid you mighta run off."

"Momma!" he shrieked.

"You know I wouldn't let the boy run off," said Dangerfield. "He's been helping me in the fields."

"I see," said Harriet softly. "Thank you for minding him. "I didn't think . . . ."

"You didn't think I'd come back? Didn't think I'd look out for Jericho?"

"No, I knew you'd come back. I just don't see him that much, not with Mistress in her condition. Spend all my time in the house lately. I don't get much sleep . . . ."

Dangerfield looked at Harriet, and in an instant, any anger he had toward her disappeared. Dark lines creased her face, and her eyes were puffy. Her chocolate skin was sallow.

"I'm sorry, Harriet," said Dangerfield.

"Don't matter. I came down here to fetch both of you. Jericho, you come on back to the cabin with me. I can't rest unless I know where you are."

She turned to Dangerfield. "Mistress Carola wants to see you in the house."

"Why?"

"Didn't say. Just told me to fetch you, and send you on up to the house. Says she wants to speak with you. Says you s'pose to knock on the door, and Lilly will show you in."

The three of them left the barn. Harriet and Jericho went to their cabin to sleep, and Dangerfield continued toward the house.

Dangerfield tapped lightly on the front door. No one answered. He knocked again. No response. He was about to leave when Lilly peered through the curtain and opened the door.

"You were s'posed to knock on the kitchen door," she said. "Didn't hear you at first." She looked him over from head to toe. "Take off your hat and come inside."

Dangerfield removed his hat and hesitantly stepped inside.

He had never been inside the Jennings house. The front drawing room was roughly twice the size of the drawing room at Henry's house. Lace curtains covered every window. The wooden floors were smooth and tightly joined, unlike the rough oak planks on the floor of Henry's house that creaked and buckled under weight. Four wooden chairs anchored the corners of the room, and an immense rocking chair in front of the fireplace presided over everything else.

Dangerfield saw four female slaves bustling about the kitchen, each carrying a pot or pan for the next meal. The women barked instructions at each other, and the clatter of pots, pans and utensils filled the house. The smell of fresh bread wafted through the air, and he started walking toward the kitchen, but stopped when he saw Lilly staring at him.

"You act like you ain't never been inside a house," said Lilly.

"Ain't never been in Marse Jennings' house," said Dangerfield, peering up the curving staircase.

"Well, I s'pect you won't be here long. Stay here while I fetch Missus." She turned and started walking up the staircase before turning back.

"Keep your hat off and brush the dirt off you," said Lilly. "You look like you live in a barn." She turned and disappeared up the stairs.

Dangerfield rocked back and forth on his heels, fidgeting with his hat. He had been working all day, and his feet ached, but he knew he couldn't sit in any of the chairs in the drawing room. He closed his eyes and allowed the smell of the bread to soothe his nerves. He wanted nothing more than to sit down in a chair, and smell fresh bread baking inside a comfortable house.

He opened his eyes and saw Carola coming down the steps. Lilly walked in front of her, holding her hand. When they reached the bottom of the stairs, Lilly spoke to Carola.

"There he is, Miss Carola. I'll be in the kitchen if you need me." Lilly gave Dangerfield a long look, then shook her head and disappeared into the kitchen.

Carola stood in front of him and looked him over as though she were inspecting a horse or prize bull. She was slender and about five and half feet tall, with luxuriant dark hair that cascaded over her shoulders. She had penetrating green eyes and a sharp, slender nose that fit her face perfectly. Her creamy skin contrasted with her black widow's dress. Dangerfield saw the outline of her hips as she inspected him, and even the widow's dress could not conceal her figure. She looked to be in her middle 40's, and far too young to be a widow. Dangerfield looked into her eyes only briefly, then stared at his shoes, fearful that her great beauty would expose something evil within him.

"You must be Henry's Newby's man," she said. Her voice was smoky and soft, and she spoke with the tone of a woman accustomed to getting her way without ever raising her voice. "Harriet has told me about you. I understand you might be staying a bit longer than planned."

"I don't know how long I might stay, M'am. That was between Marse Henry and Marse Jennings."

Carola laughed. "Don't think I don't know what's going on in my own home," she said. "I know Harriet is carrying your baby. Harriet tells me everything, you see. There are no secrets between us. She hasn't been herself these last few weeks. Always tired, always needing to sleep. I know some women think carrying a baby is hard work, but Harriet doesn't seem to understand how hard all of this has been on me. After all, I have the responsibility of maintaining the house and the farm by myself now that Augustine is dead. Harriet spends three, sometimes four hours a day sleeping and looking after that boy."

"I know she does her best to look after her boy and you, M'am."

"Well, I should hope so. Truth is, I need Harriet in the house more than ever. At least until I can get things straightened out. That's why I sent after you. I understand Augustine paid Henry for three days per week for your services."

"Yes, M'am."

"Well, I know what happens in the house. Lilly keeps an eye on things for me here, and lets me know what's going on with the house servants. But Augustine was always in charge of the farm. He never wanted an overseer. Said the overseers were always too partial to the slaves. He always wanted to be in charge of discipline."

She sighed, and her body shuddered. "Truth is, I don't know what's going on out there. I always relied on Augustine to manage the farm, and the field slaves, but now . . . ."

She began to cry, and but quickly composed herself.

"So with Harriet carrying your baby, it makes sense for you to be the overseer here. At least until my son arrives from Brentsville. Besides, you want to be close to Harriet and Jericho, don't you?"

"Yes, M'am, I do."

"Of course you do. Starting today, you will be the overseer here, in charge of the field hands. I won't ask you to whip or beat anyone, unless you think it's necessary. Augustine always said he preferred a light hand on the whip. I know how much the field hands admired him, and appreciated his light hand."

Dangerfield remembered the savage beating Jennings had given Jericho, and tried to consider what a heavy hand on the whip would look like.

Dangerfield stared at his shoes. "Happy to help, M'am," he mumbled.

"Very well then," said Carola. "You will stay for the next week, until my son

Lewis and his wife Virginia arrive from Brentsville. He had some important business to attend to in Brentsville after Augustine's funeral, but I expect him to return shortly. Lewis will take over after he arrives. I will send word to Henry Newby that you will be staying longer."

"Yes, M'am."

Carola looked Dangerfield over again, and smiled at him. "I can see why Harriet has taken a liking to you. Let's hope she can get back to work soon. Lilly will see you out." She turned and began to walk away."

"M'am," said Dangerfield.

Carola stopped as if she were not certain she had heard another human voice. She turned, slowly, to face him until her body faced his.

"Is there something else?" she said icily.

"Just that I never been any overseer to anybody. Always took care of myself and my kin, but nobody else. Don't know what you expect from me."

"As I explained, I won't ask you to whip or beat anyone unless you think it's necessary. Just keep an eye on the field hands, and remember, a light hand on the whip instills discipline. And if you hear of anyone plotting to escape, let me or Lilly know. That's all."

"Yes, M'am."

Carola turned toward the staircase. Lilly was waiting for her. Lilly opened the door and escorted Dangerfield outside. He shielded his eyes against the late afternoon sun, put his hat on and walked toward the cabins.

He opened the door to Harriet's cabin and peered in the darkness. Harriet and Jericho were both fast asleep, Harriet on the bed and the boy sprawled next to her. Lilly would be here any minute, rousing Harriet to attend to her duties in the house. He thought about waking her, then decided against it. He would walk down to the barn and finish his work, then come back and wake her if Lilly hadn't awoken her first.

He entered the stable, and saw Andrew and Micah feeding handfuls of oats to a pair of dun-colored mares.

"Well, if it ain't Old Man Reliable, come down to clean stables for his dead master," said Micah, laughing. "You changed your mind about leaving with us?"

"No, I ain't changed my mind," said Dangerfield. "Harriet's in no condition to travel, and it wouldn't take long for Mistress Carola to notice she gone. Besides, folks will notice the five of us traveling together any time."

"Five of us?" said Andrew.

"The two of you, me, Harriet and Jericho. Ain't no way all five of us go anywhere without getting caught."

"Why don't you go with us, and get Harriet later," said Micah.

"I ain't leaving Harriet, not in her condition. Ain't leavin' Jericho, either." Dangerfield looked at the mares eating their oats. "'Sides, Mistress Carola don't hardly let Harriet out of her sight. She can't hardly pass water without Carola asking for her."

"Suit yourself, Old Man Reliable," said Micah. "This time tomorrow, we won't be here."

"You might want to leave sooner than that," said Dangerfield.

"Why?" said Andrew suspiciously.

"Mistress Carola wants me to be the overseer for a spell, until her son gets here. Wants me to keep an eye on the field hands, and tell her if anybody plans on leavin.'"

"Did you say you would?" said Andrew.

"Weren't presented to me as a choice."

Micah circled around the back of one of the mares, which had stopped eating oats to bite at a black fly on its haunches.

"What are you going to tell her? 'Bout us?" said Micah.

"I don't aim to tell her anything. I aim to tell you something. Mistress Carola asked me to be the overseer. Reckon I don't have much choice. She and Lilly are in the house right now. Likely to be there for a while."

Micah crossed his arms and stared at Dangerfield.

"What are you goin' to tell your new mistress, Old Man Reliable? You go from servin' a dead man to servin' the dead man's wife. Ain't you something."

"Reckon you ought to hear what I say to you first," said Dangerfield. "If you two are smart, you ought to leave now, while there's still daylight. Saddle up them mares, and take your town papers with you. Don't go past the house, somebody might hear you. Take the mares behind the stable, and across the creek. Stay in the meadow until you both far enough away from the house so nobody hears you. Get on the path, and get to Warrenton before dark. Won't nobody believe you two got honest business takin' two mares on the road after dark."

Andrew grabbed two saddlebags and stuffed them with oats.

"You both got town papers, right?" said Dangerfield.

"Got 'em right here," said Micah, pulling two crisply folded pieces of paper from one of the saddlebags. His eyes never left Dangerfield.

"Keep those with you, and don't let 'em get wet," said Dangerfield. "I need to finish work on one of the fences, and then check on Harriet and Jericho. You both ought to be gone the next time I come into the stable. Don't give me a reason to tell Carola anything."

Micah looked at Dangerfield and smiled. "Well, Old Man Reliable, you ain't so bad after all. Reckon we'll send word once we get to Canada." Micah and Andrew each hoisted saddles onto their mares, and inspected their saddlebags.

"Reckon you will," said Dangerfield. "Don't expect to see either of you any time soon."

Dangerfield left the stable, took a long walk around Old Bull's pen, and then went back to the cabins to check on Harriet. She was gone. Jericho was still asleep. Dangerfield did not wake him.

He walked slowly back to the stable and opened the door. Andrew, Micah and the mares were gone.

CHAPTER 29

After his meeting with Damon, Turner returned to the hospital to resume his rounds. He would finish his twelve, go home and sleep for a few hours, and then meet with Roger Hillman tomorrow morning at 9:30.

His meeting with Damon strengthened his belief that nothing was wrong with him. "Everyone hallucinates," Turner said to himself out loud as he drove to the hospital after meeting with Damon. "Civil War soldiers, suburban housewives, janitors, even Oliver Sacks. We all do it," he said to himself in his car over the droning voices on his car radio. "Nothing unusual about it."

And in the face of such esteemed and ordinary company, how could anyone say there was something wrong with him? Damon's confident, knowing manner and his assessment that 10 percent of the brain's activity was a mystery provided Turner with all the evidence he needed – there was nothing wrong with his mind. If anything, he was special – his brain operated in the ten percent realm that was still largely a mystery to neuroscientists. But he was different – he would conduct his own experiments, and discover for himself what his dreams meant.

He raced through his rounds, eager to finish so he could go home and explore the next chapter in his personal mental mystery. He felt even more confident in his medical abilities than he had before. He anticipated the questions his residents would ask, and he had the answers ready almost before the question was asked. Questions about anesthesia, surgical procedures, infection risks – he handled them all, precisely and efficiently. Even the residents, jaded and full of unearned cynicism, took note of the ease with which he answered their questions.

Shortly after noon, he was speaking to a young resident about whether to use the femoral, brachial or radial arteries when performing an angiogram. He explained the pros and cons of each technique. As he finished, he spotted Hillman striding toward him.

"Afternoon, Mike. How are you feeling?"

"Fine, Roger," said Turner, perplexed at the question. "Are we still on for tomorrow at 9:30?"

"Absolutely, Mike. I hope you don't mind, but I invited a few folks to our meeting tomorrow. Ed Sorenson, chief of patient services. And Phil Evans, the medical student liaison. And Marcia Harris, chief RN."

"Sounds like you brought the band together, Roger. If I didn't know better, I might think this was a final interview."

"It isn't. I just wanted to have a few more people sit in on our meeting. Just to visit with you. Just to confirm . . . ." Hillman's voice trailed off. "Never mind. We are still on for tomorrow morning at 9:30. See you then."

"Thanks, Roger. See you tomorrow."

Turner wondered why Hillman had invited so many people to what was supposed to be an informal meeting. Although it was no secret that Roger Hillman was retiring, the chief of surgery position had not been posted nationwide. No one had been formally interviewed for the job, and Hillman would have the job for almost another year. And why had Hillman asked him how he was feeling?

"I just need some sleep," Turner thought to himself. "Get ready for tomorrow."

Turner breezed through his afternoon and evening rounds. He sat in on a resident performing his first procedure, removal of a small skin lesion. He gave a short presentation to the residents about a new and dangerous strain of staph recently discovered. After checking in on a few more residents, he finished his patient rounds and headed home.

Tracy was in her studio when he arrived at home.

"Didn't think you'd still be up," he said.

"Working on a piece for one of my favorite clients," she said. "It's taking longer than I thought. How was your day?"

"Marvelous. I am meeting with Hillman tomorrow, along with the chief of patient services, the med student liaison, and the chief RN."

"Wow. This sounds like a formal interview."

"Not really. Although Hillman told me the job is mine if I want it. Nothing has been decided."

"Why would Hillman invite all those people if he weren't grooming you for the job?"

"Don't know, but I have a really good feeling about tomorrow. I went to med school with the patient services chief, the med student liaison is one of my former residents, and I helped the chief RN out of a jam when she was new. She owes me one."

"Should we celebrate? Break out that really good wine we bought in Napa last year?"

"Let's wait until tomorrow. Hopefully we will have something to celebrate." He sat on the couch and took off his shoes. Tracy sat next to him and softly rubbed his thigh.

"How did your meeting with Damon go this morning?" she said.

"Well, Damon says I am not crazy, so everything must be fine."

"I'm not certain Damon is the best judge of crazy."

"You know those dreams I've been having? Well, everyone has dreams like that. Some range of hallucinations is normal. Civil War soldiers used to feel pain in non-existent limbs. Oliver Sacks had vivid conversations with people who weren't there. Damon has a patient who thinks Jesus lives in her closet. It happens to everyone."

"Yes, but those dreams don't sound normal. Just because someone thinks Jesus lives in her closet doesn't make it normal. Did Damon say anything else?"

"Yes. 90 percent of human activity is readily explained. The other ten percent is a mystery. I am a proud member of the ten percent group. Oh, and we are all a few loose connections away from the psych ward."

"Well, that's refreshing. Why don't you get some sleep. We can celebrate tomorrow after your successful meeting."

"Good idea. Let me have one of your pills before I hit the sack."

Tracy's face darkened. "Mike, that's not a good idea. You know what happens after you take the sleeping pills. It triggers those dreams. You don't want this, Mike. Not now. This is a really bad idea. Not before your meeting with Hillman."

"That is exactly why I want to take one tonight. I have a medical problem to solve, only this time I am the patient. For whatever reason, those pills enable me to see things. Real things, Tracy. Things that actually happened, except I wasn't there. But the pills enable me to watch these events unfold, even though they happened a long time ago. This is huge, Tracy. What if I can discover some new medical phenomenon? What if there is some part of the brain that allows us to see into the past, with a little help from modern chemicals? What if long-dead memories can be resurrected? I don't want to wait."

Tracy reached into her purse and pulled out a pack of cigarettes. She flipped it open, and pulled out a cigarette. Her hands trembled as she fumbled with her lighter.

"I thought you quit for good?"

"I just started up again. God, Mike, this is scary. I didn't mind you taking the pills at first. But now . . . ." She lit up and took a long drag.

"Mike, you don't really know what happened in that dream," she continued. "We don't know if any of this is real."

"But it is real. I saw the newspaper article. You saw it. Those men in my dream were real. I saw them in the dream. And you saw their pictures in the paper."

"Maybe it's just a coincidence. Maybe someone told you that story a long time ago, and the newspaper article just triggered a remnant memory. Maybe it's all in your subconscious. Maybe this is just old memories."

"Maybe," countered Turner, hands behind his head. "Or maybe the pills are a portal to a part of the brain we don't yet understand. Maybe that ten percent of the brain we don't understand is capable of seeing into the future, or recreating long-ago events. This could be huge, Tracy. And I want to be the first to figure it out. I – we – could be on the cusp of discovering something huge."

Tracy exhaled twin plumes of smoke. "A portal to the part of the brain we don't understand? Seeing into the future, re-creating the past? Jesus, Mike, this sounds like something from Star Trek. I can't believe I hear you saying these things. It makes no sense. You're supposed to be the rational one, and I'm the dreamer. I don't want to be the responsible one."

Turner stood up and held his wife's trembling hand.

"Alright, let's approach this rationally. How many times have I taken those pills?"

"Three or four times, maybe."

"And each time, I had some crazy dream, right?"

"Yes."

"Did I ever hurt anyone during those dreams?"

"No."

"Did I ever hurt you?"

"No, Mike, but . . . ."

"Were you with me each time I took those pills?"

Tracy sighed. "Yes."

"Did you ever notice anything wrong with me after I had taken the pills? Sweating, shortness of breath, uncontrollable physical reactions, vomiting, violent reactions toward you?"

"No, but I was sleeping too. If you had any of those symptoms, I would not have noticed."

"Did you ever notice any of those symptoms after we woke up?"

"I guess not."

"If you had noticed any of those symptoms, would you have called 911?"

"Of course, but . . . ."

"And you never worried about me before giving me the pills?"

"Mike this is silly. If I had thought anything was wrong, I would have called 911."

"Right. And you haven't worried about me since I started taking the pills, right?"

"Not until now."

"And I never hurt you, or presented a danger to myself, right?"

Tracy exhaled smoke and sighed. "No," she said softly.

"Okay, let's do this. I take one of the pills tonight, as an experiment. You can stay up and watch me. If you notice something weird – some unusual physical symptoms – call 911 right away, and I will never take those pills again. The whole experiment ends."

"Let me get this straight – you take a sleeping pill, and I get to stay up all night and watch you sleep? Lucky gal, I am."

"Trace, this could be huge. I'm not a dreamer. I don't believe in any god. I believe in science and reason. But I also know what I saw. I saw those men driving. I saw Billy wrap his car around a tree. I saw Billy and the old man shoot those guys, and put them in a truck. I saw that guy who looked like Dangerfield when we were in Harpers Ferry. It all happened, Trace. And I need to find out why."

Tracy stubbed her cigarette into a glass on the coffee table. She reached into her purse and pulled out the pill container. She flipped the container toward him, and he caught it with one hand. She pulled out another cigarette, and walked toward the kitchen.

"I still think this is a bad idea, the day before you meet with Hillman and the others," said Tracy. "Don't do this, not now. Wait until tomorrow night, after the meeting."

"No," countered Turner. "I need to do this now, so I have no doubt before the meeting. I need to have absolute confidence that I know what is happening to me, and why. I can't meet with Hillman not knowing what is happening to me."

"I can't convince you of anything," said Tracy wearily. "Guess I'd better make a pot of coffee, since I'll be up all night." She turned toward him and smiled. "Once again, you owe me, Michael Turner."

"Always will. Why don't you make that coffee, and come on back to bed. I need you to be fully awake for this experiment to work."

Tracy made coffee while Turner undressed. Tracy returned to the bedroom with a mug, and sat next to Turner while he got comfortable. He popped one of the pills, and took a swallow of water. Tracy caressed his forehead. "Sweet dreams," she whispered. Turner kissed her on the mouth, and quietly drifted off to an unknown place to continue his experiment.

—————

Turner is naked, and standing outside of a grand white house. A thin blanket of snow covers the ground. He watches the sun drag itself up from behind a distant ridge, throwing light on the house and a nearby stable. A dozen or so horses are tied up at the stable, nickering and snorting in the morning chill. A large group of well-dressed men mills about the house, speaking quietly among themselves. A stout black woman with gray hair moves among the men, offering them cups of coffee and warm bread. The coffee steams in the chill air, and Turner can smell the warm bread being passed.

The woman distributes the rest of the coffee and bread, and retreats into the house. The men grow silent. Some pull documents out of their coat pockets, muttering to themselves while reading. Others pace silently in the yard, heads down, moving quietly amongst each other. Some of the men seem to know each other, but most now keep their heads down, avoiding eye contact or conversation. Boots crunch in the crusted snow. The front door opens and a slim man in a threadbare gray suit appears. His face is deeply creased, and his mustache is equal parts black and gray. He clears his throat and addresses the group

"Good morning gentlemen," he says hoarsely. Many of you know me, or at least you knew my father. For those I know, welcome. For those I don't, I trust your journey here was safe. I know some of you have come from as far as Louisiana." The man pulls at a loose thread on his coat, and as he does, a button falls off his coat and bounces off the porch into the snow.

"As some of you may know, my father passed away unexpectedly in 1848, after a tragic accident. Since then, my mother and I have been running the farm with a varying number of field slaves and house servants." The man puts his head down and closes his eyes. "Unfortunately, our affairs have taken a turn for the worse, a fact which is neither your concern nor your problem. I can assure you that my father always paid his debts, and I intend to do the same."

"At any rate, my present misfortune is your gain, because today, with great reluctance, I am selling several of my prized house servants along with several strong young field bucks, and a young child. I can assure all of you that the house servants are docile, well-trained, and capable of providing any service you gentlemen may need inside your homes. And the field slaves are equally well trained, having been disciplined at an early age by one of my father's trusted overseers."

"The lot for sale includes six slaves in all. An adult female house servant, two young field bucks, two young female house servants, and the child, a boy who I can assure you will grow tall and strong on relatively little rations. The adult female is the mother of all the children. The father of the children was my father's overseer, and he trained his children very well. You need not worry about the father trying to reclaim his family, because he is dead. The lot originally included another young buck, also the son of the adult female, but circumstances required me to sell him earlier than I had hoped."

"I would prefer that any buyer purchase the lot, so as to keep the family intact and improve morale and discipline, but of course, I understand that some of you don't want or cannot afford the entire lot of six, so I am willing to sell each individually. And with that, let us begin the inspection."

Turner watched as the men pressed closer to the front porch. A tall woman emerged from the house sobbing, cradling a child in her arms. Next to emerge were two young dark-skinned black girls, tall and gangly, eyes red from weeping. And then two young men, lean and hard, staring coldly at the assembled mass. One of the young men clenched his fist as he emerged from the house. Turner saw him unclench his fist and say something to the other young man before taking his place on the porch. Each stood on the porch, the mother holding the baby, and the other four standing several feet apart.

"And now, gentlemen, please take a moment to inspect the inventory, and then we shall open the bidding," said the man in the gray suit.

The men jostled for position near the porch, calling out their requests. "Have that one turn around so I can see her ass," cried one. "Have the buck over there take off his shirt and turn around, back facing me," called out another. The men began swarming the porch, fighting for the best view of the black human flesh displayed for sale.

"Gentlemen, I can assure you they are not going anywhere," pleaded the man in the gray suit. "Please be careful so as not to damage my house or the inventory," he cried hoarsely.

One of the men jumped over the porch railing and spun the adult woman toward him. She jumped back and pulled her child close to her body, cradling the child in one arm. The man grabbed her other arm, pulled her toward him, and shoved his hand under her dress. "Need to see if this one can still feed a child" he said as he pushed his hand further up her dress.

The young man with the clenched fist ran over to protect his mother. He grabbed the man's coat collar, spun him around, and knocked him off the porch with a short hard right to the man's jaw. The man spun sideways and hit the railing before falling into the crowd below.

The mass was now swarming, with some men trying to storm the porch. The second young man stood in front of his mother, swinging wildly at any assailants who tried to grab her. The two girls kicked at a man who tried to approach them while their mother pulled the baby closer to her, shielded by her son.

A shot rang out. The crowd pushed away from the porch. Turner saw the man in the gray suit holding a pistol in his hand, gunsmoke curling from the barrel.

"Gentlemen, I assure you what you just saw was not what you should expect from any of this lot," he said quietly. "I will ensure that this one," he said pointing to the young man who struck his mother's assailant "is firmly disciplined."

"I will pay $3000 for the entire lot of six," said a voice from the back of the crowd. All heads turned toward the speaker.

A tall man with an enormous belly and a pistol hanging off his belt spoke again. "$3,000 for the entire lot, Jennings, and that includes that 'un there," he said, pointing to the young man who defended his mother. "I don't worry none about discipline. I take care of that better than you have, apparently. And I like the young bucks to have some fight in 'em. Gives me something to work with."

No one moved while everyone looked at the speaker.

"What will it be, Jennings? $3,000 for the whole lot. I keep the family intact, 'improve morale and discipline' as you say, and I take that troublemaker off your hands. Getting rid of that one ought to make it worthwhile for you. Take it now, or I take the first train back to Louisiana."

The man in the gray suit put his pistol back in his coat pocket. "Sold for $3,000 to the gentleman from Louisiana, the entire lot of six. You come with me, and we will complete the necessary documents."

The new owner strode through the crowd, stepped onto the porch and shook hands with Jennings. The two men exchanged quiet words, and entered the house. The stout black woman ushered the woman and her kids back into the house. The crowd began to disperse, and Turner watched as the men slowly walked toward their tethered horses.

Turner is suddenly lifted upward. His arms don't move. He continues upward, toward the morning sun. He tries to break free, but nothing happens. He stops ascending, and for a moment hangs suspended in the air. He begins plummeting toward the earth. He lets out a scream from deep within, trying to free himself from some unknown force, this malevolent thing that has taken hold of his body. His scream echoes off the side of the house. He is falling faster now. He holds out his arms, and braces himself.

⊰⊱●⊰⊱

Turner awakes with a splitting headache. He tries moving his arms. Nothing. His legs won't move. He is in a room that is familiar, but it is not his room. He looks down at his body. He is wearing a thin blue hospital gown. He looks up and sees Tracy, Damon, Roger Hillman, and several nurses milling about the room. He groans.

Hillman hears him, walks over, and touches him on the arm.

"Welcome back, Mike. You gave us quite a scare. Rest up, and we can talk tomorrow. You are going to be here for a while."

CHAPTER 30

The morning after Micah and Andrew left, Dangerfield awoke earlier than usual. He kept waiting for the sound of horses coming down the path, the slavers returning with Andrew and Micah tied together. He didn't know much about Canada or how long it took to get there, but he hoped Andrew and Micah would make it. Harriet once told him there were more slave-catchers on the road to Warrenton than anywhere else in Virginia. She and the other Jennings slaves heard rumors that the slavers patrolled all night, torches blazing, inspecting every ditch, every shack and shanty along the road, hoping to round up fugitives and sell them to the highest bidder.

Having papers and traveling during the day helped. When she sent her house servants into town to pick up supplies, Carola told them to keep their papers safe, and have them ready if the slavers or deputies stopped them. Carola once told Harriet that Jennings paid every slaver and constable in town, and they were all on notice not to confiscate any of Jennings' inventory. Now that Jennings was dead, Dangerfield wondered if the slavers would honor the agreements.

He slid quietly out of the bunk he shared with Harriet, careful not to wake her. He pulled on his boots, and looked at Jericho. The boy was sprawled across his bunk, snoring softly, with a glistening trail of spittle running down his chin. Neither Harriet nor Jericho moved. He gave them a long look, and slipped out the door toward the stable.

He stopped at the creek to wash his face and shave. He found a deep pool behind a rock pile where the water moved slowly enough for him to see his face. Foam swirled in the eddy behind the rocks. He took off his boots and pants and waded slowly into the water. He splashed his face, then pulled his soap out of a leather pouch Henry had given him. He set the pouch on the rock pile and lathered his face, then pulled out his razor. He looked into the water. Someone he did not recognize stared back at him, someone with Henry's face, and Elsey's skin color, but not quite like either of them.

At home, there was only one mirror in the house, in the room where Henry and Elsey slept. Dangerfield and his siblings got to look in the mirror once each week, on Sunday mornings before church. Now that he was spending more and more time at the Jennings farm, Dangerfield realized that it had been days since he had clearly seen his own face. The man looking back at him seemed older than the one he remembered.

He finished shaving, and washed his face. He emerged from the creek and resumed his walk toward the stable when he heard distant hoofbeats on the road. He waited for the sound of the baying dogs and the loud voices of the men who owned them. The hoofbeats became clearer as they got closer. A single rider, coming from the direction of Warrenton, riding at a brisk trot. He heard no dogs, and no human voices, just the steady double-clip of the hooves on the road. He turned and walked back toward the house.

When he arrived, he saw a slender man in his mid to late 20's, dismounting from a thickly muscled bay Morgan. The man wore a slim, elegant gray riding suit, and black gloves. A wispy, nascent mustache covered his upper lip. Dangerfield watched him dismount.

"Oats and water for the horse, and then groom him with a heavy wet brush," said the man, handing Dangerfield his black gloves. Dangerfield said nothing, and took the Morgan by the reins. The man studied Dangerfield.

"A bit old to be a groom, aren't you? My father always preferred young boys as his grooms. They seem to be easier on the horses."

"Not a groom by trade, Marse, but I am pretty good with horses," said Dangerfield. "I'll take this one down to the stable right away." The young man continued to study Dangerfield.

"When did my father buy you? You don't meet the description of anyone on my father's list."

"I don't live here, Marse, and your father never did buy me," replied Dangerfield. "I belong to Marse Henry Newby. Marse Jennings paid Marse Henry for my time and my services. I take care of things here for your family."

"I see. And what do you do for my family, if you aren't the groom?"

"Anything needs to be done, Marse. Fix fences, clean stables, fix the barn, butcher hogs. Anything needs to be done, I do it. Marse Jennings paid Marse Henry for my time."

"How long have you been here?"

"Don't know exactly. Been comin' regular for a month, maybe two."

"How much did my father pay for your services?"

"Don't know, Marse. That was business 'tween Marse Henry and Marse Jennings."

The young man eyed Dangerfield up and down.

"How much does Henry want for you? If I wanted to buy you?"

"Don't know, Marse. You'd have to ask Marse Henry."

"Yes, of course you wouldn't know that." The man folded his hands behind his back and rocked gently on his heels.

"I am Lewis Jennings, Augustine's son. I assume you know about my father's accident."

"Yes, Marse, I do. I was there when it happened."

"You were?" Lewis' voice squeaked. "I assume you tried to save him from that rampaging animal."

"Did what I could, Marse." Dangerfield saw no point in explaining that Jennings had tried to kill him by ordering him in the bull's pen.

"Yes, of course you did. And how long will you be staying with us, now that my father is dead? Has Henry Newby made arrangements for you to stay here?"

"Don't know 'bout any arrangements, Marse. Mistress Carola asked me to stay for awhile. Said something about being the overseer."

"Overseer?" Lewis' voice softened. "Well, you must be trustworthy if my mother wants you as overseer. You must have tried to save my father."

"Did what I could, Marse."

The big Morgan stamped his hooves and shook his head, rattling the reins in Dangerfield's hand.

"I'd better get him on to the stable, Marse. Oats, water, and a heavy wet brush."

"Yes, of course," said Lewis. "I have some business to attend to inside with my mother. Get the horse in the stable, and I will come down later when I need you."

Lewis turned and strode toward the house. Dangerfield took the Morgan by the reins and walked him toward the stable.

Dangerfield talked to the horse while he brushed him.

"Well, Old Man, don't know what to make of this Lewis. Don't seem as bad as Marse Jennings, but can't tell too much right now."

He continued brushing the horse, pushing hard with the brush until the Morgan's black mane shone, and the dapples in his coat shimmered. Dangerfield had worked up a sweat, and he wiped his brow with his shirt sleeve.

"Well, Old Man, you don't look so bad now. Reckon I ought to brush old Solomon the same way, so he don't get jealous. Might think I like you more than him."

Jericho entered the stable.

"You ought not talk to horses as much," said Jericho. "Folks start to think somethin' wrong with you."

"Hey, boy, where you been?"

"Out by the chicken coop, gettin' eggs for supper. Jes' came back from the house."

"Where's your Mama?"

"In the house with Mistress Carola and Marse Lewis. Mama told me to come get you. Marse Lewis wants you to come up to the house."

Dangerfield wiped his brow, and tucked his shirt in before walking to the house. When he arrived, Lewis was standing outside.

"Day, Marse."

"Yes. I spoke with my mother, who explained everything about your . . . situation. Seems you've made yourself quite at home since you've been here."

Dangerfield clutched his hat before speaking.

"I've worked hard since I've been here, Marse. Look at them fences, the shed, the chicken coop . . . ."

"That's not what I meant, although no one seems to question the quality of your work. I am talking about our house girl Harriet, who is rumored to be carrying your child. Is that possible?"

"Yes, Marse, it is certainly possible. I aim to take care of Harriet as best as I can, and the baby and Jericho too."

Lewis chuckled. "Your intent is admirable, but you don't have any say in taking care of Harriet, her baby, or anyone else, do you?"

"No, Marse. But I intend to take care of my family, any way I can."

Lewis twirled the ends of his mustache.

"As I said, no one questions the quality of your work. And Mother says Harriet's boy Jericho is much more . . . disciplined since you've taken him under your wing. I can only expect you will have the same effect on your own child. And if you remain as overseer, I would expect you to have the same effect on other younger, less disciplined field hands. I have spoken with Mother, and she is of the opinion that your presence here would greatly improve discipline."

Lewis stared intently at Dangerfield.

"You do want to stay, don't you? To be close to Harriet?"

"Yes, Marse."

"Of course you do," answered Lewis confidently. "I suspect Henry won't mind. One less mouth to feed at home, and you will be making money for him. Any smart owner would be happy with such an arrangement." Lewis stared at the sleeve of his coat, and pulled a loose thread.

"Of course, we would allow you to visit your home once a month, perhaps twice if Henry needs you. You have a brother by the name of Gabriel, correct? And a sister named Anna Mae, I believe?"

"Yes Marse." Dangerfield wondered how Lewis knew so much about his family.

"Well, with that much help at home, Henry and Elsey shouldn't need you as much. As I said, we would allow one or two visits home per month. I will send word to Henry. He and I can work out the arrangements."

"Yes, Marse," Dangerfield said weakly. He wondered if Lewis had already spoken with Henry. Dangerfield felt his stomach tighten as he watched other people plan his life, and determine his fate. Something welled up inside him as he looked at Lewis, a feeling he could not describe, not love and not hate.

"Very well, then," said Lewis. "You should plan on sleeping in Harriet's cabin, so you can be close to her and Jericho. No point in pretending things aren't what they are. Harriet will need you, and so will Jericho. It is your cabin now. Tomorrow, you and I will survey the farm, and determine what needs to be done. I will also expect you to keep track of all the field hands. I have my father's list, and his notes on which hands are the most productive. You and I will go over the list tomorrow. I will expect you to give me your honest opinions regarding the capabilities of all the field hands. Which ones are hard workers, which ones could benefit from a firmer hand and which ones should be sold. We can't afford to lose any inventory, but neither can we afford to keep non-productive inventory. Surely you understand."

"Yes Marse."

"Good," said Lewis, smiling. "I expect things will work out splendidly with us."

"Yes, Marse," said Dangerfield. He turned to walk back toward the stable.

"One more thing, before you go," said Lewis. "Harriet has been a tremendous help in the house. But she hasn't been herself. I'm afraid she might be getting sick, or perhaps she simply suffers during the early stages of pregnancy more than other women. Whatever the cause, her productivity has diminished. Why don't you take her back to your cabin. Let her get some rest. Lilly can take over in the house. You take Harriet back with you, so she can recover and doesn't get sick. Sick inventory is no better than a runaway. At least you don't have to feed runaways."

"Yes, Marse."

Lewis chuckled at his own joke.

Dangerfield stared at the strange creature before him, this master who wasn't really a master, this boy child with the wispy mustache who kept talking about "inventory." But none of his talk mattered right now. Dangerfield was not thinking about Andrew or Micah, or Gabriel or Anna Mae. He was where he belonged, with Harriet, Jericho, and his unborn child. He took Harriet by the hand and led her to their cabin, which instantly felt like he had lived there his whole life. He ignored the nagging thoughts in the back of his mind, something that made the hair on his neck stand up. He was at home.

BOOK III

CHAPTER 31

LATE AUGUST 1858, JENNINGS FARM, WARRENTON, VIRGINIA

Dangerfield awoke to the sound of footsteps outside his family's cabin. He did not know what time it was, but it was still dark. He fumbled for a match, and clumsily lit the candle next to his bunk. He sat up and took count of his family, making certain they were safe. His two boys, Dangerfield Junior and Gabriel, sprawled on their bunks. Lucy and Agnes curled up next to each other. Jericho's long legs stretching past the end of his bunk. No sign of his wife.

He pulled on his boots and took the candle outside. Harriet was walking slowly, ambling back and forth outside the cabin, breathing heavily.

"I think this baby might come early," she said. "I can feel him down low. I think he's ready to come out," she huffed.

"Go on back inside and lay down," said Dangerfield. "I'll fetch Lilly from the house."

Dangerfield dressed quickly, and ran toward the house. He knocked just once before Lilly answered.

"I think it's time," he said. Lilly said nothing, just ran her fingers through her thick gray hair. "Be right there," she said.

When they arrived at the cabin, Harriet was seated on a stool next to her bed. Gabriel was wiping his mother's face with a cloth. Jericho had retrieved a pail and some rags.

"Where's everyone else," said Dangerfield.

"Lucy and Agnes went to fetch water, and Junior went to fetch wood for a fire," said Jericho. Even the younger children knew their roles when it was time for a new baby – Lilly was the nursemaid, and everyone else fetched water, wood, clean rags, or simply got out of the way.

"Lay down and push," said Lilly.

Harriet lay down on her bunk, sweat dripping from her head.

Lucy, Agnes and the younger Dangerfield arrived. Junior quickly built up a fire outside the cabin. Lucy and Agnes took turns holding the water bucket over the flames, until the water was hot enough.

"Sit up now," barked Lilly to Harriet. "Gabriel, hold your mother's head while I get the baby out."

Harriet screamed, and then fell back on her bunk. Gabriel and Jericho held her up while Lilly tore open Harriet's dress and petticoats. "Baby almost out," she said. "I can see his head. Lucy, fetch me a hot rag."

Lilly placed the hot rag on Harriet's tumescent belly, slowly rubbing it back and forth. Dangerfield watched as the baby's wet, matted head poked out from Harriet's body. Lilly shoved her hand inside, and pulled the baby out a little farther, bit by bit. With one final pull, the baby heaved out, defenseless and bloody, gasping for its inaugural breath. A great gush of blood and placenta spilled forth onto the cabin floor. Lilly extracted a bit of birth material from the baby's mouth. She pulled a small knife from her apron, sliced the birth cord, and pushed open the baby's eyes. Liberated, the baby let loose a wail, and pissed on Lilly's dress. Harriet pushed herself up, and Lilly handed over her new charge.

"Another boy, just like I told you it would be," said Lilly wiping her hands on a rag. "I ain't never been wrong. Marse Lewis be pleased to hear that. Lucy, fetch your mother a bunch of them rags."

Harriet cradled her newborn boy, mewling and wriggling. He let loose another piercing wail and promptly began nursing. Dangerfield surveyed the chaos in his cabin and smiled. "Lucy and Agnes, clean up that mess. Gabriel and Jericho, fetch more wood for the fire. Junior, get more water."

As the children dispatched to their assigned duties, Lewis Jennings darkened the door of the cabin.

"Day, Marse," said Lilly. "Miss Harriet just finished. Got herself another boy."

"Splendid news," said Lewis. He surveyed the cabin while twirling the end of his thick black mustache. "I trust the baby is healthy, Lilly?"

"Yes, Marse. Big, loud and hungry. Shouldn't need no doctor."

"Even better. Of course, I will spare no expense to ensure healthy inventory, but if the expense is unnecessary, so much the better."

He glanced at Harriet. "And how is the proud new mother?"

"Fine, Marse," said Harriet. Tired, but happy and fine. I expect to be up and about soon."

"No hurry, of course" said Lewis. "I would expect you to take the rest of the afternoon off. Lilly and the other girls can handle things in the house until you are rested. Take a few hours to recover and nurse. Have one of the children fetch Lilly when you are ready to return."

He turned to Dangerfield. "Quite the growing brood you have. And all healthy, too. You and Harriet produce exceptional children. I don't recall having to summon a doctor more than once for any of your brood. Your children have proven so far to be a profitable investment."

Dangerfield curled his hand into a fist before speaking. "Thank you, Marse."

"Of course, if any of your family should fall ill, let Lilly know," continued Lewis. "As I said, I will spare no expense to ensure the health of your family, and my inventory. And don't think I don't recognize your contribution to my family's holdings. Jericho has become a very productive worker under your tutelage."

"He's a good boy, Marse. I treat him like he's one of my own. Try to raise him to stay out of trouble."

"And so far he has, with a few notable exceptions." Lewis turned to make certain the women and children were occupied.

"I received a letter from Henry today." He pulled the letter out of his coat pocket. "Henry has requested that you return home immediately, and that you be allowed to stay for two weeks. This, of course, is not the arrangement I have had with you or Henry."

"Did Henry – Marse Henry say why he needed me?"

"No, but he did say it was a matter of some urgency."

Lewis looked directly at Dangerfield.

"As you know, I pay Henry for your services. Henry and I agreed that you would be allowed to visit your home once a month, perhaps twice if Henry needs you. A two-week stay is far beyond what we had contemplated."

"That business is between you and Marse Henry."

"Yes, of course." Lewis cleared his throat, before speaking softly.

"My family and I have come to rely on you for your work and your positive influence on the field hands. If Henry were to cancel our agreement, take you back, it would adversely affect my interests. The field hands would become unruly and difficult to manage. I would have no choice but to sell them and replace them with more pliable and disciplined inventory. I trust you don't want to see Jericho sold to the highest bidder. No telling how he would be treated."

"No, Marse. Jericho's a good boy. Raised him like he's one of my own."

"Yes, you did. It would be a great shame to see all of your hard work and positive influence sold to someone who won't treat him like family."

Dangerfield felt his stomach knot. His hands tightened into fists, but he said nothing.

"And of course, there is the matter of Harriet. A beautiful, fertile woman like Harriet would fetch a high price on the market. If you were to leave, Harriet would quite likely become distracted, less productive. The only thing worse than a sick slave is a love-struck slave. I could ill afford to keep her if she is no longer happy. A new owner would likely relieve her of any happy family memories. I know you don't want that."

"No Marse. Harriet and my family are right here. I take care of my family,

Marse, and I always will."

"Of course you do." Lewis paused, and looked down at his riding boots. He pulled a spotless white handkerchief out of his pocket and polished the tip of his boot.

"You do like it here, don't you? With Harriet and all of your children, all together, under one roof?"

"Yes, Marse. This is home now."

"Of course it is." Lewis looked back toward the house and sighed. "Ever since my father died, I have tried to run this operation the way he would have, with discipline, compassion, and of course sound business sense. A light hand on the whip, as he used to say. Since he's been gone, I have discovered that happy inventory is productive inventory. I have tried my best to keep families together, not just because God wants it that way, but because it is good business. The men are more productive with a woman in the home, and the women feel safe with a man around. It's just the natural order of things."

"Of course, Marse."

Lewis retrieved a toothpick from his coat pocket and absent-mindedly plucked his front teeth.

"Well, of course I will honor Henry's request that you be allowed to return home for two weeks, and not a day longer. All I ask of you is that you return the trust I have placed in you."

Lewis leaned in and spoke softly in Dangerfield's ear. "My mother and I have come to trust you, and value the contribution you have made to this family. All I ask is that you return that trust. I hope you agree that it will be best for this family. And your family. After all these years, this is your family now. Think of Harriet and your children."

Dangerfield choked back the bile in his throat. He rocked back and forth on his heels, clenching and unclenching his fists.

"Yes, Marse. I aim to take care of my family."

"Very well, then. Plan on leaving first thing in the morning. I will send word to Henry that you can stay, but I expect you back in exactly two weeks."

Dangerfield awoke before dawn the next morning. He lit a candle, and surveyed his growing family's cabin. Harriet sound asleep at last after a fitful night with the baby. Baby John, finally asleep at his mother's breast. Lucy and Agnes curled up in their bunks. Dangerfield Junior and Gabriel stretched out snoring, and lanky Jericho fidgeting in his bed. Dangerfield crawled out of his bed, and kissed his wife on the forehead. She grunted, but did not awaken.

He got to the stable just before first light, and saddled up Solomon. Almost 13 years old, Solomon was no longer the strongest or fastest horse in the county. But he could still keep up a brisk double-clip trot for five miles without breaking a sweat. Dangerfield had not ridden him hard in over a year. He hoped Solomon was up for a hard ride.

Dangerfield filled the saddlebags with oats and a few handfuls of fresh sweet grass. He filled his canteen from the creek, and packed chunks of ham, two boiled potatoes, and hard bread that Harriet had packed for him the night before.

He hit the trail just after first light. He pushed Solomon as hard as he thought he could. Solomon kept up the pace, and twice broke into a full gallop before Dangerfield could slow him down. They stopped only once, for water and oats.

He arrived at Henry's farm home shortly after noon. As they rounded the final turn toward the house, Solomon knew he was home, and broke into a gallop. Dangerfield saw no need to rein him in.

Horse and rider clattered to a stop in front of the house. His brother Gabriel heard the noise and emerged from the chicken coop with a basket in each hand.

"Almost ten years of riding, and you still don't know how to ride the old man," said Gabriel. "Look like Solomon riding you, not the other way 'round."

"Like to see you do any better. No wonder why Henry won't let you ride him. An old mule's more your speed."

Dangerfield dismounted and clapped his brother on the back.

"Been a while. Boy Lewis don't hardly let you come home no more," said Gabriel. "Harriet had that baby yet?"

"Yesterday. Baby boy. Named him John. Would have named him after you, but I already named one after you. You need to start havin' babies so you can name one of 'em after me."

"Harriet just had the baby yesterday, and you came here? Why?"

"Hoping you could tell me. Henry sent word that he needed me home right away. Everything okay here?"

"Far as I know. Henry and Elsey both fine. Anna Mae's been working up at Old Man Fox's farm, up near Brentsville. Henry says Marse Fox has taken quite a shine to her. She comes home about once or twice a month. Takes after you."

"Is anything wrong? Anything I need to know? Marse Lewis said it was urgent."

"Can't think of anything urgent," said Gabriel. "Henry fell and hurt his back 'bout a week ago, but he gets around fine now."

Henry emerged from the house. Stoop-shouldered and lean, he walked with a cane toward his sons.

"Heard you two galloping in from about a mile away," said Henry. "Didn't think old Solomon still had it in him. Should know better than to expect you to rein in him." He hobbled toward his son. Henry stretched out one wiry hand and Dangerfield held his father's hand while patting him on the back.

"What happened? Gabriel says you fell."

"Nothing to worry about. I fell last week while moving some hogs. Tripped over a rock. Turned my knee and twisted my back darn near all the way around. Stopped hurting a few days ago. Elsey says I got to keep using this," he said, lifting the cane in his hand. "Don't reckon I need it, but it ain't worth fussin' about. "Sides, I just make Gabriel do all the work now, since you ain't but a stranger now."

The three men laughed until Henry began coughing, a slow, liquid rattle that convulsed him completely. Finally he spat, and straightened himself.

"Damn this cough," he said. "Makes a man feel like he's got syrup in his lungs. Gabriel, go on in the house and tell Elsey Dangerfield is home. Tell her to start fixing an early supper."

Gabriel walked toward the house. Henry watched until he was inside.

"Lewis must have told you I needed you to come home right away."

"Yes, he did. Left first thing this morning." Dangerfield studied his father.

"Ain't never seen you with a cane before. How long you been needin' that?"

"Just this past week. Like I said, this is more to keep Elsey happy. Reckon you know how that works."

"I certainly do."

Henry coughed again, gripping his cane until the convulsions stopped.

"Harriet had that baby yet?"

"Just last night. I would be with her right now, but I left as soon as I could. Lewis said it was urgent."

"Is the baby healthy?"

"Yes. Big, loud and hungry, as Lilly likes to say."

"Good. Boy or girl?"

"Boy. Named him John."

"Well, that's alright. Maybe Elsey and I hitch up the carriage and come see you in a couple of months. Thinking about buying a pair of Morgans. Hitch 'em up to the carriage and come see you and Harriet and your family. Lucy and Agnes well?"

"Yes, Lucy, Agnes, Junior and Gabriel are all fine. Harriet's boy Jericho almost as tall as I am. But you didn't send for me just to talk about the children." Dangerfield cleared his throat. "If there's something wrong at home, let me know what it is. I can stay and help with chores if that's it. Marse Lewis says I can stay for two weeks. I can get a lot done in two weeks."

"No, that ain't it. Gabriel works almost as hard as you do, although I don't like to tell him that. Something I want to discuss with you, Elsey, Gabriel, and Anna Mae all together. I sent for Anna Mae. She should be here shortly. Let's all talk over supper, after she gets here. I want everyone to be together for what I have to say."

Henry peered down at a thin black snake parting the grass in front of them. He poked at the creature with his cane, then let it go.

"Comes in handy sometimes," he muttered to himself. "Why don't you go in the house, greet Elsey, and clean up for supper. We'll eat and talk later."

When Dangerfield entered the house, his mother was filling the stove with fatwood. She looked up and smiled.

"Well, well. Look like Marse Lewis ain't fed you in weeks. Does he let you eat?"

"I eat fine, Miss Elsey."

His mother hugged him tightly for a long time. She released her grip and studied him closely.

"Harriet had that baby yet?"

"Just last night. His name is John, and he's healthy."

"And you came this morning even though your wife got a new baby at home. She got help?"

"She got plenty of help. Lilly and the other girls, Lucy, Agnes, she got plenty of help."

Elsey handed him a loaf of bread, and ham hocks.

"Set down and eat. Be a while before supper."

Dangerfield retrieved a plate, knife and fork. He dipped the bread in a jar of bacon grease that Elsey kept on the counter, and took a bite. Elsey said nothing while he finished chewing.

"Henry sent for me. That's why I came this morning, even though Harriet's got the new baby and all. Henry said it was urgent."

"I know," said Elsey as she put more fatwood in the stove.

"So you know what this is about?"

"Best to wait until Anna Mae gets here. She's gone almost as much as you."

"I heard. Gabriel said she's one of old John Fox's house girls now."

"She is, and Henry thinks John has taken a shine to her. The two of them have talked about arrangements."

"She goin' to live with Fox?"

"Let's talk after supper."

Anna Mae arrived late that afternoon. After catching up with her brothers, she helped Elsey finish preparing the family meal.

Dinner quickly assumed familiar patterns. Anna Mae gossiped about all the house girls at the Fox plantation, how Mistress Fox was silly and disorganized, and how John Fox was hardly ever around. Dangerfield discussed life at the Jennings farm, his man-child master, Lewis, and Dangerfield's growing brood of children. Gabriel talked about his job as a dock hand at one of the largest ports on the river. Henry rented him out for fifty dollars a month. Gabriel had taken a quick liking to the rigors of dock work, and was now one of the most sought-after dock hands for twenty miles up or down the river. The port manager offered to buy Gabriel at least once a month, but Henry refused, because the price was never right.

The port manager was not the only one to notice Gabriel. His hard work had attracted the attention of a pretty young cook, a light-skinned mixed slave named Eliza. She was owned by the port manager, who bought her at an auction when she was fifteen. Her previous owner had defaulted on a bank loan, and the bank sold all his assets, including his slaves. The port manager bought Eliza and two of her brothers for $275.

Eliza cooked meals for the dock hands so they had an incentive to stay at the port. Gabriel was convinced she gave him the biggest portions, and best pieces of ham. She always talked to him during breaks, and after the last riverboat had docked for the evening. Sometimes when he was working, she would slip him a hot biscuit, or a hard-boiled egg, or slices of boiled potato.

"She doesn't do that for any of the other dock hands, just me," said Gabriel as the family was finishing dinner.

"So you think," said Dangerfield. "If she's as proper as you say she is, she must have better choices than you, dear Brother."

"What would you know about choices?" said Gabriel. "You can't hardly pass water without first asking Marse Lewis."

The two brothers laughed and continued their game of insults. Henry and Elsey said nothing, but simply watched their adult children, together at family dinner table.

Finally, Henry spoke.

"That's enough, both of you. Now, you all know I have asked all of you to come home, and stay for a few weeks. Elsey and I have something we need to discuss with all of you."

The room fell silent.

Henry coughed again, and spat into his handkerchief. "Elsey and I aren't getting any younger. I haven't been feeling well lately. Nothing serious, just getting older. It isn't easy keeping up the farm, even with hiring help."

Anna Mae, Dangerfield, and Gabriel looked at each other.

"Now that all of you are on your own and can take care of yourselves, I have decided to sell the farm, and all the assets. Old John Fox says he wants to buy this place, and I have agreed to sell it to him. I intend to sell everything to Fox, take the proceeds, and move the family to Ohio. Everything is done, except for filing the deeds. We should be able to move by October. That will give us almost two months to pack, and settle our affairs before we leave. I wanted to tell you now, so it won't come as a surprise when the farm is sold. Elsey, if you could please pass the ham."

Henry tucked into another slice of ham, cradling it between two thick slices of greasy bread.

The kitchen was quiet as a tomb, save for the sound of Henry's chewing. Elsey sat with her hands folded in her lap, studying her family. Dangerfield's mind raced, and he stammered for something to say.

"Why Ohio?" said Gabriel.

"Ohio is a free state. Once we move there, all of you are automatically free. Long as everyone stays in Ohio, no man can ever lay claim to any of you."

"Why can't we stay here, in this house? All of us together now," said Anna Mae.

"We may be together now, but not for long," replied Henry. "And we will never be a free and proper family, not in Virginia. It's time for us to go."

"Why now," said Dangerfield. "Everything seems like it's going well for everyone now."

"Might seem that way, but things ain't been easy for me. Folks starting to ask questions about my family, wondering about me and Elsey." Henry sopped his biscuit in bacon grease and took another bite.

"And I'm not a young man anymore. Tired of living like this ain't a proper family."

He coughed again, and leaned back in his chair.

"I don't know if all of you been keeping track of the changes," explained Henry. "You know about Virginia's law says that any free blacks have to leave the state within a year, or else they can be caught, and sold again into slavery. Think about that. You can be free as a bird, got your papers and everything. And if you don't leave, they can catch any of you, and sell you to anyone, anywhere, highest bidder. And things been getting worse since they passed that law back in 1850. Lot of folks talking about sending all the blacks back to Africa."

Henry chuckled.

"Ain't none of you ever been to Africa, but if you was all free, they could send you there. Makes no sense, but that's how things have gotten in Virginia. That's why I didn't free you earlier. If I had freed you, you all would have had to leave, or get caught, and sold to someone else. This way, we all move together, and all of you are free as long as you stay in Ohio. We can finally be a proper family."

Henry took another bite of ham, and leaned back in his chair. Elsey said nothing.

"Where in Ohio," said Dangerfield.

"I bought a place in Bridgeport, just across the river," explained Henry. "Big enough for all of us. Some land, but not enough to farm. Figure I can get enough for the farm and all the land, maybe I can do something else. You all can get jobs anywhere. You can take care of yourselves, work, and then come home."

No one spoke. All the children had stopped eating.

"Well, you all act like this is bad news, like I was dying," said Henry. "Thought you all would be happier. Elsey, you happy about this?"

"Of course, Henry. But I don't worry about me. Our children have their own obligations now." She looked straight at Dangerfield, who was poking at his ham.

"What about Harriet and your family," said Elsey. "What are you going to tell her? What are you going to tell Lewis Jennings?"

"Don't know," said Dangerfield. "Don't know if I can tell Harriet. Don't know if I can leave her. Certainly can't leave the children with Marse Lewis. No telling what will happen to them."

He recalled Lewis Jennings' thinly veiled threats to sell his wife and children if he left Jennings' employ. Although Lewis was not as cruel as his father, he was even more ruthless when it came to business. Dangerfield knew Lewis Jennings would sell his wife and all his children in an instant if the price was right.

"Henry, what do you propose I tell Marse Lewis," said Dangerfield. "What should I tell Harriet and my children? You know I can't take any of them with me to Ohio."

"I have put plenty of thought to that," said Henry calmly, leaning back in his chair. "I never much cared for Augustine, but his boy Lewis is different. He's better at business. More reasonable. You work for him, and work someplace else when you aren't with him. Make enough to buy your family, then bring them to Ohio. I ain't saying it will be easy, or won't take long. But once you are free, you can go anywhere. I taught all of you how to work. That's why I waited until now to move us. Time had to be right. Now, the time is right. And we can't stay in Virginia any longer."

Henry looked at Dangerfield, who sat slumped in his chair.

"I know Lewis about as well as you do," said Henry. "I can talk to him, maybe lend him some money, help him pay off his father's debts. Make it easier for him to let you buy your family. I'll do everything I can to make it work."

Henry wiped his mouth on his handkerchief. "All right, let's get back to work. Anna Mae and Dangerfield are back for two weeks. Fences don't fix themselves. Anna Mae, help Elsey clean up. Boys, let's head out back and see what needs to be done. Can't expect an old man with a cane to do all the work. Let's get this place fixed up, so we can sell it."

Dangerfield stood up, and looked out the kitchen window of his childhood home. The view had not changed, but now, everything was much different than it had ever been.

CHAPTER 32

Turner tried to sit up, but something held him back. Roger Hillman sat at the edge of the bed and stared at him.

"Roger where am I? What happened? Is Tracy okay? Was there an accident, is she okay . . . ."

"Relax, Mike, everything is fine," said Hillman, patting him on the leg. "Tracy is in the cafeteria getting some coffee. She asked me to keep an eye on you. Damon is here too."

"Damon, what the hell is going on? What happened?"

Damon sat down across from the bed. "Everything is fine, Mike. As far as anyone knows, your great-uncle Billy never killed anyone. He died in a car crash, Mike, a tragic accident. Everything is going to be fine."

Turner felt his breath leave him as Damon talked.

"So you know about those dreams?"

"Tracy told us. Against her wishes, but she told us. She told us everything, all the dreams you have been having, the pills, everything. Don't be angry with her, Mike. She probably saved your life. She will be back soon with her coffee. I will let her explain."

Turner looked around the room, but did not recognize any of the nurses, or the other doctors.

"Where am I?"

"St. Mary's," said Damon. We thought it might be easier to treat you here, instead of University Hospital. Pretty awkward to have you as a patient at your own hospital. I have staff privileges here, so I pulled a few strings."

"I need some water," said Turner. "I feel okay now, I can get it myself." Turner tried sitting up in his bed, but something pushed down on his chest and waist. He looked over the edge of the bed, and saw two large leather straps buckled to the edge of the bed, holding down his arms and waist.

"Restraints? What was I doing when you brought me here? Was I unconscious?"

"Just standard procedure in this unit. We'll unbuckle you in a few minutes, after Tracy gets back, and after we run some more tests."

"Well, I appreciate everyone's concern, but the restraints seem a bit unnecessary. Normally, we only use these in the psych ward."

Damon looked at Roger Hillman, who was looking at something on his phone. Hillman looked at Damon, sighed, and stood up. Damon got out of his chair and walked over to the bed. He touched Turner lightly on the shoulder. "We have to leave them on until we complete our tests," said Damon. "I'm sorry."

"Damon, what the hell happened? Dammit, where am I?"

"Mike, you had an acute, severe psychotic episode, likely triggered by a combination of stress, and the sleeping pills you have been taking. There may be other causative factors. That's why we need the tests. Tracy tried bringing you back, but she couldn't. She called me, I talked to a few people, and I had you admitted here.

"Where is 'here'"?

"St. Mary's Hospital, Mike. One of the best psychiatric units in the Midwest. Let's finish those tests, make certain you are okay, and then we can get you up and walking around."

"Damon, I need to get out of here," Turner said loudly. "Roger and I have an important meeting this morning with Ed Sorenson, Phil Evans, and Marcia Harris. Roger, we can't keep them waiting."

Hillman was looking at Turner's chart. He turned and sat on Turner's bed.

"Mike, I don't think you understand," said Hillman softly. "That meeting was supposed to be two days ago. You've been out for two straight days." He patted Turner on the shoulder. "The meeting can wait, Mike. Everything can wait. I told Ed, Phil and Marcia that something, uh, came up in your family, and you were going to be unavailable for a few days. Dr. Prandra has agreed to take over your duties temporarily until you get better."

"I don't want Prandra taking over my workload. He's horrible with patients."

"I know, Mike, I know. But he's a great surgeon. You said so yourself. He'll have to do until you get better. It's just temporary. Just get better."

Hillman looked at his watch and stood up. "Glad to see you back. Get well and get back, Mike. I have to get back to the hospital. Damon, let me know how he's doing, okay? Tell Tracy I had to leave."

Hillman pulled his overcoat on and walked out.

Turner struggled to sit up against the leather restraints.

"Look, Damon, this is silly. I took some sleeping pills, something to take the edge off. They trigger dreams in a lot of people. It's one of the warnings, right on the bottle. Can you release the restraints?"

Damon sighed. "Let's wait until Tracy gets back. I will check with your attending, and get those tests done ASAP. Once the attending says go, we get you out of these things, and walking around. You could be back home with supervision in two or three days, maybe a week."

"Attending? Supervision? Jesus Christ, Damon, c'mon. I'm fine."

"You will be Mike, you will be. Just try to relax."

Tracy kicked open the swinging door, a cup of coffee in each hand.

"He's up," said Damon.

Damon took his coffee from Tracy. "I will leave you two alone. Thanks for the coffee, Trace. I will be back in 20 minutes or so."

Damon checked Turner's chart, looked back, and left the room without another word.

Tracy pulled up a chair and sat next to his bed. She kissed his forehead.

"God I was worried about you."

"So was everyone else, apparently. I feel like a prisoner on his way to death row. Lethal injection just around the corner. What the hell happened? How did I get here?"

Tracy took a huge gulp of her coffee.

"What's the last thing you remember after you took those pills?"

"I was standing outside of this huge house. I don't know where it was. There was snow on the ground. A bunch of men were there, standing around. I don't know why. And then another guy comes out of the house, and announces that he is selling some of his 'inventory.' And then six people come out of the house, a woman, a baby, two young girls, and two young boys. I think the woman was the mother of the five kids. One of the men from the crowd jumps over the railing and starts groping the woman. Sticks his hand up her dress and starts squeezing her."

"Jesus," said Tracy.

"One of the young boys punches the man groping his mother," continued Turner. "And then a brawl breaks out. People trying to storm the house, assaulting the woman and the girls. The two boys defending their mother and sisters. And then the guy selling the family shoots a gun into the air, and everyone scrambles. Finally, some big fat guy from Louisiana offers to buy the entire family for $3,000. $3,000 for six human beings. The seller agrees, and then everyone leaves. That's all I remember. And then I started falling, and now . . . ." Turner closed his eyes.

"Tracy, tell me what happened. For God's sake, what happened?"

Tracy took another gulp of coffee, and set the plastic cup on a table behind the bed.

"You remember taking the pills, right?"

"Of course."

"I watched you fall asleep. You seemed okay. I watched you for an hour or so, and then I went to the kitchen to get some food."

"And?"

"I was gone about five minutes. When I came back to the bedroom, you weren't there. I heard the front door open and close, and I knew you had left."

"Jesus."

"All the other times you had taken those pills, you never went anywhere, at least not very far. I didn't think you would leave, but this time you did. I never should have left you. I was only gone for a few minutes."

"What did you do?"

"I went after you, but you were running down the street, screaming. I couldn't hear you at first, but you were yelling. I caught up to you, but I couldn't stop you. You weren't there, Mike. Your body was there, but your mind was somewhere else, and it was scary."

Tracy finished her coffee, crumpled the paper cup, and tossed it into a nearby wastebasket.

"What I saw was real, Mike, real life, not one of your dreams," she said softly. "You fell, and I couldn't get you off the ground, and I could not bring you back, so I called 911. Then I called Damon."

"God, Tracy, I am so sorry." Turner lay in his bed, thinking.

"Did anyone see me?"

"Well, the cops and the paramedics, of course. And the neighbors who were home and still up. And a few other people driving past, some curious onlookers. Maybe a few others. But only a few people who actually know us. The paramedics showed up quickly. But still . . . ."

Turner contemplated the carefully built quilt of his life, all the time and energy he had spent weaving and threading different pieces of his career and life into a strong, flexible patchwork. He closed his eyes and watched everything unravel, thread by thread, piece by piece.

"When did you call Damon?"

"I called him first, and he told me to call 911. Damon got there just when the cops and the paramedics arrived. He told them he was your doctor, and that you were just having a bad reaction to medicine. They were going to take you to University, but Damon told them to take you here. Said all your treating physicians were here. Got to hand it to him, he was smooth."

"I'll bet." Turner sat up as far as he could, and sipped from a cup of water next to him.

"How long have I been here?"

"Two days. They sedated you as soon as you got here."

"Jesus."

Tracy held the water cup to his lips and dribbled out a few drops.

"You said you saw a man selling a mother and her children," said Tracy. "That sounds like a slave auction."

"Yeah, I guess it was," said Turner wearily. "I had no idea what was happening."

"Do you know who any of these people were," said Tracy.

"No", said Turner. "How would I know any of them? I remember the guy selling the family was named Jennings. The fat guy from Louisiana called him that."

"So the guy selling the family was named Jennings," she said to herself. "Do you remember anything else," said Tracy. "Any other names you remember hearing?"

"No. Why are you asking?"

"Just thinking." She paused, and then rummaged for her purse. She emptied the contents on his bed, and spread everything out, until she found a small notebook. She stuffed everything back into the purse, except for a pack of cigarettes, and the notebook.

"How many of those have you burned through," he said, nodding his head at the cigarette pack.

"More than a pack, and less than a carton. The last two days have been quite stressful." She squeezed his hand.

"So this last dream you had seems unrelated to all of your other dreams," said Tracy. "First, you saw Dangerfield at Harpers Ferry, then in our hotel room, and again in the OR. And then you saw your great-uncle Billy in a car crash, and then you saw him shoot some guys. And now, you saw what must have been a slave auction. There must be something linking these dreams."

"Well, if there is, I sure as hell don't know what it is," snapped Turner.

"Did anyone else show up at the house, or the slave auction?"

"No. What are you getting at? What the hell is going on?"

Tracy stared through the small windows of the double swinging doors.

"I don't know, babe, I don't know," said Tracy wearily. "I'm as confused as you are."

Turner rubbed his eyes. "What does all of this mean? I can't . . . I can't figure any of this out. Nothing makes sense. My head hurts. I need to . . . ."

Tracy rubbed his leg. "Right now, there is nothing you can do. You aren't going anywhere. I have an idea."

Before she could elaborate, Damon and another doctor breezed in. Damon was still in his suit, and the doctor wore his white lab coat, about two sizes larger than it needed to be, over a blue plaid shirt, rumpled khakis and white sneakers. He was plump, with an unruly tousle of blond hair that sprayed out from the top of his head. Turner saw what looked like a pimple on his chin. He did not appear to be older than 30.

"Mike, this is Dr. Herbert Cornell," said Damon. "He works here at St. Mary's. He'll be your attending. I'll let you two get acquainted, while Tracy and I talk outside." Damon pulled up the padded chair and scooted it next to Turner's bed.

"Listen, Mike, you are in the best place possible," Damon whispered. "Herb has treated dozens of high-achieving professionals. Doctors, lawyers, high-finance Wall Street guys, you name it. You will be fine." He patted Turner on the forehead, stood and took Tracy by the arm. "Tracy, let's you and I talk outside for a minute. Cool?"

"Sure. Let me talk to my husband alone for a few minutes first."

Damon and Dr. Herbert Cornell excused themselves and began a quiet conversation in the corner of the room. Tracy stood over Turner's bed and whispered in his ear. "We are going to figure this out. I don't know what the hell is going on, but I believe you. I believe in you. We are going to figure this out, whatever it is. Don't give up." She kissed him on the mouth, stood, and walked out with Damon, leaving Turner alone in the room with Herbert Cornell.

Dr. Cornell looked at his chart, and sat next to the bed.

"Dr. Turner, I must say it is an honor. I saw you present two or three years ago at the Upper Midwest conference. You were amazing."

"Well thanks, but I really don't think we need the formalities any more, do we?" he said, nodding toward the restraints. "Why don't you take these off, so I can sit up."

"Of course," said Cornell, running his fingers through the spindle of hair on the top of his head. "I will release the top restraint for now, so you can sit up and talk easier. We'll leave the leg restraints on for the time being."

"I don't think I need any restraints at all, Herbert. I am fine."

"For now, please call me Dr. Cornell."

Turner raised his eyebrows.

"Look, Dr. Cornell, I am fine, really. You know about the pills I was taking. I am quite familiar with the known side effects, and the risks. It was a risk I was willing to take to . . . ."

"You were willing to risk your career to take sleeping pills that you knew could cause the side effects you experienced?" interjected Cornell sharply. "Surely you read the warnings on the back of the bottle. I can't imagine why you would knowingly risk your career and possibly your safety to take those pills, when you knew there were other options."

"I knew what I was doing, and I know what I am doing now," retorted Turner. "I had my reasons."

"Yes, of course you did. Forgive me." Cornell stood up and unbuckled the top restraint, letting the strap fall to the floor. Turner sat up quickly, and then lay down again, feeling the blood rush to his head.

"Dr. Turner, let's get something straight," said Cornell evenly. "I have your file. I have your history. I have spoken with your wife. You are undoubtedly a brilliant man. And when you leave here, you will still be brilliant. But in here, right now, I am the doctor and you are the patient. Remember that as long as you are here. And tomorrow, I do want to hear about all your reasons for taking those pills. Since you knew of the possible side effects, I'm sure you must have had your reasons. Can't wait to hear them. Our conversation will be part of your treatment, and your answers will be part of your treatment."

Cornell stood, and retrieved his clipboard. "I will have an orderly bring you some food from the cafeteria. I will keep the top restraint off, but we will leave the bottom restraint on for now. Eat up, get some rest, and we will talk tomorrow morning." Cornell left the room, and the only noise in the room was the sound of the double doors swinging as he exited.

Turner surveyed the room. A closet, a desk, a pitcher of water on the table. A notebook, but no pens or pencils. And his legs below the knees securely strapped to the bed, with the lock unreachable.

"I fell from the sky and landed in the psych ward," he muttered to himself. "This can't be real." Then the door whooshed open, and an orderly brought him a tray of lasagna from the cafeteria. Lukewarm, gelatinous, and flavorless, just like the food at his hospital. "This is real," he said to himself after the orderly left. "Dammit, it is real.

CHAPTER 33

For the two weeks that Dangerfield and Anna Mae were back home, Henry did his best to maintain his family's routines. They rose at the same time every morning, just as they had when all the children lived at home. After breakfast, the women began their duties in the kitchen, while the men retreated to the barn, the stable, the fields. For Dangerfield, the two weeks at home felt liberating, yet oppressive. His whole family back together, talking in the kitchen, laughing in the fields, and telling stories in the evening before sleep. But he knew at the end of two weeks, he would have to explain to Harriet that his family was moving to Ohio. He knew that Lewis would not approve of him moving. The thought of being without Harriet indefinitely made his stomach boil.

One afternoon, while tending the animals, Dangerfield looked up to see Henry grimacing. Henry had bent over to pick up a lame hen, and could not straighten himself. He howled in agony, and his sons ran toward him.

"Damn this back," Henry growled. "Happens almost every time I lean over."

"Might help if you squat instead of bending your back, like I been telling you," scolded Gabriel.

"You sound like your mother. You boys grab an arm and help me over to that log. Let me rest a spell. Goes away after a while."

Dangerfield and Gabriel helped their ailing father to a fallen oak log. The men sat three abreast on the log while Henry breathed heavily. He coughed a long, liquid rattle before spitting on the ground before him.

"Boys, I know moving to Ohio was a surprise," said Henry. "That's why I wanted us all home for a couple weeks. Let everything sink in. Truth is, I can't run the farm too much longer. Don't want to. Elsey and I will make a lot of money selling this place. You all can work, and take care of your families. In Ohio, we all have a safe place to stay. Bridgeport ain't far, just across the river. Take some getting used to, but it's best for the family."

"I don't question your plan, but some of us have other obligations," said Gabriel, pointing to Dangerfield. "Why don't we just stay put? I can run the farm on my own. Dangerfield can come back once or twice a month, help out. When he's gone, we can hire someone to help out."

"Can't hire someone," said Henry sharply. "I don't want an outsider here. Start to ask questions about Elsey, about Anna." He coughed again, convulsing before being able to speak.

"You boys know the situation now," continued Henry. "I don't own Elsey. Old Man Jennings did. Now Lewis Jennings owns her. Lewis has not said a word to me in ten years about getting Elsey back, which leads me to reckon he don't know he owns her."

"Trust me, Henry, Lewis Jennings keeps track of his property," explained Dangerfield. "Lewis knows if one of the hands ate an extra egg in the morning."

"I don't doubt Lewis Jennings keeps track of his property that he knows about," replied Henry. "But Augustine and I had a handshake arrangement, a gentlemen's deal. Nothing was ever in writing. Elsey lives with me, and I agreed not to collect on some debts Jennings owed me. Jennings never could pay me back, so he left Elsey alone. Nothing was in writing, so I suspect Lewis may not know about my arrangements with his father. But I don't know how long we can just keep things going."

"I still don't see why we don't just hire someone. Let me run things. You handle the business, and I do the hard work," said Gabriel.

Henry sighed. "I wish it was that easy, Gabriel. "But Elsey and I can't live as man and wife in Virginia. Only way I can keep her legally is if I own her. And I don't. And I don't want Lewis Jennings to get any ideas if I try to buy Elsey from him. So if an outsider comes here, sees how Elsey and I live, word gets around. People in town might begin to talk. 'Old Man Henry Newby and his colored wife and colored family. Aint that something.' I don't know if Augustine Jennings told anyone else about our arrangement. But if he did, and someone were to tell Lewis about Elsey . . . ."

Henry picked up a pebble and tossed it softly toward the house. "Last thing I need is Lewis Jennings trying to reclaim Elsey. He'd win in court. And I'd have to let her go, or kill Lewis. Then we'd all be ruined." He turned toward Gabriel. "Besides, Gabriel, running a farm is hard work. I know you work hard, but there's much you don't know. And with you working at the riverport, you don't have that much time either. Fact is, you ain't around that much."

Gabriel tossed a pebble toward the house. "You don't think I can run the farm," said Gabriel softly. You don't trust me."

"Dammit Gabriel, that ain't it, and you know it," said Henry. "Three of us together, here all the time, with Anna Mae and Elsey here all the time, we might make it work. But you spend more time at the riverport than you do here. Anna Mae is likely to take up with John Fox before too long. And if things work out with you and Eliza, and Anna Mae takes up with Fox, none of you will be here. Just me and Elsey. And we can't do it by ourselves."

Henry jerked a thumb toward Dangerfield. "And we know he ain't coming back any time soon. Not with his obligations."

Dangerfield turned toward his father. "Truth is, Henry, I do have obligations. Got my own family now. You know I can't just up and take Harriet and the children to Ohio." He stood up and pulled his hat brim down against the afternoon sun.

"I don't plan on joining you in Ohio," said Dangerfield. "Maybe someday. But I can't go with you, not now. I can't leave Harriet and the children, even if it means staying with Marse Lewis."

Henry looked at Gabriel and then Dangerfield. "Well, I figured you might act that way. Understand boys, I'm just doin' what I can to keep this family together. Me, Elsey, and all of us."

"I have my own family to keep together, Henry," replied Dangerfield. "I can't just leave them."

"I don't expect you to. But hear me out." Henry grimaced, and shifted his weight while remaining seated on the log. "Tell Lewis you want to buy your family. Ask how much he wants. You go out and earn the money, long as it takes. You come back and buy them, and move up with us. I ain't sayin' it will be easy, but at least make the offer."

"You think Marse Lewis will let me buy them?"

Henry coughed and spat on the ground. "From what I know of Lewis Jennings, that boy cares about money, and nothing else. Hell, that boy would sell his mother if the offer was right. Not that anyone might offer."

"One other thing to consider," said Henry. "We sell this place and move to Ohio, me and Elsey can help you buy your family. Have some extra money on hand. We can give you some money, maybe make it worthwhile for Lewis. He knows business better than his old man. You make him the right offer, he'll let you have your family."

"And what if he doesn't want to sell them," said Dangerfield.

"If the money's right, he will sell. Like I said, the boy would sell his mother if the money was right."

Henry shielded his face against the afternoon sun, and tried to get up. He rose halfway, winced, and fell down against the log.

"Help me up, boys, we got too much work to do to sit around talking."

Gabriel and Dangerfield each took an arm and pulled their father upright. The three men walked slowly back toward the house, each son holding an arm. Dangerfield noticed how lean his father had become. His arms, always sinewy, had become thin and spindly. His back was permanently bowed, and his gait, once long and confident, was hesitant, jagged and mincing, as though Henry no longer trusted his legs to do his bidding. Dangerfield felt his father's reedy arms quiver under his grasp.

"Why don't we take you back to the house," said Gabriel. "Dangerfield and I can finish up outside, and then we join you and Elsey and Anna Mae for dinner."

"That ain't a bad idea," said Henry. "Let me set for awhile 'fore dinner. Might help."

The two boys helped their father into the house, and completed all the evening chores. The sun was halfway below the horizon when they returned home. Elsey and Anna Mae greeted them.

"I think you boys must have hurt him bad," said Elsey. "Look."

Henry sat in his favorite chair, dead asleep. Spittle trailed down his chin, and formed a delta through his beard stubble. Mouth agape, he let loose a snoring thunderclap that shook his body and set him upright. He looked at his wife and children, smiled weakly, and went back to sleep.

"Should we wake him for dinner?" said Anna Mae.

"No, leave him be" said Elsey. "The rest of can eat in the kitchen. Henry can eat when he's ready. Just leave him be." The family retreated to the kitchen for supper while Henry slept deep into the evening.

━━━━◦◉◦━━━━

The two-week family retreat quickly came to an end. John Fox had sent a carriage for Anna Mae, and she left early in the morning, after kissing her family goodbye. Dangerfield, Gabriel, Henry and Elsey stood outside the farmhouse and watched her go until the carriage had disappeared around the bend, and a thin cloud of trail dust was her only trace.

"Best be going myself," said Dangerfield. "Marse Lewis said exactly two weeks, and I know he's been keeping track."

"You know he has," said Henry. He dug the toe of his boot into the dust and dug out a small pebble. "Have you thought about what I said? About offering to buy your family?"

"I have, and I aim to ask him as soon as I get back."

"That sounds like the right way to handle it." Henry turned toward his son.

"I thought about something last night," said Henry. "Might make sense if I buy your family from Lewis. Take you out of the picture. I can handle the negotiations, the business side of things with Lewis. I will have more money after we sell the farm. You just take care of your family, and let me handle things with Lewis."

"I appreciate that offer, Henry, but I can handle things with Lewis. After ten years, I reckon I know him better than you. I spend every day with him. He knows my family. He ain't his old man. I don't mean to say I like the man, but I can handle things with him. And it's my family, not yours."

"I understand," said Henry. "Just want to help, so we can all be together some day."

"We will, said Dangerfield. "But I need to do this my way. I need to take care of my family, just like you take care of us. Just like you taught me. I need to do this my way."

Henry coughed and turned toward the house. He pulled his handkerchief out of his pocket and wiped his eyes. "Got some dust in my eye," he said as he wiped his face and shoved the handkerchief back in his pocket. "Go on, and get back to your family. Next time you come back, you let me know how things work out with Lewis. After we sell the farm, maybe I can help you with the money."

Henry shifted his feet. "Before you go, I need to give you something. Something real important. Stay here."

Henry went into the house, and returned with a leather pouch.

"I figured you might want to handle things with Lewis yourself, instead of me doing it for you," explained Henry. "But you forgot something. You ain't a free man. In Virginia, you don't have any standing to negotiate with Lewis about anything. Lewis can't sell property to a slave any more than he can sell property to an ox. You ain't free. You want to handle this yourself, you need this."

He handed the pouch to Dangerfield.

"Open it," said Henry.

Dangerfield opened the pouch and pulled out a crisp piece of thick paper, folded in thirds. The paper was unsealed. Dangerfield unfolded the paper and began reading out loud.

> *I Henry Newby, a white man of sound mind and body, and resid-ing in Culpeper County, Virginia, and being possessed of several hun-dred acres of real property, and several negro slaves, including one mulatto slave named Dangerfield Newby, born in the year 1820, do hereby declare that said Dangerfield Newby shall be and hereby is, forever manumitted and emancipated according to the laws of the Commonwealth of Virginia, effective this date, September 25, 1858.*

Dangerfield folded the paper and put it back in the pouch.

"Henry, you mean . . . . ."

"It ain't official yet," interjected Henry. "I ain't filed the deed with the county, but I intend to, a few days after September 25. By that time, we should be almost ready to go to Ohio. That will give you some time to make your arrangements with Lewis Jennings. Once I file the deed of manumission with the county, it becomes official, and you are a free man under Virginia law. For now, that should give you what you need to do your business with Lewis. Keep that safe. Keep it in the pouch, and don't never let that pouch out of your sight. I will keep another one here at home, just in case."

Dangerfield looked at his father, speechless.

"One more thing," said Henry. "Once I file that deed of manumission with the county, you have one year to leave Virginia for good. If you don't leave in a year, slavers can catch you and sell you to any bidder. 'Voluntary reenslavement,' is what they call it, though ain't nothing about it seems voluntary to me."

Henry picked up a pebble, studied it, and tossed it toward the barn. "Won't make no difference once we are in Ohio. Law says all of you free once we move to Ohio. But Virginia don't care about Ohio's laws. They catch you in Virginia one year from the date of manumission, and you get caught and sold, there ain't nothing I can do to help you. So get your business done in a year. I intend to hold off on filing 'til just before we leave, but once it's filed, you got one year." He chuckled to himself. "Course, Lewis doesn't need to know it hasn't been filed. He won't check with the county, but be prepared if he asks."

Henry looked skyward. "Best get moving now," he said. "It could rain, although it looks like it might wait 'til you get back to Jennings' place."

Dangerfield looked at the letter, folded it and placed it carefully in the pouch. "Henry I don't . . . ."

"Go on," said Henry. "Mind the weather. And keep that letter safe. Don't ever let it out of your sight. Keep it safe and dry. Now go."

Dangerfield hugged his father, and Gabriel. He kissed Elsey goodbye, saddled up Solomon, and started toward the Jennings farm. He buried the pouch in the bottom of one of the saddlebags, and latched the saddlebag tight. Henry, Elsey, and Gabriel watched him leave. They watched the trail until the double-clip of hoofbeats had disappeared, and the dust cloud had dissipated. Nothing else moved on the trail. After some time, the three remaining family members went back into the house and ate breakfast.

⟫•⟪

As he rode to the Jennings farm, Dangerfield rehearsed what he would say to Lewis. "Day Marse," he said as he rode, with Solomon as the only listener. "I need to speak to you about some business that pertains to both of us." He rejected this opening as too formal. "I want to talk with you about my family, about Harriet and my children." Solomon twitched his ear to remove a black fly, and Dangerfield took this to be a sign of disapproval. "I want to buy my family, all of them. I will pay you what you ask. Just give me enough time to earn your price, and I will pay for Harriet, and all of my children." He decided this sounded better. Satisfied with his plan and his presentation, he sat Solomon near a bend in the creek, and dismounted.

He retrieved his lunch from a saddlebag. Two boiled eggs packed in straw and sweet grass, hard bread, and thick chunks of salt-cured ham. He took Solomon's reins and led him to the creek. The old horse plunged his mouth into the creek up to his nostrils, and took in long gulps of creek water. Dangerfield sat by the edge of the creek and ate his lunch while watching Solomon. He checked the other saddlebag, and verified the pouch was still there. He practiced his speech again. "I intend to buy my family, all of them," he said to himself in between bits. Lost in his thoughts, he had scarcely noticed the wind at his back, and the dark clouds behind him.

Solomon pulled his head out of the water and nickered. He lumbered away from the water and back on the trail, stamping his hooves. Dangerfield looked and saw black thunderheads to the west. A strong gust blew leaves and sticks across the trail. The thunderheads boiled and bloomed, black dirty mushroom tops erupting and shape-shifting in the sky. Dangerfield wet his finger and held it aloft. The storm was directly behind him, heading east, and moving faster than he could ride.

He considered his options. If he rode back toward home, he would ride directly into the teeth of the oncoming storm. If he pressed on toward Jennings' place, the storm would catch him from behind, long before he arrived. Having ridden this path countless times, he knew he had at least another two hours of riding ahead of him. Solomon was too old to ride hard for two hours. He looked for a suitable place to bed down, someplace with shelter for Solomon. The trail ahead was broad and flat, and the surrounding trees were tall and widely spaced. There were no ditches or low spaces. He quickly saddled up and began riding hard toward the Jennings farm. Maybe there was shelter further along the trail, or at least a ditch or low spot. He started with a canter, and then a gallop as Solomon warmed up.

They had gone a little over two miles when the storm caught them. Silver blades of rain pelted the ground in front of him. His back was instantly soaked, and a gust blew his hat off from behind. He reached up just as hit hat flew forward, and he grabbed it before it flew over Solomon's head. The trail was wet, but hard-packed, and still passable. Solomon's hooves threw up chunks of clay and mud as he hammered on. Although early in the afternoon, it quickly became dark as midnight, and Dangerfield could not see beyond Solomon's shaggy head. A thunderclap erupted directly overhead, and Solomon reared up in terror. Dangerfield stayed mounted, and tried to rein his horse back.

Hail stones the size of robins' eggs began pelting man and rider. He pulled his hat down as low as he could over his face. Hundreds of hail mallets pounded his back, and thudded against Solomon's flanks. Another boom of thunder, and Solomon reared again. Dangerfield pressed his knees against the horse's flank and leaned forward against the saddle, trying to cover the horse's eyes. Dangerfield looked up and saw a break in the clouds, and a thin crease of daylight, through which hail and wind and lightning poured forth as from an Old Testament fable. Solomon was bucking and snorting, and in the roar of thunder, hail and horse, Dangerfield did not hear the crack of an old oak tree as it succumbed to the wind, nor did he see it falling toward him.

He felt something pushing against him, and then an enormous wooden pillar shoved him off the horse. Falling through space, he put his arm out, and landed on his side. He tried to get up, but could not move. He heard Solomon roar, looked up, and saw the tree falling in slow motion toward the horse. Solomon was in front of him, and as the tree continued falling, it pressed down on Solomon's back. The big horse's legs buckled under the falling oak, and Solomon began stumbling and falling toward Dangerfield. As the horse stumbled toward him, Dangerfield rolled away, and Solomon fell on his side under the weight of the tree. Dangerfield watched his horse, wall-eyed and screaming, scramble to stand up. He tried to stand up to calm his mount, but as he struggled to rise, Dangerfield stumbled and fell down an embankment. He rolled twice before reaching out his hand to stop his fall. He felt a searing pain in the back of his head, and saw bright yellow stars and flashes of lightning directly in front of him. And then he saw nothing.

He awoke not knowing where he was, or how long he had been there. There was no wind, and the sun shone through a gauzy film of clouds. His head pulsed, and each surge of blood through his veins brought a dull pain. He sat up slowly, and tested his limbs. His left arm was fine. He moved his right arm, and a bolt of fire shot through his shoulder. He moved it again, and this time he was able to move it forward and back. He struggled to his feet. His legs wobbled, but he was able to stand, walk a few feet, and take note of his situation.

The creek below him surged, turbid and roiled with sediment. A rock shelf jutted out from the embankment, and he could see a dark mottled clump of his own hair on the edge of the rock. He felt the back of his head, and looked at his hand. It was slick with dark blood and hair. Below the rock, the creek boiled, and man-sized tree limbs swirled in the foam eddies near the rocks. He realized that but for the rock shelf, he would have fallen unconscious into the surging water. He climbed up the creek bank and tried to get his bearings in this newly formed landscape.

Every tree in sight was blown over, all in the same direction. The trail had disappeared under countless fallen trees. But for the angle of the sun, it would have been impossible to tell east from west. Nothing moved in the sky or on the ground.

He heard a noise to his right, and saw Solomon shaking his head. His reins were tangled around the branches of a fallen tree, and he was violently trying to free himself. Dangerfield saw an enormous oak that had fallen, but not all the way to the ground. He surmised that Solomon had been knocked over, but had been able to stand up and get clear of the tree. Dangerfield walked up and stroked the horse's mane. He pulled his hand back and it was slick with blood.

Solomon's left flank from mane to tail was raked and bleeding where the branches of the falling tree had scraped him. None of the scratches was deep, or pulsing. He talked quietly to the horse while he contemplated what to do next. He took off his shirt and wrung it out in his hands. He then wiped all the blood off Solomon's flank, and watched the scratches. Each time the blood returned, he wiped his flank again, pressing hard against the animal's side and pushing his shirt against the wounds until the blood stopped flowing. He untangled the reins and dropped them on the ground. He walked to the creek, rinsed out his bloody shirt, wrung it out, and put it on. He found his soaking and battered hat under a tree branch. He checked the saddlebags. The leather pouch was still there, covered in wet oats, straw and grass. He pulled out the letter. Still intact, and dry. He folded it carefully, put it back in the pouch, and buried it at the bottom of the saddlebag.

He put his hand to his eyes and looked toward the sky. He calculated it was late afternoon. He could make it to Jennings' place before nightfall if he could find the trail, and if Solomon could still run. He walked east about fifty yards, and found the outline of the trail – a trace of hard-packed mud with wet grass and stones on either side. He walked back, remounted the saddle, and began picking his way toward the trail, riding slowly east.

He arrived at the Jennings farm before dusk. When he clattered into the yard, he saw Jericho walking toward his cabin. Jericho saw him, and ran toward him. He stopped short as he approached.

"You look like you been fighting with the Devil himself," said Jericho. "What happened?"

"Got caught in that storm. We both made it out, although Old Man here got scratched up a bit. Where's your mother?"

"In the house with Lewis and Mistress Carola," replied Jericho. "All the house servants went inside during the storm." Dangerfield dismounted. "Take Solomon to the stable. Don't brush him, just a few oats and water." Dangerfield retrieved the pouch from the saddlebag and tucked it under his arm. Jericho led the wounded horse toward the barn.

He walked toward the house, and knocked on the door. Lilly answered. She stared at him, but said nothing for a long while. "You look like you should have stayed with Henry an extra day," she offered. "Weren't no reason to ride in that storm."

"I made it out okay, Lilly. Where is Harriet?"

"Inside, tending to Mistress Carola. I will send her out."

Harriet emerged a few moments later. "Lord Almighty," she said softly as she studied him. Neither husband nor wife said another word as they embraced.

"I did sorely miss you," said Harriet finally. "Lucy and Agnes have been fine, but

Junior and Gabriel been acting out while you were gone. They missed their daddy. I told 'em they keep acting out, they'd be sorry when you got back."

"I'll get 'em right soon enough. They know where I keep the switch. How's the baby?"

"Slept fine for awhile, but lately he ain't been sleeping. Lilly says he has colick, but he eats fine. Lilly has him in the house for now, until he starts sleeping better." She kissed him, and wrapped her arms around his waist.

"I need to tell you something real important," he said. "Tell Lilly you need to step out for a bit, and come with me. Tell her to watch the baby. I need to tell you now."

They walked together toward their cabin. Inside, Agnes and Lucy were stirring the coals of the fire. They ran toward their father, babbling excitedly. He picked them up, one in each arm.

"I missed you girls," said Dangerfield. "Where are your brothers?"

"Junior went out to gather wood, and Gabriel been tending the hogs all morning."

"You girls run out and fetch your brothers. Tell them to come back to the cabin. Tell them I am home."

Lucy and Agnes scampered outside toward the stables and fields, leaving Dangerfield and his wife alone in the cabin. Dangerfield watched as the girls ran from the cabin. He sighed before speaking.

"Henry says he is moving my family to Ohio. He plans to sell the farm, take the money, and move Elsey and all of us to Ohio. Wants all of us to live like a free and proper family."

Harriet sat on the bed.

"You aim to go with him? With your family?"

"I aim to, but not without you and the children. If Henry takes all of us, I would be a free man as soon as we cross the river. And I aim to go, but not without you and the family."

"But how are going to go?" said Harriet. "Marse Lewis won't let us leave. And we can't run. Seven runaways and a baby among 'em can't hide anywhere for very long. Can't keep quiet, and there ain't no place big enough for all of us."

"Won't be runaways. I aim to buy all of you from Marse Lewis. Pay for all of you. I buy you free and clear, and we go as we please, as a free and proper family."

"How are you going to get the money?"

"Don't know yet. I might have to work it off with Marse Lewis, or work at the riverport. Might take a few months to get the money. Once I get it, I buy all of us, and we move to Ohio. We won't be runaways."

Harriet slumped on the bed. "When are you going to tell Marse Lewis? How? What if he says no, what if . . . ."

"Don't worry about any of that now. I just need to talk to him. I know him better than anyone else here. Just don't worry about anything."

Dangerfield turned to walk out of the cabin, but his legs failed him, and he fell on the bed next to Harriet. The room darkened, and Harriet's face became clouded and hazy. "I need to set for a while," he mumbled. "Hit my head on something during the storm." Harriet reached up to hold his head, and recoiled when her hand came back bloody.

"You need to rest right now," she said. She found a piece of coarse linen cloth and pressed it against the back of his head. He lay down on the bed, and closed his eyes while Harriet stanched the wound on the back of his head.

He awoke to the sound of muted voices and sobs. He sat up slowly, and the first thing he saw was Lewis Jennings, gazing at him intently, fingering his black mustache.

"You gave us quite a scare," said Lewis. "You should have considered staying at Henry's instead of riding out that storm. I would have forgiven the extra day."

"I said I'd be back in two weeks, Marse, and I keep my word." He tried to stand, but fell back on the bed.

"I think it would be best if you get some rest," said Lewis. "You can resume your duties tomorrow morning. There is no shortage of work that needs to be done." Lewis put his hand on Dangerfield's shoulder and spoke softly in his ear. "You are of more value to me healthy than ill. Rest here with your family, and we can determine what needs to be done early tomorrow morning."

Lewis stood up to leave. "Lilly can handle Harriet's duties in the house for the evening. Harriet, I assume will want to spend this evening here. I will expect you back at the house by dawn tomorrow."

He turned toward the door, but Dangerfield spoke.

"Marse, I need to speak with you now about something urgent. It can't wait."

Dangerfield stood, steadying himself against the bed. "This is important, Marse, and we should talk now, if it suits you. Let's talk outside."

Lewis twisted his mustache and stared at him, slack-jawed. "You want to discuss something with me now, and it cannot wait until morning," he said softly. "Very well, let's discuss this now." Lewis exited the cabin. Dangerfield picked up the pouch and followed him.

Outside, the last remnants of daylight hovered above the hills. Lewis flicked at a black fly on his lapel, and brushed a thread from his sleeve.

"I trust Henry is well," said Lewis not looking up from his suit. "I hope your news does not concern Henry's health."

"No Marse, Henry – Marse Henry is fine. I want to . . . there is a matter of great importance to me and I . . . ."

Lewis looked up from his sleeve. "Yes," he said evenly.

"Well, Marse, I want to buy Harriet and my children. All of them. Jericho too. I will pay whatever price you ask. I want to buy Harriet and all my children, and

Jericho. Just give me enough time to earn your price, so I can buy them from you, right and proper. That's what I want to discuss."

Lewis looked down at his brightly polished boots. A large black beetle lumbered across the ground in front of him. Lewis watched the creature for a few seconds, then crushed it with his bootheel, grinding the insect into the dirt in a half-circle.

"You want to buy your family," Lewis said not looking up as he used the toe of his boot to inter the crushed bug in the soft dirt. "You want to buy your family. Have you any idea what a Negro woman in her prime childbearing years is worth on the slave market," he said without waiting for an answer. "Have you any idea what I could get for your children, all healthy, with no evident deformities? And what of Jericho, what do you think the market will pay for a healthy young buck, with a strong back, and in need of nothing except perhaps a firmer hand, and a bit more guidance? Have you any idea what I could have already gotten for your family?"

"No, Marse, I don't. That's why I ask you to name your price. Harriet, my new baby, all my children, and Jericho. Just give me enough time to earn it, and I will pay what you ask, whatever it is." Dangerfield propped his hand against the cabin wall.

"Given your present condition, I don't think it wise for you and I to discuss this matter now," said Lewis softly. "Just an hour ago, Harriet was convinced you were going to die. I saw the wound on the back of your head – that will take some time to heal. It is evident to me that your head injury has affected your better judgment. I suggest you sleep this evening, and you can resume your duties tomorrow morning. As I said, you should have considered staying home one extra day instead of riding in that storm. I would have forgiven the extra day. Rest, and we can talk tomorrow. I will see you at dawn."

Lewis turned to leave, but Dangerfield spoke again. "I mean what I say, Marse. I aim to buy my family, right and proper. Set your price. You been a man of your word to me Marse. Ten years, and you kept your word to me. Done everything you said you would. I don't expect that to change. You been a man of your word, and I aim to be a man of my word. Set your price, and I start in tomorrow."

Lewis sucked in air through his teeth. "Did Henry put you up to this? Is this nonsense Henry's idea? I always thought him to be a man of good sense, even if a bit coarse and uncultured. But this . . . ."

"Ain't Marse Henry's doing. It's my doing," interrupted Dangerfield. "I want my family to be free. I will do what I need to do here. Work as long as we agree on. But I want my family to be free. Don't care how long it takes."

"Surely you don't think I need the money," retorted Lewis. "I could have sold your family any time I wanted during your absence. I could have sold them while you were here, in front of you. I certainly don't need the money, if that is your motivation."

"Ain't about your money, Marse. You didn't sell my family because you said you wouldn't. And you keep your word, Marse. I don't expect that to change."

Lewis paused, and looked up at the setting sun. "Yes, I keep my word," he said softly. "That is the one thing my father always taught me, a man is only as good as his word. And I always keep my word." He looked at Dangerfield. "And you did try to save my father."

"Yes, Marse, I did."

Lewis picked at his mustache. "Perhaps it would be better if I had this discussion with Henry. Although you have been invaluable to my family, I simply cannot sell property to property. The law won't allow it. It would be the legal equivalent of a man selling a cow to a pig, although surely you will understand that is not how I value you or your family. I . . . ."

Dangerfield retrieved the pouch from under his arm, and removed the letter. "Marse Henry gave me this."

Lewis squinted his eyes as he read the letter in the fading daylight. He held the letter at the end of his arms, and then pulled it closer to his face. "Forever manumitted and emancipated according to the laws of the Commonwealth of Virginia," he muttered softly to himself. "I see." He handed the letter back to Dangerfield.

"Does Henry have a duplicate of this letter with him?"

"Yes, he does. He told me he wrote out another one and has it at his house."

"Of course he does. And when does he intend to file this with the county?"

"September 25, 1858, Marse."

Lewis looked toward the house. The sun had now fallen below the top of the hills.

"Very well then, let's discuss the price of my inventory, one free man to another free man. For your wife, your four children and Jericho, I would expect nothing less than $3,000. I could easily get more for all of them on the open market, probably $4,000. Harriet alone is worth $2,000, perhaps more because she is still rather young, produces magnificent children, and she is pretty. Jericho might be worth $500. The younger four have very little value now, but in time, I can only assume your boys would be strong and disciplined. And Lucy and Agnes will likely inherit their mother's physical gifts. So although they are not of much value now, your girls will soon be of enormous value on the market. That is what I am giving up."

Lewis sucked at his teeth. "A prize thoroughbred has no practical value as a wobbling foal, but the wise man buys the future, not the present," said Lewis. "That is what you are buying, and what I am giving up. Surely you understand."

Dangerfield removed his hand from the cabin wall, and stood upright. "I ain't buying the future or the past, Marse. Just my family. Name your price, Marse, and keep your word. That's all I ask."

"Very well then. At present, I am unwilling to sell Jericho and all of your children. They are worth too much to me in the future. Because you and Harriet are obviously suited to each other, I will sell Harriet and your newborn baby to you for $1,500. Over time, I assume the girls can take on Harriet's familial duties. Lilly can help. Take as much time as you need to earn the money. We can discuss your other children and Jericho when you come back with the $1,500."

Dangerfield's head throbbed as anger surged through his veins. "I want my whole family, Marse. All of them," he hissed.

"The arrangement is Harriet and your newborn baby, $1,500. That is my offer at present. Come back with the money, and we can talk about the others."

Dangerfield steadied himself against the cabin wall. "You keep your word on Harriet and the baby, and we can talk about the others later?" said Dangerfield. "Is that your promise?"

"I am a man of my word," said Lewis. "One free man to another."

Lewis extended his hand. Dangerfield felt the heat in his mouth and the bile in his veins, but he extended his hand toward Lewis. Lewis Jennings' soft and unworked hands were no match for Dangerfield's large, calloused and farm-worn hands as the men completed their business.

"You have quite the strong grip," said Lewis. "I trust that will come in handy over the next several months."

Lewis turned and walked toward his house. Candles flickered in the windows. Dangerfield slumped against the cabin wall, and felt a small trickle of blood running down the back of his neck. He struggled to his feet, and stumbled into the cabin.

CHAPTER 34

Turner awoke early the next morning, still strapped into the hospital bed. An orderly had loosened the restraints the night before, but they were still tight enough to keep him from moving. He looked around the sparse room, saw no one, and tried to wriggle free from the restraints. Behind him, he heard the soft voice of his orderly.

"Please don't struggle, Dr. Turner. Dr. Cornell says we can remove the restraints this morning, and have you walk around today. How are you feeling?"

The orderly was a tall, thick-set man, with a barrel chest and hair on his arms that was long enough to braid. His head was clean-shaven, and he wore a small diamond stud in each ear. A neatly groomed goatee covered his chin.

"I am fine, Oliver, thank you. When can we take these off? I need to stretch and urinate like a free man."

"Dr. Cornell says I can take them off now. I brought your breakfast. Dr. Cornell will be here at 9:30 for your interview."

Oliver released the restraints. He put his hand behind Turner's back as he sat up, and helped him to his feet.

Turner began walking toward the bathroom, but his knees buckled, and he almost fell. Oliver gripped his arm, pulled him up, and began walking him toward the bathroom.

"Takes awhile to get your legs back," said Oliver. "Almost three full days in restraints, and your muscles get weak. You'll be fine by tomorrow. Just walk slowly."

Turner felt a sharp twinge as the blood slowly returned to his legs.

"I need to sit down, Oliver."

"Best to keep walking, Dr. Turner. Your legs are stiff right now, but you need to get moving. Keep walking, I'll help you."

"Oliver, my legs are burning, just let me . . . ."

"I've got you. Just keep moving. Almost there."

Oliver opened the bathroom door and escorted Turner inside. Oliver gripped his arm to keep him from falling. Turner's ill-fitting hospital gown fell off his shoulder as he sat, leaving him almost naked with Oliver holding his arm.

"I assume you'll be fine from here," said Oliver. Turner grabbed the safety rails next to the toilet seat and lowered himself. Oliver stared at him and smiled.

"Not used to being the patient, are you?"

"No. I don't intend to get used to it."

"No one does. Your breakfast is on the cart next to your bed. I'll give you some privacy. Ring the bell if you need help getting out of the bathroom. Stand up slowly, and walk slowly, back and forth." Oliver closed the door and walked quickly out of the room.

Turner sat on the toilet and contemplated his fate. Three days ago, he was Roger Hillman's leading candidate to be chief of surgery, a position he had been working toward for over ten years. He had everything lined up. Now, he was a patient in a psych ward, and needed help walking to the bathroom. He had to sit down to urinate. Forget chief of surgery, he might never practice medicine again. Everything he ever wanted, gone, because of some drug-induced dreams.

But the first dream came before any drugs. Way back in Harpers Ferry, when he saw Dangerfield Newby walking the streets. Or was it simply a reenactor? No, he knew what he saw then. And what about Frazier? Frazier read him instantly, like a comic book. And then Turner remembered what Frazier had told him back in Harpers Ferry:

"You must have the courage to accept your fate. Nat Turner and I were chosen – we did not seek. You must decide for yourself whether you have been chosen, and if so, what your path should be."

Turner struggled to lift himself from the toilet. "I am not crazy," he muttered to himself. "I know what I saw, what I felt. I know what I heard." He lifted himself and walked back to his bed, slowly and painfully at first. He continued to pace about the room, holding his gown so it would not fall off. After five minutes of pacing, he felt the strength in his legs return. He kept walking, back and forth, first slowly, and then faster while he thought. He lifted the lid off his breakfast. Lukewarm scrambled eggs, toast adorned with a rock-hard frozen pat of butter, a square container of jelly, and a pop-open cardboard container of orange juice. There was only one utensil, a small plastic spork. No sharp objects. Not even a thin plastic butter knife. He ate his breakfast standing up, and continued pacing.

He looked at the clock in his room. 9:10. Twenty minutes until his appointment with Cornell. He needed a plan. Whatever it is he was chosen to do, he couldn't do it here, in the psych ward. At least he still had Tracy. He owed her a huge dinner when this was all over.

He lifted the curtain and peeked through the window into the hallway. Doctors, nurses and orderlys rushed past. His patient ID tag was strapped to his wrist. He had no knife or scissors to cut it off. The giant hospital gown was the only clothing he had. He was naked underneath. He craned his head and looked as far as he could down the hall. There was Oliver, seated just outside the door, leafing through a magazine. Probably assigned to sit there, and monitor the room. Oliver was close enough to touch, if he simply opened the door. No chance of escape.

Stupid idea, anyway. Everyone knew who he was, where he lived, what he did. Even if he did get out, he would be running through the streets in a hospital gown, barefoot and half-naked. That would earn him a lifetime membership in the psych ward. He lowered the curtain and continued pacing and thinking.

"Think like a doctor," he said to himself. "First, do no harm. Second, what problem am I trying to solve?" He quickly determined that running or refusing to cooperate with Cornell would do great harm. "So stay put, and answer all of Cornell's questions," he thought to himself. "Do no harm."

"What problem am I trying to solve," he muttered again. Then he remembered something else Frazier had told him:

"I can't tell you whether you have been chosen to tell Dangerfield's story, or even whether he has a story. Perhaps you have been chosen to tell another story, someone else's story. Perhaps you have not been chosen for anything."

"So that's a good start," he said in a louder voice. "There are really three options. First, I have been chosen to tell Dangerfield's story. Second, I have been chosen to tell another story, someone else's story. Third, I have not been chosen for anything."

He ruled out option three. He had seen too much, and what he had seen was too vivid. He remembered what Dangerfield was wearing, and the way he slouched when he walked. Uncle Billy's yellow car, and the old man with the cane. The two men Billy shot. The car accident that killed Billy. And then the slave auction. He saw it all. And none of it made sense. Whatever it was, it made no sense, but there was a story, someone's story. So option three was out. He had been chosen for something. He had to find out what it was.

"That leaves Dangerfield, or someone else," he said as he paced back and forth. He looked at the clock. 9:20. Ten minutes until his visit with Cornell. "Think, Mike, think."

He had only seen Dangerfield three times, once in Harpers Ferry, once in his hotel, and once in the operating room. The first time was a fleeting glimpse. It could have been the heat, or maybe he was tired. Second time in the hotel was very real, but was very close in time to the first. He considered those to be one incident.

Third time in the OR was the most important. A vision at work was a sign. But he had not seen Dangerfield since then. Every vision since then was about Billy and his family. And then there was the slave auction. Who were those people?

"Maybe he was telling me something about someone else, trying to get my attention," Turner said to himself. The tumblers in his mind continued to turn, when Oliver walked in.

"Everything alright, Dr. Turner?" Oliver said. "It sounded like you were talking to someone."

"Yes, Oliver, everything is fine. I was going over some mental notes to prepare for my meeting with Dr. Cornell. Are we still meeting this morning?"

"Dr. Cornell will be here in five minutes." Oliver surveyed the room, and took a long look at Turner. "How are your legs? It looks like you have been up and about. Your strength is back?"

"Yes, Oliver, and thank you."

"Ring if you need anything." Oliver left to resume his post outside.

"Almost everything since the OR has been about Billy and Lorraine. The crash, the men who were killed. And then there was the slave auction. What was the connection?

But whatever the mystery was, he could not solve it here, at least not without help. He needed to convince Herbert Cornell to release him so he could finish his work. He would have to make Cornell his ally. He would have to convince Cornell he was well enough to go home. If not, then he needed another plan.

9:29. Cornell would be here any time. He sat in the chair next to his bed and poured himself a cup of water from the plastic pitcher.

Cornell came in a moment later. Still wearing the rumpled khaki pants and white sneakers, but he had changed his shirt. His oversize lab coat was buttoned only at the top button, while the rest of the coat flapped like seagull wings as he walked in. His spindle of thin blonde hair sprouted straight out of the top of his head like a bundle of cauliflower. A cluster of pens obscured the cursive stitching of his name. He pushed his metal-rimmed glasses on top of his head, squinted down at his charts, and sat opposite Turner.

"Good morning, Dr. Turner. I see you are up and about. How are you feeling?"

"Better, now that I don't have leather straps cutting off my circulation. Was it necessary to leave the restraints on for so long?"

"Yes, Dr. Turner it was. You do remember the events that got you here, don't you? Under the circumstances, consider yourself fortunate to be self-ambulatory."

"Not a good move, Mike," Turner thought to himself. "I need him to be my ally."

"Yes, of course, Herbert. Forgive me, and I am feeling much better. I feel ready to go home and continue my recovery."

"Please call me Dr. Cornell. And I am sure you are aware of the protocols and tests we must complete before you can even think of going home."

"Understood, Dr. Cornell. If you don't mind, I would like to begin the tests now. I understand you have a lot to go through."

"Yes. Why don't we start with some of the things you experienced after you took the sleeping pills. How would you describe those events? Would you say they were dreams? Hallucinations? Something else?"

Turner took a long gulp of water. "I would describe them as dreams, brought about in part by the sleeping pills. Hallucinations are generally caused by mind-altering drugs, chemicals that alter consciousness. Many things cause dreams, including stress, lack of sleep, alcohol."

Dr. Cornell did not look up as he jotted in his notebook.

"I see," Cornell said as he continued writing. "Have you ever taken mind-altering drugs? LSD, psilocybin, other psychedelics?"

"No. I never messed around with that stuff."

"Wise decision. What about marijuana or cocaine?"

"Pot, never. Cocaine, once or twice in med school when I needed a boost. Cocaine, as you know, is a stimulant, not a psychedelic. Not known as a mind-altering drug, but more of a performance-enhancing stimulant."

Cornell looked up from his notebook, smiled, and pulled his glasses down. "I am aware of the effects of cocaine, Dr. Turner. I was in med school once, not so long ago. I assume cocaine hasn't changed that much." He smiled again, and looked down at his notes. "Tell me about the chief of surgery position. Is that something you wanted, Roger Hillman's job?"

Turner paused, leaned back and closed his eyes. "I have wanted the chief of surgery position since my residency. I have a great deal of respect for Roger, and it would be an honor to have that job. I have wanted that job for over ten years. There were days when I thought about nothing else except being chief of surgery. Filling Roger's shoes. He's like a father to me."

"Were you nervous about the job? Afraid you might not get it, that someone else would take it from you?"

"No, not at all. I know what I bring to the table. I know I can be chief of surgery. But I also know it isn't my job. Nothing is given to anyone. Everything must be earned."

"I see," said Cornell, scribbling in his notebook. "And how will you feel if you don't get chief of surgery? What then?"

"Given where I am now, Dr. Cornell, I have to assume I won't be chief of anything any time soon. I have a higher calling."

"What do you mean by 'higher calling'?"

Turner took another long sip of water.

"Dr. Cornell, do you consider yourself to be a materialist, or a dualist?"

"What do you mean?"

"I mean do you think every aspect of human behavior can be explained by chemistry and neurophysiology, or is some part of our existence a mystery? Is everything determined by genes and chemicals, or is there something else, something we can't explain?"

Cornell removed his glasses and put his pen and notebook in his lap. "This might surprise you, Dr. Turner, but I believe in God. I believe in heaven and earth, good and evil, and moral certainties. I think the human mind is an immensely complicated thing, far more complex than science will ever explain. Much can be explained by genes and neurophysiology, but much more cannot. There is a God who knows all, who has endowed us with the power to do good and the power to do evil. That is the backbone of my faith."

He put his glasses back on, and began writing. "I don't know if that answers your question, Dr. Turner, but that is the best answer I have."

"You believe in God?" Turner asked. "Heaven, hell, Noah's Ark, creation, all of that?"

"Not all of it. I believe the Bible is very creative fiction, with a purpose – to help us understand our place in the universe. The stories may not be factually true, but the message is unassailable. We are all God's creatures, with gifts and burdens. We are responsible for using our gifts wisely, and handling our burdens with grace. God will judge us in both areas."

Cornell wrote a long passage in his notebook before continuing.

"And what about you, Dr. Turner? Do you believe in God?"

"No, Dr. Cornell, I don't. I believe in science, chemistry, logic and reason. I think everything in the human mind can be explained by genes, chemistry, and neurophysiology. There is no logic or facts that support belief in God."

"That's why they call it 'faith,' Dr. Turner." Cornell looked up and smiled.

"I don't mean to disparage your faith, or anyone else's," Turner said, quickly remembering that Cornell held his fate in his notebook. "It's just that everything I have studied, my entire professional career, has been dedicated to solving problems using the knowledge we have. 'Faith' seems to be a cop-out."

"I see," said Cornell. "So you must be a materialist."

"I think it is the only rational option. Most of the doctors and scientists I know are materialists."

Cornell laughed. "I was certainly in the minority in med school," he said. "Although there were a few of us who believed in God. Even a few other psychiatry residents, although some of them liked to experiment with psychotropics. Faith requires us to let go, to recognize there are mysteries we cannot know. I am comfortable not knowing everything about the human mind. There are simply some things that defy explanation. It takes courage to accept that. It takes even more courage to have faith in an unpopular God."

Neither man spoke for some time. The only sound was the plodding tick of the wall clock.

"Do you believe in self-determination, Dr. Turner?"

"Yes, I do. I believe most people choose their path, based on their ability and talent."

"And did you choose your path, Dr. Turner?"

"Yes. I knew early on that I had talents and abilities that I could use to help others."

"Then why are you here? Certainly no one would choose to be in your present circumstance."

"I made conscious, deliberate decisions. I chose to take the medication, because I thought it would help me find out . . . ."

"Find out what, Dr. Turner? What is it you are looking for? You have a beautiful wife, a successful medical career, a brilliant mind, and until recently, you had the inside track to be chief of surgery at a major teaching hospital. What else could you possibly want? What don't you have? And why would you give any of that up to be here?"

Turner thought, but could not articulate an answer to Cornell's simple question. Cornell set aside his notebook, and waited for an answer.

Turner sat silently contemplating Cornell's question. And then he remembered Frazier's words from Harpers Ferry:

"You must have the courage to accept your fate. Nat Turner and I were chosen – we did not seek. You must decide for yourself whether you have been chosen, and if so, what your path should be."

He thought about Dangerfield, Billy, the old man, the car crash, the slave auction. He thought about the men Billy killed. It was real, these things happened. He had to find out why. This is what mattered.

"What I want, Dr. Cornell, is courage to accept my fate, whatever it is. What I don't have is clarity on what that fate is."

"Is this the 'higher calling' you spoke of earlier?"

"I guess so," said Turner.

Cornell wrote in his notebook, turned to a clean page, and continued writing for a long time before speaking.

"Tracy told us about the dreams you had, events that seem to have happened long ago. What do these mean to you?"

"I don't know. That's what I want to find out."

"Do you think these events actually happened?"

"I am certain they happened. The dreams are too vivid, too real. These things happened. I just don't know why."

"Is it possible you knew of these events earlier? That someone told you about these things when you were a child, and something more recent has triggered these memories?"

"I had not considered that."

Cornell pushed his glasses up and rubbed his eyes.

"What do you want to happen, Dr. Turner? What's next for you?"

"I must answer my higher calling, wherever it leads me."

"What are you willing to give up to answer this 'higher calling'?"

"I don't have much else left. Not much to lose."

"What about your career?"

"I think we both know chief of surgery is out. Medicine is out. Maybe I could teach someplace, but now, even that is uncertain. A week ago, my career was everything. Now, I know what matters. My calling. And Tracy."

"Yes, Tracy. Do you see her as the answer to your problem?"

"I don't have a problem, Dr. Cornell. I have an opportunity. I know what I have lost. I also know what I stand to gain. I didn't know what I was looking for until now."

"I see." Cornell picked up his pen, started to write, and put it down again."

"Who is going to help you achieve this 'higher calling'? Tracy?"

"Yes. As soon as I get out, Tracy will help me. She has been my rock."

Cornell chuckled. "Dr. Turner, I hope you can understand why we can't release you to Tracy's care. That would be like releasing a drunk to the custody of his bartender."

"You can't keep me here forever."

"Dr. Turner, I have a legal and medical obligation to keep you here until I am satisfied you no longer pose a threat to yourself or others."

"I have never posed a threat to Tracy or anyone else. She will tell you that. So there is no threat to 'others.' And any threat to my safety was temporary, and no longer exists."

Turner poured himself a glass of water from the plastic pitcher. His hands trembled. Water sloshed on the table and the floor.

"Herbert – Dr. Cornell – I pose no threat to anyone," said Turner evenly. "I assume you have spoken with Tracy. I have never threatened her, and I pose no threat to her or anyone else. You cannot keep me here."

Herbert Cornell closed his eyes and tapped his pen against his notebook. "Alright, Dr. Turner. Let me speak with your wife, and review your file. If I am convinced that you pose no risk to others or yourself, you may be eligible for release."

Cornell stood to leave, then spun around to face Turner.

"Whatever you choose to do after you leave," said Cornell, "I hope you take the time to understand how you got here, and what you really want. I sense you are trying to solve a problem that I cannot help you with. I would love to help you solve it, but I sense you do not yet know what problem you are solving, or what you hope to learn. And if you don't know what you want, I cannot help you."

Cornell turned toward the door. "Feel free to move about, get your strength back," said Cornell.

Turner watched as Cornell exited, the door swinging softly behind him.

CHAPTER 35

MID SEPTEMBER, 1858

Dangerfield spent the next week recovering at the Jennings plantation. He intended to leave and find whatever work he could find as a freeman in Virginia. If he could not find work in Virginia, he would ride into Ohio and Kentucky and do whatever freeman's work he could until he had $1,500. Lewis Jennings was not happy about him leaving, but it was Lewis' insistence on $1,500 for his wife and one child that left him no choice. And now that Dangerfield was emancipated, he could not count on Lewis paying him a fair wage. Lewis would have him working for twenty years to earn the money. Much better to leave with his emancipation papers in hand and take his chances as a freeman, earning freeman's wages. If he earned enough, he could negotiate for the rest of his family.

The night before he was to leave, he curled up in his bunk with Harriet. The baby nursed at her breast while they talked.

"Still don't see why you can't stay here and work for Marse Lewis. Maybe he pays you enough to buy us all," said Harriet.

"I can make more money faster as a freeman than I can working for Marse Lewis. He'll always think of me as Henry Newby's boy, and pay me what he has always paid Henry, maybe even less. Lewis don't care about my papers. He and Henry had an arrangement, and I don't reckon he will change it. If I work elsewhere, I can set my own price, and get back here faster."

Harriet curled up closer to him.

"How long you reckon it will take?"

"Don't know. A year, maybe two. Gabriel does alright down at the riverport. Maybe I could work with him for a spell, least until something else comes up."

"I hear the girls in the house talk. Lilly says Virginia ain't no place for a freeman. She says they can round you up and sell you if they catch you, papers or not."

Dangerfield chuckled. "Henry told me that too. Henry says I have a year after my free date 'fore they can round me up. After the year is up, I have to be careful. 'Til then, I can go where I please, like any freeman."

The baby cried, and Harriet slid her breast toward him.

"Why not have Henry buy us all? He did offer to buy us didn't he?"

"He did, but then Henry owns you. And Henry aint been well. If something happens to Henry before he emancipates you, there's no tellin' where you all would end up."

"Why not just work for Henry? He will pay you fairer wages than Marse Lewis."

"Won't be too much different than working for Marse Lewis. Both of them see me as Henry's son. And this is my family, and I have to do this my way. I don't want to depend on Henry or Lewis to get my family."

They lay together on the bed in silence.

"Did Marse Lewis say you could buy the rest of us when you got back" said Harriet.

"'Come back with the money, and we can talk about the others,' is what he said."

"Do you believe him?"

"Marse Lewis never give me any reason to question his honesty. He has always kept his word with me."

"But do you believe him? Do you trust him?"

"Don't have a choice. He owns all of you," said Dangerfield.

"I hear what goes on in the house," said Harriet. "Mistress Carola tells us things like it was our business. Marse Lewis likes to spend money, just like his daddy. Owes people in town. He borrowed a lot of money for that big Morgan he rides. Word is he don't even own the saddle. Had to borrow money for that too. And his wife Virginia likes to spend almost as much as he does."

"Well, that apple fell right next to the tree," said Dangerfield.

They both laughed, and burrowed under the rough wool blanket.

"Thing is, I worry that he won't keep his promise," said Harriet. "He could run up too much debt, and have to sell some of the slaves. I heard Mistress Carola tell Lilly how much she would get if Marse Lewis sold her South. Mistress threatens to sell Lilly South 'bout twice a week. And I've seen his books. Mistress Carola looks at 'em every day. He has prices written down for every one of us."

Dangerfield said nothing. "Like I said, he ain't never broken his word with me. Besides, I don't have much choice right now. I have to trust him."

The baby spit out Harriet's nipple, and promptly fell asleep.

"When do you aim to leave," said Harriet.

"First light tomorrow."

"Let's not wake the children tomorrow. Best if you just leave. They know why you have to go."

Harriet put the baby in his crib, and slid in bed next to her husband. He kissed her swollen breasts, and he felt her body jump at his touch. She pulled him closer, and he covered them both with the blanket. After they had quietly eased into the paradise of each other's bodies, they both fell asleep.

Before dawn the next morning, Dangerfield lit a candle and surveyed his cabin. Harriet was naked and asleep in his bed. His baby boy John curled up in the crib Dangerfield had made out of old fence boards and barn planks. Junior and Gabriel, in their bunks, snoring. Lucy and Agnes, their spindly brown legs coiled together like vines in the bunk they shared. Jericho's arm sprawled over the edge of his bed. Dangerfield took a long look at his sleeping family and tried to create an image of them he could take with him. He kissed his sleeping wife on the cheek, pulled on his boots, and left for the stable.

He had Solomon fed and saddled and ready to ride before first light. He checked his saddlebags, and made certain the leather pouch with his papers was drawn tight. He rode past his cabin, and heard no sound from inside. As he turned up the trail, he saw candles burning in the kitchen of the main house. Lilly looked out the window and nodded toward him. He tipped his hat, but did not stop.

He arrived at Henry's farm shortly after noon. He let Solomon gallop the last hundred yards or, knowing the big horse had very few hard runs left in him. Gabriel and Henry were next to the barn, loading a wagon. The carriage horses blew and stamped in the paddock next to the barn. The door to the house was open, and Elsey emerged carrying an armful of clothes and linens.

"You all look like you about to go somewheres," said Dangerfield.

Elsey put the clothes she was carrying on the ground, and rushed to embrace her son. "Talk to Henry," she said. "There's been some changes."

Dangerfield dismounted, threw the reins over Solomon's head, and walked toward the barn.

Henry walked toward his son. "Planned on writing you, but I figured you'd be back before the letter arrived." He wiped his brow with a large stained handkerchief.

"John Fox wants to move in sooner than expected," said Henry. "He's got three hundred acres down east, but it's mostly tobacco. He's thinking about starting a cattle herd, and this place would suit him for that. I suspect he plans to take up with Anna Mae before too long. Maybe the two of them could live here." Henry coughed until his face turned purple. He spat on the ground and wiped his mouth with his handkerchief.

"'Course, his house near Warrenton is big enough for two families," said Henry. "If I had been thinking, I would have bought a place down east, got into tobacco. I could have been a retired gentleman planter. Big white house, fences, fancy horses. Instead, I spent my whole life cutting corn and standing in pig shit." Henry looked at his house, with its fading paint, small porch, and rough-planked roof. "Raised ever one of you in this house," he said to himself. "Maybe could have done more if I'd gotten into tobacco. It don't matter. Fox wants to move in right away."

Gabriel called out. "About time you got here, brother. I was fixin' to burn all your things to make room in the wagon for mine."

The brothers laughed and embraced, joking about whose belongings should get more room in the wagon.

"That's enough, you two. We got enough work to do as it is. Gabriel, finish loading up that wagon, and tie it down. I need to speak to your brother for a bit."

Henry and Dangerfield walked toward the house. "I know you can't go with us to Ohio, least not yet," said Henry. "I know you have obligations to Lewis Jennings. It's just that things happened pretty quick. And if John Fox pays what he promised, we can pay for the new house in Ohio, and live in Ohio free and clear, no obligations to anybody."

"When do you aim to leave," said Dangerfield.

"We get everything packed up, we can leave in three days. You can take care of your obligations to Lewis Jennings, and join us in Ohio after you get Harriet and your children. Things will be tight once you join us, but least most of us will be together. After we get settled in, you, me and Gabriel can build a smaller house for you and your family."

"What about Anna Mae," said Dangerfield.

"I suspect she will stay here with John Fox. He made clear he intends to take care of her. Rich as he is, no one will bother him if he takes up with her."

The two men reached the house. Henry coughed and spat again. "I need to sit for a spell. Moving all them boxes made me tired." Dangerfield helped his father into one of the chairs on the tiny front porch.

"Speaking of Prince Lewis, did you speak with him about buying your family?"

"I did, Henry."

"What did he say?"

"Said I could buy Harriet and the baby if I paid him $1,500,"

Henry's face darkened. "Just Harriet and the baby? What about the others?"

"Said the deal was only for Harriet and the baby. Said we could talk about the others after I came back with the money."

"That son of a bitch," muttered Henry. "Damn son of a bitch. No better than his father." Henry's face turned purple as he kicked at a pebble on the porch.

"What do you aim to do," said Henry.

"I intend to head out, earn the money, come back and buy my family, and join you all in Ohio."

"I see," said Henry. "What do you plan to do? What work will you do? Who will you work for? Where?"

"I don't have it all sorted out just yet, Henry. I aim to head out to Ohio first. Easier for a freeman to find work in Ohio than in Virginia. Virginia ain't no place for a freeman."

"I think I told you that. Glad you listened to that part."

"I listened, Henry, you know I did. I know I'll get better freeman's wages in Ohio than Virginia. Far as the work, I'll do harness work, repair saddles, make boots. That will pay better than simple farm work although I expect to do quite a bit of that too. Anything I need to get the money."

"Sounds like you got most of it sorted out. I expect you will make more money in saddles than farm work." Henry picked up a pebble and tossed it away from the house.

"How do you intend to get work?"

"Ask around. Pay some visits to shops in town, see who needs work to be done."

"I see," said Henry. "Might not be as easy as you think. Even in Ohio, folks might not appreciate a free black man offering his services. You got to be careful."

"How long do you think it will take to get the money to buy Harriet and the baby," said Henry.

"I don't know. I aim to have it within a year."

"Only a year," said Henry. "Might want to count on it taking longer than that. Two, maybe three years."

Neither man spoke for some time.

"What happens when you come back," said Henry. "How do you aim to get the rest of your family?"

"Don't know just yet. I intend to get more than the $1,500, and offer to buy everyone with whatever money I have."

"How much extra you think you will need to buy the rest?"

"Don't know that either. Marse Lewis said come back with $1,500 and we'd talk about the rest."

"Do you trust Lewis to keep his word?"

"He ain't never given me a reason not to trust him. Besides, I don't have much of a choice now. I have to trust him."

Neither man spoke for a long while. Henry coughed into his handkerchief.

"You ever consider just taking Harriet and the rest of your family? Lewis seems to trust you. You take Harriet, the baby, and the rest. If you leave at night, you could make good time before Lewis catches on."

"I gave that some thought, Henry, but it won't work. Me, Harriet, Lucy, Agnes, Junior and Gabriel is six people right there. Add in the baby and Jericho, and you got seven runaways and me trying to hide them all. Lewis keeps track of his property. He'd know in an hour if Harriet was gone from the house. I don't know how I'd get all eight of us out of Virginia without getting caught."

"You'd take Jericho too?"

"Wouldn't leave him with Lewis. I promised Harriet I'd look after him."

"Sounds like you got that sorted out too," said Henry.

Dangerfield pushed the toe of his boot against a loose board on the porch.

"Henry, did you mean it when you offered to buy my family?"

"I meant it then."

"Thing is, if you meant it, you could buy my family right now. I could pay you back once we are all in Ohio. Might take awhile, but I would pay you ever penny."

"I thought you wanted to do this yourself. Didn't need me."

"I didn't then, but I did not count on Lewis only selling Harriet and the baby. I can't just leave the others."

Henry studied the loose floorboard. "Thought I fixed that last week," he muttered to himself. He struggled to get out of his chair.

"So you changed your mind, then?" said Henry. "'Bout me buying your family?"

"I reckon so, Henry. You know I wouldn't ask you 'less it was important. I need you to buy my family. I will pay you back."

Henry sighed and walked stiffly toward the front door.

"Come on in the house. I want to show you something while Elsey is outside."

The two men walked upstairs into Henry and Elsey's bedroom. Henry reached into a large box on the floor, and pulled out a thick leather-bound book. He began thumbing through the delicate pages.

"What's in that book," said Dangerfield.

"Everything I own, and everything I ever did own is in this book," said Henry. "Cattle, pigs, sheep, buildings, farm equipment, and slaves. Every slave I ever owned is in this book." Henry slowly leafed through the crackling pages of the book until he stopped.

"Remember those slaves I used to own, when you, Gabriel and Anna Mae were just children? Maybe you don't. You weren't no more than eight or nine then."

"I remember them being around," said Dangerfield. "Reckon I never thought of them as slaves."

Dangerfield had only a hazy memory of his father's other slaves, souls who had been bought, sold and largely forgotten many years ago. He had vague, gauzy memories of watching them cutting corn, driving pigs and throwing piles of loose hay, laughing and cursing at 'Ol Marse.' He remembered the feeling that he was somehow one of them, a member of their dark-skinned and cursed tribe. But he never felt like them, and they never let him into their inner circle. He did not then understand the idea of owning another human being.

Dangerfield remembered one afternoon when, as a child, Elsey had sent him down to the fields to look for Henry. He could not find Henry, but he came upon a group of Henry's field slaves resting near a shade tree. He could hear them laughing, and he wanted to laugh with them, to be part of the group, to learn from these coal-black, strong men. One of the men saw him coming, and shushed the others. "Hush, you all, we don't want Ol Marse's young un tellin' him where we at." The man motioned toward the young Dangerfield and motioned him away. "Go on, young un, you got no business here. Go on back up to the house with Ol Marse and his woman. Ain't nothing for you here."

Henry spoke and interrupted Dangerfield's reverie.

"Well, I used to own five or six at any one time," said Henry. "Sold 'em when you kids started getting older."

"Why did you sell them because of us?"

"I didn't want you all to . . . ." Henry's voice trailed off. "When you all got old enough to work, I figured I could make do with my own family. Never wanted you all to see that side of life."

"Why did you buy them then?"

"I didn't buy them at first. I inherited this place from my father, and the slaves came with the farm. I quickly figured out I couldn't run this farm without them. It was just me and Elsey, and she weren't even mine. So I kept them, and bought a few more as needed. I just could not run the place without them. After you all started to get old enough, I figured I could do without."

Henry ran his bony finger down the page of the book and stopped toward the bottom of the page.

"What happened after you sold them?"

"Don't know. I sold some to John Fox's father, but I made him promise not to sell them South. The others I sold at auction. God only knows what became of them."

Henry closed the book and sat down on the bed. He coughed and spat into his handkerchief. "God only knows" he said softly.

Neither man spoke for some time.

"Is that why you don't want to buy my family now," said Dangerfield. "Seem to me if you buy them for me, you know I'll take care of them."

"No, that ain't it son." Henry sighed and rubbed his eyes,

"Do you remember when I first offered to buy your family?"

"Of course."

"And you said you wanted to do things your own way."

"Still do. Just that I need your help."

"Well, after you left, I went to a bank in town. Went to see if I could borrow enough money to buy your family. Elsey insisted. I took this book with me, and showed the bank man everything I own, and everything I ever did own. Bank man told me I didn't have enough property to justify a short-term bank loan. Said the farm wasn't worth as much as I would need to buy all of your family for what Lewis would ask for all of them. Said they could maybe lend me the money, but it would take years to pay it all back, having to borrow enough to buy seven people, including Jericho. I ain't got that much time."

Henry looked around his bedroom, all packed except for a rough linen shirt and wool trousers neatly folded on the bed.

"Bank man said something else, too," said Henry. "He said if I had more slaves, I could borrow against them. Said 'human capital' was worth more than the farm.

Said if I had kept more slaves, and maybe had got into cotton or tobacco, they might be able to lend me the money, and I could just borrow against the slaves. 'Collateral,' the bank man called it. Imagine that, needing slaves to buy more slaves, so you can buy more slaves. Damn thing never ends."

Dangerfield looked out the window and watched Elsey and Gabriel loading the wagon. The carriage horses stamped and snorted in the paddock.

"What did you do," said Dangerfield.

"I got up and left," said Henry. "Human capital" he huffed. "Bank man don't see no difference between my children and a cow, except the children are worth more on the market."

Henry picked up the book and turned to the last page. "Damn thing is, if I had kept the slaves and got into cotton, I would need even more slaves to run the place. It wouldn't never end."

Dangerfield closed the curtain.

"Henry, did you mean it when you offered to buy my family?"

"Meant every word. I just didn't realize how much it would take to buy seven slaves on the open market. It has been many years since I bought and sold any myself. I ain't been in that god-forsaken business for some time. Didn't realize how much it would cost. Didn't realize freeing slaves would imprison my own family."

Henry grasped the bedpost and pushed himself up.

"Thing is, son, I can't buy your family. I don't have the money, and the bank man says I don't have the human capital to buy them. I tried to borrow the money day after you left, only to find I don't have enough slaves to buy more slaves, even with the money I get from Fox for selling this place. But I can still help you."

"How?"

"Remember that deed of manumission I gave you?"

"Still have it safe."

"Well, I filed the original deed at the county courthouse last week, soon as I left the bank. As of September 25, 1858, you are a free man in Virginia. Deed takes effect at midnight on September 25. You can go anywhere, and if anybody checks, they will find it. You work and free your family. I can't buy your family, but I did free you. You can make more money on your own than you can here. Remember, you got a year 'fore they can sell you back."

"What about Anna Mae, and Gabriel, and Elsey?"

"I freed them too. Everyone in this family is now free. I filed everything last week."

Dangerfield paused.

"I thought you didn't own Elsey," said Dangerfield.

"I don't," said Henry. "Never owned her for a day I've known her."

"Then how could you free her," said Dangerfield. "Only Jennings can free her, and Lewis Jennings ain't the kind of man to freely give up his property."

Henry chuckled. "That's why we need to leave for Ohio now. I filed them deeds last week. For you and Gabriel and Anna Mae, there won't be a problem. But if the county clerk looks into things, he'll find out pretty quick that there ain't no records for Elsey. Might take him a while to sort it out, but anyone who checks will eventually figure out I don't own Elsey, and never did."

Dangerfield considered his father's words. "You filed a false deed with the county to free Elsey?"

"Didn't see any other way," said Henry as he pulled at a loose thread on his shirt. "'Course, by the time anyone finds out, all of us but Anna Mae will be in Ohio, and Fox will take care of her. Won't matter then. All of this," he said looking around the small bedroom, with its cracked walls, peeling paint, and rough-hewn floorboards "won't matter then. We will be free. Won't none of us have to keep living this lie anymore."

Henry hobbled toward the door. "I'm so glad to be free of this business," he said. "Be free of this damn 'human capital,' and just live. Just have all of us live like a family, and not have to worry about people finding out our secrets."

Dangerfield helped his father toward the door. "Where do you aim to go first," said Henry.

"I don't know just yet."

"Reckon you should start in Ohio. I know some people in Bridgeport, just across the river. Some folks could use some help, farmwork and the like. I will send word to them tomorrow. By the time you get there, they will be waiting for you."

"Thank you Henry."

"Start in Ohio, then try Kentucky. Don't come back to Virginia until you have the money, and only then to finish your business with Lewis Jennings. Then you and your family come join the rest of us in Ohio."

"Sounds like you have this sorted out better than I do," said Dangerfield.

"I ain't rich, but I'm still your father, no matter what Virginia law says. Now come on, let's finish packing."

The two men left the house and helped Elsey and Gabriel finish packing.

Two days later, the entire house was packed. The clothes, pots, pans, and everything in the house was safely secured in the wagon. The tools and equipment in the barn would remain for the new owner, John Fox. Anna Mae had chosen to stay behind with him. Henry hitched the carriage horses to the wagon, while Gabriel placed blankets over the contents of the wagon.

Dangerfield was saddled and ready to ride. He watched his father and brother working. Henry walked up to him and petted Solomon.

"Why don't you ride with us to Ohio," said Henry. "I know you can't stay when you get there, but we can ride together. Someone needs to ride Solomon. Just come with us. I can talk to some people when we get there. You can start working as soon as you get across the border."

"What about Harriet and my family?"

"We'll write to Jennings and let her know where you are. And the sooner you get to work, sooner you can set her free. No work to be had for a freeman in Virginia."

Dangerfield looked in the wagon at his brother and Elsey, sitting in front. "No sense in all of us going to Ohio and not going together," said Elsey. And you need to keep Gabriel in line. I'll make certain Henry sends that letter to Harriet. She don't need to worry about you. Now let's get going, Henry, we need to make good time 'fore it gets dark."

"The missus has spoken," said Henry. "Reckon we better get going."

Dangerfield took a long look at his childhood home, the small porch, the peeling paint, the rough planks on the roof. Henry spoke.

"I can't tell you what to do, son. But I think you should come with us." Dangerfield looked at his father, and Elsey sitting in the wagon. Then he nudged his toe into Solomon's flank, and on September 22, 1858, the Newby family of Culpeper County, Virginia began the long ride west to Ohio.

CHAPTER 36

OCTOBER, 1858

In the late afternoon on October 15, 1858, twenty-three days after leaving Culpeper County, Virginia, the Newby family arrived in Ohio. It had been raining steadily for two days, and the wagon was heading directly into the wind. The carriage horses snorted and strained as they pulled the wagon through the thick brown mud on Wheeling Island Road toward the west channel of the Ohio River. Just before they reached the entrance to the Belmont Covered Bridge, Henry rested the horses and surveyed his surroundings. Across the mighty Ohio lay the family's promised land, Bridgeport, Ohio.

From the bridge, the family took note of their new city. Black smoke billowed from a foundry on the north edge of town. A flour mill churned next to the river. Men unloaded provisions from a wagon next to a grocery and dry goods store. A church sat near the grocery store. Citizens walked briskly against the rain, moving from building to building, picking their way through the muddy streets. South of town were several small houses huddled together on compact, tidy lots. Further west were larger homes, some with small sheds nearby. West of these homes, standing alone near a steep cliff, was a sprawling white house, surrounded by a picket fence. This house sat on a lot that was scarcely big enough to contain it. West of this house lay steep gray hills pockmarked by holes. Soot-covered men and mules slowly made their way up the hills, leaning into the rain.

"Well," said Henry, "this is Bridgeport." He drew his coat around him and coughed into his arm. "This is our new home."

No one else spoke for a long time. Elsey stood in the wagon and took a long look at their new city. "It ain't Virginia," she said at last.

"What do they grow here," said Gabriel. "I don't see any corn fields, or wheat fields, or cotton, or anything."

"I don't see any cattle or sheep or pigs" said Dangerfield. "Where are all the farms?"

"Farms are all south of town," said Henry. "Not much grows here. It's too rocky and too steep."

"What's in those hills" said Elsey, pointing at the pockmarked cliffs.

"Coal," said Henry. "Those hills are chock full of coal. Most of the men here work as coal diggers."

"Is there other suitable work for able-bodied men?" asked Gabriel.

"There's a port on the Ohio side of the river," said Henry. "Reckon with your experience as a river hand, you could sign on there, or at another port downriver." Henry pointed to a building next to the foundry. "And there are three or four carpenter shops, and a few stovemakers in town. Between them, both of you boys should be able to find work. Man I bought the house from says they hire quite a few coloreds. Work right alongside white men, even get the same wage."

Dangerfield dismounted Solomon, and Gabriel climbed out of the wagon. The boys looked across the river at Bridgeport. Smoke from the foundry blew across the river, melting into the chalky gray sky. "It's awfully small," said Dangerfield. "Folks live right up next to each other."

"Well," said Henry. "I would have thought you all would have been a bit more excited. Once you cross that river, all of you are free forever. Go wherever you please. Imagine walking through town and not having to worry about having papers. No one asking who owns you. Go where you want."

"We are happy, Henry," said Elsey. "It's just . . . well, it ain't home yet. It ain't Virginia."

The wind blew the foundry smoke across the river toward the wagon. Henry coughed until his body shook, and he leaned over the side of the wagon and expelled the contents of his lungs on the ground. Ash flakes from the foundry melted in the rain, covering the wagon and the horses with black muddy soot.

"Let's get out of this wind," said Henry. He pointed across the river toward the large white house. "See that big house yonder, the one with the fence around it. That's our house. Big enough for all of us, and Anna Mae when she decides to come visit. May even be big enough for all of your children if we all share rooms. Let's get into town."

Henry nudged the horses forward into the semi-darkness of the covered bridge. The horses and wagon clattered across the wooden structure. Intermittent shafts of light broke through the wooden slats of the bridge. No one spoke as they left Wheeling Island and Virginia behind. When they emerged from the Belmont Covered Bridge, the family slowly made their way west down Bridgeport's rutted main street. Past the grocery and the church, and a carpenter's shop. Outside the grocery, two men unloading the wagon took note of the newcomers, politely tipped their hats, and went back to their work. The carpenter was fixing a broken wagon axle. He looked up briefly from his work, tipped his hat and continued working. The newcomers' presence did not seem to generate much interest.

They continued west until they reached their new home. The big white house stood apart from other nearby homes. It commanded nearly the entire lot, with just a thin strip of grass on all sides between the house and the fence. The fence was in good shape, with no missing boards. The fence and the house had been freshly painted. Henry sat the horses, and the wagon clattered to a stop next to the hitching post. No one got out of the wagon.

Dangerfield spoke. "Reckon we'd best start unpacking. Where do you want us to put things, Henry?"

"Let's leave everything in the wagon for now," said Henry. "We can unpack later. Just hitch the horses to the post, and leave everything where it is. Let's go for a walk."

"Walk?" said Elsey. "Where are we going?"

"We are going to walk through Bridgeport, like a free family. Leave everything where it is, and let's go."

Henry climbed down, and escorted Elsey out of the wagon.

They walked back toward town, past the church. Handbills had been nailed to a wooden post in front of the church.

"Town Hall meeting tonight at 7:30. Concerned Christian citizens are urged to attend. Learn how you can help those who have committed to abolishing the scourge of slavery from our great nation. Volunteers needed for important work in Ohio and elsewhere."

Dangerfield took one of the handbills and stuffed it into his pocket.

The family walked through town until almost dusk. They bought bread and sugar from the grocery store. Dangerfield and Gabriel visited the carpenter shops and the foundry, inquiring about work. They were told to return the next morning, properly dressed and ready to work.

As they headed back toward their new home, they passed a candlemaker's shop, still open. Henry pulled money out of his pocket and gave it to Elsey. "Go inside and buy anything you want," he said. "We are going to need a lot of candles for the new house. Tomorrow, you can go into town and get new linens. Maybe buy some new clothes for yourself."

Elsey took the money and eyed Henry. "Can't remember the last time I bought new clothes from a store," she said. "Or new candles. Might take some getting used to." She went in and returned with three new candles wrapped in wax paper. Henry wrapped his arms around Elsey as the family walked back to their new house.

They walked past the church. The doors were open and candles flickered inside. An equal mix of men and women, most well-dressed and formal, filed in. Inside, someone was playing a piano.

As they walked past the church, a small, ruddy-faced and clean-shaven white man approached them, smiling broadly.

"Good evening, brothers and sister," he said. "Won't you join us this evening for our gathering. We wish to lend our support and our prayers to our brothers and sisters fighting against slavery in Virginia and Kentucky. Won't you join us and offer your prayers and your support? There is much work to be done, and we could use as much help as is offered." He looked at Elsey and smiled. "And there are equal parts work for men and women of all races and colors." The little man's eyes twinkled as he spoke.

Henry eyed the man warily. "I suppose it won't hurt to offer prayers. What else do you want?"

The man cleared his throat. "Yes, well prayers are of first importance. But we also need volunteers, and of course money." He spoke directly to Henry. "Why don't you all come this evening and hear what we are trying to accomplish. All are welcome, and you and your servants will find an eager welcome."

"They ain't servants," said Henry. "This," he said, pointing proudly to Elsey, "is my wife of many years, Elsey. And these are two of my children, Gabriel and Dangerfield."

Undeterred by his error, the ruddy-faced man continued. "Yes, of course, forgive me. This is your family." He extended his hand. "Thomas J. Evans. I am the pastor of this humble little congregation." He shook each hand offered to him, and clasped Elsey's arm with both hands. "Forgive me for being forward, but where were you married? Was your union sanctified in a house of the Lord?"

"Not exactly," said Henry as he muffled a cough into his arm. "There was never any formal ceremony." He gathered Elsey closer to him and edged her away from the eager pastor.

"No matter, all are welcome here. We have several Negro members, and a few mixed as well. Please, won't you join us this evening? The work of the Lord knows no color." He winked at Dangerfield.

"I see," said Henry. "You will forgive us, Pastor Evans, but we are new in town. We have to unpack our belongings, and get settled in. Perhaps we will attend the next meeting."

Dangerfield spoke. "Henry, I think I might attend after we get unpacked. I don't have much, and we can unpack everything else tomorrow. I might want to hear what Pastor Evans has to say."

"Me too," said Gabriel. "Let's hear what the pastor has to say."

"Well, you boys are free now, so suit yourselves. I think Elsey and I will get settled and stay in for the evening. I ain't feeling well, and I need to rest."

"Splendid," said Evans. "I hope to see both of your fine young men this evening." Evans shook both of their hands and hurried inside the church.

The family returned to their new home and began unpacking. Dangerfield found the box with his clothes and personal effects, and quickly unpacked all that he owned. He and Gabriel changed into their Sunday suits, and walked back to the church with Gabriel.

They arrived just as the meeting began.

"Good evening, brothers and sisters," boomed Evans. Although barely tall enough to see over the lectern, he had a deep sonorous voice that echoed off the church walls.

"I see many old friends and long-time members, and some new faces as well. By now, many of you know of the troubling developments in Virginia, a state that now claims the right to re-enslave freemen who cross the Old Dominion's borders. This has led to a predictable increase in the number of slaves and freemen attempting to flee Virginia and seek refuge within our borders."

Scattered polite applause and a few derisive shouts filled the sanctuary.

"And I know that many of you have offered your support, and some of you have offered your homes to those who have fled the oppression of the Old Dominion," said Evans. "Let us continue to offer quarter to those who seek shelter from evil."

Louder applause and cries filled the room.

"And I know," he continued, "that some of you have strong feelings about Brother Brown and his vigorous efforts to rid our great country of the cancer that is slavery." His face grew redder as he spoke. "But let me declare that although this church does not support bloodshed for its own sake, we cannot fight a monstrous evil like slavery with one hand tied behind our backs."

Thunderous applause filled the sanctuary, and the parishioners stood, clapped and shouted. "Praise to God!" cried a man in the front row.

"Yes, yes, let us praise the Almighty as we work in ways great and small to eliminate this scourge, this cancer that imprisons our Negro brothers and sisters in Virginia and elsewhere," thundered Evans, red-faced and rocking back and forth on his heels.

Evans pounded the lectern with his fist. "God's work cannot be done by cowards!" he shouted. "And Brother Brown, despite his many flaws, is no coward. Let all of our right-minded and able-bodied brothers stand up, stand up and fight to free our Negro brothers and sisters, and free ourselves from this malignant blight upon our freedom-loving country!"

A woman collapsed in the pew. A tall mulatto man in the front row pumped his fists, praising God and promising to fight. The church shook with applause, cries, and shouts.

"Hosanna and praise God! Praise Brother Brown!"

Dangerfield and Gabriel sat speechless and slack-jawed.

"Who is this Brother Brown," whispered Gabriel.

"I don't know, brother. But he sure has folks agitated."

"Maybe we ought to leave," said Gabriel. "Don't seem right to move into town and gain a reputation right away."

"That don't seem to bother these folks that much. Let's sit for a spell and see what else they have to say."

Evans wiped his sweaty crimson face with a handkerchief before continuing.

"And now, brothers and sisters, it is time for all of us in this church to find out what is in us. We are but empty vessels, but faith in the Lord, and faith only, will fill us with courage to do the Lord's work. Evans paused, still rocking back and forth on his heels.

"I see some new faces here tonight." He pointed at Dangerfield and Gabriel. "Brothers, if you would, please stand and introduce yourselves. All are welcome in this sanctuary."

Gabriel stood uneasily.

"Well, my name is Gabriel Newby. This right here is my brother, Dangerfield. We just moved to this town today, by way of Culpeper County, Virginia. Took us about two weeks by wagon."

"Virginia, Virginia," shouted a woman in the front row. "Curse the wicked Old Dominion!"

"Now, now, brothers and sisters let us remember that even in Virginia, there are those who seek to end slavery," said Evans calmly. "Let us curse the sin, but not the sinner."

"Amen and Hosanna!"

"And you, brother Dangerfield. Please stand and introduce yourself," said Evans, waving his hand at the congregation.

Dangerfield stood slowly. "My name is Dangerfield Newby, son of Henry Newby and Elsey Newby. My brother and I are both freemen, emancipated just this past month in Virginia. We also have a sister back in Virginia, Anna Mae. She may join us soon."

"Blessings for your freedom!" said the tall mulatto in the front row.

"Yes, blessings indeed," said Evans. "Now tell us, brother Dangerfield, do you have a family of your own?"

Dangerfield eyed the congregation warily, then looked at Gabriel. Gabriel nodded.

"Yes, my wife Harriet is back in Virginia on a farm. She's still a slave. Man by the name of Lewis Jennings in Warrenton, Virginia owns Harriet. I have five children, Dangerfield Junior, Gabriel, Lucy, Agnes, and a baby boy, John. Marse Lewis Jennings owns them as well."

"Well, our prayers are with you, brother," said Evans. "Do you intend to bring your family out of Virginia?"

"Yes. I intend to work here in Ohio, and anywhere else I can find freeman's work. I aim to earn enough to buy my wife Harriet and all my children, and bring them here."

"Amen, brother," shouted a woman in the back of the church.

"Yes, praise the Lord," said Evans. "And tell us, brother, how much money do you need to buy your family out of slavery?"

Dangerfield paused. "Well, Marse Jennings says he will sell Harriet and my baby if I pay him $1,500. Says we can talk about me buying the rest of my family when I come back with the $1,500."

"$1,500 for only his wife and one child!" cried the woman in the back row. "Curse those who bring this sin on this man's family!"

Cries and shouts filled the room.

"Yes, brothers and sisters, let us remember to curse the sin but not the sinner," said Evans. "And now, Brother Dangerfield, when are you to complete your business with this Lewis Jennings?"

"Marse Jennings didn't set no time," said Dangerfield. "Just said come back with the $1,500, and we would talk about the rest."

"Thank you, brother Dangerfield, thank you for sharing your plight with us," said Evans. "And now, brothers and sisters, let us all pray for brother Dangerfield."

The parishioners bowed their heads and waited for Evans to begin.

"Dear Lord, hear our prayer that our Brother Dangerfield Newby may soon bring his wife and family out of the darkness and sin that is the Old Dominion, and into the fresh air of freedom."

"Amen, and praise God!"

"And Lord, we pray also for Mister Lewis Jennings, who owns brother Dangerfield's family, and presently holds them hostage," intoned Evans, "for Mister Lewis Jennings is also one of your children."

"Yes, Lord, have mercy on the sinner but curse the sin," said a man in the back of the church.

"We pray, Lord," said Evans, "that the scales may be lifted from his eyes, so that he sees the evil of his ways, and turns his back on the evil of slavery, toward the sunlight of freedom. Amen."

"Yes, lift the scales from his eyes, Lord!" said a woman.

"And now, brothers and sisters, it is time to put our words and prayers into action," said Evans wiping his brow. "Let us take up an offering for our brother Dangerfield, to help him buy his family. Be generous with your prayers, and even more generous with your money. Anything you can offer to help this child of God become reunited with his family is welcome."

Dangerfield and Gabriel stared at each other, speechless.

Ushers passed around two wooden collection platters. Coins and bills in various denominations filled the platters. The ushers brought both collection platters to Evans. He carefully examined the contents of both platters. Then he reached into his pocket and put a handful of folded bills in one of the platters. He sorted through them again, dividing the bills from the coins, and counting the contents. He then put both plates on a table behind him.

"Brothers and sisters, the Lord will bless you for your generosity," said Evans. "Tonight, we raised $37.18 for brother Dangerfield to help buy his family. It is a small sum, but a start nonetheless." Evans put the money into a small leather pouch, and placed the pouch on the table behind him.

The service continued for another 30 minutes, with Evans naming those who needed prayers, those who were ill, and those who were fighting slavery "from Ohio to New York, and also in Virginia and Kentucky."

"And now, brothers and sisters, let us end tonight's service content with the knowledge that although we cannot do everything, all of us can do something. Amen."

The parishioners filed out. The tall mulatto man shook Dangerfield's and Gabriel's hands. "I escaped here from Kentucky," he said. "My two boys were sold South right in front of my eyes," he said sadly. "Could not raise enough money to buy either of them. Marse said I could buy 'em if I raised enough money, but I could not find work away from Marse. He sold my boys at an auction, right in front of me. I escaped as soon as I could. I aim to find my boys if'n it's the last thing I do on this earth," he said.

A plump white woman wearing a large hat hugged Dangerfield and Gabriel. "I do hope and pray that you will soon be reunited with your family," she said. "Virginia is a sinful place, but prayer and faith will always banish the darkness," she said. "My name is Ann Featherston. My husband Amos has a carpentry shop next to the foundry. Both of you should inquire tomorrow about work. We are both committed to the cause." She smiled and left the church.

Evans approached Dangerfield and Gabriel. "I know of someone who may be of assistance in freeing not just your family, but all Negro families," said Evans as he pressed the leather pouch into Dangerfield's hands. "Please, take this humble offering as a small start on your quest to buy your family's freedom."

"Thank you, Pastor Evans," said Dangerfield softly. "We didn't come here asking for money, or anything else. I just saw the paper outside the church. But I do thank you and your congregation mightily."

"The money is just a small, humble start," said Evans. "There is no need to repay it. All I ask is that you consider what you can do to help not just your family, but other families just like yours." He pulled Dangerfield closer to him and whispered in his ear.

"Brother Brown has asked me to recruit able-bodied men of all races for a very important calling," he said softly. "I cannot speak of the details at present, but it involves an undertaking that could not only free your family, but every Negro family currently living in shackles. I can say no more, but ask only that you consider traveling north to Oberlin College to meet Brother Brown and other like-minded men. Arrangements will be made for your travel and accommodation if you and your brother are interested in learning more."

"Please do me the courtesy of discussing what I have told you only in the privacy of your home," said Evans. "If word of Brother Brown's intentions becomes known, innocents could be harmed."

"Who is this Brother Brown," said Dangerfield.

"Ah, yes of course," said Evans. "Brother John Brown, author of the Missouri and Kansas campaigns. He has worked to end the scourge of slavery for many years. He wishes to embark on a more . . . shall we say ambitious campaign that will strike a dagger through the beating heart of the serpent," whispered Evans. "Please discuss this with your family in the privacy of your home, and visit me at the church if you are interested."

"Don't reckon I can help much with any campaign," said Dangerfield. I just want my own wife and children back."

"Yes, and that is why I think you would be ideal for this venture," said Evans. "You have a personal stake in this venture. Your blood and the blood of your family is at stake. You understand the consequences."

Evans greeted a parishioner, then leaned in closer to Dangerfield. "The good people of this town can of course offer their support and sympathy, but few of us left family behind in shackles to seek freedom. You did. Your family is still enslaved. And given your rather unique circumstance and your imposing physical presence, I believe strongly that Brother Brown could make use of a man like you."

"Where is Oberlin College?"

"North of here, near Cleveland. Again, arrangements will be made for your travel and lodging, for you and your brother if you are interested."

Dangerfield shuffled uneasily. "I do thank you Pastor, but I have to work to earn the $1,500. Can't hardly afford to take time away from my work to meet this Brother Brown."

"Yes, yes, of course. As I said arrangements will be made," said Evans. "And I know Featherston the carpenter eagerly accepts Negro employees. Some of us can afford to simply donate money while others employ those who need money. I assure you, there will be no shortage of work."

"You seem awful quick to trust us with this information," said Dangerfield. "Reckon you don't know us, and we don't know you. How do you know we won't just take the money and leave? How do you know we won't tell somebody else what you are doing? And how do we know you ain't trying to fool us into something dangerous?"

Evans smiled wearily. "Brothers, let me be clear. The money this congregation has raised tonight is yours to keep, to spend as you please. I may not know you, but I know men's hearts. Your story of trying to free your family from enslavement is exactly the kind of story my congregation needs to hear."

Evans waved to another parishioner, then turned toward the brothers and spoke in hushed tones. "With a few exceptions, most of the good people of this congregation are at a remove from the brutality of slavery," he whispered. "They mean well, but they have never felt the lash, never had their ears cut off for disobedience, never had their fingers cut off for stealing a cup of sugar, never had their heels cut for trying to escape, never had their children sold South right in front of them, never seen their children beaten nearly to death, and powerless to stop it. I don't know you, but I suspect you have some personal experience with these matters."

Dangerfield closed his eyes and remembered the beating the elder Jennings had given to Jericho, and the sizzle of the brand as it seared Jericho's skin. Although it happened many years ago, Dangerfield could still recall the sickly-sweet smell of burnt human flesh as Jennings drove the brand into Jericho's fragile body. He could still hear Jericho's screams as the brand burned its way home. And he could see the steaming brand soaring through the air after he grabbed it from Jennings' hand and threw it as far as his strength would allow.

"And," continued Evans," you telling that story to my congregation provided more motivation than a hundred of my sermons. They have heard first hand from a former slave how this evil institution has torn families apart. Your story has spurred my congregation into action, and for that I thank you."

Evans waved at a middle-aged woman lingering near the door, then continued speaking. "Of course, Brother Dangerfield, I believe every word of your story, because the details seem too vivid to have been hastily manufactured. I mention this only because your short visit here this evening has provided my congregation with motivation that I could not provide. The money is yours to keep. I ask only that you consider using your considerable talents and physical gifts to help free others. And please remember that your family is not the only enslaved family. Consider the good you could do in the larger world outside your home. Consider the lives you could save. And please, speak only of Brother Brown in the privacy of your own home."

Dangerfield said nothing. No one had ever suggested to him that his talents could be of use away from his own home, or the Jennings plantation, or the occasional farmer who would rent his services from Henry, or someone else's business. He knew that he was a skilled carpenter, fence builder and harness maker, but he had never once considered that any of his talents could save lives. He had thought only of his birth family, and his family with Harriet. For the first time in his life, he was being asked to save the lives of people he had never met.

"Thank you again, Pastor," said Dangerfield. "Please allow me to discuss this with Gabriel and the rest of my family."

"Yes, yes, of course, do discuss this with your family. But again I ask that all discussions remain within the walls of your house."

Evans pulled away from Dangerfield. "Do use the money to buy your family. And please get back to me in two days' time if you and your brother Gabriel are interested. You can find me in the church during the day. Come back earlier if you wish. Bless you brothers. Please, both of you take a candle for your walk home."

Evans gave Gabriel and Dangerfield candles from the pews, then turned and walked toward the front of the church. Dangerfield put the leather pouch in the pocket of his waistcoat, and walked back home with Gabriel. The boys walked home in the dark, each holding a candle.

"Well, that Evans is something," said Gabriel. "I reckon he means well, but there is something about him, I can't place. I mean, he don't know us from Adam, and here he is, offering us money, and asking us to join this Brother Brown. And asking us to go to – where was it – "

"Oberlin College," interrupted Dangerfield.

"Right, Oberling College," said Gabriel. "I ain't never heard of no Oberling College before."

"Me neither," said Dangerfield."

"In fact, I ain't never heard of no college that accepted colored folk, least not in our part of Virginia. Can't help but think this might be some kind of trick, but I don't know what kind of trick."

Dangerfield did not respond. The boys walked toward their new house in silence.

"And Evans seemed keen on helping you buy your family," said Gabriel. "What do you make of that?"

"I don't know yet," said Dangerfield. Evans' words rang in his ears – "Consider the lives you could save."

"Something about this don't seem right," said Gabriel. "Can't place it, but it don't seem right. Don't know anything about this Brother Brown. Don't know what he's selling."

"I think we need to discuss this with Henry tomorrow," said Dangerfield. "Help us make sense of this."

"I don't like it," said Gabriel. "Not one bit. I think we go back tomorrow and give back that money."

Let's hear what Henry thinks," said Dangerfield.

They arrived at their new home well past dusk. Elsey had put her new candles in the parlor. Candles illuminated the rooms upstairs. The boys found their rooms, undressed and went to bed. Gabriel fell asleep immediately – Dangerfield could hear him snoring across the hall. But Dangerfield lay in his bed, unable to sleep. He kept thinking of Evans' words – "Consider the lives you could save." But then he saw Harriet and his children, trapped on the Jennings farm. He would have to save them first – no one else mattered until his family was free.

Were there other families like his? Were there other men like him, free men with wives and children owned by another man? Were there other free men desperate to raise money to buy their families, buy their own children? He remembered the words of the tall mulatto man in the church that evening: "He sold my boys at an auction, right in front of me. I escaped as soon as I could. I aim to find my boys if'n it's the last thing I do on this earth," the man had said.

Dangerfield had never considered whether his circumstance was unique. He had never thought about other families' struggles, apart from the Jennings' family, which had become his family. He thought only of Henry and Elsey, and now, Harriet and his children.

Was Evans right? Was he capable of saving lives outside of his own family?

"Maybe I can save lives," he thought to himself as he lay in bed. "But first my own family. I bring them home, then I can worry about other people."

He thought of Harriet, and the scent of her coffee-colored skin. He saw his boys outside their cabins, poking at grasshoppers or chasing black snakes. He saw his girls sleeping, arms and legs entangled like vines. He thought of the tall mulatto man and his lost children. Then he drifted off to sleep.

——◦«(◦)»◦——

He awoke early the next morning in a strange bed, in a new house. Nothing was where he expected it to be. The box with his clothes and belongings was on the floor. The room was smaller than the one he had shared with Gabriel back in Virginia, but it was his room. For the first time in his life he had his own room.

He walked downstairs and surveyed his new house in the early morning daylight. Elsey's pots were spaciously arranged on hooks. The kitchen floor was smooth and even, with no cracks between the floorboards. The floor did not sag beneath his weight, and did not groan or creak with every step. Henry's new maple rocking chair, a gift from the previous owner, presided over the parlor. Everything about this house was bigger, softer, and more comfortable than their old house. Everyone had more room to move.

And then Evans' words rang in his ears – "Consider the lives you could save." He thought of Harriet and his children, and how long it would take to earn the money to free them. He thought of this house, with its strange new comforts, and how easy it would be to live here in Ohio, as a free man. He thought of Jericho, coming into his manhood under the bootheel of another man, his surging masculinity straining against the iron grip of enslavement. His own boys, Junior and

Gabriel, would start to become young men without their father. And what of Lucy and Agnes, becoming young women without his protection? He thought of his new baby, and realized that he might not see the child again until he was walking, maybe running. He tried to imagine how different his family would be in two or even three years, when he had the money to buy them outright.

He surveyed the house again, and realized how small it was. He couldn't breathe. He had to leave right away if he was going to save the lives that mattered most to him.

Henry limped into the kitchen, leaning heavily on his cane.

"You are up early," said Henry. "You have plans for today?"

"I do now," said Dangerfield. Dangerfield explained the past evening's events, the church meeting, the money, and the urgent message Evans had given him. He told Henry about Evans' invitation to travel to Oberlin and meet the mysterious Brother Brown. Henry frowned, but said nothing.

"Do you know who this Brother Brown is," said Henry.

"Never heard of him 'fore yesterday," said Dangerfield.

"Well, you will," said Henry as he hobbled to a chair in the kitchen. "He's got all the rich planters and cotton barons from South Carolina to Virginia all riled up. Wants to end slavery any way possible. Created quite a stir out west in some of the new territories, from what I heard."

"You must agree with him, at least the part about ending slavery," said Dangerfield. "That's why you brought us here."

"I don't care so much about ending slavery as I do about taking care of this family right here," said Henry. "Brown has all these big ideas, but all he's done so far is scare the hell out of the planters. They are all so afraid of him, they keep their slaves under lock and key. He's done just the opposite of freeing them."

Dangerfield had never seen this side of Henry.

"Well, maybe someone needs to scare the planters and the cotton barons," said Dangerfield. "Nothing is going to change unless someone does something. You freed us, Henry. Shouldn't everyone else be free?"

Henry snorted. "I don't pretend to know what's best for someone else's family. I know what's best for this family. I freed you all because I know things were never going to get better for you in Virginia. But all of you have skills, can take care of yourselves. Some slaves can't take care of themselves. They might be better off on plantations, least for awhile."

Henry coughed into his sleeve. "I don't disagree with ending slavery, but Brown has no right telling other people how to run their affairs. I know what is best for this family, and I don't need Brown or anyone else telling me how I should run my affairs."

Dangerfield considered this statement.

"What about old man Jennings, and the way he treated his slaves," said Dangerfield. "You don't agree with how he used to treat his slaves, do you?"

"Jennings was a miserable, cruel man," snapped Henry. "But I had no right to tell him how to run his business, just as he had no right to tell me how to run mine."

Henry looked out the window.

"You should have heard what that Pastor Evans said last night, about us," said Dangerfield. "The church raised almost $40 for me. Said I could keep it and use it buy my family. Said there are thousands of families just like mine, with men trying to buy their families out of slavery. Maybe this Brother Brown has a plan to help us."

Henry laughed. "You are a grown man, but my advice to you is to keep your family business private. Most folks ain't interested in helping anyone but themselves, and if this Evans says Brown has a plan to help you, you'd best believe he expects something in return."

"Maybe he does," said Dangerfield. "But I won't know unless I see for myself. Maybe it's time for all of us to think about things outside of this family, things bigger than all of us."

"Ain't nothing more important than your own family," snapped Henry. "Ain't nothing bigger than that." Henry struggled to stand, leaned hard on his cane, then let out a sharp cry before collapsing in his chair. "Dammit," he muttered to himself.

"I know what I have to do, Henry," said Dangerfield. "Everything I've done since I made my arrangements with Lewis Jennings has been for my family. Everything, from the time I get up to the time I fall asleep. It's just . . . ."

"Just what," said Henry.

"Ain't nobody ever told me I could do something bigger than me. That there was something else outside of this family and my family, outside of this house. That somebody besides you and Jennings needs me for something."

"I don't think there is anything else," said Henry.

Neither man spoke for some time. Henry stared out of the window for a few minutes than closed his eyes. He started to breathe heavily, rhythmically, eyes closed. A thin sliver of drool escaped the corner of his mouth. He slumped, then started. He gripped the head of his cane, tried to stand, then sat down again.

"You ever try to do something bigger than yourself, Henry," asked Dangerfield. "Ever think of what you could have done to fight against slavery?"

Henry looked out the window again, and sighed.

"When I first met Elsey, Old Man Jennings said I could have her in exchange for two mules and $100," said Henry. "I never told you that. At first, I just needed the help around the house. But Elsey, she wore on me. Didn't never act like a slave, not from day one. Said she wasn't going to let no man treat her like Jennings did. Said she'd kill me if I tried."

"Sounds about right," said Dangerfield. Both men laughed.

"Well, after a time, she took a shine to me, reckon because I treated her like she was a person, and not like a mule. But the law is the law. And the law in Virginia says Elsey is worth two mules and $100, no matter how kind I treat her. That's the way it is, and would always be, unless we left Virginia."

Henry pulled out his handkerchief and coughed, then wiped his mouth.

"Ain't no way I can change that system," said Henry. "Anything I do is a drop of water in a flood. Won't make no difference. But I can say truthfully that I did end slavery. I, Henry Newby, ended slavery. I ended it for the people who live in this house. You, your brother, Anna Mae, and Elsey. Abolition is already here, least in this house. I can't do no more than that."

Henry pulled at a loose thread on his woolen shirt.

"I don't know much about this Evans," said Henry. "I figure he means well, wanting to free the slaves. Same with Brown. But the way I see it, abolition starts at home. Free those close to you. Let others take care of their own. You do the same. Free Harriet and your children. Let Brown worry about the rest. They ain't your responsibility."

"I aim to free my family, Henry. But some can't help themselves. Reckon if there's anything I can do . . . ."

"There ain't nothing you can do for others," said Henry. "You can't buy another man's family. You can't raise another man's children. Sure as hell don't want to free another man's wife. And if you get yourself killed fighting for someone else's family, what happens to your own? I don't care what Brown says, there ain't enough gunpowder on earth to free every slave. Best thing you can do is free your own, and take care of 'em. You do that, you've done more than most. Damn near killed me."

Dangerfield sat down next to his father. "I know what you did for us, Henry. All of us. I aim to do the same, but my own way. "

Henry gripped the head of his cane with both hands. The veins in his hand pulsed through his pale skin. He ground his teeth inside his jaw.

"Reckon you made up your mind about taking this damn fool trip to meet up with Brown," said Henry.

"Reckon I have," said Dangerfield.

"When do you aim to leave."

"Soon as I can. I need to visit with Evans first."

"What about Gabriel? He going with you?"

"If he's of a mind to. If not, I go on my own."

"I figured as much. What are you going to tell Elsey?"

"Same thing I told you. I need to save my family. But I can't help but think there's something bigger than me, bigger than all of us. Maybe it ain't my problem to solve. But maybe I can do something."

"Maybe you can," said Henry. "Maybe you can. But save your own first. Just remember that. Now help me out of this chair. I need to fix that front gate."

Dangerfield held his father's slender bony arm and eased him out of the kitchen chair. The two men walked arm in arm toward the front door of their new, strange house.

CHAPTER 37

Cornell entered Turner's hospital room at 8:30 the next morning, briefcase in hand. Turner was finishing his breakfast, softly pacing about the room. Tracy sat in a chair across from the empty bed, holding two cups of coffee.

"Dr. Turner has advised me that he no longer poses a threat to himself, or others," said Cornell firmly. "Before I can release him, I need to confirm that is the case."

Cornell turned to Tracy. "I have interviewed Tracy privately, and she has advised me that she does not feel you are a threat to her or others. I hope you can understand, Dr. Turner, why I needed to conduct this interview privately."

"Of course," said Turner.

"Good," said Cornell. "Now, let's discuss the dreams you had. You saw Dangerfield three times, you saw what you think was your great-uncle and another man in several other dreams, and then you saw what appeared to be a slave auction. Can you think of any link between these dreams?"

"No, Dr. Cornell, and I am not certain there is a link."

Cornell scribbled in his notebook. "Do you think what you saw was real?"

"What I saw was very vivid, Dr. Cornell. I could see things, smell things, even touch things in those dreams. So yes, what I experienced was as 'real' as any other dream."

"And you only experienced these dreams after taking the pills Tracy gave you?"

"Yes."

"And I am sure you now understand the risks of taking those pills," said Cornell. "However, the sleeping pills you took are frequently prescribed by doctors, and readily available. I cannot keep you in the psychiatric ward because of the possibility, however strong, that you might take pills that are perfectly legal. I trust you understand the risk. As much as I would like to study you, I cannot keep you in the psychiatric ward because you might do something that is both legal and common."

"Yes, Dr. Cornell, I am obviously acutely aware of the risks," replied Turner. "As you know, many people have experienced hallucinations or sleep-walking events after taking sleeping pills. Most don't wind up in confinement, as you know. My event was isolated, and unlikely to repeat."

Cornell continued writing. "Did anyone ever threaten you during these dreams?"

"Never. I was invisible to all. No one knew I was there."

"You mentioned that your grandmother passed away quite recently. Was she close to you?"

"Not as close as I should have been. I was not around much. Busy with med school and life."

"What do you intend to do once you are released?"

"Dr. Cornell, I think we all know my medical career is over. Chief of surgery is definitely out. Maybe I can teach somewhere, or consult, but practicing surgeon is out. Medicine is out. I don't know what I will do, but I will find something.

"How will you define yourself if not as a doctor?"

"I don't know. I should probably start with being better to Tracy than I have been."

Cornell wrote furiously for several minutes.

"Why do you think you had these dreams now? What do you think is motivating this?"

"I don't know. There does not seem to be any link. Maybe there is no immediate explanation."

"Your answer seems out of character for a pure rationalist, Dr. Turner. Are you able to accept that there may not be an answer?"

"I know what I saw and felt, Dr. Cornell. It was real. I saw things, felt things, smelled things in each of my dreams. I just need to find out why. And maybe there is no 'why.'"

"I think I can shed some light on at least one of Michael's dreams," interjected Tracy. "Mike, you said the man selling slaves at the auction was named Jennings, right?"

"Jennings, Jensen, something like that, yeah," replied Turner. "Why?"

"Your grandmother told you about Dangerfield when she was in her last days in hospice, right?"

"Yeah, she said we might be related somehow. Said he left behind a wife and some children."

"And she said no one really knows what happened to his wife and kids after he died, right?"

"She said that, but I don't know how much of that is true. Her mental state had declined in her last days."

"Yes, but remember you did your own research after she died, and everything she said was true. Dangerfield's family, his wife's owner backing out on the deal to sell his family, Dangerfield joining up with John Brown, and how he died. You confirmed all this for yourself."

"The historical part of what she told me was true," replied Turner. "What are you getting at?"

"Your grandmother did not know what happened to Dangerfield's family after he died. Did she tell you who owned his family?

"No, and I don't think she knew. Just that they were probably sold to someone else. Not uncommon for that to happen."

"I went home last night and did some research," Tracy said. "Dangerfield's wife and children were owned by a doctor named Jennings. That's the guy who refused to sell the family to Dangerfield. Here, look at this."

She handed Turner a piece of paper, which Turner read aloud. "Although the historical record is unclear, many scholars believe that Harriet Newby and her family were 'sold South' after Dangerfield's death, most likely to a new owner in Louisiana or South Carolina."

Turner handed the paper back to Tracy.

"So that dream you had about the slave auction was Jennings selling Harriet and her children," continued Tracy. "And you said the guy who bought them was from Louisiana, right?"

"Sold to the gentleman from Louisiana," said Turner softly to himself. "That is what he said."

"I think your grandmother would love to know what happened to them," said Tracy.

Cornell closed his notebook. He sat down across from the bed and leaned his head back, eyes closed. He did not speak for some time."

"Dr. Turner, one of my defining memories happened to me when I was seven or eight," said Cornell. "I was rummaging around in our family's basement when I came across an old box filled with pictures. They were black and white pictures of soldiers. I recognized one of the soldiers as my father. I had seen some old photos of him in his army uniform."

Cornell poured a glass of water and paused before speaking. "I knew my father had been in the Korean War, because my uncles had mentioned it. I would over-hear comments about Korea at family gatherings, usually when the adults had had a few drinks, and they thought the kids were in the basement watching TV. But my father never talked about Korea, or his time in the army. Whenever I would ask him, he would say he would tell me sometime. But he never did."

"Anyway," Cornell continued, "when I found this box, I was excited. Here was a box full of pictures, and medals and awards. There were lots of ribbons in the box, and medals I had never seen. I thought this was time for my dad to tell me about Korea. So I brought the box upstairs, and I showed it to my dad. He was watching TV, drinking a beer. I showed him what I had found. He reached over, grabbed that box out of my hand, slammed it shut, and told me never to open that box, or look at it again. His face was red, and I remember spit flying out of his mouth when he yelled at me. I started crying."

Neither Turner nor Tracy spoke.

"Well, he saw me crying, and then he started crying," said Cornell. "He apologized, and said he did not want to hurt me. He just wasn't ready to talk about that box. So I closed it up, and put it back where I found it. I never saw it again."

"My father died three years after that," said Cornell. "Self-inflicted gunshot wound to the head. I never knew what was in that box, and I will never find out. And my uncles are all dead, so I have no way of knowing his story."

"Oh my God," said Tracy softly.

Cornell leaned his head back and exhaled deeply.

"I have no way of reconstructing his story, except through news clippings and incomplete research," said Cornell. "But if I could take myself back to when he was in Korea, if I could see what he saw, if I could smell what he smelled and see what happened – if I could see his past in real time, as you have apparently seen your grandmother's past in real time – maybe I could find peace for him. Maybe I could give him the peace he could not find when he was alive."

Turner stared at his feet. Tracy wiped her eyes with a napkin.

"That is why I became a psychiatrist, Dr. Turner. To help people find that peace before they consume themselves. And that is why I believe in God, Dr. Turner – because all the science and medicine in the world could not save my father from himself. Maybe nothing could. I will never know. But that's why they call it faith."

Cornell pulled a book out of his briefcase. He thumbed through the pages, flipping back and forth until he found what he was looking for.

"I always get that one wrong," he said to himself. "Failing memory."

"More Shakespeare quotes?" said Turner warily.

"Not quite," said Cornell. 'You did not choose me, but I chose you, and appointed you that you should go and bear fruit and that your fruit should abide, so that whatever you ask the Father in thy name, he may give it to you.'"

Cornell closed the book. "John Chapter 15, Verse 16. I always get the chapter and verse mixed up." Cornell strode to his desk and sat down.

"Michael, have you considered the possibility that God has chosen you to be the messenger for something bigger than any of us?"

Turner laughed. "No, I have not. I have come to respect your faith, but I don't accept it, and don't believe faith in God, Buddha, or the Devil ever helped anyone. I don't think God has chosen me or anybody else for anything."

"Fair enough," said Cornell. "Do you believe in fate? Destiny? Dumb luck? Things that just cannot be explained?"

"If it can't be explained, it just means science does not yet have the answer," said Turner. "I'll put any faith I have there, not in God, Elvis, or Buddha."

"What I am asking you to consider," said Cornell, "is the simple possibility that something or someone has chosen you to be the vehicle for someone's story."

Turner closed his eyes. "No, Herbert, I have not been chosen by anyone or anything. Fate and religion are the refuge of those who have abandoned reason. There is a scientific explanation for everything."

"Perhaps there is," said Cornell. "But not all are qualified to find those explanations. Not just anyone could discover and articulate the principles of gravity, thermodynamics, light years, or dark matter. It took the right man in the right place, at the right time, whether he wanted to be there or not. Sometimes it is just fate."

Turner was about to speak when when he heard Frazier's voice in his head, thundering and clear:

"I can only hope that you achieve the same certainty. I can only hope that you have the courage to accept whatever destiny is presented to you."

He saw Frazier sitting in his squalid little house, empty coffee cups everywhere. He saw the overgrown yard, and the windows covered with black garbage bags. He saw the leaning tower of books and newspapers in Frazier's house, and the single dim bulb that provided the only light in the house. He remembered the story Frazier told him about Nat Turner, and how Frazier was Nat Turner's link between the past and present. He remembered thinking that Frazier was simply a crackpot.

Turner recalled his grandmother's stories, stories he first heard when he was very young. Her stories of ghosts and spirits, of long-dead aunts and uncles who came back from the dead, of rooms in the old house that were haunted, of distant relatives who could find no peace. Her tales about Uncle Billy, and how he died in a car crash. Dead babies. Dead slaves who were distant relatives, who died seeking freedom for themselves and their families. He remembered all those stories, and he thought he knew all of them. He never wanted to hear them again.

Frazier spoke to him again:

"I can't tell you what you want to know, Mr. Turner. I can't tell you whether you have been chosen to tell Dangerfield's story, or even whether he has a story. Perhaps you have been chosen to tell another story, someone else's story. Perhaps you have not been chosen for anything. But I can't tell you what that story is. You must have the courage to accept your fate."

And then he heard his grandmother's dying words:

"I always wondered what happened to that poor man's wife and children. Seems like nobody knows."

Turner opened his eyes, and looked at Tracy and Cornell. And then he knew that Cornell was right. Tracy was right. His grandmother was right. In that moment, Turner knew what he had been chosen to do, and what he had to do. He accepted his fate.

CHAPTER 38

Dangerfield, Henry and Gabriel spent the morning repairing the fence that surrounded the new house. They finished around noon, then had their usual midday meal – salt-cured ham, eggs, and bread. But unlike every other meal the family had taken together, the ingredients for this meal were purchased from a store. Elsey had gone into town while the men worked on the fence, and bought everything from the local grocer and butcher.

Henry wiped his mouth, and leaned back in his chair.

"That was wonderful, Missus," he said. "Our first meal together in this big house. Soon enough Anna Mae will visit us, and we eat together like we did back home."

Elsey brought the dishes to the washtub in the corner of the kitchen. "Reckon it was a fine enough meal," she said softly. "Didn't take no effort to make it. Just buy everything and bring it home."

"I thought you might enjoy not having to butcher chickens and knead dough every day," said Henry. "Leave us more time to do other things."

"Like what, Henry?"

"Go into town, walk by the river. Look inside some of them stores. Maybe just spend an hour or two on the front porch. You can knit, while I read or sleep. Soon as Dangerfield buys his family and brings them back, we can chase his little ones around."

Elsey allowed herself a smile. "Would be nice to have some young'uns around the house," she said. But for now, I . . . ."

"What is it, Missus?"

Elsey put her washcloth on the kitchen table and sighed.

"I knew what I was in Virginia," she said. "Didn't like most of it, but I knew what I had to do. Butcher chickens. Make bread. Tend the garden. Fix the buttons on your shirts. Butcher hogs. Cure hams. Clean the kitchen. Every day. Anna Mae and I made sure you men had food on the table when you came in from the fields. Most days, it was just me and Anna Mae in the kitchen, cooking and cleaning. Weren't nothing else to do, and it all needed to be done. Every day. You men didn't know half of what we did. Now I know you took care of everything else outside, and dealt with the business things, but you never worried none about having food on the table when you came in from the fields."

Elsey picked up the dishes and deposited them in the tub. "And now we can just buy everything from a store. Grocery man and the butcher do all the work," she said as she poured water from a wooden bucket into the tub.

"Elsey, it ain't that bad, is it?" said Henry. Soon as things settle down, we can get a few chickens, if that's what you want. Didn't think you'd mind having less to do."

"I don't mind having less to do, I just don't . . . ."

"What is it then?"

"Everything is different now. We got this big house, and I don't know what to do with it. Anna Mae has taken up with John Fox, and she might not never live here again. I don't mind taking care of things around the house, but Anna Mae was always there with me."

She paused.

"And Dangerfield won't be 'round much longer, what with trying to buy his family from Lewis Jennings. "I'll be fine Henry, it's just everything new happening all at once. At least the boys will be here for a few weeks, right?"

She turned toward Dangerfield and Gabriel. Neither spoke. Henry cleared his throat loudly and gestured toward the boys.

"Boys, now would be the time to tell your mother your intentions."

"What intentions," said Elsey.

Gabriel and Dangerfield stared at each other, neither speaking.

"Boys, tell me what's going on, and I mean now," demanded Elsey.

"We intend to leave first thing tomorrow morning, head up north to a place called Oberlin College," said Dangerfield. "Pastor Evans says there's a man we should meet up there by the name of Brown. Says he could help me free my whole family, and other families too. Gabriel might go as well, if he's of a mind to."

"Gabriel, is this true?" said Elsey.

"Yes, Miss Elsey, it is," said Gabriel softly.

Elsey stared out the window toward town.

"Henry, do you approve of this plan?"

"No, and I told the boys I think it's a damn fool idea," said Henry. "But they are both grown, and I reckon they can make their own decisions."

Elsey sopped the dishcloth into the wooden bucket, and then wrung every single drop of water back into the bucket. Her veins popped from the backs of her thin black hands.

"Dangerfield, what about buying your family? I thought you were going to set out to work in Ohio, get some freeman's money and buy your family. How is this Brown going to help you free Harriet and the children? Is he going to pay you?"

"I don't know just yet," said Dangerfield. "Pastor Evans said he wants us to keep our intentions secret, least for awhile. Said if a lot of folks knew, innocents could be harmed. But Evans said Brother Brown – Brown – has a plan. Said he wants to free not just my family, but other families like mine. Other freemen trying to buy their families, just like me. Said he thinks I can help. Said people need me."

Elsey wiped a dish.

"Is Evans the man you met last night at church?"

"Yes."

"So this Evans says he knows of this Brown, who can help you free your family, and other families you ain't never met. Says you need to go to this Oberling place to meet Brown. Can't tell you why, or what to expect once you get there. But you and Gabriel aim to leave out of here, first thing tomorrow, to meet this Brown. And Evans, who you just met last night, can't say more because someone might get hurt."

"Reckon that sums it nicely, ma'am," said Dangerfield.

"Boys, this sounds like a fool idea. "You'd best stay here among family, and not trust strangers. Remember, we ain't been here but two days. Nobody knows us. You'd best save your own family first, 'fore you start thinking about somebody else's family."

"That's what I told them," said Henry, as he closed his eyes and leaned back in his chair.

"I know you don't approve," said Dangerfield. "But I don't see why I can't save my family and other families, too. Maybe it's about time we all started to think about something bigger than just this family."

Dangerfield walked toward the kitchen table and picked up Henry's Bible. "From what Evans says, slavery ain't going away on its own. Slavery just gets bigger and bigger. And as long as there is cotton and tobacco, there's always slaves. Cotton and tobacco get bigger, plantations get bigger, and need more slaves. It won't never end, unless someone makes it end."

"Why do you care about somebody else's family," said Elsey. "You, me, Gabriel, Anna Mae, all of us free now. We live in Ohio, right and proper. All you need to do is get money, buy your family, and let others do the same. Don't see no need to step back into something we spent our whole lives trying to leave."

"Oh, I told them that too," said Henry as he leaned his head back and rubbed his temples.

"Except we ain't all free, Elsey," countered Dangerfield. "Harriet and my children ain't free. Jericho ain't free. And even if Marse Lewis sells all of 'em to me, there's thousands of other Harriet's and Jericho's that won't be free. I can't buy them all."

"Aint your problem to buy them all," said Elsey. "You just need to buy yours. Let others take care of their own."

"Some of them can't take care of their own," said Dangerfield. "We met a man last night from Kentucky. Said he left two of his boys behind, but he promised he would find 'em. Ain't found em yet. No man should have to live like that."

"I still don't see this as your problem," snapped Elsey. "And this Evans and Brown sound like trouble for all of us. What if you get killed? What happens to your family then?"

"I told them that too," added Henry.

"I aim to take care of my family, Miss Elsey, just like Henry took care of us. But I aim to do it in my own way. I think I can help others, too."

Dangerfield leafed through Henry's Bible and then stared out the window. "There's a world outside of this house. I ain't never known much outside of our house."

Elsey sopped the washcloth in the bucket and began washing another dish.

"I don't approve," she said softly. "Not one bit. Don't want strangers meddling in our business, and you aim to go off meddling in someone else's business. Don't like it one bit."

She turned toward Henry.

"Do something," she said.

"What would you have me do, Missus? Chain the boys to a wagon till they stop acting up?" Hobble 'em like a old mule? Cut their heels, keep 'em from running like a proper slave owner? Boys are grown, Elsey. They got to leave sometime."

"Not like this, and not this way," she said. "What if both of them get killed? You want that on your head, Henry?"

Henry leaned forward in his chair, and slowly stood up.

"Reckon it won't be," said Henry. "They got to leave sometime. We don't get to pick the time or the reason."

"Do something, Henry," said Elsey again.

"Boys told us their intentions, Elsey. They could have just as easily left without telling us. But they told us, and now we know. We can't stop them, but we can help them in our own way."

Henry picked up his Bible and tucked it under his arm.

"When do you boys aim to leave," he said.

"First light tomorrow," said Dangerfield.

"Come upstairs now. We need to discuss a few things before you go."

Dangerfield looked at his father. "You aren't going to stop us?"

"No," said Henry. "Come upstairs, please."

The boys followed their father upstairs into Henry and Elsey's bedroom. Henry sat on his bed and rubbed his eyes.

"I reckon you boys know what this damn fool idea will do to your mother," said Henry.

"Weren't my intention to have her worry," said Dangerfield. "Just wanted to be honest."

"Reckon you also know Elsey will hold me to account if anything happens to either of you."

Dangerfield and Gabriel said nothing.

Henry pulled a small box from his nightstand and opened it.

"You both will need a few things on this trip," said Henry. "We may be in Ohio, but you ain't completely safe here. Slave catchers can still come after you."

He pulled two leather pouches out of the nightstand. "Gabriel, take these. Your freeman's papers. Proves you are free, and have been freed under the laws of Virginia. Living in Ohio ain't enough. You could be just a runaway. These papers prove you were freed in Virginia, which means you ain't a slave anywhere, and ain't a runaway. Never let these out of your sight. Dangerfield, I assume you still have those papers I gave you in that pouch?"

"Yes, Henry, I do," said Dangerfield patting his coat pocket.

"Good. Both of you never let them papers out of your sight."

Gabriel took the papers carefully.

"Take this too," said Henry, handing Dangerfield the Bible. "You might need this more than me and Elsey. Keep it safe. It's the only one we have."

Dangerfield took the Bible.

"One last thing," said Henry. "You will need this too."

Henry reached into the bottom of the nightstand and moved some papers toward the back. He pulled out a wood-handled Colt pocket revolver and handed it to Dangerfield.

"Take this everywhere," said Henry. "And these too." He handed over four small sacks of powder, two pouches of lead balls, and five percussion caps.

"Keep the powder and balls dry, and keep the extra caps somewhere safe," said Henry. "Keep it loaded, and leave the hammer uncocked if it's in your pocket. Leave the pistol half-cocked when you need to load a new charge. There's an extra rod in the ball pouch."

Dangerfield admired the heft of the stout little Colt, with its black barrel and brass trim. The barrel was just three inches long, and the gun would fit easily in the breast pocket of a coat.

"Henry, can you afford to part with this," said Dangerfield as he flipped open and spun the cylinder.

"I can part with that faster than I can part with my Bible," said Henry. "I got a few other pistols, but only one Bible." Henry coughed into his arm. "Reckon you boys need these more than I do."

"Thank you, Henry," said Dangerfield. "Reckon we will be just fine. You and Elsey don't need to worry about us."

"One last thing," said Henry. "I can't stop you boys from this fool adventure. But Gabriel is your responsibility now, Dangerfield. If anything happens to him, I will hold you responsible as his older brother. I don't care what Cain said, you are now your brother's keeper. Mind that always."

"You don't need to worry about me, Henry," said Gabriel. "Old Man here needs me more than I need him. I will make certain we both get home safe."

"You do that Gabriel, you do that," said Henry.

Dangerfield surveyed his freeman's papers, the family Bible, the Colt and the equipment, and his father.

"Henry, when we get back, Gabriel and I will put up a new fence around the shed in the back," said Dangerfield. "Maybe help you and Elsey start a garden."

"Don't worry about that," said Henry. "I have plenty of fences I need to mend while you two are gone, and ain't one of 'em outside the house."

The three men laughed. Henry said a short prayer, and the men went to their separate responsibilities.

<hr />

At dawn the next morning, Gabriel and Dangerfield walked to the church to meet Evans. When they arrived the church doors were open.

Evans was inside, putting fresh candles in the holders. Dangerfield and Gabriel removed their hats and stepped inside. Evans turned when he heard them.

"Good morning, Pastor Evans," said Gabriel.

"Well, good morning," boomed Evans in his incongruously loud voice. "What brings brothers Dangerfield and Gabriel to the Lord's house so early this morning?"

"We came here to accept your offer to travel to Oberlin," said Dangerfield. "We want to learn more about how we can help you. I want to free my family. And we want to meet this Brother Brown."

Evans' eyes twinkled. "Splendid," said Evans. "As I said yesterday, Brother Brown could use men like you, physical specimens that you are. And Brother Dangerfield, I can assure you that Brother Brown will quickly take a personal interest in helping you free your family. Yes, yes, he will."

Evans patted his forehead with a handkerchief. Sweat beaded on his ruddy face, and he tugged at his collar.

"Have you discussed this with your family," said Evans.

"Yes, Gabriel and I told them our intentions last night," said Gabriel.

"And your parents – Henry and Elsey I believe, correct? Henry and Elsey approve of you joining us on this trip?"

"Well they don't – "said Gabriel.

"Yes, they approve," said Dangerfield.

"Splendid," said Evans. "And to make my intentions perfectly clear, neither of you is obligated to join Brother Brown. We simply want you to meet him and decide for yourself if his course of action is right for you. If you decide not to join us, we will pay for your safe transport back to Bridgeport, if that is what you truly want."

Evans eyed both men and smiled. "Of course, Brother Dangerfield, I firmly believe that with your help, we can quickly free not only your family, but hundreds of families like yours," said Evans. "The whole world will know your name, and recognize the good you have done for hundreds, thousands of families like yours. This campaign won't work without dedicated men like you and your brother. God Bless both of you."

Gabriel glanced at his brother, turned his head toward the door, and rocked back and forth on his heels. Dangerfield eyed the large painting of Jesus on the cross that hung on the wall.

"Yes, brothers, our Lord and Savior Jesus Christ made the ultimate sacrifice for all of us," said Evans, noticing the direction of Dangerfield's gaze. "Of course, we aren't asking you to make that kind of sacrifice. You shall return soon enough to your families. And your families shall be free, brothers. What a glorious day that will be."

"Glorious indeed," said Gabriel under his breath.

"Just think, Brother Dangerfield, soon you and Harriet and your children will be united in freedom," said Evans, waving his arms. "You won't have to worry about what sinful acts are happening at the Jennings plantation in your absence. Never again will you go to sleep at night wondering whether your wife and children have been sold, or worse." Evans eyed Dangerfield directly.

"Can't say I love Marse Lewis Jennings, but he has always been fair to me," said Dangerfield. "Kept his promises to me so far."

"Yes, yes of course," said Evans. "Forgive me, I in no way meant to trouble you, or suggest that Lewis Jennings might sell or harm your wife or children. Please forgive my assumption. It's just that as a man of God, I know that the serpent speaks with two tongues. And brother Lewis Jennings, despite his intentions, is a slave owner. He has been bitten by the serpent of slavery. And that venom is not easily removed from the body. Once a man understands the power he has to buy and sell another human being, the venom takes hold until there is no human blood left. There is only the serpent's venom. And the only way to remove that venom is to cut off the head of the snake. There is no cure for the serpent's venom. The serpent must be killed. There is only one path, brothers." Evans removed his handkerchief and patted the sweat from his forehead.

Gabriel glanced at his brother, and took two large backward steps toward the church door.

"Forgive me, brothers," said Evans. "I am filled with anger at the mere thought of how slavery has torn this country apart. As you can see, God has given me this mission to end this evil, and to kill the serpent. I cannot rest until the task has been completed."

Evans pulled his watch from his pocket. "Well brothers, are you ready to begin?"

"Pastor Evans," said Gabriel, "my brother and I would like a few moments in private to discuss your . . . generous offer. Please allow us a few minutes . . . ."

"We are ready to begin when you are, Pastor Evans," said Dangerfield. "My brother is sensible and cautious, which is why I have asked him to join me. He will be of great help to us. When do we begin?

"Right now," said Evans. "Let me lock up the church, and then we will walk to Featherston's carpenter shop. The two of you will ride with Featherston in his wagon to Oberlin. All arrangements will be made. Featherston is transporting some supplies to Brother Brown, but there is plenty of room in the wagon for both of you."

Evans locked the church door, and led the group down the main street toward Featherston's shop. Gabriel pulled Dangerfield toward him and let Evans walk ahead.

"I don't know what to make of this Evans," said Gabriel. "I don't know what we are getting into."

"You heard Evans," said Dangerfield. "We are simply going to meet Brown. We meet him, and decide if we want to join him. If we don't join him, we come back home. No risk."

"You seem awful certain," said Gabriel.

"Yes, I am."

They arrived at Featherston's shop. Evans knocked three times on the door, two sharp quick raps followed by a pause, then another rap. Evans stepped away from the door. A latch moved on the other side of the door, and the door slowly swung open.

"Good morning, Amos," said Evans. "You will have some company on your journey."

"Come in, Pastor, said Featherston.

The men entered Featherston's shop. Featherston quickly closed the door behind them.

Amos Featherston stood just over six feet tall, with a thick brush of gray flowing hair, and a luxuriant white beard. He was stout, and his belly strained against his workmen's clothes. Though it was cool and dim in the workshop, Featherston's shirt was damp with sweat, and he was breathing heavily.

"Amos, meet brothers Dangerfield and Gabriel Newby," said Evans. "They are new to Bridgeport. I spoke to you last night about Brother Dangerfield. His wife and children are imprisoned in Virginia."

"Yes, of course," said Featherston. "You are saving money to buy your family. You hope to buy your wife and children and bring them to freedom. Thomas told me your story. I hope we can help. And with your help, we can not only free your family, but all families like yours."

Evans glanced toward a large carriage wagon behind them.

"Do you need help loading the supplies," said Evans.

"No," said Featherston. "I loaded everything this morning. The carriage has not left the shed since the supplies arrived. Everything has been loaded inside." Featherston cracked open a window and fanned his shirt in the faint breeze.

"Thomas, I assume you have explained the reason for this journey to these fine young men," said Featherston, still breathing heavily.

"Yes, of course," said Evans. "All has been explained, and these brothers are eager to join us.

"What kind of supplies are we bringing to Oberlin," said Gabriel, eying the wagon. "I don't see anything in that wagon."

"No you don't see anything in the wagon," said Featherston. "The cargo is very sensitive, and has to be specially packed. We don't want it to move around during the journey."

"What kind of cargo is it," said Gabriel, warily.

"Come on up, and I will show you."

Dangerfield and Gabriel stepped into the carriage and sat down. The inside of the carriage was completely empty. A thick woolen blanket covered the floor.

"Now if you gentlemen would put your feet up on the seat," said Featherston. Dangerfield and Gabriel obliged.

Featherston pulled back the blanket and slid the end of a crowbar into the floorboard. He pushed the crowbar away from him, and the entire floorboard slid back into a hidden chamber. Dangerfield peered into the bottom of the wagon and saw perhaps a dozen long bundles, each bundle individually wrapped in a gray wool blanket. All the bundles were nestled in a thick straw bed.

Featherston pulled out two of the bundles and unwrapped two gleaming new rifles. He handed one rifle to Dangerfield, and another to Gabriel.

"Lord Almighty, said Dangerfield softly. "What kind of gun is this?"

"This is a Sharps rifle," said Featherston. "One of the most accurate weapons made. A skilled marksman can shoot the stem off an apple from 100 yards with this gun."

Dangerfield cradled the heavy gun and peered down the sight. Gabriel held his gun, looked at his brother, and quickly returned the gun to Featherston.

"Brother Brown is in urgent need of supplies," said Evans. "Although an adequate supply was sent to Kansas, the new campaign will require even more tools. Featherston and I are simply transferring necessary supplies. Think of it as a religious mission."

"How many guns are in that wagon," said Dangerfield.

"Twenty-four rifles, each wrapped in blankets," said Featherston. "From the outside, the wagon appears empty. Road agents will have no reason to suspect anything."

"What does Brother Brown aim to do with 24 new rifles," said Gabriel.

"Brothers, as you know the anti-slavery forces have been under continuous attack since the unpleasant events in Kansas," said Evans. "Abolitionists have been beaten and killed. Now, we are a peaceful and God-fearing group – ours is a mission of mercy, of peace. But the pro-slavery factions, they will have no peace until the stain of slavery has spread over the entire nation. We have no choice but to defend ourselves."

Pastor Evans took the rifle from Featherston's hands. "And the Sharps rifle," he said, admiring the dark wood of the stock, "has proven its worth in Kansas and Missouri. I once saw a man with a Sharps gun down a slaver from 100 yards, shooting into the wind." Evans thumbed back the hammer and looked down the bore, smiling. "Magnificent weapon," Evans said to himself. He then closed the hammer, and returned the rifle back to Featherston, who wrapped it in the blanket and returned it to the hold.

"Pastor Evans, you know an awful lot about guns, for a man of God," said Gabriel.

Evans chuckled. "Even angels have swords," said Evans. "And the Lord honors those who defend themselves."

"Brother, may I have a word with you," said Gabriel. "Now."

Gabriel pulled Dangerfield to one corner of the shed.

"I don't like this, not one bit," hissed Gabriel. "I think we need to leave, and now. We go back home and tell Henry and Elsey we changed our minds."

"Brother, you whisper like you was raised in a forge. Keep your voice down."

"This ain't right, and you know it," said Gabriel. "I don't know what this Evans is up to. Right now, I ain't even certain he is a pastor. Ain't never met a man of God knows so much about guns. But whatever he and this Brown are up to, it ain't no Sunday church picnic. I say we leave now, and go home."

"What do you aim to do at home, Gabriel? Spend the rest of your days with Henry and Elsey? Fix fences, chop wood, work for other people? Wait for something good to happen? When do you plan on doing something bigger than you?"

"Bigger than me? I don't give a damn about doing anything bigger than me. I got no one to save. I just don't want us to go off and get killed."

Dangerfield grabbed his brother's shoulder. "You ever have anything in your life worth fighting for? I mean really worth fighting for?"

Gabriel shifted uneasily. "I can't say I have. Henry and Elsey always took pretty good care of us."

"Look around, Gabriel. Things are changing. We ain't in Virginia any more, but a lot of us still in Virginia, waiting for someone to set them free. And it won't happen by itself. You heard what Evans told us. Cotton keeps getting bigger, and the plantations keep getting bigger, and it don't never end. Someone has to make it end."

"You may be right, but it ain't worth getting killed over," said Gabriel.

"What makes you so certain we won't survive?"

You may be the older brother, but I know that any trip that begins with a wagon load of guns won't end well for somebody. And we don't know this Evans or Featherston well enough."

"You want to go home, Gabriel, then go. I aim to go with these gentlemen. If they wanted us dead, they could have killed us by now."

"Ain't them I'm worried about," growled Gabriel.

"Suit yourself, brother, but I aim to go with them. You can stay with me if you want."

Evans and Featherston stood near the window, peering out at the town.

Gabriel looked at the wagon, then looked at Evans and Featherston, who was lifting saddles onto a post.

"You aim to go without me," said Gabriel.

"If I have to," said Dangerfield. "I'd rather have you with me, so I can keep an eye on you. Henry will have my hide if something happens to you."

"You still have that gun Henry gave us," said Gabriel.

"In here," said Dangerfield, patting his chest.

Gabriel spat into the sawdust on the floor.

"Well, can't have you getting yourself killed," said Gabriel. "And since it seems you ain't got enough sense to recognize trouble even when it slaps you in the face, I guess I better go with you. You seem like you done lost your mind."

"Harriet and my children need me. And I think some other families need me too."

The two brothers walked back to the wagon and climbed in. Featherston opened the shed door, hitched the horses to the wagon, and nudged them forward down the main street, and then north, toward Oberlin College.

CHAPTER 39

O<small>CTOBER</small> 17, 1858

Once the wagon left Bridgeport, Featherston nudged the carriage horses forward and they settled into an easy rhythm, the double-clip of each horse's stride sounding in unison. Featherston held the reins and spoke constantly to the horses as he drove the wagon, clicking his tongue, and occasionally flicking the horses on their flanks to control them. Dangerfield and Gabriel sat on either side of him. Their bags were stacked on the floorboard behind them, covering the sliding floorboard that concealed their cargo.

The road out of Bridgeport was narrow and steep, winding through the coal hills. In some places, the road was scarcely wide enough for two wagons to pass. Dangerfield looked up at the soot-covered men harvesting coal. An equal mix of black men and white men worked the hills, each reduced to a dull gray equality by their occupation. Dangerfield looked at the laborers and realized that in Virginia, he had rarely seen white men working in fields. And he had never seen white men and black men laboring side by side. Then he wondered who built the road if there were no slaves in Ohio.

No one spoke for some time. Featherston was lost in his conversation with the horses, while Dangerfield and Gabriel took note of the surroundings in the free state of Ohio. As the wagon proceeded north, the steep hills receded, and the road became wider and flatter as it entered the valley.

"How far until we get to Oberlin," said Dangerfield.

"About three days," said Featherston. "A man riding could make it in two, but we have a heavy load. And we don't want this cargo damaged, so we will take our time where we can."

Featherston stroked his thick white beard before speaking.

"I assume Thomas – Pastor Evans – explained the nature of this trip to both of you."

"Yes," said Dangerfield. "We are going to meet Brother Brown and see if he needs us, and how we can help him."

"And you will bring us back home safely if we decide not to join Brown in whatever it is he is doing," said Gabriel quickly.

"Yes, both points are true," said Featherston. "However, I believe you will find Brother John Brown to be an honest and forthright man, dedicated to freeing all of us from the stain of slavery."

"We can decide that for ourselves," said Gabriel.

"Yes, of course," said Featherston. "Both of you must decide whether and how you can help your people. This country. We all must decide. And doing nothing is its own decision."

"What does Brown want us to do?" said Dangerfield.

"I think Brother Brown can best explain his intentions," said Featherston. "I do know that most of his efforts have been defensive. Protecting those who have been viciously attacked by slavers. His mission – our mission – is a mission of peace."

"And what about those guns?" said Gabriel.

"Purely for self-defense," said Featherston sharply. "As Thomas said, even angels have swords."

No one spoke. The wagon wheels groaned under the weight of the cargo. The double-clip of the horses sounding in unison echoed throughout the valley. Featherston clicked his tongue at the horses and eased them toward the center of the road.

"Why do you care so much about ending slavery," said Gabriel. "It don't affect you. Your wife and kids are safe. You got nobody in Virginia to rescue."

Featherston clucked at the horses before speaking.

"We are all children of God, Brother Gabriel," said Featherston. "And God tells us that whatsoever we do to the least of our brethren, we do unto him. What slavery does to the black race, it does to all of us."

"I could take the easy path, and allow others to do the work," continued Featherston. "I could simply pray that slavery ends, and have faith that good will prevail over evil. But as you know, brothers, faith without works is dead. And I am too old to embark on some of the more ambitious campaigns. So I have chosen to help in whatever way I can, with whatever strength I have."

Featherston flicked the lead horse gently with his riding crop while speaking softly to the horses. No one spoke over the rhythmic sound of the horses' hooves and the groaning of the wagon. Featherston continued his conversation with the horses. Gabriel leaned back and closed his eyes, his body bouncing in rhythm with each bump in the road.

Dangerfield gazed at the passing Ohio countryside. There were no plantations. There were no slaves working bareback in the broiling sun, and no mounted overseers. There were no black-skinned women looking for a shady spot to hide their babies before bending over to pick cotton meant to be worn by others. There was no burning flesh, and the only whip in sight was used on the horses. He wondered if there was any place in Virginia like this.

"I assume both of you have your freeman's papers," said Featherston. "Ohio may be free, but slave catchers still patrol these roads. If you don't have your papers, they will claim you are escaped. God knows where you might end up."

Dangerfield reached into his coat pocket and felt for the leather pouch with his papers. He reached into the other pocket and felt the smooth wooden grip of the little Colt. He had not considered which would prove more useful.

Gabriel opened his eyes and retrieved his papers from his coat pocket. He looked warily at Featherston.

"How many slave catchers patrol this part of Ohio," said Gabriel.

"Enough. Always best to have your papers," said Featherston. "Since you both are free men, with papers, we should not have any problem. We travel by daylight, and you two will always sit with me. Even a fool would not risk smuggling fugitives in the open in broad daylight."

Gabriel caressed the leather pouch that Henry had given him. He rubbed his chin while looking at the passing countryside.

"You ever see any slave catchers on this road," said Gabriel.

"Often enough," said Featherston. "I make the trip from Bridgeport to Oberlin twice a month. Sometimes, I don't see any slave catchers. Other times, I get stopped two or three times in the same trip. They get quite active if a owner offers a big reward. Word gets out quickly."

"Why do they stop you?" said Gabriel.

Featherston smiled and stroked his thick white beard. "This wagon carries more than just guns, brothers. I sometimes make the trip with more delicate cargo."

"You mean runaways?" said Gabriel.

"We prefer to call them fugitives from injustice. Slavers call them runaways, among other things."

Gabriel surveyed the wagon as it bounced over the rutted path.

"How many runaways fit in that hold?" said Gabriel.

"Depends. It can hold four small children, or two adults, depending on how they are arranged. If we can lay the boxes side by side, we have more room for other cargo. And of course, transporting human cargo takes more time. It requires frequent stops, and of course more discretion when traveling in the open."

Gabriel began to slide the wooden door open, and then stopped.

"Can they breathe in there?"

"Yes, through the air holes in the front of the hold. Not visible from the road, or even from the wagon."

"What if they have hounds," said Gabriel. "Cain't hide 'em from hounds if the hounds start sniffing the wagon."

"We hide the human cargo in pine coffins," said Featherston. "Inside each coffin we place sacks of pepper or gunpowder. The coffins have air holes. That is often enough to throw the dogs off, for a few minutes. I make the coffins myself," said Featherston proudly.

Featherston resumed his conversation with the horses, clicking and chiding as the wagon left the coal hills and descended into the valley. The road was now flat and wide enough for two wagons to pass easily. A thick canopy of trees shrouded the sun.

Dangerfield considered what goes through the mind of a runaway packed into a coffin seeking freedom. He wondered how many runaways never escaped those coffins.

"Why do you do all this," said Dangerfield finally. Why do you take the risk?"

Featherston smiled. "If not us, then who, brothers? When the Lord summons you to his work, that summons cannot be ignored. Eliminating the scourge of slavery is God's command. I am simply following orders."

Featherston looked out at the trees shrouding either side of the road. He tapped the lead horse with his crop and urged the wagon ahead faster.

"How much do you get paid," said Dangerfield. "Who pays you for this work?"

"Our reward is in heaven," said Featherston sharply. He stroked his beard and scanned either side of the road before nudging the horses ahead. The wagon rocked back and forth as it picked up speed.

Gabriel held onto the side of the carriage as it bounced over the rutted trail. "Why are we going so fast? Feel like I might fall right over the side."

"This is not a good place to stop or tarry," said Featherston, scanning the road.

The wagon crossed a rickety bridge that spanned a shallow creek. The horses were now moving quickly and the wagon rocked violently as they crossed the bridge.

Featherston eased the horses to a walk as soon as they crossed the bridge.

"Are you armed, brothers?"

"I have a small Colt," said Dangerfield. "Why?"

"Keep your gun handy," said Featherston. "Make certain the ball is in, and make certain the gun is cocked."

Dangerfield remembered Henry's instructions and retrieved the Colt from his breast pocket. He loaded a powder charge and a ball into the front of each cylinder. He retrieved a cap from his pocket and thumbed it down onto the nipple at the back of the barrel.

"You expect somebody might be after us?" said Gabriel.

"This is the worst part of the trip" said Featherston. "Road agents own this territory. Brother Gabriel, you might need this." Featherston retrieved a short-barreled shotgun from beneath his feet and handed it to Gabriel.

"Charged and primed," said Featherston. Keep that close by."

"Does someone aim to kill us" said Gabriel.

"Not you," said Featherston. "This is just a precaution."

"Reckon you could have told us about this precaution before we started," said Gabriel. "Might not have joined you."

Featherston said nothing, but retrieved another short-barreled shotgun from beneath his feet. He checked the charge, then put the gun back.

"Brothers, you are free men, and your papers prove it," said Featherston. "Any danger that exists is for me, not you. If we are stopped, have your papers handy."

Featherston held the horses at a walk as the wagon crested a small hill. The canopy of trees now completely blocked the sun, creating a tunnel. The road vanished into blackness.

"Why didn't we take the side roads," said Dangerfield.

"Sometimes it is best to hide in the open," said Featherston. "Be mindful of what you see."

Dangerfield patted the Colt in his breast pocket. And then he remembered Henry's warning: "Gabriel is your responsibility now. If anything happens to him, I will hold you responsible as his older brother. I don't care what Cain said, you are now your brother's keeper. Mind that always."

Dangerfield closed his eyes and contemplated Henry's warning. And then he saw his family back in Virginia. Harriet was directly in front of him. She was thinner than he remembered. She wore a ragged blue dress, and walked about the cabin, cradling their new baby while singing softly. Lucy and Agnes were in the cabin, playing with dolls they made out of straw, sticks, and old corn cobs. He heard the baby crying weakly.

Dangerfield saw Junior and Gabriel in the field behind the corn crib, gathering wood, laughing and joking. He heard them telling stories about Lewis Jennings. Both had grown taller, and more muscular – they were no longer boys. Jericho was moving a stubborn hog from the pen to the butchering shed while Lewis Jennings looked on from a distance, stroking his thin mustache while he watched Jericho work. Dangerfield could see Jericho had a fresh set of scars on his back, some still bleeding. He was wearing a pair of Dangerfield's old breeches, dirty and even more tattered then when Dangerfield owned them.

Lewis Jennings wore a threadbare gray riding suit. His boots were scuffed and unpolished. Dangerfield had never seen Jennings without polished black boots.

Jennings rocked back and forth on his heels while watching Jericho prodding the hog. Jennings' face was lined, and the skin under his eyes was sagging. Jennings looked older and more haggard than Dangerfield ever remembered. And in that moment, Lewis Jennings looked like his dead father.

Dangerfield emerged from his reverie when Gabriel began tapping him furiously on the shoulder. "Wake up, brother. Somebody is up ahead of us."

A lone rider emerged from the trees in front of the wagon. He was clothed from head to toe in black, and wore tall cavalry boots. An enormous black hat covered his face. He prodded his horse and stopped in the middle of the road. He held a rifle aloft and fired a single shot into the air. Featherston's horses bucked, and the wagon lurched to one side.

"Keep your weapons close, but don't draw them," hissed Featherston.

Dangerfield turned toward Gabriel. "Nothing will happen to us, Brother. We will get home safely. They don't want us."

"I ain't so certain of that," whispered Gabriel. "I don't know what we got ourselves into."

The lone rider advanced his horse toward the wagon and the screaming horses. Featherston struggled to calm the horses, but was unable to turn the wagon around. From behind, another rider emerged, blocking the road, and preventing any escape. He wore a long cloak, a soldier's light blue riding trousers, and a tattered infantry officer's dress cap. This rider held aloft a long-barreled revolver, but fired no shots. The riders closed in on the wagon. Featherston struggled to calm his wall-eyed horses. The first rider dismounted and approached the wagon, rifle in hand.

"State your business," said Featherston.

"We are looking for runaways," said the man. He was tall, and as he approached he pushed his hat back from his face. He had a faint jagged scar on the left side of his face that ran from just under his left eye to the corner of his mouth. Dangerfield had seen him before, but could not remember where.

"We have no runaways here," said Featherston. "These are free men." The second man approached from the other side of the wagon. He held his revolver aloft, and stepped onto the wagon. This man had full lips, and soft, almost feminine features. Curly blond hair crept out from under his infantry cap. Dangerfield had seen him before, but again could not remember where.

"Produce your warrant before you set foot on my property," said Featherston.

"We don't need a warrant to search for runaways," said the first man. "And if you have no runaways, you have nothing to fear."

"These are free men," said Featherston. "They can show you their papers."

Dangerfield reached into his pocket and pulled out the leather pouch. He handed it to the tall man with the scar. Gabriel handed over his papers. Dangerfield kept his hand on the Colt while the tall man inspected the papers. He read Dangerfield's papers, then Gabriel's, then read both papers again. He looked up at Gabriel and Dangerfield, carefully studied their faces, then looked back at the papers.

The second man spoke. "Should we search the wagon?" he asked as he began climbing aboard the wagon.

"Produce your warrant, or get off my property," growled Featherston. The second man continued climbing aboard. Featherston waited until both of the man's hands were on the side rails, and both feet were on the boarding plank.

Featherston grabbed the shotgun at his feet, thumbed back the hammer, and pointed the barrel at the blond man's forehead. With both hands on the side rails, he could not draw his own weapon. The man froze.

The tall man continued reviewing the papers. He finally looked up and saw Featherston holding the shotgun at his partner's head. He carefully folded both papers and put them back in their leather pouches.

"Stand down," said the tall man. "We don't need to search this wagon." He returned the leather pouches to Dangerfield and Gabriel. "And you put your gun away. He means no harm." The tall man gestured to his partner. "Get off the wagon."

Featherston lifted his shotgun and allowed the man to descend. The blond man fell to the ground, trembling.

Dangerfield put his papers in his pocket and surveyed the situation. Gabriel did the same. The tall man spoke.

"Both of you Henry Newby's boys, according to your papers, ain't you? Used to live in Culpeper County. One of you worked over at the Jennings farm."

"That was me," said Dangerfield. "Worked for Jennings – Marse Jennings for many years. Still do some work for his son."

"So I have been told," said the tall man. "Is Henry Newby still alive?"

"Yes," said Dangerfield.

"He still live in Culpeper County?"

"No. He moved to Bridgeport just last week."

The tall man scratched at his scar.

"He leave anything behind in Culpeper? Any property?"

"No," said Dangerfield. "He moved everything to Ohio. Nothing left in Culpeper. How do you know Henry Newby?"

The tall man chuckled. "Me and my partner used to catch fugitives in Virginia, years ago," he said as he jerked his thumb toward the trembling blond man. "Used to run into Henry from time to time when we were searching. I remember once we stopped at his house and told him we were looking for two young half-breed field hands had got loose. He told us he owned two half-breed boys, but they belonged to him free and clear. Told us if we went after his property, he'd find us and kill us, and wait for the hangman."

Dangerfield and Gabriel looked at each other.

The tall man continued. "We told him we only took runaways. Didn't want no trouble with Henry Newby, least not from what we heard of him. Promised to leave his boys alone. He told us enough about both of you, so we'd know enough to leave you alone. Word got out not to mess with Henry Newby's property, 'specially after he killed a man went after one of his house girls."

The tall man scratched at his scar, and pointed at Dangerfield. "He still let you ride that big old horse he had, Old Solomon?"

And then Dangerfield remembered where he had seen these men. Years ago, when he first started working for Augustine Jennings. He had been on the road from his house to the Jennings plantation, riding Solomon harder than he should have. The tall man and his partner had stopped him, looking for runaways. And then he remembered their bounty from that day – a beaten and whipped captured fugitive tied up on horseback. Dangerfield remembered the lash marks on the Negro man's back, long red fingers dripping blood from his coal black skin. Lash marks covering his back from his shoulders to his waist, stretching from rib to rib. He could still see the black flies covering this wretched soul's body, feasting on his wounded and open flesh. And he remembered the smile on the blond man's face as they continued.

Dangerfield felt for the Colt in his pocket before speaking.

"Old Solomon don't ride much any more."

"I do recall he was a splendid horse. Thought that the first time I saw you riding him. Don't often see slaves trusted with a mount like that."

The tall man pushed his hat down low over his face, so the scar was not visible. He mounted his horse and motioned to his partner.

"Good day, gentlemen," he said as he turned his horse toward Bridgeport. The tall man tipped his hat. Both men rode away.

The three men in the wagon watched in silence as the riders disappeared. Featherston sat slack-jawed and motionless, watching the dust cloud as the riders receded.

"Lord Almighty, what just happened," Featherston said to himself softly. "The Lord has delivered us from evil."

"I ain't so certain about that," said Gabriel. "I think we just got lucky once. No telling what happens around the next bend."

"Brothers, do you understand what this means," said Featherston. "Word has gotten out among the road agents that you two are to be left alone. Whatever Henry Newby has done, his reputation has spread among the devil's workers. They leave you alone. Brothers, the hand of the Almighty rests lightly on your shoulders. You are protected by angels."

"The Almighty can keep his hand on my shoulder in my own bed," said Gabriel. "I don't know what you got us into, Featherston, but I don't want no part of it. I want to go back home. If this Brother Brown is in the same business as you, then it ain't none of my business. I want to go back home, like you promised. Ain't worth me getting killed to free somebody else."

"Please hear me, Brother Gabriel," pleaded Featherston. "The work we do is hard, and it is dangerous. Forgive me if I did not explain that beforehand," said Featherston. "We are under constant threat whenever we move supplies or human cargo. But you two are blessed. The slavers fear you and Henry Newby.

Think of the good you could do if you helped us. We could move supplies and help those fleeing injustice. With either one of you aboard our wagons, and with your papers and Henry Newby's reputation, we could move freely from Bridgeport to Oberlin, maybe even through Virginia for a time. It's as though the Lord has delivered our own personal angel. Please, Brother Gabriel, consider the good you could do. Consider how you could help others."

"I don't want no part of this," said Gabriel. "This ain't my fight. I want to go back home."

Featherston slumped. "I will take you to the next safe house north, and you can return home on the next wagon," said Featherston. "But let me tell you this, Brothers. You have been chosen. Both of you have been chosen by the Lord to do this work. I have known many brave men. But you have been chosen by God. Man ignores the Lord's commands at his peril."

Featherston urged the horses toward the side of the road while he talked softly to them. "And what about you, Brother Dangerfield?"

Dangerfield had not been listening to Gabriel's plea, because the tall man's words echoed in his head – "word got out not to mess with Henry Newby's property, 'specially after he killed a man went after one of his house girls." Dangerfield turned this over in his mind.

"Let me have a word with my brother," said Dangerfield. Featherston left the wagon, hobbled the lead horse and walked to the side of the road to piss.

"I told you this was a damn fool idea," said Gabriel. "Told you that before we left. We ain't but a few miles down the road, and we got people with guns threatening us. We go back home now."

"They weren't threatening us, Gabriel. Soon as they saw our papers, we were safe."

"A bullet can't read no papers," said Gabriel. "What if the next ones we meet shoot before they know who we are?"

Dangerfield watched Featherston as he finished pissing.

"Did you hear what that man said about Henry? Said he killed a man who went after one of his house girls," said Gabriel. "Henry never told us about that."

"I reckon there's quite a few things Henry never told us," said Dangerfield. "Henry did what he needed to do."

"And we can thank him properly when we get back home," said Gabriel. "This ain't our fight, brother. Henry did what he needed to protect us. Be a damn shame if we get ourselves killed on some fool mission after everything he done for us. Think of everything Henry did for us, Elsey, and Anna Mae. You think Henry moved us out of slavery in Virginia so we could get ourselves shot as free men in Ohio?"

Dangerfield closed his eyes and saw Harriet and his children in the yard at the Jennings farm. He could smell Harriet's skin, and the rough soap she used to bathe. He remembered the first time he was with her, in the hayloft at the Jennings farm, and the time they had almost been caught by Old Man Jennings. He remembered how she quickened at his touch, and the feel of her beautiful coffee skin. He wanted to be with Harriet more than anything. That was all that mattered.

And then the words of Pastor Thomas Evans intruded on his reverie – "Of course, Brother Dangerfield, I firmly believe that with your help, we can quickly free not only your family, but hundreds of families like yours. The whole world will know your name, and recognize the good you have done for hundreds, thousands of families like yours."

Dangerfield thought of his own family, and hundreds of other families just like his. Black children playing in yards in Virginia, Tennessee, and Kentucky, always aware that they could be sold South any day. Masters more cruel than even Old Man Jennings with his brands. The smell of burning black flesh, and the crack of the whip echoing across the South. Beaten and whipped black men riding bound and shirtless while black flies devoured their bleeding flesh.

He tried to push these thoughts out of his head. This wasn't his fight. He was a free man, with papers to prove it. Let others do what Henry had done for them. Maybe Gabriel, Elsey, and Henry were all right – let others save their own. He would get Harriet and his family, and live quietly in Ohio. Let Brown save the rest. This was not his fight.

And then he considered how the slave catchers had retreated as soon as they discovered he was Henry Newby's son. They left without searching the wagon. A wagon load of guns and two black men riding in the open in broad daylight, and they were not searched, just because of his father's reputation. He thought of the hundreds of other families like his. What if they had no one like Henry? What if there was no one willing to sacrifice, willing to kill for their freedom? What if there was no Henry for any of them?

But he couldn't save everyone. Saving just his own family had damn near killed Henry. Henry had done enough. Maybe he couldn't do any more.

And then Featherston's words echoed in his heart – "But let me tell you this, Brothers. You have been chosen. Both of you have been chosen by the Lord to do this work. Man ignores the Lord's commands at his peril."

Dangerfield opened his eyes and gazed at his brother. "You can go home if want to, Gabriel. I am going with Featherston."

Gabriel stared at him. "You aim to leave me?"

"I ain't leaving you," said Dangerfield. "You aim to leave us. If you want to go, then leave. I aim to get my family, and help others get theirs. Somebody's got to do it. Not everybody has someone like Henry."

Gabriel looked down the road and spat in the dirt. "Well, I don't want no part of this. I aim to catch the next wagon going back to town."

Featherston approached the wagon apprehensively. "Brothers, whatever decision you make, please consider carefully what the Lord needs from you. You have been chosen."

"My brother wants to go home," said Dangerfield. "I intend to go with you."

"Splendid," said Featherston. "Bless you." Featherston removed the hobble from the lead horse, climbed aboard the wagon and took the reins.

"Brother Gabriel, we will take you to the next safe house and leave you there. You can ride home on the next wagon heading back to Bridgeport."

"How far until we get there?" said Gabriel.

"Another four miles," said Featherston.

"I ain't going another mile on this road," said Gabriel. "Reckon I will walk home from here."

"You aim to walk home alone," said Dangerfield.

Gabriel considered his brother's words, then said nothing as he climbed back into the wagon. Featherston waited for Gabriel to take his seat, then clicked his tongue, and the three men and wagon proceeded north, toward Oberlin.

CHAPTER 40

Dangerfield, Gabriel, and Featherston rode north in silence until the first safe house, about four miles north of where they had encountered the road agents. The house sat about ten feet from the road, and was visible from a great distance. It was nothing more than a rickety log cabin, with a slanting roof, large gaps between the logs, and a wooden door that hung unevenly from its hinges. There were no windows. Featherston sat the horses and dismounted.

"Well Brother, Gabriel, here is where we leave you, unless you have changed your mind."

Gabriel eyed the cabin warily. From inside the wagon, Gabriel looked through the gaps in the logs and saw grass on the other side of the structure. Unlike most cabins that sat elevated on large beams, this cabin was flush with the ground.

"Don't look like much of a house, and it don't look real safe, neither," muttered Gabriel. He did not get out of the wagon.

"It may not look like much, Brother Gabriel, but it serves its purpose well," said Featherston. "Come on down and let me show you."

Gabriel did not move from the wagon. Dangerfield dismounted, and walked to the side of the road to piss.

"You ain't having second thoughts, are you Brother," said Dangerfield as he buttoned his pants. "Looks like a fine place to rest for a bit. Unless you want to come with us to Oberlin." Dangerfield walked up to the cabin and gently nudged one of the logs with his toe. Despite the cabin's unstable appearance, the log did not move.

"Yes, well it does not look like much, but this little shack has sheltered hundreds of people," said Featherston. "Let me see if the girls are home."

Featherston put his fingers to his mouth and let loose a piercing whistle. Two young women emerged from behind the cabin. When they saw Dangerfield and Gabriel, they bowed politely.

"Did you see anyone pass recently, girls," said Featherston.

"No Papa," said one of the girls. She was perhaps 17 or 18, tall, thin, and very pale. She wore a starched white dress, and a scarf that covered her blonde head completely. "We were working in the garden and gathering greens from the field. Haven't seen anyone from either direction for over an hour."

"Any news from below?" said Featherston.

"No, Papa," said the second girl. "No messengers." She was shorter than her sister, plump, with darker hair. She had a fresh scar under her left eye, which did not seem to trouble her. She wore nothing on her head.

"Brothers Gabriel and Dangerfield, these are my daughters Louise and Mary. They assist me in my work."

Both girls again bowed politely.

"Girls, why don't you show Brother Gabriel inside. He will be staying here for just a few hours until a wagon arrives from Oberlin."

"Good day, ladies," said Gabriel as he tipped his hat politely. He did not dismount from the wagon.

"Brother Gabriel, I can assure you that my daughters won't harm you," said Featherston. "Please let them show you inside. Unless you really have changed your mind and wish to join your brother and me, in which case we can let the girls to their work."

"How much longer till we get to Oberling," said Gabriel.

"Another day's ride, and someplace to rest for at least one night," said Featherston.

"What if we see more slave catchers?

"We almost certainly will see more slave catchers on our journey, both there and back."

"How many?"

"Could be one or two teams, or could be dozens. It depends on how many runaways are on the loose."

Gabriel paused as he remembered the two men who had attempted to seize the wagon just a few miles outside of Bridgeport. "Reckon I will stay here," he said as he climbed down from the wagon. "Can't be no worse than having people shooting at me."

The interior of the cabin provided no surprises – it was as timeworn as the outside. A single rough-hewn log table occupied the center of the room, with a chair on either end. A collection of shovels, rakes, and hoes were neatly gathered in one corner of the cabin. Two large buckets sat in the opposite corner. Freshly-cut field greens were on one end of the table, waiting to be cleaned. A package of long candles sat on the other end of the table. Although there were no windows, the gaps between the logs provided enough sunlight so that Gabriel could see the lines in Featherston's face. The floor was incongruously solid, with tightly-packed oak boards that did not creak despite the weight of five people inside the cabin.

"This ain't much more than a hog shed," said Gabriel as he studied his surroundings.

"The humble appearance is purposeful," said Featherston. From the road, this looks like nothing more than a simple woodsman's cabin. When the girls are here, they use it as gardening shed, and storage for the tools. Nothing about this building is intended to convey its purpose."

"Where are the beds," said Dangerfield.

"No one sleeps here, not even my family," said Featherston. "We use it as a gardening shed and lookout post. From inside, you can see well down the road in either direction, even without windows. Come look."

Gabriel peered through a crack in the logs, looking toward Bridgeport. He could see almost a quarter-mile down the road. He turned in the opposite direction, and could see an equal distance north. Nothing blocked his view of the road in either direction.

"The gaps in the logs are intentional," said Featherston proudly. "From inside the cabin, you can see and hear horses and wagons from a great distance. And because there are no windows, travelers cannot see into the cabin until they are very close."

"What is this for, if nobody sleeps here," said Gabriel.

Featherston chuckled. "Let me show you. Louise, come help with the table."

The girl with the fresh scars picked up the table and moved it to one side. Featherston pulled a knife from his pocket and gently loosened one of the floorboards. Underneath the floorboard was a metal handle. He loosened another floorboard, revealing another metal handle. Featherston gripped one handle while Louise gripped the other. They lifted in unison, removing a large square segment of floor. They lowered the segment and Featherston pointed.

Dangerfield and Gabriel saw a hole in the floor about four feet in diameter. Featherston retrieved a candle and a striker from his pocket, struck the flint, and lit the candle. "Look down," he said.

The hole led to a tunnel under the cabin. As wide as a man's body, the tunnel went straight down for about three feet, then disappeared.

"Where does this lead," said Dangerfield.

"Look through that gap," said Featherston.

Dangerfield peered through a gap in the rear wall. About 100 feet away sat a small house, almost completely hidden by a thick grove of trees. The house sat just below the top of a rolling ridge, so that only the roof was visible from the cabin.

"This tunnel goes to that house," said Featherston. "That is where my family stays when not in Bridgeport. You cannot see the house from the road."

Gabriel knelt and peered into the hole while Featherston held the candle. The entrance was lined with brick and stone, held in place with mud and mortar. A ladder led straight down for three feet until the tunnel turned toward the hidden house.

"Louise, Mary and I and some men from town made this ourselves," beamed Featherston. "It took us over a year, accounting for the time we could not dig during the winter. The whole thing is lined with brick and stone to keep it from collapsing during rains."

Gabriel squinted as he peered into the hole. "How many runaways been in that rathole," he said.

"Hundreds," said Featherston. "We bring them here in the hidden compartment of the wagon, as you have seen. We bring the wagon behind the cabin, unload the runaways, and send them down the tunnel. We can send ten at a time. Louise or Mary guide them toward the house. One guides, and the other one stays behind and replaces the trap door and the table. If any strangers pass by, it's just Louise or Mary in the shed, cleaning greens."

Gabriel stood and brushed off his pants. "Don't reckon I would ever climb down into that rathole. Don't know what might happen."

Featherston smiled. "Brother Gabriel, many of the runaways have traveled hundreds of miles, in coffins, empty whiskey barrels, and wagons with hidden compartments. A tunnel where they can crawl is a welcome relief."

"Won't nobody shoot at you inside that tunnel," said Dangerfield.

Gabriel eyed the tunnel entrance warily as he stepped backward. "Wouldn't never go in that thing," he muttered to himself. "Ain't you worried something might happen to your girls, all alone in this cabin?"

"The risk of harm is great for all of us," said Featherston. "You saw that yourself on the way here. I have been attacked many times by slavers. That's why I carry the shotguns in the wagon."

"As for the girls," said Featherston, "I have taught them to defend themselves. I don't worry about them when I am gone." He turned to Louise. Dangerfield and Gabriel watched as she pulled a long, thick-bladed and curved knife from within the folds of her dress.

"Watch," said Louise. She gripped the knife by the blade, flipped her wrist, and flung the knife toward the back wall of the cabin. The knife sailed blade over handle for several revolutions until finally the blade sank deep into the log wall. The handle quivered for several moments afterward.

Louise grabbed the handle, placed her foot against the wall, and heaved the knife out of the wall. She wiped the blade against her dress, and returned the weapon inside the folds of her dress.

"Slavers never see that coming until it is too late," said Featherston proudly. "Now, Mary and I prefer less subtle means of protection." Featherston retrieved a blue-barreled Colt five-shot pistol from inside his vest pocket, and held it aloft. Mary retrieved an identical pistol from inside her dress. "I bought matching pistols for me and Mary. I keep this with me even when I sleep."

Gabriel eyed Featherston and his gun-toting, knife-wielding daughters and backed toward the cabin door.

"All this seems mighty dangerous for a man who ain't got no family in slavery," said Gabriel. "Seems like it might be easier to just be a carpenter, and keep your family safe."

"To act on behalf of others is dangerous," said Featherston. "To do nothing on behalf of others is a sin against God. As for me and my house, we would rather face the danger of confronting slavers than face the wrath of the Almighty." Featherston flipped open the cylinder on his Colt, and examined each chamber. He closed the cylinder, returned the Colt to his pocket, and eyed Gabriel evenly.

"There is still time to change your mind, Brother Gabriel. There is danger in what we do, but there is great reward. There is no reward in doing nothing. Consider the example that Henry set for you. Consider the sacrifices that Henry made for you."

No one spoke. Gabriel stared at the ground, shuffling his feet against the oak floor. Louise and Mary bowed their heads in polite silence.

"If I had family to save, it might be different," said Gabriel. "But I don't. And I ain't Henry. Seems like an awful waste to come all this way for freedom, and then get shot trying to get freedom for someone else."

Gabriel looked through the gaps in the log walls. "I ain't never been free before, at least not legally," he said. "It ain't like Henry beat us or anything, but we still weren't free under the law. Now we are. Got papers to prove it." He kicked the toe of his boot against the floor. "Reckon I want to enjoy some freedom first 'fore I risk my hide for somebody else. Maybe someday, but not now. Freedom ain't worth much if you dead."

Gabriel retrieved his hat and pulled it low over his eyes, even though the inside of the cabin was dimly lit. "I ain't Henry," he said flatly. "I don't have to do the things he did. Maybe I will someday, but I don't have to do those things now. I want to go home, with Henry and Elsey."

"Very well, Brother Gabriel," said Featherston. "We will see to it you are returned home safely. We are expecting a wagon from Oberlin any time now. You can ride on that wagon back to Bridgeport."

Featherston turned toward Dangerfield. "And what of you, Brother Dangerfield? You are free to return home as well if you like."

Dangerfield turned toward Louise and Mary, and wondered how many times Louise had buried that knife in a slaver's chest. He wondered how many bullets Mary had fired into slave catchers intent on hurting her. He wondered if he could do that. Then he thought of his children, and realized that Louise and Mary were just a few years older than Dangerfield Jr. He wondered whether any of his children could kill if they had to, and whether he could do for his family what Henry had done for him.

He turned toward Featherston. "Reckon I will go with you, Featherston. Reckon you need me and my freeman's papers. You better off with me than without me."

The distant clatter of a wagon coming from the north clarified the issue. As soon as he heard the wagon, Gabriel left the cabin and stood by the road. Featherston and Dangerfield went with him.

The wagon stopped, and Featherston spoke to the driver. Gabriel and Dangerfield stood next to each other, neither man speaking. Gabriel looked south down the road back toward Bridgeport, toward his new home, while Dangerfield looked north. After a few minutes, Gabriel turned toward his brother.

"Reckon you know what's best for you," said Gabriel.

"As much as anyone does," replied Dangerfield.

"Just don't go and get yourself killed," said Gabriel. "Henry and Elsey won't never forgive me if something happens to you."

"Henry said the same thing to me," replied Dangerfield.

"Looks like Henry only raised one of us with any sense," countered Gabriel. "I don't aim to get killed."

"Neither do I."

"Then just come home. You can work and free your family."

"I am just going to meet Brown. I might not like him. I might come home soon as I meet him. "Sides, it looks like Featherston needs us. Slavers leave us alone, they leave him alone. If they are afraid of Henry, they are afraid of us. We can help him even if we don't spend a minute with Brown."

"And you might never make it to Oberlin, let alone make it back home," said Gabriel. "You could get shot two miles up the road."

"That possibility don't seem to bother Featherston and his family."

"You ain't Featherston, and he ain't your family."

Featherston approached the men as they talked. "The driver is ready to leave. He has rather important cargo to pick up in Bridgeport, and he needs to be off the road before nightfall. Whenever you are ready to leave, Brother Gabriel."

Gabriel turned toward Dangerfield.

"Tell Henry and Elsey I will be home soon. Tell them not to worry," said Dangerfield.

"I will tell them. It won't do any good," said Gabriel.

Gabriel climbed into the wagon, and pulled his hat over his face. The driver clucked his tongue, and the horses nudged forward, back toward Bridgeport.

Dangerfield watched the wagon as it rumbled toward Bridgeport. He watched until it disappeared from sight. Then he turned toward Featherston, but he was already in his wagon, readying the horses. "Let us not tarry, Brother Dangerfield. We have no time to lose."

Dangerfield climbed aboard, Featherston tapped the horses with his crop, and the wagon proceeded north toward Oberlin.

CHAPTER 41

October 20, 1858

Dangerfield and Featherston arrived in Oberlin, Ohio late in the morning after another full day's ride. They entered the town from the south, and soon reached the campus of Oberlin College. Dangerfield saw elegant red brick buildings shaded by tall canopies of trees. As they rode through the campus, he saw well-dressed black men with polished boots walking side by side and conversing with equally well-dressed white men. He saw men and women sitting and talking outside the red brick buildings. At one corner, he saw a tall coffee-colored black man wearing a top hat. He had a luxuriant waxed mustache, and he was conversing freely with a young white woman wearing a brilliant white bonnet. Dangerfield wanted to warn him, but he looked about and sensed no danger. He saw no one with a whip or a gun. The top-hatted man black man and the white woman looked at the wagon as it passed. The man nodded politely, and continued his conversation with the woman. Dangerfield heard her laugh softly.

"What is this place," said Dangerfield as they rode past a gleaming white church. Sunlight struck the steeple such that it appeared the very hand of God had dropped the steeple in place.

"This is the campus of Oberlin College," said Featherston, bringing the horses to a halt. "It is a beautiful place."

Dangerfield saw a dark-skinned young black man walking down the street. He carried a bulging satchel full of books, and strode confidently into one of the red brick buildings.

"Where are the slave catchers," said Dangerfield. "Seems like they'd have easy pickings here. These fancy negroes can't run very fast carrying all them books."

Featherston laughed. "The slave catchers won't bother us here, Brother Dangerfield. Oberlin is a safe place, an abolitionist stronghold."

Dangerfield eyed the well-dressed students milling about, chatting and holding their satchels of books over their shoulders.

"It ain't Sunday, is it," said Dangerfield. "Why is everyone dressed up?"

"That is how the students on campus dress, Brother Dangerfield," said

Featherston. "They don't work with their hands like you and I. Here, you will find men and women whose hands have never known hard labor." Featherston clicked his tongue, and nudged the horses forward until he found a hitching post. He dismounted, and tethered the horses to the post.

"Let's leave the horses here," said Featherston. "There are a few people you should meet while we are in Oberlin."

Featherston pulled a piece of paper from his breast pocket, examined it, and put it back in his pocket. "The building is this way."

They walked for a block until they reached a single story red brick building. Smaller than the surrounding buildings and set back from the main campus road, it was easy to miss. Featherston knocked twice at the front door, waited, then knocked twice again.

The wooden door creaked open, and a hand motioned them inside.

"Hello, Lewis," said Featherston. "I hope all is well. I have someone you should meet." Featherston closed the door behind them. Inside, the building was well-lit – windows on all sides provided ample light.

A slim, light-skinned negro man with enormous copper-colored eyes and a thin mustache approached Dangerfield and held out his hand. "I'm Lewis Leary. Pleased to meet you." Dangerfield gripped his hand.

Another man approached. "This is my nephew, John Copeland," said Leary. Copeland, like his uncle, was a tall and light-skinned negro, but stouter than his uncle. He had a thick and unruly head of hair, and a robust black mustache that blanketed the whole of his upper lip. Although introduced as Lewis Leary's nephew, John Copeland appeared to be about the same age as his uncle.

"Brothers Leary and Copeland have been working with us to fight the scourge of slavery," said Featherston. "And Brother Dangerfield," said Featherston "is new to Ohio. He seeks to free his family from slavery."

"You have enslaved family?" said Leary.

"Yes," said Dangerfield. "Wife and children back on a farm in Virginia."

"I see," said Leary. Leary exchanged glances with Featherston.

"Brother Brown would certainly be interested in how he could help you free your family," said Leary. "Please wait here."

Leary went into a small side room, and closed the door. After a few moments, the door opened and a lean, compact and gray-haired man entered the room. He had a sharp nose, a long, waving, cream-colored beard, and penetrating gray eyes the color of a catbird's feathers. He had a full head of hair that was closely cut on the sides, making his enormous ears appear even bigger. From the front, his ears appeared half as large as his face. His luxuriant beard covered every facial feature below his nose.

"Good to see you Featherston," said the man. "I hope your journey from Bridgeport was uneventful."

"Splendid. Gentlemen, let us sit down and I can share my plan with all of you. Lewis and John, please make certain the door is locked."

Leary and Copeland secured the room, and the men sat at the table. Brown spoke.

"Brother Dangerfield, as you may know, we struck a decisive blow against the slavers in the Kansas Territory, at Pottawatomie Creek. Some say we committed murder, but the shedding of blood in defense of freedom is not a crime. It is justice, and it is God's will."

"I ain't never been to Kansas, and ain't never heard of Pottawatomie Creek," said Dangerfield.

"Yes, of course," said Brown. "That is just as well. Now I intend an even more powerful strike against the slavers, one that will bring them to their knees, and will free not just your family, but every enslaved family across this nation. It will take time, but I think your family could be free in less than one year if my plan succeeds. But I need men like you, and Leary, and Copeland, and Featherston."

Brown stood and began pacing again, the pounding of his bootheels against the wood floor accentuating his words.

"Consider just the men in this room," Brown thundered. "Black men working alongside white men, side by side, brothers united in cause, and not divided by race or skin color. White men working to free black men from slavery, and black men working to free white men from the shackles of evil. Consider having your name alongside the great men in history."

Dangerfield heard Brown's words, but the words that echoed were "your family could be free in less than one year if my plan succeeds."

"How do we make my family free in less than a year," said Dangerfield.

"What I have in mind," said Brown, lowering his voice to husky whisper, "is a nationwide slave insurrection, an uprising that will make Nat Turner's rebellion seem like a schoolyard fight. Slaves in every slave-holding territory will rebel, and we will help them, we will arm them. From the Kansas Territory to the shores of South Carolina, every slave will be armed, trained, and ready to fight to the death for their freedom. We will arm them and train them. The slavers will be overwhelmed, and we will finally cast off the shackles of slavery from this great country."

Brown leaned in close to Dangerfield. "What I intend," he whispered, "is nothing less than a slave revolution that will overthrow this corrupt government, and replace it with the seeds of freedom. We have even prepared a new Provisional Constitution and Ordinances. It will be the law of the land until the army of liberation can create a new government. I have been elected Commander In Chief of the new army."

Leary and Copeland exchanged glances. Featherston scratched at his beard while listening to Brown.

Dangerfield closed his eyes as he listened to Brown. He imagined Harriet and his children in a yard with a garden surrounded by a fence he built himself, living in a cabin he built himself.

"How do we get the guns to the slaves," said Dangerfield. "How do we train them to use guns if they still live on the plantations?"

Brown leveled his gaze at Dangerfield and scowled. "The plan is of course still in its infancy," said Brown. "I – we – will have to work out many details. But let us not allow details to derail us from the grand vision."

"Where do we get that many guns," said Dangerfield. "Where do we keep them?"

Leary, Copeland, and Featherston twisted uncomfortably in their chairs.

Brown's thin lips curled into a tight smile. "Brother Dangerfield, you are strong, brave, and wise. The questions you pose will need to be answered."

Brown continued pacing. "I know of a place in Virginia where we will obtain the guns. A federal armory in Harpers Ferry. It is poorly defended, and will be easily overtaken. And Harpers Ferry is near mountains, which will provide shelter and cover for our operations. It is only 40 miles from the free state of Pennsylvania. With enough men, we can capture the armory. Once inside, we will control the armory, and with it, we will have enough weapons to overthrow the government. The mountains will shield us."

"How many people know about this plan," said Dangerfield.

"Only the people in this room and a select few others know of the grand plan," said Brown. "After our victory at Pottawatomie, our enemies have become more vocal. I cannot speak freely about our plans, even in a bastion of freedom such as Oberlin. Thus the secrecy, the closed rooms, even here. My words would fall on kind ears in Oberlin, but surrounding areas in Ohio are less fertile ground to plant the seeds of freedom."

Brown began pacing again. "I went to Canada in May of this year to discuss the plan with free Canadian blacks," said Brown. "I gathered more recruits, and of course raised quite a bit of money. Canada has proven to be more fertile ground than even Ohio."

Brown turned toward Dangerfield. "Have you been to Canada? Chatham is not far from here. There are numerous free black settlements there," said Brown. "There, you would see what real freedom is like. Black families like yours, with no masters, no shackles. You would be free to go where you please. You would never need freeman's papers – such papers don't exist in Canada, because there are only free men. That is the type of freedom that we will bring to this country. American blacks will know the type of freedom that Canadian blacks already enjoy. But I need strong men like you, and Featherston, and Leary and Copeland."

Dangerfield tried to imagine a place where freeman's papers did not exist, because all men were free. He could imagine no such world.

"When do you intend to start," said Dangerfield.

"As soon as we have the necessary recruits, and refine the plan," said Brown. "Perhaps a month, perhaps eight months, perhaps longer. But as soon as we have the recruits, we will gather in Harpers Ferry for the final preparations. The insurrection will begin shortly thereafter."

"I ain't real keen on going back to Virginia, except to buy my wife and child," said Dangerfield. "I understand they can capture free negroes and sell 'em back into slavery. Henry told me not to go back to Virginia unless there ain't any other choice."

"Yes, of course," said Brown. "I understand your reluctance to accompany all of us on such a long journey, especially after your recent escape from Virginia. I don't wish to keep you from your family any longer. If you wish to return to Bridgeport, Featherston will take you home. I ask only two things of you."

"What two things," said Dangerfield.

"First, I would ask you not to reveal the details of the slave insurrection to anyone. After Pottawatomie, we must be discreet. Second, I ask you to consider joining us if . . . ."

"If what," said Dangerfield.

"If your plan to buy your family does not succeed," said Brown. "I have no doubt that you will do what is necessary, and that this Lewis Jennings is as honest as any slaver can be. But if you cannot secure your family by lawful means, I ask only that you consider a more forceful effort. Good does not vanquish evil with pleas and requests. Good vanquishes evil with the sword, and the blood of those who offend God's will."

"I promise you that I will not discuss your plans with anyone, even my family," said Dangerfield. "And I will come back if Jennings don't keep his word. But I promised my wife I would earn the money to buy her, and our family. I have to keep that promise first."

Brown smiled. "You are a brave, honest and trustworthy man, Brother Dangerfield. We need men like you, and I can only hope that you are soon reunited with your family. But you must keep your promise to your wife and family. I understand. Featherston will take you back to Bridgeport whenever you are ready."

Brown extended his enormous hand. The two men shook hands, and then Brown clutched Dangerfield's shoulder.

"If our paths never cross again, may the grace of God bless you, and the wrath of God inspire you. One is useless without the other."

Dangerfield considered these words. Although he had been a slave almost his entire life, he had never been motivated by wrath. Instead, his goals had always been to please Henry and Elsey, take care of his siblings, and take care of his wife and family. Wrath had never been his inspiration. He wondered if it ever could be.

"Please heed my words," said Brown. "If you are unable to secure your family, we will have a place for you. Consider joining us in Harpers Ferry. God Bless you, Brother Dangerfield. Featherston will take you back whenever you are ready." Brown crossed the room again, pulled apart the curtains, then quickly closed them.

"Brothers Leary and Copeland, we have much work to do today," said Brown. I have some sources that can supply us with more weapons."

Brown paused, then turned toward Dangerfield and Featherston.

"Amos, were you able to bring the supplies we spoke of at our last meeting?"

"Yes," said Featherston. "The cargo is safe in the wagon."

"Splendid,' said Brown. "Bring the wagon to the supply shed next to this building. We will unload, and then you are free for the day."

Featherston brought the wagon to a small nondescript shed that stood next to Brown's makeshift headquarters. Brown and Leary opened two heavy wooden doors, and Featherston drove the wagon inside. Brown quickly closed the doors behind him. Featherston brought the horses to a halt, and dismounted. Brown leaped aboard the wagon, removed the woolen blanket from the floorboard, and slid back the wooden panel that concealed the hidden cargo area below. He pulled one of the wool-wrapped rifles from the hold and examined it lovingly.

"How many of these, Amos," said Brown softly as he extracted the rifle from the wool blanket.

"Twenty-four rifles, each individually wrapped in blankets to prevent damage," said Featherston.

Brown slid the breech lever forward and dropped the breech block. He peered down the barrel, smiled, then closed the breech. He cradled the gun for a few moments, then put it to his shoulder and swung the barrel toward the window, aiming at an invisible enemy.

"Beecher was right about these," said Brown. "These weapons are a truly moral agency. I think Beecher was right when he said there is more moral power in one of those instruments than in a hundred Bibles. "

Brown opened and closed the breech lever several more times, admiring the heavy metallic thud each time the breech closed. "Truly a gift from God," said Brown as he gently cradled the rifle in his arms. He closed his eyes for a few moments as if recalling fond memories, then he handed the rifle to Dangerfield.

"Hold this for a few minutes, Brother Dangerfield, and feel the presence of God in your hands."

Dangerfield took the gun and drew it to his shoulder. It was heavier and more solid than any weapon he had ever used.

"All of these will need to be oiled before we put them to good use," said Brown. "The breech levers are sticking, and of course we need to make certain we have enough primer tapes," said Brown. "Leary and Copeland, please unload the cargo, check each weapon, and store them in the usual hiding place."

Brown turned toward Dangerfield. "Brother Dangerfield, I hope you agree that the Sharps rifle is a magnificent weapon."

"Yes, it is," said Dangerfield, admiring the craftsmanship. "Ain't never had one like this. Henry mostly keeps old shotguns and a few pistols."

"Brother Dangerfield, I want you to keep this weapon. You and Amos Featherston may need it on your return journey. If we never meet again, consider this a gift from John Brown. And if we do meet again, you will need that weapon to carry out God's work and free your family. Think of the good you can do for all of us."

Brown turned toward Leary, Copeland, and Featherston. "Gentlemen, when you have secured the weapons, please return to my office. We have much planning to do before we leave for Harpers Ferry."

Brown turned on his heels and left the shed, his bootheels echoing against the wooden floor. Dangerfield watched him leave.

"Brother Dangerfield, if you would help us unload the rest of these weapons," said Featherston. "When we have finished, we will eat, and rest here for a few days. I will then take you back to Bridgeport."

The men unloaded the weapons in silence. Brown's words echoed in Dangerfield's ears – "your family could be free in less than one year if my plan succeeds." Everything else Brown said about the insurrection and arming slaves faded away.

He thought about Harriet and his children living in freedom in one year. He would build a cabin for him and Harriet and the baby, and a larger cabin for the older children. They would have their own garden, a few hogs and chickens, maybe a milk cow. Of course, they would all live in Ohio, close to Henry and Elsey. He could help Henry with chores, and keep an eye on his brother Gabriel. He decided he would look into a few acres of land in Bridgeport, near Henry and Elsey, when he returned home. He could see the cabins and the garden, and the children playing in the yard.

These thoughts occupied him for the next week in Oberlin. After spending the week helping Brown and learning about his plan, Dangerfield and Featherston left Oberlin, and Dangerfield returned to Bridgeport, seeking freeman's work to finally buy his wife and family.

CHAPTER 42

O𝖼𝗍𝗈𝖻𝖾𝗋 30, 1858

When they reached Bridgeport, Amos Featherston dropped Dangerfield off in front of his house. Dangerfield gathered his belongings, and bid farewell to Featherston.

The return trip to Bridgeport was uneventful – a few slave catchers had made menacing approaches toward the wagon, but aborted their efforts when Dangerfield brandished the Sharps. Toward the end of the trip, Featherston had put away his shotguns, content to let Dangerfield sit next to him, Sharps in hand, a silent warning to all those who would approach. Oncoming wagons gave them wide berth, and polite tips of the hat as they passed. Travelers on horseback stopped and let them pass, staring slack-jawed at the bearded white man and rifle-toting black man sitting next to him. One such rider, a ruddy-faced teenaged white boy, sat his horse as they approached. As Featherston passed, Dangerfield heard him mutter, "Lord Almighty, I ain't never seen no gun like that round here." Dangerfield began to understand Brown's reverence for the mighty Sharps. He had never held a weapon that commanded such respect.

Henry was sitting in his rocking chair when Dangerfield walked in the door. Henry looked up and smiled.

"So you decided to come back home," said Henry. "Elsey told me she thought you'd up and run off to join Brown. Said we'd never see you again."

Dangerfield leaned the Sharps against the wall. "I met Brown, and he don't seem as bad as everyone says," says Dangerfield. "But I decided I'd best come home and start working. I aim to bring Harriet and the rest of the family to Ohio by this time next year, maybe sooner."

Henry eyed the rifle leaning against the wall.

"Where did you find a gun like that," said Henry.

"Brown gave it to me as a gift. Said I could keep it."

Henry slowly pulled himself out of the rocking chair. He picked up the rifle and studied it.

"Quite a gift," said Henry. "What does Brown expect in return?"

"Didn't say he wanted anything in return. Just thought I might need protection on the ride home."

Dangerfield watched his father handling the heavy rifle. Henry turned the gun over, trying to figure out how to open the breech block. Dangerfield realized that Henry had probably never owned a gun like the Sharps.

"Where is everyone," said Dangerfield.

"Elsey is in town, looking to buy some bread and eggs. Seems she's taken quite a shine to buying things in town. First, she bought new candles. Then she bought some table linens. Today, it's bread and eggs. She won't never admit it, but I think she don't mind being able to buy some things instead of making everything." Henry chuckled. "I might have to get a job in town if she keeps it up."

"Where's Gabriel?"

"He's at work. After he left you, he got a job with the blacksmith in town. Seems to enjoy it. He ain't hardly been home since he got back."

Henry leaned the Sharps against the wall and sat down.

"Gabriel says you ran into some road agents on the way up to Oberlin," said Henry. "Slave catchers looking for trouble."

"We did. Featherston was aiming to shoot them, but they stood down when they read our freeman's papers. Said they knew of you, and didn't want no trouble with you."

Henry laughed. "Don't think I could put up much fight against road agents, or anyone else now."

"They said you'd killed a man went after one of your house girls," said Dangerfield. "Said you killed him, and were aiming to kill anyone else went after your property. Said you put the word out to leave us alone."

Henry rubbed his eyes and looked out the window. "I reckon I said all those things. Thank God I never had to kill anyone else."

Neither man spoke for a few moments.

"Did you kill anyone," said Dangerfield.

"I did," said Henry. "Ain't proud of it, but would do it again if I had to." Henry stood and began slowly pacing the room.

"Back in Culpeper, probably 30 years ago. You weren't but 15 or so, Gabriel was 13. Anna Mae weren't but 11 or so. I had you and Gabriel running some hogs down to another farm. Elsey and Anna Mae had gone into town to get a few provisions."

"Well, Elsey and Anna Mae come running back home, screaming and crying. A man in town had attacked them as they were walking home from town. Hid in an alley and knocked Elsey down, and grabbed little Anna Mae. Grabbed her, and took her into the alley, started taking her clothes off right there in the alley. Elsey got up, and stabbed him in the eye with a sewing needle just before he could do his business. He started hollering, and Elsey and Anna Mae, they ran all the way home."

Henry pulled his handkerchief from his pocket and blew his nose.

"Elsey told me what he looked like. Well, I saddled up and rode hard to find the bastard. Found him in the tavern, drunk with a bloody patch over his eye. Short little red-haired Irish bastard. I spun him off his chair, and punched him in his good eye. He stood up and pulled a little flintlock from his pocket. I knew he was too drunk to shoot, so I grabbed the gun from his hand, and shot him in the forehead. Left him lay there. Told everyone in that filthy tavern to leave Henry Newby and his family alone. Not a single one of those cowardly drunks got up off their chairs. I saddled up and rode home."

Henry wiped his brow and sat down heavily in his chair.

"From time to time, slave catchers would come to the farm, looking for run-aways. I told 'em I didn't keep no runaways, and that I would kill any man who touched my property. You and Gabriel must have run into one of them on the way up to Oberlin."

Henry closed his eyes. "That was 30 years ago, in Virginia. And now, 30 years later in Ohio, and my family still ain't safe."

"We are safe, Henry," said Dangerfield. "Those slavers, they left us alone 'soon as they heard your name."

"I mean your family," said Henry. "Harriet, all your children. Still in Virginia."

"Not for long," said Dangerfield. "I aim to bring them all to Ohio within a year."

"I know you do," said Henry.

Henry opened his eyes and looked directly at Dangerfield.

"You aim to join up with Brown, and whatever new mischief he has in mind, don't you?"

"No. I plan on bringing Harriet and the children to Ohio. Hope I won't need Brown for that. But if things don't work out . . . ."

"What promises did Brown make to you?"

"Didn't make no promises to me."

"You don't think Brown would part with a gun like that without expecting something in return."

"Don't know what Brown expects. I just know what I have to do."

Henry stood and looked out the window.

"You know I would buy Harriet and your family if I could afford to."

"I know you would," said Dangerfield.

"I could probably buy Harriet and one or two. But not all of them," said Henry.

"They ain't your responsibility, Henry. I intend to get them back, and we all live in Ohio. I might even start looking at some property in Bridgeport near you and Elsey. We could all live close by. Gabriel and I help out around the house. Anna Mae can help Elsey when she visits. You and Elsey could help Harriet mind the younger children if she needs help."

"That would be nice," said Henry. "We could use some help, although Elsey don't need any more excuses to buy things in town."

Henry looked out the window.

"Elsey should be home soon. You should stay until she gets here."

"I only came home to get a few more clothes, and saddle up the horse," said Dangerfield. "Featherston gave me some names in Ohio and Kentucky. Some people who would hire on a freeman, and pay good freeman's wages. I work for them, then go back to Virginia, get Harriet, and come back to Bridgeport. Be back within a year. Maybe sooner."

"Featherston gave you these names?"

"Yes. Gave me names, towns, and addresses in Ohio and Kentucky. I can get freeman's wages."

"You won't wait until Elsey gets home?"

"Reckon me leaving again would be hard on Elsey. She already saw me leave once. Best if I just saddle up and leave now."

Henry peered out the window again, then closed the curtain.

"That's probably best," said Henry. "I'd stay out of Virginia as best you can. They catch you in Virginia a year from now, and they can sell you right back into slavery. Can't no one help you then."

"I intend to have the money and my family back here within the year, before my freeman's papers expire."

"That sounds about right," said Henry. "You go on and gather your things. I will saddle up the horse, and you can get started straight away."

Dangerfield walked into the room that had been his for just a few days. It didn't feel like his room, and the house didn't feel like his house. He realized he had spent very little time in this room since arriving in Bridgeport.

He gathered his clothes, provisions, and the Sharps rifle, and met Henry near the barn. Henry had the horse saddled, bridled, and ready to ride.

"Where you aim to go first," said Henry.

"Here in Ohio, then down to Kentucky. Get my family in Virginia, then back to Ohio."

"Stay out of Virginia as best you can."

"I will."

"Write home, and let Elsey know where you are. And send me those addresses, in case I need to find you."

"You won't need to find me. I will be back within a year."

"I know you will do your best."

Dangerfield spurred the horse, and began his journey out of Bridgeport. Henry watched him ride until he disappeared into the hills.

CHAPTER 43

October 30, 1858

Dangerfield rode north out of Bridgeport, towards Martins Ferry, Ohio. Featherston had given him the name of a man who ran a coal mine. "Never enough men to work the coal seams," Featherston had said. The man was an abolitionist, and sympathetic to Dangerfield's plight. With winter at hand and a shortage of workers, Featherston said the man would pay Dangerfield eight dollars per day. Not enough to buy his family any time soon, but it was a start. Featherston had also told him about a farmer who needed help slaughtering pigs, and a harness maker who needed an apprentice. If he could make and sell his own saddles and harnesses, he would have the money in less than a year.

Two miles north of Bridgeport, it began to snow. The flakes fell softly at first, then the wind picked up from the north, driving the snow into his face. Dangerfield dismounted, and adjusted his horse's blinders to keep out the snow. He rode for another mile or so, until he could no longer ride. Wind-driven snow caked his eyelashes, and he could only see a few feet down the road. Dangerfield dismounted, took the horse by the reins, and walked the horse along the snow-covered road, shielding its face from the driving snow. He checked his saddle bags, and made certain the Sharps was covered and strapped tight.

There was no place to bed down, and no shelter. He kept walking, leading the horse by the reins, looking for any safe space. He crested a hill, and saw a woodsman's cabin on the side of the road. He recognized it instantly – it was Amos Featherston's cabin, the one his daughters used as a gardening shed and way station for runaway slaves. The snow was now blowing horizontal, and the horse's ears were filled with snow. He would have to stop here.

He walked the horse to the south side of the cabin, out of the wind and snow. He dropped the reins, hobbled the horse, and fed it a double ration of oats from his saddlebag. The big bay nickered contentedly, and shook his back, spraying Dangerfield with ice and snow.

Inside, Dangerfield remembered the simple layout of the room – the single rough-hewn log table that occupied the center of the room, with a chair on either end. No beds, just shovels and garden tools. Everything in the cabin was just as Dangerfield remembered. He took one of the candles from the package at the end of the table, struck his flint, and assessed his options. Although he was inside, the wind blowing through the gaps in the logs nearly extinguished the candle.

He went back outside and walked behind the cabin. He could see no trace of Featherston's house – no lights in the windows, and no sounds in the distance. In the blowing storm, he could see no trail or footpath leading to the house. He thought about prying open the trap door and taking the tunnel to Featherston's house, but then he would have to leave his horse and his saddlebags at the cabin. He would have to stay here for the night. He retrieved his blankets and bedroll from his saddlebags and went back inside.

There was no stove in the cabin, so he would have to sleep without a fire. He lit another candle and jammed it into a large crack in the table. He unrolled his blankets and took off his snow-caked woolen coat. He shook the snow from the coat, folded it in half, and set it on the floor as a pillow. As he drifted into an uneasy sleep, he thought of Harriet. He could smell her smoky brown skin, and the flowers she sometimes wore in her hair. He heard her soft, raspy voice as she wished him goodnight, and it was the last voice he heard before falling asleep alone on the floor of Featherston's cabin while a storm raged outside.

He awoke later that night after dreaming of being with Harriet in the hayloft of Old Man Jennings barn. So many years ago, and he still remembered his first time with her, the smell of the hay in the loft and the musky horses below. He thought about how long it would take before he would see her again. Less than a year. Then they would all be free.

So deep was his sleep that he did not remember where he was when he awoke. The candle he had jammed into the log table was dark. Shards of moonlight pierced the gaps in the cabin wall, and it was only when he heard his horse nickering outside that he remembered where he was. Featherston's cabin. The storm. Harriet in the hayloft, and her earthy scent.

He unrolled his woolen coat and went outside to piss, and check on the horse. The snow had stopped falling, but the wind still came strong from the north. The sky was clear, with a bright full moon. The bay was still behind the cabin, out of the wind. Dangerfield fed him a handful of oats, and then checked on the Sharps. Still tightly bundled, and secured fast to the horse. He thought about bringing it inside the cabin with him, but he would then have to secure it again in the morning. He checked his breast pocket, and felt the reassuring presence of Henry's Colt.

As he turned to re-enter the cabin, he heard muffled hoofbeats coming from the north. A single horse, moving at a good clip along the snow-packed trail. Dangerfield checked his Pitkin watch in the bright moonlight. 2:48 a.m. Only road agents and the truly desperate would be out on the road at this hour.

He picked up the hobble and moved the horse toward the back of the cabin, completely out of sight of the southbound rider. The horse nickered and shook its back, anticipating the saddle.

"Best hush now, Old Man. We ain't going nowhere just yet." Dangerfield reached for the Sharps, but it was tightly wrapped against the horse. No time to unwrap, charge and load. He felt again for the Colt.

Dangerfield pushed himself hard against the cabin wall. If the rider passed by at a good clip, he would not notice Dangerfield or his horse hiding behind the cabin. The horse would be wearing blinders, and a skilled horseman riding alone at night would push his horse hard past an unfamiliar cabin, fearing an ambush. He would be safe if they kept riding.

The hoofbeats grew closer, and began to slow. The wind carried the rider's voice toward Dangerfield as he slowed his horse. Dangerfield pressed his face against a gap in the cabin wall. He could see the faint outline of a smallish horse clattering to a stop in front of the cabin. If the rider brought his horse around the cabin, Dangerfield would have no cover. He pulled the Colt from his breast pocket and waited.

"Well, looka here," said the rider. "Room for the night. Get down now." The rider dismounted with a heavy thud against the deep snow.

Dangerfield heard a grunt from the horse, but it was no noise any horse made.

"I won't hurt you if you keep quiet. Get down now, and let's get inside."

Dangerfield heard the grunt again, this time louder and higher pitched, as though a child were screaming into a sack wrapped tightly against its mouth.

He heard another thud and peered through the gap in the cabin wall. He saw a second rider standing next to the horse. This rider was short, wearing a scarf, and appeared to have no coat or shawl. Long dark hair flowed out of the scarf – a woman. Dangerfield could see something covering this rider's mouth.

"Now, you make nice with me and don't fight back, I might take that scarf off your mouth. 'Course, you don't need to talk much any time soon. Get inside, and the two of us get warm together."

Through the gap in the cabin wall, Dangerfield saw the taller rider pull the other rider's head back as he held a knife against her throat. Again he heard her grunt, desperately screaming into the gag that silenced her.

The first rider pushed open the door, and shoved the woman inside. Dangerfield heard a struggle, and the scrape of wood on wood as someone pushed the heavy wooden table across the floor. Something heavy fell off the table and clattered onto the wooden floor.

His blankets and bedroll were still on the floor, and the dead candle was still in the table. It would not be long before the strangers figured out someone else had recently visited the cabin. And if they moved the table, they might discover the trap door. There was no cover behind the cabin, and Dangerfield knew he could not run or hide in the new fallen snow. He could not saddle his horse without making noise.

He pulled the Colt from his breast pocket and slowly approached the front door. Inside, the struggle continued, and he heard again the scrape of wood on wood, and the high-pitched grunt, this time more desperate. The visitors had not bothered to close the door, and it swung open slowly in its uneven frame. This was good – he could enter the cabin without making a sound.

Dangerfield stepped across the threshold, gun drawn. The woman was bent forward over the table, her dress torn and her petticoats ripped. The man was on top of her, pants at his feet, grunting as he pushed himself inside her. His hands gripped the edges of the table as he sought leverage, moving the table across the floor as he pushed himself inside the woman.

Dangerfield crouched as he entered the cabin. The man did not see him enter, and when he looked up, Dangerfield pointed the barrel of the Colt at his forehead.

"Get up, and get your hands off her. Move real slow."

"Who the hell are you?"

Dangerfield said nothing, and thumbed back the hammer on the Colt.

"I didn't mean no harm. Didn't know anybody lived in this cabin. Just thought it was a old hunter's shack. Didn't mean to trespass on a man's property. I didn't mean no harm to nobody. Please don't kill me."

"Get up real slow and move away from her, or I scatter your brains on that wall."

"You might let a man have some dignity. Let me pull my britches up."

"You stand up slow, and you get away from her. Then maybe you pull up your britches."

The man stood up slowly, and pushed himself off the woman. In the dark cabin, Dangerfield did not see the man's knife resting on the table. The man stood, and as he rose, he grabbed his knife and spun toward Dangerfield in one motion.

He swung his knife hand against Dangerfield's hand, sending the Colt flying toward the open door. Dangerfield saw the blade glint in the moonlight as it moved toward him. The blade softly brushed his throat, and he felt a slow warm trickle run down his neck. He stopped the blade just before it cut deeper. He grabbed the man's arms and shoved him back, sending him sprawling against the table.

Dangerfield looked behind him for the Colt. He did not see where it landed. The man was on him instantly, launching himself off the wooden table. The force of his body knocked Dangerfield to the ground, his attacker on top of him, the knife point inches from his throat.

Dangerfield scrabbled one hand against the floor, hoping the Colt had landed nearby, while his other hand gripped the knife handle, pushing it away from his throat. He could not find the Colt. He swung hard with his free hand, driving his knuckles into the man's temple. The man grunted and loosened his grip on the knife. Dangerfield grabbed the knife handle with both hands and turned the blade against his attacker's throat. As he did so, he heard a great rush of air and something heavy landing from above on the man's head.

The force of the blow pushed the man's chin onto the point of his own blade. Dangerfield heard a soft pop and then a click as the blade cut through the bottom of the man's jaw, sliced through his tongue, and pierced the roof of his mouth. The man's jaws slammed shut and his teeth clacked together as the blade sliced upward through the roof of his mouth, stopping only when the hilt of the knife slammed against his chin.

Dangerfield grasped the knife handle and pushed up, throwing the man's head back. The man stumbled to his feet, grasping at the knife handle jammed underneath his chin. He pulled at the knife handle, but the blade was solidly lodged in the roof of his mouth. He grunted, and was trying to speak, but no words could come from his locked jaws.

Blood began to flow in a great stream from his mouth and the wound in his head. Again he tried to speak, but he could only grunt as blood gurgled from his wounds. He stumbled backwards and sat heavily in one of the chairs, as though considering what to do next. A great stream of blood and snot spewed from the man's nose, burbling as it flowed onto his chest. He made one last weak effort to remove the knife from his jaw before falling sideways onto the floor, his hands still clutching the knife handle. He lay on the floor wheezing through his death wound before emitting a great moan. His body convulsed, then all was silent.

Dangerfield pulled himself to his feet. Before him stood a woman with a ripped dress, and torn petticoats. She was holding a shovel, pointing it at Dangerfield.

"Don't you come no closer to me, or I do to you what I did to him. Lay this shovel right alongside your head."

"Wasn't my intention to bother you, or anyone else. Seems to me I just saved your life. Put the shovel down, I won't hurt you."

The woman did not move, and continued pointing the shovel at him. Dangerfield ignored her, and looked for the Colt. In the moonlight of the open door, he found his Colt against the wall. He picked it up, carefully closed the hammer, and put it in his breast pocket.

"Are you hurt?" said Dangerfield.

"No. He didn't get real far." The woman slowly put the shovel blade on the ground. "Reckon I owe you some thanks. Don't know what would have happened if you hadn't come along."

"Reckon you would have fought back just fine. Let's get some light in here."

Dangerfield took his flint striker and lit another candle. He held the candle and examined the woman carefully.

Her skin was the color of molasses, and just as smooth. She was about Harriet's height, but a bit more stout. Her scarf was pulled tight over her head, emphasizing her huge dark eyes. She was prettier than almost any other woman Dangerfield knew.

"You a runaway?" said Dangerfield.

"Yes," said the woman. "Came here from Kentucky. Trying to get to Canada."

"How'd he find you," said Dangerfield, pointing to the dead man on the floor.

"Group of us was holed up in a safe house outside Martins Ferry," said the woman. "But it weren't as safe as we thought. Slave catchers got wind of us, and raided the house in the middle of the night. Some of us scattered, some got caught. Last I saw, my son was running out of the house into the woods, two slave catchers hot on him. I ran to save him, but that one and his partner jumped on me. Said they was going to take me back to Kentucky first thing in the morning. That one yonder took me, and his partner took my daughter. Don't know where they went."

"How old is your boy," said Dangerfield.

"He's 12."

"Is he strong?"

"Like a mule."

"Reckon he might be fine. Young boy like that can outlast anyone in the woods."

The woman threw the shovel on the floor and sat on a chair. She began crying.

"My daughter ain't but 15. Lord knows what they will do to her." She sobbed into her hands.

"I'm real sorry," said Dangerfield clumsily. "They can't get too far in this weather. Maybe you catch up to them soon."

"And what if I do? I can't do much against slave catchers with guns."

Dangerfield considered the woman's plight. A runaway, alone, separated from her children, unarmed and defenseless. He felt the Colt in his breast pocket, and thought of the Sharps tethered to his horse. He could fend for himself. He had always assumed that others could do the same, or had someone who could fend for them.

"Reckon we – you – can't do much to fix anything tonight," said Dangerfield. "Best you stay here tonight. It ain't much, but it's better than outside."

Dangerfield took one of his blankets and his bedroll and unrolled it on the floor away from the door. "You sleep here," he said. "I will make do over here." He placed his remaining blankets on the floor across the cabin, and folded his wool coat in half. He stretched himself out and had lain down when he looked across the cabin. The woman was holding the shovel.

"I ain't sleeping here. Not with you, and not with him," she said, pointing to the dead man in the corner.

"I don't aim to hurt you, and I reckon he can't do much harm anymore." Dangerfield retrieved the Colt from his pocket, and made certain it was loaded and charged. "And if I aimed to hurt you, I could. That shovel ain't much good against a bullet."

The woman slowly put the shovel blade against the floor. Dangerfield ignored her, and tried to make himself comfortable on the cold wooden floor. He rolled up his wool coat and put it under his head. The woman picked up the candle from the table and examined him.

"You a runaway? Don't see too many runaways with guns and nice blankets like this," the woman said.

"I ain't no runaway. I am a free man in Ohio, by way of Virginia."

"Free man? Why you on the road at this hour of the night?"

"Looking for work. Trying to buy my family back in Virginia. They ain't free."

"Whose your family?"

"Wife, five children, and a new baby. Man back in Warrenton, Virginia owns all of them."

"You aim to buy all of them?"

"Every one."

The woman said nothing for a moment. Dangerfield was almost asleep when she spoke again.

"How long will it take 'fore you earn enough to buy your wife and six children?"

"I expect to have the money in a year, maybe less."

The candle in the woman's hand began to flicker, and the cabin grew darker. The woman walked to the table, picked up another candle, and lit the wick with the dwindling flame of the first candle. The fresh candle popped and hissed before shedding a yellowish light in the cabin. The woman held the new candle and sat down.

"You aim to be away from your family for year? Reckon it'd be easier to just run away, take your chances on getting to Canada."

"I thought about that, but hiding seven runaways ain't easy, and mind that one is a new baby," said Dangerfield yawning. "New babies don't keep quiet. And I won't have my family get split up. Least now I know they are all in one place while I work to buy them."

Dangerfield turned toward the woman. "'Sides, being a runaway don't always work out either. How do you aim to get your son and daughter back?"

"I don't know," said the woman. "I don't even know where to look." She began sobbing quietly.

Dangerfield silently considered her plight. Having lived his entire life under Henry's protection, he now realized that he had never had the experience of being alone, helpless, and completely undefended. He could not imagine that experience.

"Your children will be just fine," said Dangerfield, unable to think of anything else to say. "And I know of someone who can help you."

Dangerfield got up and moved the table against the wall, and used the point of the shovel to pry open the trap door. He held the candle over the tunnel.

"This cabin is a safe house. Man named Featherston helps runaways. You go into that tunnel, it takes you to his house. Featherston and his family take runaways to Canada. First thing tomorrow, we use this tunnel to travel to Featherston's house. He will take care of you."

The woman took the candle and peered down into the tunnel.

"How far is it?"

"I don't know. We will find out tomorrow. Best get some sleep tonight." Dangerfield replaced the trap door and walked back to his makeshift bed.

"I ain't sleeping here, not with him in here," said the woman, pointing at the dead man in the corner.

Dangerfield walked toward the dead man. "You hold the candle while I move him. Reckon he won't mind sleeping outside."

The woman held the candle while Dangerfield lifted the dead man under his arms and began dragging him outside. In the dim light, the man's face seemed familiar. Dangerfield took the candle and held it close to the man's face.

The dead man's face was ghostly white, except for the blood caked around his mouth and nose. He had full lips, and soft, almost feminine features. Curly blond hair covered his shoulders. His pale blue eyes were wide open and looking downward, as though he were examining the knife handle lodged in his chin.

Dangerfield stood up and returned the candle to the woman.

"Something wrong?" she said. "You look like you know him."

"No I don't know him. Least I don't know his name. You said he had a partner who took your daughter. What did his partner look like?"

"He was real tall, with a thick mustache. And he had big scar on his face, from just under his eye all the way to the corner of his mouth. I remember that real well. Looked like somebody had cut him open from his eye all the way to his lips. Real ugly. I remember that when he burst into our cabin."

Dangerfield knew then where he had seen the dead man and his partner – the slave catchers who had threatened him while he was riding with Featherston. He knew them all the way back to Virginia, when he was still Henry's property.

Dangerfield grabbed the man by his arms and resumed dragging him outside. He laid his body in the snow behind the cabin. He then retrieved the man's horse and hobbled it behind the cabin, beside his own horse. The two horses nickered, and the smallish horse nipped Dangerfield's horse in the rump. Dangerfield fed both horses a large handful of oats, and the animals ate contentedly. He went back inside the cabin and closed the door.

"You act like you know that man," said the woman suspiciously.

"I said I don't know him by name. Just know that he and his partner, the one you saw, been catching slaves here and in Virginia for a long time. The other one might come back this way. I knew who it was when you said he had a scar. I would know that man anywhere."

Dangerfield made certain the door was latched closed. He peered through the gaps in the cabin wall looking northward, looking for another rider.

"You think he might come back here," said the woman.

"Not likely at this hour. He might come back tomorrow looking for his partner. "Reckon we – you – are safe for the night. Best get some sleep. First thing tomorrow you take that tunnel to Featherston's house."

Dangerfield walked to his bed and lay down. He closed his eyes, but sleep would not come. He heard the woman rustling in the bed he had made for her, and he knew she was not sleeping either.

"You aim to go with me tomorrow, to look for this Featherston? I ain't never met the man."

"I can't leave my horse alone. And I can't have you ride with me, if slave catchers are looking for you. I got no wagon, and no way to hide you on a horse. Best thing is for you to take that tunnel to Featherston's house. He knows what to do."

The woman rustled in her bedroll, and let out a deep sigh.

"Thank you again," she said.

"Best get some sleep," said Dangerfield.

Dangerfield heard the even sounds of the woman breathing, and he knew she was finally asleep. He heard the horses grunting and nickering behind the cabin. The wind sliced through the cabin walls, and he watched as the candle flickered, then died. He thought about Harriet, Jericho, and his family. He wondered what Henry was doing now. He thought about his brother Gabriel, safe and warm in his new house.

Dangerfield realized he could never live with his family in Henry's house. He would look for his own house, near Henry and Elsey, so he could look after them. They would all live nearby. Henry could teach his boys how to make harnesses, and how to shape metal in a forge. He would help Elsey with the garden. And Harriet would have her own garden, and her own chickens. The girls would help gather eggs every morning. They might even have breakfast with Henry and Elsey two or three times a week. He smiled at this thought, and it was enough to bring an uneasy sleep.

The wind howling through the cabin walls woke him. He sat up, and reflexively felt for the Colt in his breast pocket. The table was pushed against the wall, and the trap door was flung open. The woman was gone.

He went behind the cabin and checked on the horses. Both animals were still hobbled. The Sharps was still tightly wrapped against his horse. Everything was where he had left it. He fed the horses a half ration of oats, then surveyed his surroundings. There was a creek nearby. He would have to get his horse some water soon.

The dead man lay where Dangerfield had dragged him. Snow covered his face, and only the pale blue of his eyes pierced the snowy veil. Dangerfield went inside the cabin and retrieved his blankets, bedrolls, and woolen coat. He went back outside and covered the man's body with a blanket. There was nothing else he could do.

He had almost completed packing his horse when he heard a noise from inside the cabin. He pushed open the door to find Featherston's daughters Louise and Mary emerging from the tunnel. The girls pulled themselves up and surveyed the room. Both girls bowed politely when they saw Dangerfield. Louise spoke.

"Good day, Brother Dangerfield. My father sends his thanks. He is sending a wagon this morning to retrieve the horse and the . . . body of the deceased."

"Where is the woman who was here last night," said Dangerfield.

"She is safe in our home. Our mother is feeding her and getting her clean clothes. She will stay with us for a few days until she is ready to continue her journey."

"You aim to take her to Canada?"

"If that is where she wants to go, we will take her there."

"We expect the slavers to return this way very soon," said Mary. "We need to act quickly to hide the horse and dispose of the body. Please show us where the body is."

Dangerfield led the girls behind the cabin, and pulled back the blanket. Mary gasped softly. Both girls closed their eyes while Mary prayed.

"Lord, our Father, bless this man's soul even as we condemn his sin, and condemn the evil he has brought upon your children. Amen."

Louise then inspected the man's death wound. She tried to pull the knife from his chin, but it would not budge. She placed her bootheel against his chin, and pushed his head down with her foot while she pulled on the handle. The knife was lodged too deeply in his chin. After several tries, the knife slid out of the man's head. Louise wiped the blade against her dress and inspected the knife.

"This is a sturdy blade. Do you want to keep it, Brother Dangerfield?"

Dangerfield shook his head. Louise wiped the knife again, and placed it in a fold within her dress. Mary searched the dead man's pockets. She pulled out some loose coins, a few pieces of paper, and a small curved knife. Mary turned this knife in her hand, then placed it in her dress.

The trio turned at the sound of horses coming from the south. Featherston's wagon creaked up the hill as the horses struggled to pull the wagon through the fresh snow. Featherston pulled up and sat the horses.

"Good day, Brother Dangerfield. Alma sends her thanks for saving her last night. And we thank you for your service. I know you have other obligations, but I thank you."

"Sorry I can't help you more."

"You have already helped greatly. Louise, take the slaver's horse back to our stable. We will keep it in the barn until we decide what to do with it." Louise picked up the hobble, mounted the slaver's horse, and rode off toward her home.

Featherston dismounted and removed a casket from the false bottom of the wagon.

"Brother Dangerfield, will you help us load this man into the casket?"

Dangerfield lifted the man by his feet while Featherston and Mary took hold of his arms. They dropped the man in the casket, then loaded the casket into the false bottom of the wagon. Featherston closed the sliding wooden door.

"Thank you again, Brother Dangerfield. May the Lord keep you."

Dangerfield shook Featherston's hand, and tipped his hat toward Mary. He finished saddling his horse and rode north toward Martins Ferry without looking back.

CHAPTER 44

November 16, 1858

Dearest Harriet,

I hop you and children are healthy and warm. I found work in the cole mines near martins ferry ohio. A kind gentleman named Amos Featherston helped me find work here. It is vary hard work, but we are paid 8 dollers per day. Black and White get the same pay, which is strange. All of us workers are treated farely. But the work is hard, and dangerous. Yesterday, a man and two mules fell off the cliffs and dyed. Do not worry, I am vary carefull.

I aim to work here for a few more days, then move north. Hopfully, I can find work as a blacksmith, or making sadles or harneses for farmers and such. I think it will pay as much, and will not be as dangerous.

I do not know when you will get this letter, as I don't have a home to stay in. I maled this from martins ferry, but I will not be here long, so do not try to send letters here. If you get this and want to write back, send a letter to Henrys new house in Bridgeport. I aim to go back to Bridgeport to gather my belongings before I come to Virginia to get you and the children. I hope to see manny letters from you when I go back to Bridgeport.

I expet to have the money Marse Lewis asked for by next summer. I will come to Virginia and buy you and the children as soon as posible. You and the children will like Ohio. But it is vary cold in winter.

I hop Marse Lewis is treating you and the children well. I have met manny runaway slaves on the road. It seems most get caut real quick.

Tell the boys to mind you and Marse Lewis. I hop the baby is well.

Your loving Husband,

Dangerfield

Terrance C. Newby

Terrance C. Newby

DECEMBER 18, 1858

Dearest Harriet,

I have vary good news. Last month, I mad almost 200 dollars working in the cole mines. Today, I put that monny in the State Bank of Ohio, in which I have an account. I expet to make even more monny once I find blacksmith or harness work.

I have saved a lot of monny, but still not enough to buy you and the children. And the cole mines are dangerous. Last week, two more men fell off the cliff and dyed. I am carefull, but so were the men who fell.

I heard of a man in Kenntucky who needs help making fences and such. I hop to work for him for one or two weeks, and then go back to Ohio. I have been told it is not easy to find work in Kenntucky, as most of the farmers own slaves. There are not manny free coloreds in Kenntucky, and it is hard for a free colored man to find work. I hop I can work for the man for a few weeks and then go back to Ohio and find other work. If not, I can work again in the cole mines. The cole mines are vary dangerous, but the pay is fare. But it will take longer to get the monny to buy you and the children.

If you get my letters and want to write back, I expet to be back in Bridgeport in one or two munths, and I will read your letters then. Please send letters to Henrys house.

I made Chrismas presents for you and the children. I hop you like them. I hop to see you and the children soon.

Your loving Husband,
Dangerfield

FEBRUARY 5, 1859

Dearest Harriet,
I hop you and the children are well.

I have been searching for work not in the cole mines. It is not easy for a free colored man to find work. Last month, I went to Kenntucky to find the man who needs help making fences and such. He said he found someone else to help him. He also said he could not hire a free colored, because there were White men who needed to work. And most of the farmers who have monny also have slaves.

I am back in Ohio. I was able to save almost 200 dollers, which I will soon put in the Bank. But it is still not enough to buy you and the children. I hop to find work making harnesses and sadles and such.

I aim to return to Virginia to buy you and the children this summer. I will bring all the monny I have. I hop it will be enough. But if it is not, I think Marse Lewis will treat me farely. He has always been fare to me.

I will be back in Bridgeport at Henry's house next week. I hop to see manny letters from you. And I will see you this summer when I come to Virginia with the monny.

Your loving Husband,
Dangerfield

MARCH 9, 1859

Dearest Harriet,

I have vary good news. I have been back in Bridgeport with Henry, Elsey and Gabriel since last month. The man Featherston who helped me find work in the cole mines has hired me on in his shop. I make sadles and shoes for his draft horses. I also smith for some farmers who need shoes for their horses. Featherston pays me vary well. I aim to keep working for him until I have the monny to buy you and the children. I hop to have all the monny by July or August. I put 450 more dollers in the bank yesterday.

I am glad to be back in Bridgeport. Henry is not well. Gabriel and I help him with chores and such, but Gabriel is working, and not at home. He helps when he can. Elsey is fine. She still misses Virginia, but has taken a shine to Ohio. She buys most of the food in town. She also buys new clothes. She says she does not miss having to make her own clothes. Henry says she spends too much monny on store bought clothes and linens. But she still buys them.

My bones still ache when it gets cold and wet. Somtimes my knees and elbow make noises when I am working in the cold or rain. Featherston says it is something called rumatism. I think Henry has it too, as his back always hurts. Sometimes he cant get out of bed. Elsey says he needs to see a docter. But Henry wont go. He says he will be fine. I don't know if he will.

I will see you and the children soon, maybe even September. Tell the children to mind you and Marse Lewis. You can send letters to Henrys house in Bridgeport, as I will be here until I come back to Virginia.

I found a house for sale in Bridgeport. It is big enough for all of us. It has a fence and room for chickens and a garden. After I buy you and the children, we can save some monny to buy it. Henry says he can lend me a small amount of monny too. Hopfully, I wont need to borrow monny from Henry, so he and Elsey can keep there monny.

Your loving Husband,
Dangerfield

CHAPTER 45

BRENTVILLE Aᴘʀɪʟ 11 1859

Dear Husband

I mus now write you apology for not writing you before this but I know you will excuse me when tell you Mrs. gennings has been very sick she has a baby a little girl ben a grate sufferer her breast raised and she has had it lanced and I have had to stay with her day and night so you know I had no time to write but she is now better and one of her own servent is now sick I am well that is of the grates importance to you I have no newes to write you only the chrildren are all well I want to see you very much but are looking fordard to the promest time of your coming oh Dear Dangerfield com this fall with out fail monny or no money I want to see you so much that is one bright hope I have before me nothing more at present but remain
   your affectionate wife
   HARRIET NEWBY
   P S write soon if you please

BRENTVILLE Aᴘʀɪʟ 22 1859

Dear Husband

I received your letter to day and it give much pleasure to here from you but was sorry to hear of your sickeness hope you may be well when you receive this I wrote to you several weeks a go and directed my letter to Bridge Port but I fear you did not receive it as you said nothing about it in yours you must give my love to Brother Gabial and tell him I would like to see him very much I wrote in my last letter that Miss Virginia had a baby a little girl I had to nerse her day and night Dear Dangerfield you Can not amagine how much I want to see you Com as soon as you can for nothing would give more pleasure than to see you it is the grates Comfort I have is thinking of the promist time when you will be here oh that bless hour when I shall see you once more my baby commenced to Crall to day it is very dellicate nothing more at present but remain

your affectionate wife.

HARRIET NEWBY

P s write soon

July 15, 1859

Dearest Harriet,

I received your letter with much joy. I have been working vary hard with Featherston and with local farmers near Bridgeport who need a smith and sadle maker. I made three sadles and shoes for five horses for a rich farmer in Kenntucky. He owns slaves, but thay dont know how to make sadles or harneses or shoes. And Featherston has told people that I am the best blacksmith in Ohio, White or Black. He is vary kind. Manny people now want me to make things for them.

I have now saved over one thousand dollers, which I have put in my account in the State Bank. I hop this is enough to buy you and the children. Marse Lewis said it would be enough.

I will come to Virginia in August to settle my affiars with Marse Lewis, and to buy the family. Dont tell the chilren just yet, so it will be a suprise when I come.

Henry says I have to be careful in Virginia, because they could catch me and sell me back into a slave. But I have my papers from Henry. And I aim too stay in Virginia only long enough to buy you and the chilren, and then leave.

Please start packing your clothes, and clothes for the children. You will need warm clothes as it can be vary cold in Ohio. Also pack cooking pots, spoons, knives, forks, ect, salted ham, smoked beef, bread, biscuits, sugar, and other food that Mistress or Lilly will let you take without asking too manny questions. Best not tell anyon you are leaving until I settle my affiars with Marse Lewis and he signs your freemans papers.

I hop the baby is well, and lerning to crawl and stand. Looking forward to see-ing you and the children and the baby. My rumatism is much better, and my bones do not ache ecxpect when it is vary cold and rainny. I think the rumatism goes away when it is hot.

Your loving Husband,

Dangerfield

CHAPTER 46

Bᴙɪᴅɢᴇᴘᴏʀᴛ, Oʜɪᴏ, Aᴜɢᴜsᴛ 1, 1859

D angerfield arose at dawn and began packing for his trip to Virginia. He packed both saddlebags evenly so the horse would not pull on the long trek, then tightened the straps on the saddle. He pulled out the leather pouch that Henry had given him, and checked its contents: his freeman's papers, notarized and signed by Henry; $1,500 in bank notes, to be used to buy Harriet and his family; and the letters Harriet had written him in the last year.

He read her letters again in the early morning light, starting with the first, reading slowly, savoring every word, every sentence. He stopped when he read this passage from her April 22 letter:

> Dear Dangerfield you Can not amagine how much I want to see you Com as soon as you can for nothing would give more pleasure than to see you it is the grates Comfort I have is thinking of the promist time when you will be here oh that bless hour when I shall see you once more

He kissed the letters, then gently folded them and put them in the pouch, along with the bank notes and his freeman's papers. He put the pouch in his right breast pocket. He flipped open the cylinder on Henry's Colt, checking to make certain there was a round in each chamber. He closed the cylinder, then inspected his powder bag, lead balls, and percussion caps. These he put in his left breast pocket, alongside the fully loaded Colt, positioned handle up so he could retrieve and fire with one motion.

He strapped the Sharps that Brown had given him to his saddlebag, fastening it tight. He was about to mount and ride off when Henry hobbled out the front door.

"You aim to leave without saying goodbye?"

"Reckon there ain't much to say. I have what I need, and we both know what I have to do. We talked about everything last night. No point in troubling Elsey."

Henry leaned on his cane and squinted out at the early morning sun.

"Should be a good day for riding. How far you aim to go today?"

"Twenty, maybe twenty-five miles. See how the Old Man is doing." Dangerfield patted Solomon's flank. "If the weather holds up, I should be back in Marse Lewis' place in Brentsville in twelve days or so. I can ride faster than the wagon we took to get here."

Henry held his hand to the sun, examining a small cut on his wrist. "How you aim to bring your family back to Bridgeport once you buy them. Harriet and the children won't all fit on one horse."

"I will ask Marse Lewis to let me borrow a wagon and one horse. Solomon can pull alongside another horse. Marse Lewis has been fair to me. If he needs money, I will work for one week at his farm, enough time to buy or trade for one horse and an old wagon. He has a few run-down wagons need some work. I can buy one, and fix it up. That will give Harriet and the children time to get ready 'fore we leave."

Henry sucked at a tooth and looked skyward. "Well, let's hope that works out. You might want to take my wagon. Solomon can pull an empty wagon with one rider, but he can't go too fast. Buy one horse when you get back to Brentsville. That way, you already got the wagon."

"That's a fine idea Henry, but a wagon will slow me down. I need a horse that can ride hard and fast to Brentsville if need be. Won't matter on the way home. Reckon a fully loaded wagon with women and children on board won't attract as much attention as a single rider on a wagon. Slavers can't capture all of us, but if it's just me driving a wagon by myself in Virginia . . . ."

Henry considered this point. "You have your papers?"

"Right here." Dangerfield patted his right pocket.

"And the Colt?"

"Right here." Dangerfield patted his left coat pocket.

"Good," said Henry. "Keep the barrel pointed . . . ."

"Down, handle up, so I can pull and fire in one motion," said Dangerfield.

Henry closed his eyes and sighed. "Remember, you have one year from . . . "

"One year from September 25, 1858, the date of emancipation, to leave Virginia forever," said Dangerfield. "I have 56 days from today to get my family and get back to Ohio. Should take me twelve days or so to get to Brentsville if I ride steady and the weather holds. That's about 23 miles per day. Don't want to push Solomon harder than that. Get to Brentsville by August 13 or so. I figure it will take one week for the family to pack and for me to settle my affairs with Marse Lewis, maybe a bit more. Enough time to rest and mend the horse, and earn the money to buy another horse and an old wagon. I can work a few days extra if need be. And twenty-four days to get back to Ohio, considering a fully loaded wagon don't travel as fast as a single rider. That's as long as it took us to get here from Culpeper. That's about twelve miles a day, a nice, easy pace even with a fully loaded wagon.

That's why I can't take your wagon with me on the way to Virginia – it would slow me down. Whole trip should take 43 days. I should be home by September 12. That gives me some time if things don't work out as I planned."

Henry arched his eyebrows and allowed a thin smile to crease his lips. "Reckon you have put some thought into this ride back to Virginia. That's good. But you ain't leaving yourself a lot of extra time. Might take a few weeks to work to get that wagon and settle up with Prince Lewis."

"It's all the time I have, Henry. Took me that long to earn the $1,500."

"You have the $1,500," said Henry.

"Right here," said Dangerfield, patting his right pocket.

Neither man spoke for a moment. Solomon nickered and stamped his hooves.

"Reckon I should go now, Henry."

"I should have waited to sign them papers," said Henry. "If I had waited til December or January, you would have more time now. Would not have to worry about getting back before . . . ."

"You did what you needed to do, Henry. No one knew how much it would cost, or how long it would take to free my family. Didn't even know if Marse Lewis would sell them. Now, we know the cost, I have the money, and I know how much time I have before I have to be out of Virginia. You did everything you needed to do."

Dangerfield mounted his horse and pulled his hat low against the early morning sun.

"I will see you and Elsey September 12, if not before," said Dangerfield. "Tell Gabriel we might need his room for the baby til I can buy my own house in Bridgeport. That house across town looks nice. Had my eye on it since we moved here. Big yard with a fence. Me and Harriet and the kids aim to visit on Sundays."

"That will be nice," said Henry, looking off into the distance. Henry pulled his kerchief from his pocket and wiped his brow. "Got something in my eye. Anyway, you'd best get going."

Dangerfield tipped his hat and rode east, back toward Virginia.

⸻ ◉ ⸻

He crossed the Belmont Covered Bridge over the Ohio River, crossed Wheeling Island, and rode into Wheeling, Virginia. It felt no different than Bridgeport, but as soon as he crossed the bridge, he sat Solomon and pulled out the leather pouch with his freeman's papers. He read the words on the paper out loud, then carefully folded it and returned it to his pocket. He checked each chamber of the Colt, and returned it to his other pocket. No slavers would be out this early in the morning – most runaways moved at night, and this segment of road offered few buildings and little shelter. Solomon flicked his tail at a black fly on his flank, and stamped his hooves. Dangerfield nudged his heel into Solomon's flank, and they continued riding east.

He rode twenty-five miles the first day at an easy pace, not wanting to push Solomon too hard. Solomon could no longer ride hard for ten miles at a clip, but he was still fit, and able to easily cross terrain that would make other horses turn back or toss their rider. Dangerfield knew that once they got close to Culpeper, Solomon would remember the trails he had run countless times between Culpeper and Warrenton. From Warrenton, it was only another day's ride to Jennings' smaller farm in Brentsville.

By dusk, he was well into Virginia. There were no inns that would accept a colored freeman, so he made camp in a field near the road. He hobbled Solomon and fed him a single ration of oats mixed with alfalfa. The big bay ate quickly, and could have easily eaten a double ration, but Dangerfield wanted to save his provisions. And he wanted Solomon to be lean in case they had to gallop to escape slavers.

He dipped his hat in a nearby creek and brought a hatful of water for Solomon. The horse drank the hat dry, and two more hatfuls of water after that, until he snorted contentedly, snot flying from his nostrils.

Dangerfield surveyed his surroundings in the rapidly dying light. He saw no houses or barns nearby, and no sign that anyone had tended this field recently. He had seen no one on the road in over an hour. A row of trees shielded his camp from the road.

He left Solomon and walked back to the middle of the road and turned toward his camp. He could not see or hear Solomon, and the last embers of daylight revealed no trace of his entrance into the field. He picked his way carefully through the trees so as to leave no trace of his entrance, and back toward his camp.

He took his blankets and bedroll from the saddlebags, and made his bed on a soft tuft of fieldgrass. He unwrapped the Sharps and laid it next to his bedroll. He felt the heft of the Colt in his breast pocket, and exhaled deeply. He was cold, but dared not light a fire. He had memorized Harriet's letters, and did not need light to read them:

> *Dear Dangerfield you Can not amagine how much I want to see you Com as soon as you can for nothing would give more pleasure than to see you it is the grates Comfort I have is thinking of the promist time when you will be here oh that bless hour when I shall see you once more*

Harriet's voice was the last thing he heard before he drifted into a cold, fireless sleep.

He was up at dawn the next morning. He fed Solomon a full ration of oats, bolted down a breakfast of salted ham and bread, and was on the road before the sun had dried the dew in the field.

At midafternoon, he passed a small roadside shack that reminded him of Featherston's safe house back in Ohio. He stopped and peered inside through a cracked window. There was a small table pushed against a wall, and two chairs at opposite ends of the table. There was no one inside.

By dusk, he had ridden another twenty-five miles. Again there were no sheds, inns, or homes where he could stay. He led Solomon deep into a wooded area until he found a clearing. He dismounted, fed and brushed his horse, and set up camp for the night. He took note of his provisions, cut a piece of salted ham in two, and ate while staring at the rising moon. Again, he slept without a fire. The night before, he fell asleep while dreaming of Harriet. Tonight, and for the rest of the nights of his trip, he fell asleep while dreaming of his soft bed in Henry's house.

August 16, 1859

Dangerfield rode into his birthplace of Culpeper, Virginia late in the afternoon. He had not slept under a roof, or in a bed, or rested his head on a pillow since leaving Bridgeport. But it had rained hard four times since he left Bridgeport, and as a result, he had not made good time – it took him four days longer to reach Culpeper than he had planned. He considered pushing on to Brentsville and Harriet, but first he wanted to see who was living in his old house.

He rode down the path toward his old home. Solomon picked up speed and began cantering in recognition of a familiar destination.

Dangerfield rounded the bend and pulled up when he saw his childhood home. Two windows on the first floor were boarded up. The paint was peeling, and the front porch sagged. A broken porch railing dangled from a post. An unboarded second floor window was broken. Two sparrows darted into the broken window, and quickly darted out. A torn curtain flapped in the broken window.

He dismounted and walked gingerly across the front porch. A floorboard creaked as he walked across it. He pushed open the front door, and slowly walked in.

The front parlor was exactly as it was when his family left Culpeper. Henry's old rocking chair, deemed too fragile to survive the move to Ohio, was next to the fireplace. Thick dust covered every surface.

Upstairs, someone had left a hammer and several nails next to one of the boarded up windows. He walked around every room on the second floor.

His bed was as he left it – his room was undisturbed from his last day in the house. A dusty pair of children's shoes sat in the middle of Gabriel's room. He did not recognize them.

The window in Henry and Elsey's room was also boarded up. Another hammer, and several bent nails were on the floor, along with a dust-covered pair of a child's leather boots.

Dangerfield picked up the boots, looking for a trace of ownership. He blew off the dust, and recognized the shoes as his from many years ago. Elsey must have saved them under her bed, and whoever had boarded up the first floor windows must have found them while searching the rooms.

"Old John Fox must have decided not to move in after all," muttered Dangerfield to himself.

He peered under the bed and saw a small dust-covered object laying against the baseboard. He pulled it out and held a bone-handled penny knife that Henry had given him for his seventh birthday.

When he was six, he had begged Henry to get him a penny knife, just like Henry used every day. Henry had refused, telling him he was not yet responsible enough to care for a nice knife. Dangerfield begged Henry every day, then Elsey, until Elsey had finally ordered Henry to "get the boy a knife so we can have some peace." Henry relented, and on Dangerfield's seventh birthday, Henry presented him with a small curved blade with a sharp point, full belly, and handles made of deer bone.

"Don't lose that knife, boy," Henry had told him. "Show me you can be a responsible man."

Dangerfield used the knife every day, working alongside Henry and Henry's bought slaves. One of those bought slaves, Alfred, borrowed and promptly lost the knife. Dangerfield knew Henry would whip him for losing the knife, but he would whip Alfred harder. Of all Henry's bought slaves, Dangerfield liked Alfred the best – Alfred would tell him jokes and sing songs while they worked together in the fields. Not wanting to see Alfred whipped, Dangerfield told Henry he had lost the knife. And Henry did indeed whip him, telling him to be more responsible "and don't let anybody borrow your tools if you ain't sure you will get them back."

Dangerfield sat on the floor in his old house, holding his long-lost prized penny knife. He wondered how Henry knew he had let someone else use the knife. He wondered how Henry had found the knife when Alfred had sworn he lost it. And then he remembered that Henry had sold Alfred later that summer, telling the family that he no longer trusted him. Henry must have quickly figured out that Alfred had taken the knife, and he had simply never told Dangerfield or returned the knife to him.

Dangerfield flipped open the knife, which still opened smoothly. He flipped it closed, then put it in his pocket. He would give it to Junior when he got to Brentsville, and tell him to keep track of it like a responsible young man. "Don't let anybody borrow your tools unless you trust them," he would tell him. He thought of the look he would see on Junior's face when he saw his father after almost a year away. He would sleep in the same cabin with Harriet, with Lucy and Agnes and the baby nearby. He would make certain Jericho was minding his manners, and within a week, maybe two, the family would be heading west, back to Bridgeport.

He went outside and surveyed the rest of the farm. The barn door hung on one hinge. Every window was broken. He went inside, and saw no immediate trace of squatters or inhabitants. He climbed the ladder to the hayloft. Someone had made a nest in the hay – a torn pair of breeches and a linen shirt were rolled up in a tight ball, a makeshift pillow in the hay. He saw no other human traces. Probably runaways, and probably a few weeks old.

He checked the stable, the corn crib, and the hog shed. When he opened the stable door, an old tomcat snarled at him before running off. He saw no traces of any human in any of the other buildings.

Runaways were probably using the barn at night. It was far enough from the house that no one inside would see them enter or leave. There was no place in the stable, corn crib or hog shed to bed down for the night. And no runaways would be bold enough to enter the house, even if it appeared deserted.

He walked the perimeter of the yard. Just behind the stable he found the remains of a campfire, the embers cold and disintegrating. The remnants were at least a week old. The fire would not have been visible from the road or the house, but a passerby would have smelled the woodsmoke. Only a very brave or inexperienced runaway would have dared to light a campfire here, even at night.

He kicked his boot in the embers and then picked up a piece of partially burned wood. The maker of this fire was likely long gone, or already captured.

He returned to the house, and surveyed the ruins of what used to be his home, the only home he had known for all but one year of his life. That night, he slept under a roof for the first time since leaving Ohio.

August 18, 1859

He arrived at Brentsville early in the afternoon. It had been almost a year since he had seen Harriet, his family, or Lewis Jennings.

As he rode through the gate, a stout gray-haired black woman emerged. She glowered at him, then spat on the ground. He tipped his hat.

"Day, Miss Lilly. Ain't seen you in a while."

"Surprised you came back," said Lilly. "Figured once you got a taste of freedom, you'd find some woman in Ohio to marry. Leave us back here. Didn't expect to see you ever again. "

"Sorry to disappoint you, but I came back, and intend to stay for a spell. "Where is Harriet and the rest of my family?"

"Your wife and baby is in the house, with Mistress. Your other children are in back." Lilly looked toward the house and barn. Seeing no one, she leaned in and spoke in a raspy whisper.

"Good thing you came back when you did. Marse Lewis looking to make some changes since you been gone. Word is he owes some money in town, and can't pay it back. Been looking to sell some slaves, including some of yours. You need to find him quick, if you aim to buy your children."

"Where is Marse Lewis?"

"Out by the stable."

"I will find him now. Please tell Harriet I am here, and will get her and the children shortly."

Dangerfield marched toward the stable. He turned the corner and saw Lewis Jennings and another white man examining a tall, light-skinned young Negro man. As he drew closer, Dangerfield recognized the man – it was Jericho.

"Now, you will see that this young lad has very good teeth, and is exceptionally strong, despite his lean frame," said Jennings. "Also, I can assure you that he is very disciplined. One of my most experienced and trusted field hands has brought him up, and taught him the penalties for misbehaving. I think you will find him worth every penny I am asking for him."

"Marse Lewis, I need a word with you."

Lewis Jennings turned and saw Dangerfield. Jennings' face drained, and he stammered as he spoke to the potential buyer."

"If you will excuse me, uh, Robert, I have a bit of personal business I must attend to. Please feel free to inspect young Jericho, especially his teeth. And although illiterate, he can communicate and understand any orders you give him. Please excuse me."

Jennings walked slowly toward Dangerfield.

"You have returned sooner than I expected," said Jennings. "Surely you cannot have the money we agreed on already. I would have expected it would take far longer than this . . . ."

"I have the $1,500 Marse, just like we agreed. You aim to sell Jericho?"

"Well, perhaps not right away, but I am entertaining some offers. I don't expect anything to happen today, or even tomorrow, but I do have to maximize my assets . . . ."

"Where is Harriet and my family?"

"Harriet is in the house, with your youngest child, no longer quite a baby. They are healthy and well."

"What about the rest of my children? Lucy, Agnes, Junior, Gabriel?"

"The rest of your children are also well, and still under my roof." Jennings cleared his throat. "Of course, you do remember that our agreement was that I would sell only Harriet and your newborn baby to you for $1,500. No one else is part of the transaction."

"Yes, Marse, and you also said we would discuss my other children and Jericho when I came back with the $1,500. I have the money. Reckon we need to talk about all of my family."

"Yes, of course. Let me conclude my business with Robert, and I will meet you in the house."

"Don't sell Jericho until you and I finish our business. You gave me your word, Marse. I kept my word. I expect you to keep yours."

"Yes, of course," said Jennings. Please give me a minute. I will meet you in the house."

Dangerfield turned and walked toward the house. Before he could enter, Harriet ran out the front door screaming. She leaped into his arms, knocking him to the ground as she wailed with joy.

"I knew you would come back, I knew it! I don't care what Lilly thinks, I knew you would come back! Do you have the money? Did you get my letters? What does the house in Bridgeport look like? How is Brother Gabriel? How is Anna Mae? Are Henry and Mama Elsey still well?"

Dangerfield pulled himself up slowly, and pulled his wife close to him. He smelled her hair, and nuzzled his favorite place on her neck. He inhaled her smoky skin, and it was just as he dreamed it would be each night he had gone to sleep for the past year. He gave her a long, wet kiss, then pulled back and admired his wife.

"Yes, I have the money. Yes, I got both of your letters. Brother Gabriel is fine, and so are Henry, Elsey, and Anna Mae. I haven't bought the house in Bridgeport just yet. Been saving money to buy you and the children."

Harriet pulled back. "Both of my letters? I sent you three letters. You only got two?"

Dangerfield retrieved Harriet's letters from his pocket. "April 11, 1859, and April 22, 1859. I can almost recite them from memory."

Harriet's face darkened. "I wrote you another letter after those two, just a few days ago," she said. "You must have left before it arrived." She pulled him closer and spoke in low tones. "Things here ain't real good. Rumor is that Master is in want of money, and has to sell servants, or else the bank will take his house."

"Lilly told me about that."

"It is worse than I have ever seen. Every day, strange white men come to the house and farm, inspecting field hands, putting their hands on the house girls. Last week, he sold two field hands, and one house girl. Today, Lilly told me he has someone looking to buy Jericho. I pleaded with him, but Jericho is tall and strong. And Jericho don't listen to Marse since you left. I plead with Jericho every day to behave, so he don't get sold South. And I plead with Marse every day not to sell him South. I tell him every day to wait til you get home, and you will buy us and take us to Ohio."

She hugged him again. "Please don't leave without us."

Inside the house, a small child wailed. Lilly stepped out, with the child holding on to Lilly's finger. The boy toddled outside, holding Lilly's finger with one hand, grasping a wooden doll in his other hand.

"Ma Ma," said the boy, gently patting Harriet with his doll.

"The last time you saw Baby John, he wasn't but a newborn baby," said Harriet." Now, he still cannot walk yet, but he steps around by holding on to things. He's just like Agnes when she was a baby."

Dangerfield picked up his child, a baby he had seen only briefly before leaving almost a year ago. Dangerfield saw his own face in this child – long, sleepy eyes, coffee-colored skin, and a smoldering gaze that drilled directly into his father's soul.

"Ma Ma," he said loudly, batting his father with the wooden doll. "Ma Ma."

Dangerfield gently handed back his child to Harriet.

"I have the money Marse Lewis and I agreed to," said Dangerfield. "I aim to settle up and we can begin packing."

"What about Jericho," said Harriet. "Is he going with us?"

"I aim to take all of ours, and Jericho with us," said Dangerfield. "Just need to settle up with Marse Lewis."

He went back outside, and found Lewis Jennings alone, pacing back and forth behind the stable.

"I have the money, Marse. $1,500 in bank notes. That should buy Harriet and my baby, like we agreed. Now I want to buy all the rest of my children, and Jericho too. Reckon I can work here for a week or two, do whatever you need me to do. I will stay until September 1. When I leave, I take Harriet, all my children, and Jericho with me. You name your price, and I work to buy the rest of my family."

"I see," muttered Lewis Jennings softly. "You have obviously put some thought into this . . . plan. But how do you intend to transport all of your children and Jericho? Are they all going to walk?"

"No, Marse. I buy that old wagon you had behind the barn. I buy it fix it up, and we include that in the price for my family. When I leave September 1, you and I are even, and I have my family. Here is the $1,500 for Harriet and the baby."

Dangerfield reached into his pouch, and handed the bank notes to Jennings. Jennings slowly thumbed each note, counting the value to himself until he reached the end of the stack.

"Now, you draw up the papers for Harriet and the baby. We can make arrangements for me to buy the rest of my family after we sign the papers."

Jennings exhaled, and slowly handed the pouch back to Dangerfield.

"You know I am a man of my word, and always have been," said Jennings.

Dangerfield did not reply.

"And because I am a man of my word, I am obliged, indeed compelled, to explain to you the difficult circumstances under which I find myself."

"What I hear is you need money," said Dangerfield. I just gave you $1500, like we agreed. You give me my family, and we both get what we want."

"I see you have learned the fundamental aspects of business during your short time as a freeman," said Jennings. "But although you may now understand the value of a dollar earned through sweat, the realities of running a farm and managing inventory are far more . . . sophisticated than a simple laborer can hope to understand."

"As you know," continued Jennings, "I have tried to run this operation the way my father would have, with discipline, compassion, and of course sound business sense. A light hand on the whip, as you know from experience."

Dangerfield recalled the elder Jennings "light hand on the whip," and the sizzle and smell of burning human flesh when the elder Jennings had branded a young Jericho.

"To run an operation like this requires human capital," said Jennings. "And the cost of new inventory continues to climb, especially healthy inventory, like your family. To fund this operation, I have borrowed money from several banks. The money I borrow allows me to buy more inventory, while also paying for non-human inventory, draft horses and equipment and the like."

"Looks like you also pay for nice clothes, and fancy riding horses," said Dangerfield, pointing to Jennings' fine woolen suit, polished black boots and black leather riding gloves. "Them Morgans in the stable ain't cheap, and they ain't for work."

"Yes, well a man of my station is entitled to some fineries," muttered Jennings. "And money borrowed from banks must eventually be paid back. That, regrettably, is the situation I find myself in. The bank must be paid. And, for reasons that are not completely within my control, I don't presently have the liquid capital to repay my most . . . . pressing obligations."

"Why don't you sell them Morgans? You take the $1500 I brought, give me my family, and use that money to pay the bank."

Jennings chuckled. "As I said, you have a skilled laborer's understanding of finance. But my operation is considerably more sophisticated than a day laborer's income and expenses. I have already sold several of my less profitable inventory, and I am considering selling one or two of my more valuable inventory, including young Jericho. But I cannot sell my most valuable and prized assets, including Harriet and your children. They are worth more to me as inventory and collateral."

Dangerfield's gut tightened. "What do you mean "inventory" and collateral" said Dangerfield angrily.

"You see," Jennings continued, "I owe one bank a large sum of money. I intend to take out a loan from another bank to pay the first bank. Harriet and your children are the collateral for that loan. If I sell them, I have no collateral. This way, I can keep Harriet and your children, pay back the first bank, and continue to run my business. I trust you can see this is the best arrangement for all concerned. Harriet and your children remain with me. Your family remains intact, and under my roof. I get the money I need to pay off my debts. I keep my collateral. And you will be free to visit your family whenever you wish, just as we had agreed previously."

"What about Jericho? You promised you would not sell him."

"Jericho is not your child, and I have never fully understood your attachment to him, although I do appreciate the tutelage and guidance you have given him," scoffed Jennings. "Thanks to your instruction, he is a more disciplined servant and field hand than he ever would have been. As a result, he is worth more on the open market than he otherwise would be. I would only consider selling him because of your influence."

Dangerfield pulled out the pouch. "Take the money, Marse. Count it again. Keep your word."

Lewis Jennings counted the money again, sighed and returned the pouch to Dangerfield.

"I have always kept my word. Regrettably, I cannot sell your wife and baby to you at the present time. If I did, I would have to sell the rest of your children to someone else, and neither of us wants that. Rest assured, your family will remain intact – they are worth more to me as human capital and collateral than they would be on the open market. I can get more from a bank in one loan than I would in a week's worth of auctions and inspections. I will preserve your family, you have my word on that. Now, if you would like to see the rest of your family, I am sure we can make a business arrangement for your services. . . ."

Dangerfield pulled out his Colt, and drove the barrel into Jennings pale forehead. Dangerfield's hat quivered as he held the gun.

"I want my family. All of them."

Beads of sweat dribbled down Jennings' forehead into the collar of his shirt.

"I was afraid you would not understand the complicated economics at work," Jennings whispered. "But now you have lost your mind. I could have you hanged by sundown . . . ."

Dangerfield thumbed back the hammer on the Colt. "You won't see sundown, Marse. Make your peace now." He wrapped his finger around the trigger.

"Wait, please," whispered Jennings. "Think of your family. If you kill me, what then? You can't simply kill me and take seven people with you. My wife, my baby, and my mother are in the house. You won't kill them. You aren't that kind of man. And it won't be long before my absence is noted. They will find all of you on the road by tomorrow at the latest. You will be hanged, and your family will be scattered to the winds. If you kill me, you have doomed your family. I am giving you my word that I won't sell them. I can't sell them now. I will keep them here, under my roof. I just can't sell them to you."

"Your word don't seem to be worth much."

"Think of your family. You pull that trigger, and you will be hanged. And you will never see your family again. I give you my word I won't sell them."

Dangerfield rammed the barrel into Jennings' forehead, pushing him back until Jennings was backed into the stable wall. He held the gun while Jennings gurgled.

"Say your prayers, Lewis Jennings."

Jennings closed his eyes, and began muttering softly to himself. "Heavenly Father, please forgive my sins," he said weakly.

Dangerfield pulled back the gun, and slowly released the hammer, bringing it slowly forward. Jennings leaned forward, coughed and spat on the ground. He rubbed his hand over the round red dent in his forehead.

"You go and tell my children I need to see them," said Dangerfield. "Bring them right here, all of them. Bring Jericho too. I am going back to the house to get Harriet and my baby. You bring them all back here, right where we are standing. You ain't back by the time I get back, I hunt you down and shoot you like a sick dog."

Jennings stumbled off toward the slave cabins.

Dangerfield went back to the house. Harriet was inside washing pots.

"Tell Lilly Marse Jennings needs to see you right away," said Dangerfield. "Bring the baby, and follow me."

Dangerfield took his wife and baby back to the stable. When he arrived, Junior, Gabriel, Lucy, Agnes and Jericho were there. Jennings stood next to them.

"Thank you, Lewis," said Dangerfield. "If you would give me a few minutes to speak privately with my family." Jennings glowered and began to speak, but Dangerfield patted his breast pocket with the Colt inside. Jennings walked slowly back toward his house. Dangerfield waited until Jennings was gone.

"I came here today to buy all of you and bring us all to Ohio," said Dangerfield. "But Lewis won't sell you to me, at least not today." The baby began mewling, and Harriet began sobbing.

"And I can't stay in Virginia, or else they can catch me and sell me back into a slave. I won't let that happen."

"What happens to us," said Junior.

"All of you will continue to live here, with Marse Jennings. He won't sell any of you, including Jericho. All of you will live here until I get back."

"What are you going to do?" said Gabriel.

"I can't stay here, and Jennings won't sell you, least not now. I aim to go back to Ohio until I can figure out how to get all of you back with me. I know a man who will help me. In the meantime, all of you will be safe here. Lewis promised me he would not sell any of you. And he intends to keep this promise."

Dangerfield pulled out the pouch with the bank notes and the penny knife.

"I have something for all of you. Junior, I want you to keep this knife. My daddy gave it to me, and now it is yours. Don't lose it, and don't let anybody borrow it unless you trust them. You are the man of the family now, until I get back."

He pulled out the bank notes. "I am giving each of you $200 in bank notes. Your mother will keep them in a safe place in the house or the cabin."

"When you come back to get us Daddy," said Lucy.

"Soon, Lucy. You listen to Mama, and stay out of trouble. Junior, Gabriel, you take care of this family. Lucy, you look after Agnes and the baby. Jericho, you take care of your mother like I took care of you."

Harriet cradled the baby, who was tugging at her hair. "Who is this man who will help you? Is he going to buy us? Can he make Jennings sell us?"

"Man I know says he will help me free all of you and many others. Don't care about the others, just you."

"When will you be back next?"

"Don't know. Before winter, one way or the other. I aim to have us all back in Ohio before snow falls."

He patted the baby and kissed Harriet on the cheek. He drew her closer to him, but she pulled away from his touch.

"You ain't never coming back," she said."

"Yes I am. Said I would, and I did. I kept my word to you and this family."

"Promises of men don't seem to be worth much. Men make a lot of promises they don't intend to keep."

"Maybe Lewis Jennings and men like him. Not me. I told you I would come back, and I did."

"Who is this man says he wants to help you? Why should you believe him any more than you believed Marse Lewis?"

"Man's name is Brown. And he has already helped me. Gave me a nice rifle, and people he knows in Bridgeport gave me money to help buy all of you. Didn't ask for nothing in return. I kept the rifle and the money. So if he does that for me, I trust him to help me again."

"You trusted Marse Lewis, and we ain't no closer to Ohio than we were before."

"I know. I don't know what else to do. Henry can't buy all of you. I asked him, and he don't have the money. And can't nobody order Marse to sell if he don't want to sell."

He held Harriet and the baby close. Harriet pushed him away, before relenting and drawing him in.

"You ain't never coming back," whispered Harriet. "You can come and go as you please. We can't just leave, like you can."

Harriet pulled the baby closer to her body. "You saw freedom, and now you ain't never coming back."

"Yes I am," snapped Dangerfield. "I will see you before the snow falls."

He kissed her on the cheek. "Keep these bank notes in a safe place in the house, or the cabin. Won't do you much good here, but if you and the children . . . If I don't . . . it don't matter, just keep them in a safe place. We will need them when I come back.

I need to talk to Lewis before I leave. See you before the snow falls. Write me and tell me how the children are doing."

Harriet did not respond. She took the baby and walked back to the house without saying a word.

Dangerfield found Lewis Jennings and the other white man talking in low tones in front of the house. Both men stopped speaking when Dangerfield approached.

"Lewis, I need a word with you again."

Lewis stepped forward hesitantly.

"I can't make you sell my family to me, even though you said you would," growled Dangerfield softly. "And I can't take them all with me as long as you and your family are alive. And I won't kill your wife, your mother or your children. I would kill you in a heartbeat, but I won't kill your wife, mother or your children. You ain't nothing but a lying snake. I would shoot you like a dog if I thought it would help my family, but it won't. I can't make you sell them, but I can make you keep them here. You keep my family right here, under this roof. Don't sell any of them, including Jericho."

Dangerfield glanced at the other white man, who was nervously looking into the kitchen window.

"Henry is still alive, and so is my brother Gabriel, and my sister Anna Mae. They all know where you live. If I get word that you sell any of my family, I will find you, kill you, cut off your head, and wait for the hangman. Don't care how long it takes. Don't care where you run off to. Don't care how many men you bring in to protect your cowardly hide. Don't care if you beg for mercy, or cry like a sick baby. Don't care how far you run. If I find you sold one of my children or Jericho, you are a dead man. I will kill you and feed you to the hogs. Do you understand, Lewis Jennings?"

"Yes, of course," said Jennings weakly. "Please understand, this is simply an unfortunate turn of economic events that makes it impossible for me to presently honor my word, but I fully intend . . . ."

"I will shoot you like a dog, Lewis. Do you understand?" Dangerfield retrieved the Colt from his pocket and pressed the barrel through his coat against Lewis' ribs. He pulled Lewis by the arm toward him so the Colt was firmly against Lewis' ribcage.

""Do you understand, Lewis?"

"Yes, of course."

"Good. Go back to your business. Tell that man that Jericho ain't for sale, and none of my other family is for sale. Do your business with the bank. Next time I see you, I leave with my family."

Dangerfield released his grip, and returned to the house. Lilly gave him some hard bread, salted pork, biscuits, and water for his canteen. Harriet would not look at him. He went to the barn and filled his saddlebags with oats and alfalfa. Then he mounted his horse, and began the long journey home.

CHAPTER 47

Dangerfield knew he could not push Solomon hard on the return trip. He would ride as far as his old house, rest there for a few days, and try to get back to Ohio by early September. He would rest at home, then meet up with Brown in Ohio. Maybe he could convince Gabriel to join him.

He arrived at his old house in Culpeper just before dusk. As he approached, he smelled woodsmoke. Wisps of smoke curled up from behind the stable. He pulled the Sharps from the scabbard, and made certain it was loaded. As he brought Solomon to a halt, a man approached from the behind the stable, holding a pistol in his hand.

"State your business," shouted the man. "Who are you?"

Dangerfield did not respond, but dismounted. He put the loaded Sharps back into the scabbard, and patted his breast pocket.

"I said who are you," said the man. "Speak, or I shoot."

"This is my home," said Dangerfield. "My family lived here for many years. Who are you?"

Dangerfield drew closer and his gut turned to water when he saw the man. He was tall, with a faint jagged scar on the left side of his face that ran from just under his left eye to the corner of his mouth. It was one of the slave catchers he had encountered when he was riding with Featherston on the way to Ohio, and before that, countless times when he lived in Virginia.

"Reckon we have met more than once," said the man, putting his pistol in his vest pocket. "You are Henry Newby's son. This your house?"

"Used to be," said Dangerfield. We lived here for years. Henry packed up the whole family and moved us to Ohio last fall."

"I remember now," said the man. Me and my partner saw you on the road in Ohio last year. You were with Amos Featherston. Is he with you now?"

"No, I ain't with Featherston now, just me," said Dangerfield. "And last time I saw you, you were with a partner. That young blond feller, long hair, wearing a cavalry cap. He with you?"

The man's eyes narrowed. "No. I haven't seen him in almost a year. He just up and disappeared. Don't know what happened to him. You ain't seen him on the road, have you?"

"No, I ain't seen him. Last time I seen him was when the two of you jumped Featherston's wagon. Featherston almost shot him."

The man chuckled. "Well, Ellis was young, and a bit too eager sometimes. Always wanted to whip the runaways. I always told him, our job is to catch 'em and return 'em. Let the masters whip 'em if they choose. If we bring 'em back whipped and bloody, masters get mad at us. Catch 'em and return 'em, nothing else."

"Mighty kind of you," said Dangerfield. "What brings you here? This is still Henry Newby's house."

The man looked toward the ruined house. "Don't look like nobody's house anymore. And you said Henry moved all of you back to Ohio. Reckon this house is there for any tired soul who needs a place to bed down for the night."

The man eyed Dangerfield. "Mighty dangerous for a free colored to come back to Virginia. You stay too long, you won't be free any more. Plenty of slave catchers willing to team up two or three and capture a strong fella like you and sell him on the market. Best not to stay in Virginia too long. Just a friendly word of advice from someone who has known Henry Newby for many years."

"Obliged." Dangerfield looked up and his heart dropped to his boots when he saw someone walk past one of the broken upstairs windows. The person stopped, peered out the window, then quickly disappeared.

"So you ain't found your partner yet," said Dangerfield. You got a new partner?"

"No," said the man. "Lately, I been working alone. Working alone now."

The two men eyed each other silently.

"I knew Henry Newby when I first started in this business," said the man. "Always promised I would leave his children alone. Now, I am getting too old to catch slaves any more. I am almost 60. Been doing this for a long time, and it don't get easier. It's a young man's business. Thinking about getting out."

Dangerfield said nothing.

"Like I said, Virginia is no place for a free colored," said the man. "And I know plenty of bad people won't think twice about trying to sell you back into slavery. Won't care if you got papers. So as a favor to Henry, why don't you show me your freeman's papers. Let me review them. Just to make certain you are safe until you leave Virginia."

The man smiled, creasing the faint jagged scar under his left eye.

"Much obliged," said Dangerfield. He reached into his left breast pocket, and as he did so, he saw the man's hand move slowly toward his vest. Dangerfield pulled out the Colt and pressed the muzzle against the man's head. He fired once, sending a spray of blood and brains out the back of the man's skull. The man stumbled backwards, and Dangerfield shot him in the chest as he fell backward.

Dangerfield ran toward his horse and the Sharps. When he reached Solomon, a bullet flew past his ear, hissing and popping the air as it passed. He pulled the Sharps from its scabbard, and looked toward the house. A figure was on the second floor, shooting toward him. Another bullet hit the ground in front of Solomon, and the big bay reared up, scraping air with his hooves. Dangerfield knelt and fired at the window. The person in the window fell backwards.

Dangerfield flipped open the breech, reloaded the Sharps and waited. A man stumbled out of the broken front door, clutching his shoulder. Dangerfield raised the Sharps and fired, hitting the man in the forehead. His head exploded, bursting apart in a florid display. He fell backward and slumped against the house, blood pulsing from the remnants of his skull and flowing down the door frame.

Dangerfield shoved the Sharps into the scabbard, and mounted Solomon. He checked his breast pocket for the Colt, and rode low and hard until he was out of sight of the house. He rode as hard as he could until Solomon began to falter, blowing and snorting as he slowed to a canter and then a walk. Dangerfield dismounted, and turned toward the road. There was no one following him.

He sat Solomon, and fed him a half ration of oats. Solomon's breathing calmed. Dangerfield mounted, then rode west until nightfall.

CHAPTER 48

September 1, 1859

Dangerfield arrived in Bridgeport twelve days after shooting the slave catcher in the yard of his family's Virginia home. He had ridden Solomon harder than he should have, starting before dawn and riding until nightfall. He had taken little-used trails and spur roads, and had seen few other riders during his escape from Virginia. But it had not rained, and he was able to make better time leaving Virginia than he had on his trip to Brentsville.

He awoke at dawn, having spent the night in an abandoned barn just outside Wheeling, Virginia. He crossed Wheeling Island from the east, crossed the Belmont Covered Bridge over the Ohio River, and rode back into Bridgeport. The sky was ashen, and the boiling clouds that had held two weeks of rain seemed about to explode. Bullet-sized droplets began falling as soon as he crossed into Ohio.

He reached Featherston's shop at 8 am. Featherston was moving framing timbers out of the rain and into the shop when Dangerfield approached.

"Well," said Featherston, pulling his hat low against the rain." "I see you made it back from Virginia." Featherston looked behind Solomon. "Don't see anyone else with you. Did you bring your family home?"

"No," said Dangerfield as he dismounted. "Lewis Jennings refused to sell them, and I had to leave Virginia without them."

"I am sorry, but I can't say I am surprised," said Featherston. The word of a slaver is worth as much as a dust mote. They have been thoroughly corrupted by the institution . . . ."

Featherston paused. "I am sorry. You don't need to hear me preach. Is there anything I can do to help?"

"Brown said he was willing to help me. I wasn't willing to join him last year. Now I am. Please take me to see Brown. I am ready to do whatever Brown needs me to do."

Featherston pulled his hat lower against the rain, which now descended from the heavens in sheets.

"I see," said Featherston. "Perhaps we should go inside to continue this discussion. We can move the rest of the wood inside later. Please come in." Featherston pushed one of the timbers against the wall of the shop, and quickly went inside.

Dangerfield dismounted and hobbled Solomon behind the shop. He went inside and shook rain from his hat and coat.

"Your arrival is fortuitous," said Featherston as he walked past a wagon with a broken axle and row upon row of stacked and finished wood. "There is someone here who may also join us . . . if you are serious about joining Brown in his cause."

Featherston escorted Dangerfield past the stacks of finished wood and carpentry tools and into the carriage house attached to the shop. He quickly opened the heavy double doors, escorted Dangerfield inside, and closed and locked the doors behind him. He pushed against the door to make certain it was locked.

"Brother Gabriel, there is someone here you will be pleased to see," said Featherston.

Dangerfield saw his brother Gabriel loading a box into a wagon. Gabriel stood and hugged his brother, clapping him on the back.

"You made it back," said Gabriel excitedly. "I told Henry and Elsey you would return. I had no doubt in my mind." Gabriel looked behind him. Where is Harriet and the children? Did you bring them back to the house already? Elsey found some dolls for the girls, and Henry made some toys for the baby. I'd wager they are already tearing the house up, but Elsey won't mind. And I suppose you and I can share a room if Harriet and the baby need my room, long as you don't snore like you always do . . . ."

"Harriet and the rest of my family are safe in Virginia," said Dangerfield. Lewis Jennings would not sell them, at least not yet. And I could not stay in Virginia, so I came back without them."

Gabriel sucked in his breath.

"Where are they now," said Gabriel softly.

"In Brentsville. All of them are safe. And the baby is fat and healthy. Harriet takes good care of them all."

"When do you aim to bring them back here?"

"Jennings says he won't sell them, at least not yet."

"Did you bring the money with you?"

"Every penny. Jennings would not take the money. Said he needed my family as collateral for some money he owes the bank. So I had to leave without them."

Gabriel shook his head. "Damn that man," he muttered softly.

"Brother Dangerfield, I am sorry for your troubles," said Featherston. "And I will pray for you and your family, as I have every day since we last parted. Perhaps now is a good time for Brother Gabriel to explain his presence here."

Featherston bowed his head and gestured toward Gabriel.

"After you left, I got to thinking," said Gabriel. "You going off to meet Brown, then going to Virginia to get your family, while I stayed behind. I know you wanted me to go with you when you went to Oberling, but I . . . well, I wasn't ready. So after you left, Featherston told me he needed some help at his shop. I been helping him out with some things, carpentry and fixing wagons and such. And he told me more about this Brown and what he's trying to do. Got me thinking maybe I should have gone with you to meet Brown last year."

"Reckon you had your reasons for staying, just like I had my reasons for leaving," said Dangerfield.

"I know, and I don't regret staying," said Gabriel. "But Featherston got me thinking, about something bigger than me. Henry may be old, but he can still take care of himself. And Elsey is tough as a old mule. And after I saw you leave without me . . . ."

Dangerfield shot his gaze at Featherston, who had opened a box next to the wagon, and was inspecting its contents.

"What do you aim to do, Gabriel," said Dangerfield.

"Well, if you aim to join up with Brown, I aim to go with you," said Gabriel. "Two of us go together, and we join up with Brown. You need Brown's help, and I aim to help any way I can."

"Do Henry and Elsey know about you leaving," said Dangerfield.

"I told 'em if you didn't come back, I would go and find you. Elsey fussed, and Henry said it was a damn fool idea. Then Henry took me aside, and gave me this." Gabriel pulled out a small blue-barreled Colt revolver from his coat pocket. "Reckon Henry knows we can't stay home forever."

Gabriel smiled and put the Colt back in his pocket.

"What's in them boxes," said Dangerfield, jerking his thumb towards the box Featherston was inspecting.

"Ah, yes. This is familiar cargo for you," said Featherston, unwrapping a gleaming Sharps from a thick wool blanket. "Brother Brown has located another supply of Beecher's Bibles from a sympathetic friend in Kansas. He has asked me to deliver them to his current location as quickly as possible. Do you remember these?"

Featherston passed the Sharps to Dangerfield. Dangerfield admired its heft, and smoothly polished wooden stock. Gabriel reached out for the Sharps, but Dangerfield glared at him, and passed the Sharps back to Featherston.

"I still have mine," said Dangerfield. "It came in handy more than once during my trip to Virginia, and on the way home."

"As it will on this trip," said Featherston as he wrapped the Sharps in a blanket and returned it to the box. "As you know, our work is dangerous and hard. I appreciated your help. But since you were not available, I took the liberty of discussing our mission in greater detail with Brother Gabriel. And I am pleased to say that Gabriel is eager to join me. It would be splendid if you wish to go as well."

"Is this true, Gabriel? You changed your mind?"

"Yes," said Gabriel. "I am ready to leave when you are."

Featherston was once again inspecting the box, and had turned his back toward Dangerfield.

"I see," said Dangerfield." "Gabriel, I need a word with you in private."

Dangerfield pulled his brother toward a corner of the carriage house. The rain pounded the roof, and water leaked from the roof onto Dangerfield's coat.

"What did Featherston say to change your mind?"

"Same thing he told you," said Gabriel. "Think about something bigger than yourself. Think of the families you could save. And today, when I saw you come back without your family, that was all the convincing I needed. We go join up with Brown, and we don't come back without Harriet and your family. Featherston says it shouldn't take more than a few weeks."

Dangerfield sucked in air through his teeth.

"I appreciate you wanting to help me," said Dangerfield. "But I need you to stay home, with Henry and Elsey. Things have changed."

"I ain't letting you go by yourself. I wasn't ready last time, but I am ready now. We go together, and we get Harriet and your family. Be back in a few weeks' time, Thanksgiving at the latest."

"Listen to me, Gabriel," said Dangerfield as he grabbed his brother's overcoat and pulled him closer to him. "I need you to stay here. I told Lewis Jennings you and Henry would track him down if he sold my family. And I don't know if . . . how long it will take for Brown's plan to work. And right now, at least I know Harriet and the kids are safe at Jennings' place."

"You still trust Jennings after he backed out on his promise?"

"No, I don't trust him, not at all, but I put a gun to his head and told him I would kill him if he sold my family. Told him you and Henry would keep track of him, and if he sold my family, you would let me know. And if he sold my family, then I would move mountains to find him and kill him. I told him you would track him down. So I need you to stay close by, to keep track of my family."

Gabriel closed his eyes. "You put a gun to Jennings' head? What did he do?"

"Whimpered like a damn baby. I was close to killing him, but then I would never see my family again. I don't think Jennings is a God-fearing man, but I know he saw his maker down the barrel of my gun. Don't think he would risk selling them now."

Gabriel looked at Featherston, who had gently eased himself closer to their conversation while pretending to inspect the axle of his wagon.

"If I don't go with you to join Brown, what do you want me to do?"

"Write Harriet every week. Tell her to write back. If she does not write back at least twice a month, tell Henry to write Jennings. Tell Jennings that Henry wants to discuss buying my family, and needs to see them to make certain they are well.

You and Henry can go back to Virginia safely. If Jennings don't write back, you and Henry pay him a visit in Virginia. Slave catchers won't bother you if you go with Henry."

Gabriel pulled at a loose cloth on his coat. "Write Harriet every week," he muttered softly to himself. "I reckon I can do that. Make certain she writes back at least twice a month. Reckon I can do that, too. Might even pay Jennings a visit on my own, without Henry. Got my own papers, just like you." Gabriel patted his breast pocket.

"Don't do anything to get yourself caught," said Dangerfield. "Remember, them papers ain't no good in Virginia after one year. You'd best go with Henry. Don't go by yourself."

"Reckon I should pay Jennings a visit sooner rather than later," said Gabriel. "While these papers are still good."

"Wise man once told me a bullet can't read no papers," said Dangerfield. "Best heed that advice."

The two brothers laughed quietly at their private joke.

Featherston had now eased himself within arm's reach of Dangerfield and Gabriel. Gabriel coughed loudly, and Featherston quickly retreated back toward the wagon."

"There is something else," whispered Dangerfield. "If . . . if something happens . . . if . . . I don't come back from Brown's mission, I want you to promise me that you will get Harriet and my children. And if something happens to them before you get them, I want your solemn promise that you will find Lewis Jennings and kill him."

Gabriel looked into his brother's eyes.

"You think you might not come back?"

"I aim to come back, but . . . . Gabriel, just promise me that if something happens to me, you will get Harriet and my children. Jericho too. And if something happens to them, whatever happens to them, you find Lewis Jennings and you kill him."

Gabriel patted the breast pocket that held the Colt.

"After what you told me about Jennings, I was half a mind to kill him without you asking me."

"Promise me, Gabriel."

"You have my word," said Gabriel softly. "Speaking of letters, I almost forgot something. Harriet sent you a letter. Came to the house while you were gone. Henry asked me to hold on to it."

Gabriel reached into his breast pocket and handed the letter to Dangerfield.

"This must be the one she sent after I left," Dangerfield said. "Harriet said she sent me three letters, but I only got two. This must be the other one." He folded the letter and put it in his breast pocket, next to the other two. "I will read it later. Right now, reckon we'd better explain things to Featherston."

The two men walked toward Featherston, who was still feigning interest in the axle of his wagon.

"After discussing the situation with my brother, I have decided that I should stay here," said Gabriel. "My family needs me, and I must think of them first. I thank you for your kind offer."

"Yes, of course, Brother Gabriel. You must think of your family first."

Featherston turned toward Dangerfield. "And you, Brother Dangerfield? Do you still want to join Brother Brown's mission?"

"I want to leave as soon as you are ready," said Dangerfield." I have considered my options, and I want to help Brother Brown, so he can free my family. Gabriel is of better use here at home. His family needs him here."

"Very well," said Featherston. "We can leave as soon as the guns are packed, and the rain lets up."

As he spoke, the rain thrumming on the rooftop began to wane, then died. An eerie orange and red light blasted the windows of the carriage house.

Featherston pulled back the curtains and peered through the small windows of the carriage house. "Surely, this is a sign from God," he said softly. He closed the curtains and turned toward the wagon. "Let us finish loading the Bibles, and we shall depart."

"Are we going back to Oberlin," said Dangerfield.

"No, Brother Dangerfield," said Featherston solemnly. "We are going back into the stinking belly of the Serpent. We will meet Brother Brown near Harpers Ferry, Virginia. We will strike from within the Old Dominion, and we shall rid this country of the poison that is slavery."

The three men quickly loaded the guns into the false bottom of the wagon. When they finished, Gabriel wiped his brow and turned toward a window.

"What should I tell Henry and Elsey," said Gabriel.

"Tell them I will be home with my family by Thanksgiving," said Dangerfield.

"You don't think you should at least come home for a short spell, explain what you plan to do?" said Gabriel.

"No. I can't go home," said Dangerfield. "Truth is, Gabriel, I am ashamed that I could not bring my family home the way I intended. I tried to do things the way Henry told me I should do them. That way didn't work. I know Henry won't approve of me joining up with Brown, but Henry's ways don't work for a black man, not even a free black man, and not even Henry's son. And there ain't no point in troubling Elsey. I aim to bring my family home. Reckon this is the only way I can finish what I started."

Dangerfield looked toward the window and the strange red sun blasting the carriage house. "Besides, this ain't home for me. Not without Harriet and the kids. Henry's ways don't work, but mine will. This will be home soon enough."

Dangerfield hugged his brother while Featherston stood a polite distance away.

"Remember that promise you made me, Gabriel," said Dangerfield.

"I will," said Gabriel. "I will tell Henry and Elsey you will be home by Thanksgiving."

"And take care of old Solomon," said Dangerfield. "Bring him back home, and don't ride him real hard."

Gabriel laughed. "I always rode him better than you did."

At 10:01 am on September 1, 1859, Dangerfield and Featherston began riding east toward Harpers Ferry, Virginia.

⸺◄(●)►⸺

That evening, Dangerfield and Featherston made camp in a field 15 miles east of Wheeling, Virginia. There was no moon. Saucers of blue and orange light flashed across the sky, and the steady orange and red glow from the morning had returned. The horizon was a violent clash of swirling purple, blue and yellow. At 10 pm, the sky was so bright the men could read without a fire. Dangerfield retrieved Harriet's letters, and read the latest to himself:

BRENTVILLE, August 16, 1859

Dear Husband.

your kind letter came duly to hand and it gave me much pleasure to here from you and especely to hear you are better of your rhumatism and hope when I here from you again you may be entirely well. I want you to buy me as soon as possible for if you do not get me somebody else will the servents are very disagreeable thay do all thay can to set my mistress againt me

Dear Husband you not the trouble I see the last two years has ben like a trouble dream to me it is said Master is in want of monney if so I know not what time he may sell me an then all my bright hops of the futer are blasted for there has ben one bright hope to cheer me in all my troubles that is to be with you for if I thought I shoul never see you this earth would have no charms for me do all you Can for me witch I have no doubt you will I want to see you so much the Chrildren are all well the baby cannot walk yet all it can step around enny thing by holding on it is very much like Agnes

I mus bring my letter to Close as I have no newes to write you mus write soon and say when you think you Can Come.

Your affectionate Wife
HARRIET NEWBY.

Dangerfield put the letter in his breast pocket, next to the others. He looked out at the iridescent sky, while Featherston calmly read his Bible by the light of the nighttime sun.

"Ain't never seen the sky like this," said Dangerfield. "Wonder what all this means."

"It is a sign from God," said Featherston, speaking without looking up from his Bible. "It means that the Almighty will keep his hand on our shoulders, and our path toward Virginia will be graced by the cleansing light of God. No evil shall befall us. The hand of the Almighty rests firmly on our shoulders, and He shall guide us on our path. The end of slavery is upon us. Freedom is nigh."

Dangerfield pulled out all three of Harriet's letters and arranged them in order. He looked out at the blinding nighttime sky. "Reckon that's what it means," he said softly to himself as he began reading them again.

CHAPTER 49

Dangerfield and Featherston arrived in Harpers Ferry late in the afternoon on September 18, 1859. Featherston eased the wagon and its cargo down the cobblestone streets. Dangerfield sat next to him with a short-barreled shotgun at his feet, not visible from outside the wagon.

Residents eyed the pair warily as Featherston rode slowly through town. He tipped his hat with an exaggerated flourish to every woman they passed.

"Where do we meet Brown," said Dangerfield as the wagon passed two very well dressed white women carrying packages. The women eyed the pair nervously. One whispered to her companion as she looked at Dangerfield, and they both laughed to themselves as the wagon passed.

"Keep your voice down," hissed Featherston. "Word of Brother Brown's plans must not escape. From this point on, do not say Brown's name in public. You know nothing of John Brown, have never met him, and know nothing of his whereabouts. John Brown does not exist, as far as we are concerned. Only speak his name when we are in private, amongst those we know."

Featherston clicked his tongue and the horses quickened their pace as the wagon rattled through Harpers Ferry.

Dangerfield peered out as the wagon passed townspeople bustling about their affairs. An old man sat on a porch watching them pass. He spat a stream of tobacco on the porch without taking his eyes off the wagon as it climbed the hill.

"If anyone asks, you are in my employ," said Featherston. "We are carpenters on our way to see Isaac Smith, in Washington County, Maryland." Remember that name. And remember that for now, you are no longer a free man. You are a Negro in my employ. You work for me as a carpenter."

Dangerfield spat over the side of the wagon and nudged his toe against the shotgun.

"It will be far better if no one asks," said Featherston. They crossed the Baltimore and Ohio railroad bridge, and began climbing out of town, north toward the Maryland hills. Once safely across the bridge and out of town, Featherston exhaled deeply.

"We will meet at the Kennedy farmhouse, about five miles from Harpers Ferry, in Maryland," said Featherston. "Brother Brown has assembled a group of like-minded warriors to carry out our mission. The others are already there. Brown is waiting for us. We will train for a month or two, and then strike."

Featherston clicked his tongue and the horses slowed, but continued climbing.

"Have you used the rifle Brother Brown gave you? Perhaps done some target shooting?" said Featherston.

"Oh, I have used it," said Dangerfield. "It came in handy not too long ago," he said, remembering the thump against his shoulder and the slaver's head exploding with a single shot in the center of his forehead.

"Good. Our opportunities to shoot live ammunition will be very limited at the Kennedy farmhouse. We don't want to attract undue attention. We will train with the guns, but probably won't fire live balls. If you have already fired the gun, that will help us tremendously."

Dangerfield looked over his shoulder at Harpers Ferry as it receded into the distance.

Featherston slowed the horses as the hill became steeper.

"Have you ever used a pike to butcher a hog?" asked Featherston casually.

"No," said Dangerfield. "I use a sharp knife and slit its throat after shooting it once in the head. Don't know anyone who would use a pike to butcher a hog. Why? Does Brown need me to butcher hogs?"

"No, that would also attract too much attention," said Featherston. "Brother Brown has ample provisions at the farmhouse, enough to feed twenty men for two months. And we have one milk cow, and dozens of chickens. Brown's daughter and daughter-in-law are fine cooks."

"Then why did you ask about butchering hogs?"

"Brother Dangerfield, we have to plan for the possibility of hand combat with our enemies," said Featherston. "Brother Brown has provided us a bountiful supply of sharpened pikes which we will carry along with our rifles. If ammunition runs short, you must be prepared to run your enemy through with a pike. We will practice on stuffed pillows and a calfskin stuffed with old blankets."

Featherston nudged the horses forward as the terrain leveled out. "Only another few miles until we reach the farmhouse."

Dangerfield considered having to run a man through with a pike. "Not certain what you got me into, Featherston," said Dangerfield.

"I hope I have been abundantly clear about the dangers presented by this mission," said Featherston. "But the danger of doing nothing is far worse. Think of your efforts to free your family thus far," said Featherston. "And I assure you, every man in this mission is committed to the cause. Freeing your family will be one of the top priorities of this mission, from Brother Brown down to the youngest warriors."

Featherston clicked twice, and the horses quickened their pace.

"I trust you are not having doubts about this mission," said Featherston.

Dangerfield considered his options, and thought of his enslaved family trapped on the Jennings plantation. "No doubts at all," said Dangerfield as he surveyed the countryside.

Dangerfield patted his breast pocket and felt the reassuring heft of the Colt.

"Of course, if the plan goes as executed, we won't need to run anyone through with pikes. The slavers will be no match for the Sharps, and slaves from miles around will answer the call to freedom. The slaves will complete the task for us," said Featherston. "If all goes according to plan, you will be with your family in a little more than a month's time."

Dangerfield allowed himself to envision Harriet tending her garden in their new house in Bridgeport. She had the baby strapped to her back while she harvested a fall crop of greens and potatoes. Chickens scratched furiously in the dirt, while Junior and Gabriel repaired the white fence that surrounded the garden. Agnes and Lucy were in the kitchen washing vegetables. He saw Henry teaching Jericho how to plant corn, while Elsey supervised all. A milk cow lowed in the barn. He closed his eyes. A little more than a month's time.

Featherston clucked twice, and the wagon clattered to a stop. "Now, Brother Dangerfield, I must ask you to lower yourself out of view until we arrive at the farmhouse. I am told there are very inquisitive neighbors who will no doubt question why Negro men are arriving at Kennedy's farm. Best not to attract attention. Please lower yourself, and use this blanket."

Dangerfield crouched beneath the footboard while Featherston tossed a blanket over him. The wagon groaned and continued forward. Dangerfield could hear the axles grinding against the wheels as the wagon moved forward.

The wagon slowed, then rumbled to a stop. From beneath the blanket, Dangerfield heard voices speaking above him.

"Good evening, Amos. I hope your trip was uneventful. Is the cargo safe?"

"Good evening, Owen. We encountered no trouble on our journey, and spoke to no one while passing through Harpers Ferry. We saw a few curious townspeople, but we moved quickly, and spoke to no one."

"Splendid. Is there anyone with you?"

"Yes, a fine new recruit, a free colored man. Let's move the wagon in the barn, and we can make our acquaintances then."

"Excellent. Our second Negro warrior. Commander Brown will be pleased."

Featherston clucked once, and the wagon creaked forward. From his hiding place in the wagon, Dangerfield heard a heavy metal latch lift, then wooden doors being pulled open. The wagon lurched forward, stopped, and the wooden doors closed, followed by the latch slamming shut. One of the horses nickered, and shook its head, rattling the harness.

"Brother Dangerfield, you may come out now," said Featherston.

Dangerfield eased himself up, and saw a tall dark man with a round face, bushy eyebrows, an impenetrable, luxuriant beard, and shiny brown hair pressed close to his head. The man approached eagerly and extended his hand.

"Welcome. I am Owen Brown, Commander Brown's son."

"Good day, Marse. I am Dangerfield Newby, son of Henry Newby of Culpeper, Virginia." Dangerfield extended his hand, and Owen Brown grabbed it eagerly and shook vigorously.

"The first rule you must know is that no one on this mission is 'Marse,'" said Owen. "All men are equal, and none is above another, except by way of rank within the militia. Commander Brown has first rank, and there are several captains and lieutenants beneath him. But none are superior simply by virtue of race."

"Obliged for the explanation," said Dangerfield.

"I must also apologize for having to conceal your presence as you arrived," said Owen. "We have very inquisitive neighbors, and the constant arrival of wagons and equipment has aroused their curiosity. Mrs. Huffmaster has come by three times this week, poking her head in the kitchen and asking Annie if she can have fresh milk. Either she has birthed a calf, or she is fishing for information about the new arrivals."

Owen and Featherston laughed quietly.

"The only other rule you need to know now is that we address each other by last name, except when in militia training," said Owen. "Then, it is 'Commander Brown,' 'First Lieutenant Kagi,' 'Lieutenant Stevens,' 'Captain Brown,' etc. Your rank will be determined after you meet with Commander Brown, and he determines your role."

"Obliged again," said Dangerfield.

"Yes of course," said Owen. "House rules will be explained once you are inside. Now, let's get you inside and fed. Annie and Martha have made a marvelous beef stew, and fresh bread."

"I will join you as soon as I remove the tack from the horses," said Featherston, as he loosened the harness and removed the bit from the lead horse's mouth. "Don't wait for me."

Owen and Dangerfield exited the barn through the back door, and quickly entered the house.

⟫•⟪

Every window was covered with heavy curtains. Although still early in the evening on a cloudless day, virtually no sunlight penetrated the kitchen.

Dozens of candles burned on tables and in the kitchen while two young women hurried about the room, serving the evening meal. The cramped house smelled of beef stew and oven-hot bread, of sweat and unwashed men, of damp wool and leather, of woodsmoke and tobacco.

There were a dozen men around a long wooden table, ravenously consuming the meal. The only sound was the clank of spoons against bowls, and knives scraping butter against bread. While the men ate, a young woman in a bonnet refilled their bowls, and delivered more bread. The men ate by candlelight.

"Gentlemen, we have a new arrival," announced Owen. "Please welcome Brother Dangerfield Newby to our ranks."

Each man stood and bowed. Dangerfield removed his hat. The promise of beef stew and hot bread felt like a warm blanket on a frigid night.

"There is an open spot between Brothers Stevens and Green," said Owen. "Gentlemen, please make room."

Dangerfield squeezed himself between a tall, thickset white man with immense shoulders and curly black hair, and a stout black man with piercing gray eyes and a bird's nest of thin, wispy hair that grew straight up from his skull. The white man introduced himself as Aaron Stevens, and the black man introduced himself as Shields Green. "Shields is my given name, but I call myself 'Emperor,'" said Green. "Direct kin of African royalty," said Green proudly.

"Pleasure to meet both of you," said Dangerfield.

"Annie, please get Brother Newby some food," said Owen. "Brother Newby, meet Annie Brown, Commander Brown's daughter, and my half-sister." The young woman curtsied, and returned with a bowl of steaming beef stew, and a plate of soft hot bread. Dangerfield remembered that he had not eaten since that morning, and tucked in quickly.

"Commander Brown is upstairs, and will join us shortly," said Owen. "We will make our introductions then, and have the evening prayer before we all go to bed. After you eat, I will show you to your quarters."

"Obliged again," said Dangerfield. He looked down and his bowl and plate were both empty, although he did not remember finishing his meal. Annie took plate and bowl from him and returned moments later with refills.

He quickly finished his seconds and upon finishing the last bit of bread, Annie instantly removed his bowl and plate and refilled both. He was about to start in on his third bowl of stew when Stevens clapped him on the shoulder. "Commander Brown is descending from his headquarters," said Stevens. "He will want to meet you."

The men stood at the table, while Annie and Martha adjusted their bonnets. The stairs creaked as Brown descended. Martha lit another candle.

"Good evening, all, and please finish your supper. I was reviewing maps and preparing for tomorrow's exercises, but Annie's beef stew and Martha's bread proved to be too great a distraction. I thought it best to join you all, if there is room."

Brown entered the crowded kitchen and the men made way. Dangerfield did not recognize him at first. The long, flowing white beard was gone, and only an inch or so of closely cropped, milk-white hair covered his face. His hair was shorn almost to the scalp around his ears, while a thick salt-and-pepper bristle adorned the top of his head. He twitched as he walked, and his catbird-gray eyes flickered about the room, toward the drawn curtains, to the door, to the side of the kitchen, and then back to the men.

"Yes, of course there is room," said Owen. "Father, we have a new recruit who has joined us, a colored man out of Virginia. Brother Dangerfield Newby has come to join us."

Dangerfield stood and extended his hand. Brown's iron grip numbed his fingers.

"Welcome, Brother Newby. We met last October, at Oberlin College in Ohio. You came up with Featherston. As I recall, you were reluctant to join us then. We welcome you now."

"Yes, well I aim to free my family. I tried to buy them, but the man who owns them would not sell them."

"Yes, a Lewis Jennings owns your family, if I recall," said Brown. "You have two boys, Dangerfield Junior and Gabriel. Two girls, Lucy and Agnes. You also have a baby boy, John, who must be almost a year old now. And your wife is . . . Harriet, correct? And I think you told me you were raising Harriet's son, a young man named Jericho. Not your child, but you raised him like he was yours. I admire a man who will sacrifice for the children of others. Noble indeed."

"Reckon you know my whole family," said Dangerfield.

"Yes, well you were a notable man when we met last October," said Brown. "I had prayed that our paths would cross. Did you offer to buy your family? What did this Jennings say?"

"Said he could not sell them. Said they was collateral for money he owed the bank. Said they was worth more to him as collateral than I could pay him."

Brown closed his eyes and bowed his head, and his whole body convulsed. The other men murmured. "Damn the border ruffians and all those who support them," yelled Stevens.

"The evil these slavers practice every day is the reason we are here," said Brown as his face reddened. "And here, we prepare for the battle that will kill the Serpent and bring freedom to all," said Brown. The men roared.

"Gentlemen, let us briefly introduce ourselves to Brother Newby," said Brown. "Then we shall finish eating, say the evening prayer, and prepare for bed.

The men stated their name, place of birth, and reason for joining the cause.

Then it was Stevens' turn.

"I am Aaron Stevens, born in Connecticut, fought in the Massachusetts Volunteer Regiment, and served in the Mexican War. I joined this cause because you will always find me on the side of human freedom. And there is only one just cause in this great battle."

The men cheered, and pounded the table.

Next was Shields Green. "I was a slave in South Carolina, and after my wife died, I ran away in 1856," said Green. "I am direct kin of African kings, so I call myself Emperor. I left my son in South Carolina, 'cause he was little, and I couldn't care for him proper as a runaway. Went to Canada for a spell, then Rochester, New York. That's first time I met Mr. Frederick Douglass. First time I heard him speak, I knew I had to fight. And I know Mr. Douglass ain't real keen on us taking up arms against folks. He tried to talk me out of coming here. But I don't see no other way. As I told Mr. Douglass at that quarry up in Chambersburg, if it's 'tween doing nothing and joining up with John Brown, I believe I will go with the old man every time," he said, pointing to John Brown. "Might be a perfect steel trap like Mr. Frederick Douglass say, but I reckon the only way I ever see my son again."

The men clapped and cheered, pounding the table and sending plates and bowls flying. "To War!" they shouted. "Let the battle begin!" The uproar continued until Brown stepped forth, hands raised.

"Gentlemen, your resolve is just, but we are not as isolated as we would like. Please keep your voices down, unless you want nosy Mrs. Huffmaster and her ragged barefoot children to pay another visit. We cannot allow ourselves to be discovered. Now, let us pray."

Brown lowered his head and began to speak.

"Our Father, we ask for courage as we carry out your wishes to eliminate the scourge of slavery, and bring freedom to all of your children. We ask for your guidance and strength as we seek to destroy the Serpent, and cleanse this country of the venom that has spread from the Old Dominion to the bloody fields of Kansas and Missouri. We go forth secure in the faith that only fire and the blood of sinners will purify our souls and rid us of the evil of slavery. There can be no freedom without blood."

"Amen" rose softly from the room.

"And finally, Heavenly Father," said Brown, his voice trembling, "we ask that you lift up Brother Dangerfield, and provide him with courage as he seeks to free his wife, his children, his baby, and countless other wives, children and babies from shackles and chains. Let his cause be our cause. Let his pain be our pain. And let his quest for his family's freedom be our guiding light as we vanquish the darkness. Amen. Men, let us finish eating."

"Amen" rose louder from the room, and the men turned when they heard weeping.

Dangerfield sat at the table in a room full of white men and one black man, all committed to the freedom of his family. He looked at Annie and Martha, Brown's daughter and daughter-in-law, committed to a cause that was not their own. He began sobbing, overcome with a feeling he could neither name nor control. He wept into his napkin, until Brown walked up to him and put a hand on his shoulder.

"Your family's freedom is near. Finish eating, and Owen will show you to your quarters."

Annie brought her father a bowl of stew and a plate of bread. Brown sat next to Stevens and began to discuss the best way to bring another cow and some hogs to the farm without raising suspicion.

Owen touched Dangerfield on the shoulder.

"You have had a long journey. Your quarters are upstairs. We start tomorrow."

Dangerfield finished his third helping of beef stew and bread. Owen showed him to a small bed made out of cotton sacks and stuffed with straw. Dangerfield threw off his boots and collapsed onto the bed, asleep almost instantly.

CHAPTER 50

OCTOBER 1, 1859
KENNEDY FARMHOUSE, WASHINGTON COUNTY, MARYLAND

The men lay in their beds upstairs, windows closed, shades drawn. October brought mercifully cooler air, but the house was closed up from dawn until late in the evening, and only Annie and Martha and Brown and occasionally Owen were free to come and go as they pleased. Neither Green nor Newby were allowed out during the day for fear of alarming the new neighbor. Annie and Martha were now purposefully visible during the day, hanging laundry, chasing chickens, milking the cow, and tending the garden behind the house. About seventy yards distant from the garden was a tangled and unkempt plot of scrub brush, rented since August by the Huffmaster clan.

During the day, Annie made certain the men remained upstairs, checking the curtains and making certain the men were quiet. If they were good, Annie would open the windows to allow a breeze, but any loud conversation or laughter would bring Annie upstairs immediately, to close the windows and chastise the men.

"Gentlemen, now you know we are quite isolated here, except for one neighbor, Mrs. Huffmaster, who rents near the garden," Annie said as she peered out the window. "She knows several hired men are here, but she knows not how many. A large number of white men will arouse some suspicion, but any colored men in any number will frighten her dearly. If she alerts the townspeople, Father's plan will be compromised. Please be quiet until night, when we can move about under the cover of darkness."

Annie opened the windows slightly, allowing a welcome breeze to cool the room. "Please leave the curtains closed, and do remember to be quiet. I will bring your food upstairs shortly."

Annie again peered out the window toward the garden, then closed the curtains and went downstairs to bring the men their food.

Dangerfield lay in his straw bed, reading Harriet's letters in order, over and over again. Stevens sat in a small chair, reading maps. Green lay in his bed looking at the ceiling, tapping his foot against the bed. The other men cleaned their rifles or sharpened their pikes.

"I can't wait for freedom," said Green. "Can't wait for the battle, so's I can find my son back in South Carolina. Reckon he'd be almost 13 now. Almost a man. Can't wait to see him."

"The battle will begin when the time is right," said Stevens. "Brother Kagi is in Chambersburg, ordering in more supplies and gathering information. Commander Brown and I are studying the maps, preparing the route of attack on the armory. We have every step planned. Keep preparing, keep your weapons primed and oiled, and your pikes sharpened. When the hour comes, we will strike like a serpent, without warning."

"This serpent 'bout ready to strike now," said Green. "Can't wait. Don't like sitting around. I am a man of action, not sitting around. I am direct kin of African royalty, kings and warriors every single one. That's why they call me 'Emperor.'"

"I have heard no one call you 'Emperor' except you," said Stevens, laughing softly. "Although the warrior will certainly come in handy soon. Best to keep practicing with those pikes." The rest of the men laughed heartily. Green sneered, then allowed a smile to break his face. "Ain't fitting for royalty to be sitting up here with commoners," said Green. "The Emperor don't eat with his subjects." The rest of the men laughed louder.

A thunderous crash from the kitchen below interrupted the good-natured banter.

Green sprung from his bed and bounded down the narrow stairs, taking them two at a time.

"Green, wait, don't go downstairs unless Annie says it is clear," yelled Stevens.

Green was downstairs by the time Stevens had finished talking.

"Miss Annie, are you alright," yelled Green from the kitchen. Dangerfield descended the stairs and stopped halfway down when he saw the scene in the kitchen.

Plates, cups and bowls were scattered about the kitchen. Coffee ran across the floor, and dripped between the cracks in the floorboards. A pitcher of milk lay on its side. Annie crouched, putting bread back onto a large platter.

"Yes, Brother Green, I am fine," said Annie. "I was simply carrying too much, and dropped your food. I am so sorry, men. Let me clean this up, and I will bring your food shortly."

"Let me help you, Miss Annie," said Green as he picked up pieces of bread and put bowls and forks back on the platter. Annie looked up and leveled her gaze at Green.

"Brother Green, I thought I told you to stay upstairs," said Annie in a low whisper. "The kitchen windows are open during the day, and only Martha and I are to be seen from morning until evening. If anyone sees you or any colored man . . . ."

There was a loud rap at the front door. Annie whirled. From his position half-way down the stairs, Dangerfield could see a short fat white woman with matted dark hair peering into the kitchen through the open front window. Her dress was torn and filthy. Dangerfield slowly backed up the stairs and out of sight.

"Brother Green, please go upstairs now," growled Annie. Green muttered something under his breath about "royalty," and a "caged rat," and skulked back upstairs. Dangerfield, Green, and the rest of the men stayed at the top of the stairs, out of sight of the kitchen, but well within earshot of the front door.

"Good morning, Mrs. Huffmaster," said Annie. "What can I do for you this morning?"

"Well, Miss Annie, I don't mean no harm, and don't pry into no one's business," said a raspy woman's voice from outside. "I come over to see if you could spare some milk and a few eggs for a poor widow and her hungry children."

"Yes, of course, Mrs. Huffmaster. This is the fourth time this week you have paid us a visit. I trust you and your family are well."

"Well, we ain't as rich as you all. You know my husband was real sick, and then he up and died. Something with his lungs, but his drinkin' didn't help neither. With him gone, it's all I can do to pay rent on this land behind your place. Ain't real good farmland, neither. Ain't even good for chickens, let alone cattle or hogs. Don't nothing grow on it 'cept briars and scrub, although your family seems to make do with this shit-poor land. You all got chickens and a milk cow. Your land must be better than mine. Well, anyway, I sure do appreciate your kindness, Annie Smith."

"Certainly, Mrs. Huffmaster. Let me get you a pitcher of fresh milk and a few eggs so you can get back to your children."

"What was all that noise I heard? Did I frighten you?"

"No, Mrs. Huffmaster, I simply dropped a platter of food. I am fine. Let me get you that milk and those eggs, so you can be on your way."

"Obliged, Miss Annie Smith. I will tell your father Isaac what a fine young woman he is raising."

Mrs. Huffmaster coughed.

"Now, I don't mean to pry, Miss Annie, but was that a colored man I saw helping you pick up that mess?"

"Why yes, Mrs. Huffmaster, that is one of our hired men. He helps with the farming operations."

"You all pay colored men for farm help when there's white men in town ain't working?"

"Yes, Mrs. Huffmaster. My father – Isaac – believes that colored men make better laborers. Easier to control, and they can be whipped when necessary. Can't whip a white man if he won't work."

"I see," said Mrs. Huffmaster. "Why don't you all just buy some slaves? Whip them as much as you want."

"Slavery is immoral – I mean to say slaves are expensive. We can't afford to buy even one slave, Mrs. Huffmaster. We prefer to pay only what we can when we need it, instead of buying slaves."

"But you can afford to pay 'em a few pennies for farm work. That don't make no sense to me."

"We try to run our farm as efficiently as we can, Mrs. Huffmaster. Now, here are those eggs and the milk. You can keep the pitcher. And the egg bucket. Good day Mrs. Huffmaster." Annie tried to close the door.

"Obliged for the eggs and the milk," said Mrs. Huffmaster, as she put her foot inside the door. "How many other colored men you got working for you?"

"It depends on how much help we need for each season."

"Well, Miss Annie Smith, like I said, I don't mean to pry, 'cause it ain't Christian. Bible says spreading lies and such is a sin. I ain't but a poor widow with four hungry children, but I am a Christian, and I always tell the truth, no matter how much it hurts. And I like you, Annie Smith, so I am going to tell you something I heard in town. Some say they's a bunch of runaways in town, and some folks been hiding 'em. Runaways, in town, Miss Annie Smith."

"Mrs. Huffmaster, the colored man you saw was not a runaway. He is a hired man. He works for us, and has been in our employ for years. And the other men are also hired men, and friends of ours who help with the farm."

"I tell you what else I heard," said Mrs. Huffmaster. "Some in town say the local niggers and the slaves plan on rebelling. They plan on killing us all, slaves and free niggers united. Kill every white in town, rich or poor, man and woman. They says we need to be real careful about letting free niggers into our business."

"Oh, Mrs. Huffmaster, you can't believe everything you hear. People say lots of things that are not true."

"Reckon that is true, Miss Annie. But I also heard that devil John Brown was up to no good. I heard they could not kill him in Kansas, and now he is up to more mischief. That's what I heard in town. Don't nobody know where he'll strike next."

"As I said, Mrs. Huffmaster, you can't believe everything you hear or read."

"Well, I cain't read, so's I just believe what I hear if'n it comes from someone I trust. Tell you what else I heard. People in town paying a reward for any information about suspicious activity. They says to be on the lookout for runaways, suspicious niggers and such. Offering five dollars for any information."

"Mrs. Huffmaster, I don't know anything about this John Brown person, or Kansas, or runaways, or what people in town might say. We are just trying to build a farming business, and we need as many men as we can find. We have been very kind to you and your family, Mrs. Huffmaster. I hope you won't betray our trust."

"Course not, Annie Smith. You all been real kind to me. I am just telling you, people in town payin' money for information about suspicious activity. It don't bother me one bit if you hire free niggers for your business, but it might bother some."

"What else do you want, Mrs. Huffmaster?"

"Well, Miss Annie, you a real pretty girl. My oldest girl is about your size. Got the same body as you. Ain't' none of my kids got shoes. I got just one set of clothes for each of 'em. And now that it's about to get cold, I don't know where I can get shoes for my children. Obliged if I could have a pair of your boots. Just one pair, for my girl, that's all. So she can go in town and not have people laugh at her."

"Of course, Mrs. Huffmaster. You can have these boots. Give them to your daughter. And in exchange for this kindness, I trust that you won't tell anyone in town about my family's decision to hire free colored men. I will keep the colored men out of sight, if you promise not to tell anyone in town about my family's business arrangements."

"No, Miss Annie, I won't tell a soul. These are real nice boots, and I thank you for giving them to me. They should fit my daughter real good."

"Good day, Mrs. Huffmaster. And thank you for protecting my family's privacy. I trust you will keep your promise, as a Christian woman."

"Of course, Annie Smith. I may be poor, but I am a God-fearing woman. I won't tell anyone in town about your hired colored men. You have my word as a Christian. Ain't nobody's business but yours. 'Taint none of my concern. I won't tell a soul."

"Thank you, Mrs. Huffmaster."

"Obliged for the eggs and milk. And the egg bucket and the pitcher too. And the boots. Reckon this should keep us fed, least for a few days. I will pay you a visit real soon, Annie Smith. And next time, I will tell your father what a fine young woman he is raising."

"Good day, Mrs. Huffmaster."

Annie closed the door, and locked it behind her. The men could hear her quietly picking up the food from the floor, wiping up the spilled coffee and milk. She retrieved what she could, poured fresh milk and coffee, and brought the food upstairs, moving softly in her stocking feet. She did not speak, and did not look at the men as she delivered their morning meal. The men ate in silence, the scrape of fork against plate the only noise in the house.

⸻ ◉ ⸻

Brown paced the floor, his jaw quivering as he walked. The men sat at the long wooden table, hands clasped, some with heads down. Brown walked back and forth, not speaking. The candle flames flicked back and forth as he walked past. A sliver of moonlight penetrated one of the windows. Martha lit another candle, and gently pulled back one of the curtains. From his spot at the table, Dangerfield could see a bright white moon, low and heavy, a fat round sentry keeping watch over the countryside. Martha closed the curtains.

"Men, we must consider this a sign from God," said Brown. "We have to assume that Mrs. Huffmaster, though she may be raggedy and poor, has her suspicions. Annie, I want you and Martha to pay Mrs. Huffmaster a visit once a day. Give her what she asks. Keep her quiet. Milk, eggs, whatever she asks for. Visit her every day. And ask what else she has heard. Keep track of every rumor. We can use her to our advantage."

"Yes, Father" said Annie.

"And I can confirm that townspeople have heard rumors about some slave uprising, though none know the true nature of our plans," said Brown. This morning, I was speaking to the grocer, Thomas Boerly, who told me that a slave rebellion in South Carolina was put down. The rumor is that some of the escaped slaves made their way to Virginia, but no one knows where."

Brown continued pacing, grinding his jaw as his boots clicked across the wooden floor.

"And I talked to a tanner in town, who told me he had heard that slaves in Maryland were planning a rebellion," said Brown. Said abolitionists from Massachusetts had delivered ten thousand guns to an unknown location, just waiting for the slaves to strike."

Green stood and addressed the group. "I think we strike soon, maybe even next week," said Green. "Time is now. If they don't know what our plan is, the longer we wait, the more likely someone finds out the true plan."

"Sit down, Green" said Stevens. "It was you almost got us discovered."

"Brother Green should have used more discretion, but he is right," said Brown. "The grocer thinks the next slave uprising has already started in in South Carolina. The tanner thinks the slaves in the east of Maryland will revolt. I spent all day in town, and I heard no one mention the armory, which is our quarry. If the townfolk are looking elsewhere, this could be to our advantage. They won't expect a strike from within."

"What are we waiting for," Stevens muttered under his breath.

"Patience, men, patience," said Brown. "I heard something else while I was in town. The armory has only two guards, a head watchman and a night watchman. The tanner's uncle is one of the guards. The tanner says his uncle guards the armory for 48 hours at a time, and then he is relieved by another guard. But at all times, there is only one guard. They pull 48 hour shifts. Brother Cook, can you confirm this?"

"Yes," said John Cook. "The entire armory, the rifle works, the forge, the factory, all of it, is guarded by just a few old men. And they carry no guns, only swords. The night watchman is Daniel Whelan. I know Whelan. I speak with him every time I visit Harpers Ferry. He has told me everything about the layout of the armory, where the finished guns are stored, when the head watchman takes over. I would say under different circumstances, we are friends, but I can tell you that Whelan knows nothing of our plans," said Cook.

"How does this help us," said Green.

"The tanner told me that the guards have been instructed to be on the lookout for fugitives coming from the western part of Virginia, or from the low country down south and the east," said Brown. They won't expect an attack from the north."

The men began to rise up. "Let us strike, now, said Stevens."

"Whelan and the head watchman are both old men," said Cook. "Whelan will be alone on his shift. It won't take much to overpower one man. This is a critical flaw in the armory's defense, and it works to our advantage."

Brown gently pulled back the curtain on the front window, then closed it. He spun on his heels and turned toward the men.

"Brother Dangerfield, do you have anything to add? You have as much of a stake in this operation as anyone else."

When do they change the guard," said Dangerfield.

At precisely 7 am, which is the end of each 48 hour shift," said Brown.

"Then we should strike the night before the shift change," said Dangerfield. "Guard will have been on duty almost 48 hours, and will probably be asleep, or close to it," said Dangerfield. If we strike at midnight before the 7 am shift change, that gives us seven hours to secure the armory and take the weapons before the townfolk wake up. We have the guns and the armory before anybody knows what happened."

Green turned and looked at Dangerfield. Stevens looked up from the map he was reading.

"Lieutenant Stevens, would that plan work?" said Brown.

Stevens carefully unrolled his map. "If we move out from here between 8 pm and 10 pm, everyone in town will be asleep. It will take us two or three hours to walk into town carefully under cover of nightfall. If we arrive at the armory as late as midnight, that gives us plenty of time to capture the armory, move the guns into the hills, and put our men into position. By 7 am, we will have the armory, and we will have men and guns surrounding the city."

Stevens examined his map again. "We have enough men to establish a thin perimeter around the entire city," said Stevens. "We will have high ground, and we can shoot down into the city and up into the surrounding hills if troops arrive."

Brown looked at Dangerfield and smiled. "Brother Dangerfield, you are a quick study. Featherston was right about your abilities."

"We must also consider the watchmen along the bridge," said Cook. "There are two men who guard the bridge, Patrick Higgins and Billy Williams. I am friends with Higgins. We converse every morning when I cross the bridge. The bridge watchmen work 12 hour shifts. Higgins works midnight to noon, and Williams works noon to midnight. If we take the bridge between 10 and 11 pm, we can capture Williams easily. Someone will have to stay behind to guard the bridge entrance and capture Higgins when he arrives for his shift. From there, we will have an easy path to the armory."

"Brother Cook, are the bridge watchmen armed," said Brown.

"No," said Cook. "They carry only lanterns. Not so much as a sword, let alone a gun. Once we capture them, the armory will fall easily."

Brown smiled, then bowed his head. "And now, men, let us pray."

Brown bowed his head and paused before speaking.

"Almighty God, we thank you for your guidance, and the divine act of Providence you have given us. Nosy Mrs. Huffmaster has given us valuable information, and an advantage we needed."

A low rumble spread across the room.

"And now, Holy Father, give us the patience to strike when the time is right, and the wisdom to know when that time comes."

"Amen" said a voice.

"And finally, Father, give us the courage to strike, with anger and righteous vengeance. Give us the power to behead the serpent with the fury of angels, with justified rage, and without fear or regret. Give us the power to slay thy enemies, so we can purify this cursed soil with the blood of those who have sinned against you. Amen."

"Amen" roared the room.

"Amen," said Dangerfield softly to himself. "Amen."

CHAPTER 51

KENNEDY FARMHOUSE, WASHINGTON COUNTY, MARYLAND,
OCTOBER 16, 1859, 7 PM.

The men were crowded together around the large table in the kitchen, jostling for space. Brown paced back and forth, clicking his heels and grinding his jaws as he walked the room. Leary and Copeland had arrived the previous day. They stood near the front door, their gear still unpacked.

"Men, I have gathered you all here for this moment," said Brown. "The time to strike is now. Featherston has taken Annie and Martha back home, so the women will not be in danger. And now we welcome our two newest arrivals, Brothers Leary and Copeland."

Dangerfield saw the men he had met previously at Oberlin College. Lewis Leary, the slim, light-skinned negro with egg-shaped copper-colored eyes and a thin mustache leaned against the door frame. John Copeland, Leary's nephew, sat on a box of guns. Copeland was also tall and light-skinned, but stouter than his uncle. His heavy black mustache curled up into his nose. Copeland tipped his hat and smiled when he saw Dangerfield.

"With the arrival of Brothers Leary and Copeland, we now have enough men to complete our mission," said Brown. It would have been better if Brothers Leary and Copeland had been able to join us before yesterday, but God has brought them here now for a reason."

"Amen," murmured someone from the room.

I have heard rumors in town that an insurrection is expected from the west," said Brown. "But I have heard no one mention the armory. Our plan has not been revealed."

A low murmur spread across the room.

"Lieutenant Stevens, explain the plan of attack to all in the room," said Brown.

"After the wagon is packed, we will march south, along Elk Mountain, toward Harpers Ferry," said Stevens. Each soldier will be equipped with one Sharps rifle and one sharpened pike. You will carry the rifle slung over your shoulder, to allow your hands to be free as we walk into town. Commander Brown will carry the pikes in the wagon. We will distribute them just before we cross the bridge into Virginia. You will enter battle with a rifle and a pike. Your rifle is your primary weapon."

"At last, the battle," roared Green, pounding his fist against the table.

"Cook and Tidd know the route best. They will be our forward scouts," explained Stevens. "Cook and Tidd will cut the telegraph lines on the Maryland side of the river. Tidd will carry a lantern, which will not be lit until the Maryland telegraph lines have been cut. After you cut the Maryland lines, light the lantern at the entrance to the bridge, and leave it lit for five seconds. That will be the signal for the rest of us to join you at the entrance to the bridge, where we will capture Williams, the first bridge guard."

"We will take only one wagon, with Commander Brown holding the reins," continued Stevens. "The pikes and tools and extra weapons will be in the wagon. Commander Brown will lead us down the mountain. The rest of us will march two abreast, five paces behind the wagon. First Lieutentant Kagi will lead the march. Give yourselves plenty of room between the two men ahead of you. Owen Brown, Francis Meriam, and Barclay Coppoc will stay here to guard the farmhouse and weapons. Those three will be our rear guard, and will bring additional supplies as needed for the battle."

"How long will it take for us to reach Harpers Ferry," said Leary.

"It is five miles from the farmhouse to Harpers Ferry, essentially straight south," said Stevens. But we will have to move slowly due to nightfall. We can carry no torches or candles as we approach Harpers Ferry. We will have to rely on moonlight and stars to guide our path. I expect it will take two to three hours."

We will cross into town from the east, over the Baltimore and Ohio Bridge," continued Stevens as he consulted a map. "If we leave by 8 pm, we should arrive between 10 pm and 11 pm. Once we have captured Williams, we continue across the bridge, and head south toward the armory."

"What about the other bridge guard," said Copeland.

"Taylor and Watson Brown will stay behind and guard the bridge, and capture the second bridge guard Higgins when he arrives at midnight for his shift," explained Stevens. "Once Higgins is captured, Taylor and Watson Brown will bring him to the armory, which by that time will be in our complete possession."

"The armory is locked," said Hazlett. "How do we get in?"

"Though the armory is locked there is but a single lock and chain that secures the gate, and it will be easily broken," said Cook. "I have scouted every day for the past month, and know every piece of equipment and shift change by heart."

"The shift change at the armory occurs at 7 am," explained Stevens. "If we arrive by midnight, the guard will be at his weakest, 41 hours into a 48 hour shift. As Brother Dangerfield has pointed out, this will make it easier for us to capture the armory. By the time the second armory guard arrives, we will have captured the armory, and will be in possession of the guns."

"What do we do with the guns in the armory," said Copeland.

"We take as many as we can into the surrounding hills under cover of night. After we suppress any rebellion from the townspeople, we will send word to the local farms and plantations that freedom is nigh," said Brown. "We can hold the town for three or four days until help arrives. When the slaves arrive, they will overrun the town, and we will distribute the arms to all who wish to fight slavery. The great battle will have begun," said Brown, his raspy voice quavering.

No one in the room spoke.

"How will the slaves know we have captured the town," said Dangerfield. "How do we communicate with them?"

"One of you will be appointed as a messenger," said Brown. "Once the town has been captured and we have set up headquarters, we can then decide who is best suited to leave the militia and alert local farms and plantations. I don't know who that will be at present, but it will likely be one of the white men, simply to avoid suspicion. I will make that decision after the town has been secured, the first battle has been won, and we have established a provisional headquarters. The messenger will alert the slaves while we hold the town."

The room was silent, save for the scuffle of boots on the wooden floor and a watery cough from one of the men. "How do we carry that many guns outside of town," someone muttered.

"Men, I know this is a dangerous endeavor," said Brown. "I hope I have been clear to all of you that this mission is the most perilous and important thing any of us has ever done. I am fully prepared that this mission may be my last act on Earth. Each of you should be prepared to die, and accept that this mission may be your last act on Earth. We are called by God to eliminate slavery, and if God chooses to sacrifice us in this battle, it will be because we have helped win the war. If there is any discontent among this group, let's have it out now. Any man with second thoughts is free to leave right now."

Brown stopped his pacing, and sat heavily in his chair, waiting for someone to speak.

Someone coughed. Stevens opened the window nearest his chair and spat outside.

"What if the slaves don't join us," said Leary after a long pause. "What if they can't leave, or won't leave?"

"Then we wait until reinforcements arrive," said Brown. "If the slaves cannot join us in battle, we shall bring the battle to them. We shall bring them guns and weapons. We will help them be the source of their own liberation."

"What if that don't work," said Copeland.

"Then we die knowing that we have carried out God's duties," said Brown. "There is no more honorable death than fighting this land's original sin."

The men began murmuring and arguing among themselves. "Ain't no way to alert every plantation in Maryland and Virginia with one messenger," said a voice from the room. "Need more than one wagon to deliver that many guns," said another.

The rumble grew louder, until Green stood and spoke.

"Mr. Douglass told me this was a perfect steel trap," said Green. "Begged me not to go. But when I heard Mr. Brown tell me he was willing to die for my freedom, I had no choice. 'I believe I will go with the old man,' is what I told Mr. Douglass. And I will either see my son again, or die trying. So everyone say your prayers, and let's leave soon as we can."

Green sat down, and the rumble of discontent grew quieter. Brown sat heavily in his chair and closed his eyes.

Dangerfield listened to the animated conversations among the men. He retrieved Harriet's last letter and read it again:

> *Dear Husband you not the trouble I see the last two years has ben like a trouble dream to me it is said Master is in want of monney if so I know not what time he may sell me an then all my bright hops of the futer are blasted for there has ben one bright hope to cheer me in all my troubles that is to be with you for if I thought I shoul never see you this earth would have no charms for me do all you Can for me witch I have no doubt you will I want to see you so much the Chrildren are all well the baby cannot walk yet all it can step around enny thing by holding on it is very much like Agnes*
>
> *I mus bring my letter to Close as I have no newes to write you mus write soon and say when you think you Can Come.*

Dangerfield folded the letter and put it back in his pocket. He studied the room. Leary and Copeland were arguing about something that happened at Oberlin. "I told you we needed to leave earlier," said Leary, while Copeland angrily shook his head in disagreement.

Kagi and Stevens were debating how long they could hold the town before reinforcements arrived. "We can't count on any large number of reinforcements," said Kagi. "We must plan for an extended siege."

Brown did not speak as he sat in his chair. His eyes were closed, and he almost appeared to be sleeping amidst the tumult.

Dangerfield stood and addressed the room.

"Men, I ain't no soldier, or warrior. I ain't nothing more than a freeman from Virginia, and the only thing I want is to free my family. That is still the only thing I want. But I remember something Amos Featherston told me on my way up here, and something Pastor Thomas Evans told me back in Ohio. 'Think of the lives you could save,' they told me. 'Think of the other families like yours,' they told me. Well, I ain't never met these other families, but if they are like mine, I suspect there's men like me who would do anything for them. I would kill for my family, and I know all of you are willing to do the same. And now I understand that there must be hundreds of other men just like me, all across Virginia."

The men muttered their approval.

"And when Brown – Commander Brown – told me about his plan, I started to think about why a white man with no slaves and no reason to fight would risk his life for colored men and women like me," said Dangerfield. "Didn't make no sense at first. Why fight for somebody who ain't kin? But when I look around this room, and I see white men like Kagi and Stevens ready to fight and die for colored men like me and Green and Anderson and Leary and Copeland, I reckon I can start to understand what Commander Brown means."

Stevens nodded and tipped his hat toward Dangerfield.

"And I will see my family again, in this life or in heaven," said Dangerfield. "This is bigger than all of us. I told my brother I would be home by Thanksgiving. I aim to keep that promise, or die trying. Too late for any of us to turn back. All of us will see our families again, one way or another."

Dangerfield sat down. Each man except John Brown stood and clapped, softly at first, then louder, until the room shook. Dangerfield looked at Brown, who remained seated, eyes closed. Brown opened his eyes, rose slowly out of his chair as if emerging from a long nap, and looked out the window into the night. He raised his hand, and the room grew quiet.

"Men, you have heard me speak of vengeance, and the fury of angels. And I believe that righteous fury is not a sin, but a virtue. But you all know how dear life is to you, and how dear your life is to your friends," said Brown softly, almost in a whisper. "Do not, therefore, take the life of anyone if you can possibly avoid it. But if it is necessary to take life in order to save your own, then make sure work of it."

No one spoke. Brown closed his eyes and bowed his head. He opened his eyes and looked out the window again. He checked his pocket watch.

"It is 8 pm. Men, get on your arms. We will proceed to the Ferry." Brown turned on his heels, and walked outside. He climbed into the wagon. Owen Brown, Francis Meriam, and Barclay Coppoc, all of whom would stay behind, went outside and began loading the pikes and tools into the wagon. The rest of the men stood, gathered their arms, and took their places behind the wagon. Dangerfield was the last to leave. He surveyed the room, then pulled out Harriet's letters.

> *"Oh Dear Dangerfield com this fall with out fail monny or no money I want to see you so much that is one bright hope I have before me."*

"Come boys!" boomed Brown from the wagon. The horse rattled its harness. Dangerfield folded the letter and returned it to his breast pocket. Then he gently closed the door behind him.

CHAPTER 52

OCTOBER 16, 1859, 9 PM

The men marched behind Brown, two abreast, down Elk Mountain. Dangerfield marched next to Leary. Ahead of him were Copeland and Hazlett, and behind him Green and Watson Brown. Kagi and Stevens led the marchers, walking exactly two yards apart and five yards behind Brown's creaking wagon.

The cold and persistent mist that welcomed them at the beginning of the trek had turned into a soft rain. Each man was outfitted similarly – long woolen shawls to protect the rifles, and conceal the pikes when they made their final assault on the town. For over an hour, no one spoke – the only sounds to intrude on each man's thoughts were the creak and groan of the wagon and the occasional owl. Somewhere below in Harpers Ferry a dog let out a mournful wail.

Dangerfield turned when he heard a soft voice. Behind him, Green was muttering Bible verses under his breath – "Our Father, who art in heaven, hallowed be thy name," Green croaked in his high raspy voice.

Leary tapped Dangerfield on the shoulder. "Looks like the Emperor done found religion," said Leary softly.

"Both of you hush," said Watson Brown.

By 10:35 pm, the men had reached the hill overlooking the town. Dangerfield could see faint light from a lamp on the Maryland side of the Baltimore and Ohio Railroad bridge that led into Harpers Ferry. Brown raised his hand and clicked at the horse. The wagon rattled to a stop. Kagi and Stevens spoke to Brown in hushed voices, and then turned to the men behind them.

"We wait here for the signal from Tidd and Cook," said Stevens. "While we wait, each man will receive a pike from the wagon. Keep your rifles slung over your shoulders, and carry the pikes underneath your shawls."

Kagi and Stevens retrieved pikes from the wagon and passed them back through the ranks until each man was armed. The men waited silently. Green rocked back and forth on his heels. Leary and Copeland stood together. Osborne Anderson said a soft prayer under his breath. Dangerfield recalled Harriet's plaintive wish – *"Oh Dear Dangerfield com this fall with out fail monny or no money I want to see you so much that is one bright hope I have before me."*

"I will be home, without fail,' he said to himself.

Osborne Anderson tapped Dangerfield on his shoulder. "Look at the bridge," whispered Anderson.

A shadow emerged from the entrance to the bridge on the Maryland side. The shadow walked a few paces away from the entrance, stopped, and held something aloft. A weak yellow glow emerged from the shadow's arm, briefly piercing the river fog. The light flickered and popped for five seconds, then died. The shadow vanished into the bridge tunnel.

"March now, men" hissed Brown.

The group quickly reached the Maryland entrance. Stevens and Kagi leapt ahead of the wagon and snuffed the lamp that swung at the bridge entrance. Dangerfield and the other men waited behind.

Stevens and Kagi entered the utter blackness of the tunnel and waited. A dim light approached from the Virginia entrance. As the light grew closer, Dangerfield could hear a man whistling loudly as he swung his lantern in a wide arc, passing the light over the tracks and then the wagon path, pausing for a moment on each side of the bridge. Stevens and Kagi crouched on each side of the entrance. As the light grew closer to the Maryland entrance, Stevens drew his gun, and Kagi his pike. Fifty feet from the entrance, Stevens raced towards the man holding the lantern, Kagi right behind.

"Set down your lantern, and raise your hands," growled Stevens. "You are now a prisoner of the Provisional Army of the United States. Do not fight us, and your life will be spared."

"Please don't kill me, I have a wife and two children at home. I have no money. I only watch the bridge at night, looking for fires, and checking switches."

"Then you have nothing to fear," said Stevens. "Pick up your lantern and walk slowly. Stevens grabbed the man's left arm, and allowed him to hold the lantern in his right hand. Kagi walked behind, with the pike in the man's back.

Kagi whistled, and the others entered the bridge.

"Please don't kill me," pleaded the man.

"Now, Bill, you have my word that these men will not kill you, if you listen and do as they say," said a voice from the darkness.

"Who is it speaking?" said the watchman. "Show your face, like a man."

Cook approached and held the watchman's lantern at eye level and stood in front of the man while Stevens and Kagi held him.

"You know me, Bill. We have spoken many times. You have my word and the word of Commander John Brown that your life will be spared if you listen and don't fight," said Cook.

"Why yes, I recognize you, John Cook," said the watchman. "Now please tell these men to release me. And whatever trick this is, I would advise you not to do it again. The people in town are quite wary of strangers. You and your friends could be hurt."

Brown had stepped down from the wagon and now stood in front of the watchman while Cook held the lantern.

"Mr. Williams, you are now a prisoner of the Provisional Army of the United States, with these men under my command," said Brown. "I can assure you this is no trick."

"I recognize you, Isaac Smith," said the watchman. "What is this nonsense?"

"I am not Isaac Smith. I am John Brown, and you are my prisoner. Hold your lantern aloft and do as these men tell you. We are proceeding to the armory."

Stevens again grabbed the man's left arm, and allowed him to hold the lantern in his right hand. Kagi walked behind, jabbing the pike in the man's back.

"Watson Brown and Stewart Taylor will remain on the bridge and wait for the second watchman," said Brown. "Tidd and Cook, proceed across the bridge and cut the telegraph lines on the Virginia side. We will take this prisoner to the armory. Kagi and Stevens, begin marching. I will follow in the wagon. The rest of you, march behind the wagon. Tidd and Cook, after you have cut the Virginia telegraph lines, meet us at the armory."

Kagi nudged the pike into the watchman's back while Stevens held his arm. The watchman began walking slowly, and then Kagi nudged the pike harder. Brown's wagon and his men rumbled forward, to the armory. Watson Brown and Stewart Taylor took their positions just outside the Virginia bridge entrance.

October, 16, 1859
11:45 PM

The men reached the armory gate at 15 minutes before midnight. Kagi and Stevens held Williams, who was now sweating and muttering to himself.

"Lord, I ask that you forgive me for my sins, and keep watchful care over my wife and children," croaked Williams as he looked toward the black sky.

The armory gate was ten feet tall, and topped with sharpened metal pikes. A thick chain encircled both doors of the gate, fastened with a heavy lock.

"Unlock the gate," said Stevens to Williams.

"I cannot," said Williams. "I am but a night watchman on the bridge. I have no keys to the armory. I am not in the employ of the armory."

Kagi jammed the pike into Williams' ribs. "Unlock the gate now, or else I will see to it that you deliver your prayers to God in person," growled Stevens.

"As God is my witness, I have no key to the armory," said Williams. "Only the two armory watchmen can open these gates."

"Help yourself, then," said Stevens. "Do you know the night watchman?"

"I believe his name is Daniel Whelan," said Williams.

"Stand down, Stevens," said Brown from his wagon. "Let us spill no blood until absolutely necessary. Hold the captive tight. Newby and Leary, break the gate open with the bar."

Dangerfield retrieved the crowbar from the wagon and he and Leary began twisting the crowbar into the chain, grunting as they tried to break the lock.

A tiny stooped man carrying a lantern emerged from the armory guardhouse and began walking slowly toward the gate, holding the lantern aloft in one hand and carrying a short curved sword in the other.

"Miller, is that you?" said the man as he approached the gate. "I heard a wagon and voices, and I supposed you needed help. Did you forget your key to the gate?"

Dangerfield and Leary continued twisting the crowbar into the chain as the man grew closer.

"Who are these men, Miller," said the man.

"Whelan, open the gate," said Stevens.

"Who are you, if not Miller? And how do you know my name if you are not Miller?" The man held his lantern in front of him, and pointed his sword toward the entrance.

Green, Jeremiah Anderson, and Hazlett pointed their rifles at the man's head.

"Open the gate now, and you will not be harmed," said Kagi.

Whelan took a step back from the entrance, then another, back toward the guardhouse.

"If you run to summon help, you will be shot instantly," said Kagi. Green, Jeremiah Anderson and Hazlett shouldered their rifles and took aim. The man froze.

"Whelan, open the gate now," roared Stevens.

Whelan stood where he was, immobile, the sword in his hand quivering. A puddle of liquid pooled at his feet.

Dangerfield and Leary continued twisting the crowbar in the chain. The chain began to creak and pop, until it gave way, shattering the lock and sending metal fragments into the armory yard. Dangerfield unraveled the chain, and Leary pushed open the gate, which swung open silently. Green, Jeremiah Anderson and Hazlett burst through the entrance and shoved their rifles into Whelan's back and ribs. Whelan's sword fell to the ground. Brown drove the wagon through the armory yard, and the rest of the men followed.

"Men, this is the Harpers Ferry armory," said Brown. "Within this yard and the rifle works, we now have possession of over 100,000 guns and countless munitions. Your hard work and your trust in me have paid their reward. As soon as the rifle works and forges have been secured, we will control one of the largest supplies of guns in the world, enough to arm every slave in Virginia two times over." Brown looked at the row of darkened buildings and lowered his head.

The men turned when they heard footsteps approaching rapidly. Cook and Tidd ran through the open entrance, breathless.

"Brothers Cook and Tidd, were you successful," said Brown from the wagon.

"Yes, replied Cook panting. "All telegraph lines on the Virginia side and the Maryland side have been cut. We confirmed there are no other telegraph lines in Harpers Ferry. All lines have been cut."

"Very well," said Brown. "The occupation now begins in earnest. Oliver Brown and William Thompson, you will secure the bridge over the Shenandoah River. Hazlett and Edwin Coppoc will begin to inspect and secure the buildings in the arsenal. Stevens, you will lead Jeremiah Anderson, Kagi, Copeland, Tidd, Cook, and Green to capture the rifle factory on Hall Island. Newby, Leary, Leeman, Dauphin Thompson and Osborne Anderson will stay here with me to guard the prisoners, and the main entrance to the armory, and begin sorting and distributing the guns."

The men gathered in groups and quickly began carrying out their orders.

"What in God's name is this all about," said Whelan as he looked at the intruders assembled in the armory yard. "Who are you murderers, and what is this business?"

Brown climbed down from the wagon and held a lantern at eye level as he addressed his prisoners, Williams and Whelan:

"I came here from Kansas, and this is a slave state. I want to free all the Negroes in this state. I have possession now of the United States armory, and if the citizens interfere with me, I must only burn the town and have blood."

Brown turned toward Leary and Dauphin Thompson. "You two take the prisoners to the guard house and keep them there. Newby and Osborne Anderson, guard the entrance against all save for those we know."

Leary and Dauphin Thompson leveled their guns at Williams and Whelan, and began marching them toward the guard house. Brown held the lantern aloft and watched them leave before turning toward Dangerfield.

"Brother Newby, I have a special mission for you, one that I believe will suit your talents and our objectives," said Brown as he put his arms around Dangerfield's shoulders. "I want you to be the lead sentry at the armory gate. By this time tomorrow, we will have secured the town, but we should expect resistance. The armory is our crown jewel. We now possess more guns and munitions than most countries. I want you and Osborne Anderson to guard the gate. And I want you to be lead sentry."

"Why us," said Dangerfield.

"I want the townspeople to see armed black men," whispered Brown. "I want them to know that the plan to distribute weapons to the slaves has already begun.

I want them to know that the slaves and former slaves already have guns, and the fate of this town rests in the hands of armed black men. And I want them to know that if they resist, their lives will be taken by armed black men. I want fear to be our primary weapon."

"Why me," said Dangerfield.

"Of all my men, you have the strongest motivation. Your family's freedom is at stake. Your presence will send a message. You and Osborne patrolling behind the locked gate will strike fear into all who come near."

Brown surveyed the black slumbering buildings surrounding the armory.

"Have you fired the Sharps I gave you last year," said Brown.

"Yes, I have."

"Have you shot anyone? Have you killed a man?" demanded Brown.

Dangerfield recalled the slave catcher's head exploding in the doorway of his old home.

"Yes, I have killed, but only when necessary."

"That is good," said Brown. "As I said, we will encounter resistance. You must be prepared to kill tomorrow, and as long as necessary to protect what now belongs to us. Be mindful of how precious life is, and take life only when necessary. When necessary, make short work of it. We are now defending what is ours. Your family's freedom is in these buildings."

Brown turned east and held the lantern high above his head.

"This Lewis Jennings has your family in Brentsville, correct?"

"Harriet and all my children are in Brentsville."

"Brentsville is but 50 miles from here," said Brown. "When this portion of the rebellion is complete, I will see to it that you are allowed to travel to Brentsville to join your family. I don't expect you to join us in the second phase of the rebellion, arming the slaves. Your work will have been done. As soon as the town is secure, you may leave to join your family. Your family and their freedom are but a few hours away."

Brown patted Dangerfield softly on the shoulder. "I only wish that Douglass could see what we have done," said Brown. "Perfect steel trap, indeed. And we did it with negroes and white men, armed, and fighting for a just cause. When next I see Douglass, I shall remind him of his words."

Brown turned to his other men. "Leeman, come with me, and we will determine how best to distribute the weapons," said Brown.

Brown and Leeman began walking down the empty black streets of the armory.

Dangerfield surveyed the rows of buildings that held hundreds of thousands of guns, tons of munitions, and the key to his freedom.

"I will be home before Thanksgiving," said Dangerfield to himself. "Harriet, I will be home soon."

OCTOBER 17, 1859
12:10 AM

Ten minutes late for his shift, Patrick Higgins was sweating and out of breath as he approached the Maryland side of the Baltimore and Ohio Bridge. There was no sign of anyone when he arrived at his post.

"Where in God's name is Williams," Higgins muttered to himself. "He could not have left already – I am but ten minutes past time." Higgins looked up and saw the lamp hanging from the bridge entrance was broken. He peered into the abyss but no light came from the other side. He swung his lantern over the watchman's board – the last peg had been placed at 10:30 p.m. on October 16.

"Not like Bill to leave early without leaving a note," said Higgins. He held his lantern aloft and looked up at the broken lamp and saw a hole in the frame. Shards of glass crunched under his boots.

"Bill, I am here now," called Higgins into the blackness.

No one answered. Higgins checked his pocket watch – it was now 12:15 a.m. Williams should have been waiting on the Maryland side by now.

"Bill, I am here. Please speak and state your location," said Higgins into the bridge. His voice bounced off the walls before disappearing into the tunnel.

Higgins checked the oil in his lantern and began walking toward the Virginia side. He swung his lantern from side to side in high sweeping arcs, looking for any sign of Williams.

"Bill, where are you," said Higgins, his voice splintering into the absorbing darkness.

Only the river replied, jostling and gurgling below Higgins' feet as he crossed.

As he approached the Virginia side, he looked up and saw that the lamp hanging at that entrance was also broken.

Two men emerged from the shadows, wearing large hats that shielded their faces. Both men carried long walking sticks.

"Hold your lantern aloft," said one of the men.

"Bill, is that you? Where have you been," said Higgins. "And who are you with?"

"Which way," the other man growled at Higgins.

"Not far. I am at my station, if I am to start on the Virginia side. But my shift begins at midnight on the Maryland side. I was not told of any changes to my shift, my location, or my start time. Did Bill send you?"

One of the men held forth his walking stick, which Higgins now realized was a spear. The other man swung out a rifle from underneath his shawl, and pointed the rifle at Higgins' head.

"You are now a prisoner of the Provisional Army of the United States," said the first man in a low raspy growl. "Do as we say, and we will not hurt you. Hold your lantern aloft with your right hand."

The man with the pike approached and grabbed Higgin's left hand. Higgins dropped his lantern, spun and struck the man hard with his right hand. The man cursed and stumbled backwards, grabbing his pike to keep from falling. Higgins ran toward the Virginia entrance.

A shot exploded behind him. Higgins heard the ball hiss and snap as it flew past his left ear.

Another blast from behind. Something hot and sharp ripped open the crest of his scalp. He kept running as the warm flow of his own blood trickled down his forehead.

Higgins ran out of the bridge into Virginia. He turned left, sprinting across the railroad tracks. Candles were burning in the parlor windows of the Wager House Hotel. Higgins raced toward the largest window he saw and leapt forward, sending a spray of glass, wood fragments, and his own blood through the empty hotel lobby.

The night clerk looked up from the hotel's ledger. Higgins lay on the lobby floor, bleeding, and gasping.

"Lock your doors," Higgins wheezed. "There are robbers on the bridge."

October 17, 1859
1:25 AM
Harpers Ferry Armory

Dangerfield and Osborne Anderson patrolled the entrance to the armory, even though there would be no foot traffic at this hour. Row after row of buildings were dark, except for the guardhouse where Whelan and Williams were being held.

Brown emerged from one of the buildings where he and Leeman had been inspecting the weapons by lantern, taking inventory.

"Have you seen anyone or heard anything," said Brown.

"No, Commander Brown. All has been quiet," said Dangerfield as he shouldered his rifle.

""Prepare now for the conflict in the morning," said Brown. "We should expect resistance, but the townspeople are poorly armed. They count on the guns in the armory for their protection. And now we have those guns."

The shriek of a train whistle shattered the quiet. Dangerfield heard the hiss and thunder of the steam train as it entered town.

"That would be the 1:25 eastbound from Baltimore," said Brown. "The Baltimore and Ohio bridge is the only way for that train to enter the town. And our men now have control of that bridge," said Brown. "Perfect steel trap indeed."

The train hissed and snorted before coming to a stop. "That is a good sign," said Brown. "At this hour of the evening, there would be no passengers disembarking. The train would normally slow as it enters town, cross the bridge slowly, and then continue eastbound without stopping. If it has stopped, our men must have captured the train before it crossed the bridge."

A man shouted in the distance. Another man responded, and then more shouts. "Let us pass, or I will run you over," said a voice.

A gunshot shattered the town's early morning slumber. "Halt now," said a voice from much closer. "I said halt." Another gunshot, then a man screaming. "I am hit, I am hit!" Two more gunshots, then the sound of breaking glass and a woman wailing.

Dangerfield looked at Brown, who held his lantern at eye level. "I can only hope that our men take life only when necessary," said Brown. Brown picked up his lantern and walked quickly toward the armory gate.

"I must see what is the matter," said Brown. "You and Anderson keep your wits about you. Let no one enter save those we know. Kill only if you need to."

Brown left the armory yard and ran in the direction of the railroad bridge, leaving Dangerfield and Osborne Anderson alone. Dangerfield and Anderson watched him leave.

"What do we do now," said Anderson.

"We do as Brown says," said Dangerfield. I will patrol the area in front of the gate. You take a position in one of the buildings, near a window facing the gate. Anyone who tries to enter will see me first, and you will be hidden. If you hear me shoot, you shoot at anyone entering. Try to find a second or third floor window."

Anderson ran toward a dark building next to the guardhouse and disappeared inside. Dangerfield looked east, toward Brentsville and his family. "Perfect steel trap," he said softly to himself.

—=◦《◎》◦=—

October 17, 1859
7:00 am
Harpers Ferry Armory

Dangerfield watched the sun break the crest of the mountains to the east. He paced back and forth in front of the armory gate. The head watchman and the rest of the workers would be arriving any time. Osborne Anderson emerged from his watch station next to the guardhouse.

"Has Brown returned," said Anderson.

"No," said Dangerfield. "I have heard nothing in town except for a few more gunshots, and men shouting."

"What do we do when the armory workers arrive," said Anderson. "The seven of us cannot capture the hundreds of men who work here every day."

"We capture as many as we can, and we kill the rest," said Dangerfield.

"There are hundreds of men who work in this yard," said Anderson. "They will arrive by the dozens. We cannot kill or capture that many men."

"Then we capture and kill as many as we can," said Dangerfield. "Take your position next to the guardhouse. Leary and Thompson have control of the prisoners and the guardhouse. They can shoot from the guardhouse, and you can shoot from your building. We should expect resistance."

Anderson looked at Dangerfield and smirked. "Yes sir, Captain," said Anderson as he turned to leave.

Church bells rang near the armory. Isolated at first, then hundreds of separate peals, fast, insistent, each one sounding before the previous one had stilled. The noise echoed off the buildings in the armory, until there was no distance between each peal, no distinction between the bells or the churches, simply a solid wall of metal clanging and hammering against the glass windows in the armory.

"Awful early for a church service," said Anderson.

"And it ain't Sunday," said Dangerfield.

Dangerfield looked toward the armory gate and saw two men standing on the opposite side, about 60 yards away. One of the men leveled a shotgun and fired through the gate. Buckshot bounced off the brick buildings and shattered one of the windows in the guardhouse. Anderson ran toward his station, while Dangerfield ran behind a machine shed.

The man with the shotgun fired again, sending another spray of buckshot toward the machine shed. A pellet bounced off the brick wall and lodged in Dangerfield's woolen shawl.

Dangerfield knelt and took aim at the man with the shotgun. He leveled the Sharps and fired, hitting the man squarely in his balls. Blood erupted from the man's groin, and he crumpled to the ground. The man screamed, and began crawling away from the gate.

A rifle cracked from somewhere in the guardhouse, above Dangerfield. Dangerfield saw the second man at the armory gate look up just as the rifle bullet exploded his skull. The man fell backward as pieces of his skull landed behind him.

Dangerfield kicked open the door of the machine shed and knelt below the window. He crept up and peered out the window. There was no one else at the gate. The church bells continued their urgent alarms, vibrating the windows in the machine shed.

<hr>

October 17, 1859
Monocacy, Maryland Train Station
7:05 AM

URGENT MESSAGE. Express train bound east, under my charge, was stopped this morning at Harpers Ferry by armed abolitionists. They say they have come to free the slaves, and intend to do it at all hazards. Train was captured at approx. 1:25 this morning, and was held captive for six hours until allowed to continue eastward. All telegraph lines into Harpers Ferry have been cut. Armed men in this party are on both sides of the B & O Bridge, allowing no one to pass in either direction unless on word of their leader. They also possess the armory, and have killed at least one man. The exact size of this force is unknown – I estimate at least 150 men, many of whom are well armed negros. The leader of those men requested me to say to you that this is the last train that shall pass the bridge either East or West. It has been suggested you had better notify the Secretary of War at once.

Andrew Phelps, B & O conductor

October 17, 1859
Harpers Ferry Armory
12:00 PM

Brown had still not returned. Throughout the morning, Dangerfield heard bursts of gunfire and loud men's voices during the brief moments when the church bells stopped ringing. The bells were now silent.

Dangerfield emerged from the machine shed when he saw Stewart Taylor sprinting toward the armory gate.

"There are soldiers attempting to take the Potomac bridge," gasped Taylor. "Watson Brown and I need help. With two men on either side and a marksman behind, we can hold the bridge. Come now."

Dangerfield and Taylor ran out of the armory yard and into the tunnel.

Watson Brown was at the Maryland entrance, firing at three men who were climbing up from the towpath. Dangerfield and Taylor knelt and took aim. More men were scrambling up from the towpath, firing blindly into the tunnel. Dangerfield saw dozens more men racing down the mountain toward the Maryland entrance, firing into the bridge tunnel, sending wood fragments everywhere.

"We cannot hold the bridge," screamed Taylor. "Back to the armory."

The three men retreated toward the Virginia entrance. The dark tunnel gave them cover as they ran back toward the armory.

As they emerged into daylight in Virginia, the soldiers closed in and continued firing. Taylor and Watson Brown turned right, and ran toward the Wager House hotel. Dangerfield turned left, sprinting toward the safety of the armory. One of the soldiers leveled his rifle at Dangerfield and fired. The bullet screamed past his ear and blew an apple-sized crater in the brick wall of the machine shed in front of him. From inside the armory, someone fired back at the advancing soldiers, dropping them back for only a moment.

The soldiers returned fire toward the armory as they closed in. Dangerfield heard two more gunshots from the armory aimed at the advancing soldiers. When a bullet flew past him and shattered one of the metal bars on the armory gate, Dangerfield knew he would not make it past the gate.

He took a hard left before reaching the gate and ran down Shenandoah Street, away from the armory and his pursuers. Dangerfield turned and fired one last shot toward the gate, hoping to take out one of the soldiers. He would find a place to hide in one of the buildings on Shenandoah. If he could find a building with a small hidden back room, perhaps the soldiers would not find him. He would wait until they left, then make his escape. A bullet flew past his ear and splintered a wooden door in front of him. The door swung open.

"I will hide here," he thought to himself as he raced toward the open door.

From a window in a tall building just outside the armory gates, a man cradling a shotgun looked down into the armory yard. He saw a tall negro, armed with a rifle, sprinting down Shenandoah Street, away from the armory gate and the advancing soldiers. The man in the window rammed in an extra charge of gunpowder, loaded his shotgun with a heavy metal spike, and locked the gun against his shoulders. He aimed the shotgun a few paces ahead of the sprinting man and fired at a pre-ordained spot in the universe where man and missile had always been scheduled to collide. Neither man knew the other. Yet they had been destined to meet at this place and this time since the beginning of time.

The gun bucked as the double charge of gunpowder exploded. The spike blew open the barrel of the gun as it wobbled toward its target. The man watched from his perch as the heavy spike and the running man collided at the exact spot that had been written in the stars since the beginning of time. The spike tore open the man's throat, ripping his head backward as a spray of blood shot upwards. The running man fell in his tracks, his rifle clattering across the cobblestoned streets. The man in the window watched as a river of blood flowed from the dead man's neck, slowly meandering through the cobblestones. He lowered his shotgun and left the room.

October 17, 1859
Brentsville, Virginia
12:00 PM

Harriet was mending clothes in the cabin when she felt something sharp and heavy hit her neck. She stood and coughed, and looked around. She rubbed her neck, but there was nothing there. Lucy and Agnes were working in the house. The boys were in the field. She heard footsteps outside the cabin door.

"Marse Jennings, is that you? Mistress?"

There was no one there. She walked around the cabin twice, and saw no one.

"As God is my witness, I heard footsteps," she said to herself. She came around the cabin toward the front door, and saw Dangerfield leaving the cabin. He looked just as he did the first day Harriet met him, and he was wearing the same clothes. He turned and looked toward her, no more than twenty years old. He said nothing. Harriet ran toward him, but he had disappeared by the time she reached the cabin door.

She went into the cabin and saw a drop of blood on the floor. She knelt and dragged her finger through the blood. She tasted the blood on her finger, swirled it around her mouth, then spat out the window. She walked toward the house to gather her children.

—◦◉◦—

Dangerfield watched his family from a distance. Harriet tended her garden. She had the baby strapped to her back while she harvested greens and potatoes. Chickens scratched furiously in the dirt, while Junior and Gabriel repaired the white fence that surrounded the garden. Agnes and Lucy were in the kitchen washing vegetables. He saw Henry teaching Jericho how to plant corn, while Elsey supervised all. A milk cow lowed in the barn. Henry stood tall and upright. He looked no more than twenty.

Dangerfield did not know where he was. And then he felt incredibly light, and he realized it did not matter where he was. He closed his eyes and allowed light to wash over him, cleanse him, purify him. He smelled Harriet's skin one last time before letting the light wash everything away.

CHAPTER 53

Turner knelt next to his grandmother's grave. A few plastic flowers still clung to a wreath someone had placed on the headstone. Turner touched the headstone, and laid fresh flowers on the ground. He read his grandmother's name out loud, then began speaking to her.

"Well, Gran, it has been a little over a month since we lost you, and a lot has happened to me since we last talked when you were in hospice. I am taking a break from medicine, probably permanent. Tracy and I are going to do some traveling, and I am going to help her fix up the studio. Don't worry about me. Even if I never practice medicine again, I will be fine. I have been looking at some teaching gigs, and I might even be able to do some consulting. I don't think I will ever be a surgeon again. Never thought I would say this, but that might actually be for the best. I was a damn good surgeon, but not always the best grandson, cousin, or husband. I have a lot of time to try to fix those things now."

He looked around to see if anyone could hear him, then realized he did not care if anyone heard him.

"I told Vernita I would help her and Frank with the baby two days a week, while Frank is at work. I thought it was long overdue that I spend more time with family. Vernita said she could use the help. You were always telling me to spend more time with family, but I was too stubborn to listen. I think I get it now. Tracy wants to come with me when I go to Vernita's. She says she needs all the practice she can get holding babies, for when we have our own children. She is not very subtle, but you always liked that about her. 'That gal says exactly what's on her mind, like a young woman should,' you always used to say. You were right."

Turner closed his eyes while he considered what to say next, before realizing that his audience wasn't going anywhere.

"You remember those stories you used to tell when we were kids? Great Uncle Billy, the little boy who died in the house, the ghosts of escaped slaves? You used to get so excited telling us those stories. I have to be honest, I got sick of those stories after awhile. Could never figure out why you and everyone else loved them so much. Could not figure out how anyone could believe them. I think I get it now. They were true to you. And if you believed them, that's all that matters. Tell you something else, with what has happened to me in the last month, I think I believe your stories too. "

"Speaking of Uncle Billy, I think I know what happened to him. The car crash I mean. Maybe you do too. Maybe you always knew, but just told us kids he died in a car accident to spare our feelings. I know you know more than you told us. Next time I come, I will tell you what I know, what I saw. I saw some things that you might like to know. I know it sounds weird for me to say I saw anything, but you have to believe me, I know what I saw. Billy was complicated, but you already knew that. I know there are lots of other things you did not tell us."

"Oh, and thanks for telling me about Dangerfield. That was a great story. I am glad we were able to have that conversation. I . . . ."

He paused while gathering his words.

"I think I know what you want from me now. Remember when you told me about Dangerfield's family, and how no one knows for certain what happened to them? I remember you saying 'I always wondered what happened to that poor man's wife and children. Seems like nobody knows.' Well, I think I can find out what happened to them, or at least try. This sounds weird, but I think I have a way of getting first-hand information about Dangerfield's family. Almost like I could be right there with them. I know you probably don't believe that, but . . . well, maybe you do believe it. I am starting to anyway."

"I remember what you said about Dangerfield – 'when a good man dies before he can keep an earthly promise, his spirit won't rest until he keeps that promise.' Well, I promise you this, Gran, I will find out what happened to that man's family and report back to you. I think he deserves to know, and his family deserves to know. And you deserve to know, because it's your family too, our family. You always wanted to know what happened to his wife and children, and I will find out for you. I don't have anything else more important to do."

Turner laughed softly at his inside joke to his dead grandmother, then stood up slowly.

"Well, Gran, that's it for now. I promised Tracy I would take her out for a nice dinner. The last month has been hard on her too. Anyway, I will report back next time I visit."

He walked away from his grandmother's grave and toward his new life.

⸻ «◉» ⸻

All men are born knowing their destiny. It is written in time for every man ever born, and for all those to come. Some men run from their fate, while some choose to ignore it. The foolish ones try to change their destiny, but time cannot be rewritten. Stars cannot be moved by the breath of men.

Wise men confront and then embrace their fate, knowing that it is set in stone. Whether it be glory or failure, it is fixed and unchanging. Wise men embrace their destiny not because they can change it, but because it is the only noble path. And all those who choose this path are rewarded in time.

CPSIA information can be obtained
at www.ICGtesting.com
Printed in the USA
LVHW060826030522
717810LV00034B/929